ENEMY WITHIN

Tom Whitehead had never heard of Operation Gold Dust. Why would he? No reason for a respected academic, loving husband and father of two to be aware of an international investigation into internet paedophilia. Until he finds himself at the centre of it . . . Raided by the police at dawn, and in the full glare of the paparazzi, Tom is hauled away for questioning. About the pornography found on his computer at work. About the fact it was paid for with his credit card. About the overwhelming, conclusive evidence against him . . . He discovers that he has been under investigation for some time. The police acquired his details from the National Criminal Intelligence Service — via the FBI. But why? And how?

PAUL ADAM

ENEMY WITHIN

Complete and Unabridged

CHARNWOOD
Leicester

First published in Great Britain in 2005 by
Time Warner Books
London

First Charnwood Edition
published 2006
by arrangement with
Time Warner Books, an imprint of
Time Warner Book Group UK
London

British Library CIP Data

Adam, Paul, *1958* –
    Enemy within.—Large print ed.—
    Charnwood library series
    1. Historians—Great Britain—Fiction
    2. False arrest—Fiction 3. Suspense fiction
    4. Large type books
    I. Title
    823.9′14 [F]

    ISBN 1–84617–381–7

Published by
F. A. Thorpe (Publishing)
Anstey, Leicestershire

Set by Words & Graphics Ltd.
Anstey, Leicestershire
Printed and bound in Great Britain by
T. J. International Ltd., Padstow, Cornwall

This book is printed on acid-free paper

Prologue

The unmarked white van came to a halt at the end of the track. Craven switched off the headlights and for a time the two men sat in silence, letting their eyes adjust to the darkness. Out here, away from human habitation, from street lamps and houses, the night had an intense, oppressive quality. Finch looked out of his window. He could see bushes close by, then a few shadowy tree trunks, but nothing beyond. He suppressed a shiver. He wasn't looking forward to this.

'You fancy a smoke first?' he said, trying to put off the moment when they would have to begin.

Craven shrugged. 'Why not?'

Finch took out his cigarettes. The flare of his match momentarily illuminated the cigarette packet, the words 'SMOKING KILLS' printed on the front in stark black letters. The health warning seemed to get bigger every year. It was like a statement of defiance from the tobacco company, a symbolic raising of two fingers to the nanny state. Finch inhaled, glancing round uneasily into the back of the van. It wasn't only smoking that killed.

'I suppose we'd better get this done,' Craven said after a while, but he didn't move.

'Yeah.' Finch smoked his cigarette almost to the filter, then wound down his window to throw out the stub.

'In the ashtray!' Craven said sharply.

'What?'

'We leave nothing behind at the scene.'

Craven opened his door and swung his legs out, squeezing his paunch past the steering wheel. It was a cool, overcast spring night. The wood had an earthy smell, the pungent odour of damp soil and decomposing vegetation. Craven shone his torch over the ground, picking out the rotting carpet of beech and sweet-chestnut leaves that had fallen the previous autumn. The surface of the track was hard and dry. That was good. The van would leave behind no tyre marks.

Craven opened the rear doors and took out the two spades they'd bought that afternoon from a garden centre near York. The spades were clean and shiny, like the ones they gave royalty at tree planting ceremonies. The blades glinted in the torchlight.

'You carry them,' Craven said.

He led the way into the trees, one hand shielding the torch to keep the beam low as he swung it to and fro across the ground, searching for a suitable spot. Twenty yards in, he stopped in a small clearing.

'This'll do. You start that end.'

They began to dig. It was harder going than they'd expected. The topsoil was easy enough to remove, but a couple of feet down they encountered a layer of earth that was packed tight with rocks and stones. It was difficult getting the spades in. The rocks had to be forced out of the way or broken up, a tiring process that sent jarring vibrations up the two men's arms.

2

Finch grunted resentfully. 'We should have bought a bloody pickaxe 'n' all.'

After fifteen minutes strenuous work they were ready for another cigarette. Finch sat down on a fallen log and stretched his aching shoulders.

'It's quiet here, isn't it?' he said, sucking on his cigarette and flicking ash away into the undergrowth.

'That's why it was chosen,' Craven replied.

Finch looked around. He didn't like the silence, the blackness, the sense of the forest closing in on them — dark, claustrophobic, unnerving.

Craven studied the hole they'd been digging. It was surprisingly shallow, considering the effort they'd expended. It was going to be a longer job than he'd hoped. He took a last drag on his cigarette, stubbed it out on the trunk of a tree and put the butt carefully away in his jacket pocket. He picked up his spade.

'Let's get this finished.'

They were getting tired. Neither man was built for even light exercise. They'd spent too many years sitting at desks, in cars, in the pub. Their waistlines had long since turned to flab, their arteries and lungs silted up with fat and tar. Yet this was physically arduous work. Their arms and backs were sore, their breathing laboured. Finch was hot, sweating freely beneath his shirt. He paused to remove his jacket, deliberately taking his time to give himself a break. Craven wasn't falling for that one. He stopped digging too, his thick forearms resting on the handle of his spade.

3

'That's deep enough, isn't it?' Finch said. 'How deep do we have to make it?'

'Good and deep. That's what Templeman said.'

'It's all right for him. He's not the one doing the fucking digging.'

Finch looked around for somewhere to put his jacket. It was leather, expensive. He wasn't going to muck it up by simply dropping it on the ground. He walked to one of the trees at the edge of the clearing and draped the jacket over a low branch.

'You done this before?' he said, coming back to his spade.

'What, dug a hole?' Craven said.

'Dug a grave.'

'No.'

'It doesn't seem right. You've got kids too. It makes you think, doesn't it? What about the parents? How are they going to feel?'

'One of the things I've found in this job,' Craven replied brusquely, 'is that it doesn't pay to think too much. Now let's get a move on. We want to be well away from here before dawn.'

Finch stayed where he was, staring down at the pit in the forest floor.

'That's enough, surely?' he said. 'Who's going to find them here? Let's get this over with. Just dump them and get out.'

Craven murmured doubtfully.

'I'm knackered,' Finch went on. 'It's like digging through concrete. We won't get much deeper now without a pick, or a pneumatic drill.

4

What's the point of scraping out another few inches?'

Craven took a moment to consider. Then he gave a quick nod. 'Yeah, OK.' He moved away towards the van, as if now the decision had been made he was even more anxious than his companion to get it all over with.

They lifted the first body bag out of the back of the van and carried it to the clearing. It wasn't very heavy. Either one of them could have managed it on his own, but there was an unspoken agreement — a pact between them — that they would do this last bit together. Shared responsibility, shared guilt.

They put the bag down beside the hole and Craven unzipped it.

'Can't we just leave him in the bag?' Finch said.

'You know what Templeman said. They'll rot faster out of the bags. Give me a hand.'

They took an end each. The unzipped slit in the body bag fell open a little. Finch caught a glimpse of pale flesh inside and averted his eyes.

'Ready?' Craven said.

They tipped the bag over the edge of the pit so the body tumbled out. There was just enough light to see it sprawled at the bottom of the hole. It was a boy's body, a boy in his early teens. He was naked, his skin glistening faintly in the darkness.

The second corpse went in next to the first. Another young boy, the wounds on his chest crudely patched up.

'Shit! This is all wrong,' Finch said. 'They're

just kids, not much older than my own.'

'Shut up!' Craven said harshly. 'A conscience isn't part of the job description. You knew that when you joined.'

'Poor little buggers,' Finch said.

The two men picked up their spades and began to shovel earth in on top of the bodies.

1

The alarm went off like a firecracker exploding inside his head. Tom's eyes snapped open with a jolt, blinking several times before focusing blearily on the illuminated display of the clock next to the bed. Seven o'clock. Not an unreasonable hour by most people's standards, but still far too early for any sensible man to be woken. He stared at the glowing red figures for a couple of seconds, aware that the alarm was still beeping, then summoned the energy to reach out and press the 'sleep' button. He needed just a few more minutes under the duvet before he could face the day.

Rolling over, he slipped his arm around his wife and pressed in close to her back, feeling her naked skin warm and soft against his chest. His hand cupped one of her breasts. Helen stirred and murmured sleepily. Tom's hand strayed down across her stomach, slow, tentative, waiting to see how far she'd let it go. Not far. Her fingers found his, clasped them tight and brought them back up to her breast.

Tom closed his eyes and held her, making the most of the moment, the warm, drowsy intimacies of marriage. Then the alarm went off again, a second, more insistent warning that could not be ignored. Tom retreated to his side of the bed and swung his legs out, one finger hammering down on the button to cut off the infernal beeping noise. In his student days he'd had an alarm clock shaped like a tennis ball, sheathed in tough rubber so you could hurl it across the room when it rudely interrupted your slumber. It could take any amount of punishment, was practically indestructible, but he'd got rid of it when one morning it had ricocheted off two walls and smashed his bedroom window. He'd mellowed a lot since then, but there were still moments when he missed that alarm clock.

He threw on a sweatshirt and a pair of tracksuit bottoms and went downstairs without putting the landing light on — to let the children sleep undisturbed for as long as possible. The kitchen was cold and dark. The central heating was on — he could hear the soft growl of the boiler on the wall — but the air was still tainted with the chill of the night.

He put the kettle on to boil, poured Shreddies and Cornflakes into bowls for Hannah and Ben, then took a cup of tea and a bowl of muesli upstairs for Helen. She was in the shower, her hair dripping wet, her body gleaming. Tom put her breakfast down on the windowsill and went to rouse the children. Hannah was already up, sitting on the edge of her bed getting dressed. Ben was only just coming round, tousle-haired, bleary-eyed, struggling to extricate himself from his duvet.

'Breakfast's on the table,' Tom called briskly from the doorway before going back downstairs.

He was making toast when Hannah came into the kitchen, composed and efficient, her hair brushed, school blouse tucked neatly into her dark trousers. Ben appeared five minutes later, clad in a school uniform which seemed to have been crushed in the back of a municipal dustbin lorry. The trousers — which had knife-edge creases everywhere except the knees — were smudged with dirt. The sweatshirt was liberally smeared with some unidentified white stuff — possibly paint, or glue, or even toothpaste.

'My spellings,' Ben said anxiously, rummaging in his school bag.

'Have your breakfast,' Tom said.

'No, my spellings. I forgot. I've got a test today.'

'Eat your Shreddies.'

'You have to test me. No one's tested me,' Ben said, his voice rising in a panic.

'It's nothing to worry about,' Tom reassured him.

'Yes, it is. I don't know them.'

Tom sighed. 'Give me the list. I'll test you while you eat.' He ran his eye over the sheet of paper. 'You know most of these, I'm sure.'

'No, some of them are hard,' Ben said, his mouth full of Shreddies.

'OK. Boat.'

'B-o-a-t,' said Ben.

'Said.'

'S-a-i-d.'

'Immigration.' Immigration? What a strange word to expect an eight-year-old to be able to spell.

'I-m-m . . . ' Ben paused. 'E?'

'I.'

'I-g-r-a-t-i-o-n.'

'Good, well done, that was tricky.'

Tom glanced at the kitchen clock and passed the sheet of spellings to Hannah.

'I have to get ready. Hannah will ask you the rest.'

Tom gulped down a last mouthful of tea and hurried out. As he went upstairs he heard Hannah saying, 'Come on, you must know 'because', it's *easy-peasy*.'

Helen was finishing off her make-up in the bathroom mirror, wearing only bra and pants. Tom watched her reflection while he washed and shaved, the curve of her back, her hips. Then, rubbing his face dry with a towel, he wandered over to her.

'Don't even think about it,' Helen murmured quickly, inclining her head towards the door. Hannah was just outside on the landing. Tom glanced at his daughter. She'd reached that age when children acquire a quiet, unsettling stealth, the ability to creep up on you unawares. One of these days they were going to get caught.

Ben was next. No danger of him sneaking up on you unexpectedly. You could hear him coming upstairs from half a mile away. Helen took one look at his uniform and drew in her breath sharply.

'Ben, what on earth have you done to your clothes?' Then to Tom, 'Have you seen the state of him? He can't go to school looking like that.'

'He'll be OK,' Tom said casually. 'Put clean clothes on him and they'll only come home looking like that tonight.'

Helen's mouth tightened. She gave her

husband a look, more exasperation than anger. It reminded Tom of the times before the children started school when he'd occasionally take them to playgroup, dressing them in clothes that were soiled or had colours that clashed and Helen would threaten to put a sign around their necks reading, 'Daddy dressed me today.'

'OK, OK,' Tom said, surrendering. 'I'll find him some clean stuff.'

They were late dropping the children off — as usual. The whistle had already gone and the school playground was almost deserted, only a few laggards straggling in through the gates. Tom gave Hannah a kiss and a cuddle, then Ben a more discreet hug. Ben was fine at home, but was getting funny about overt displays of parental affection in public, particularly anywhere near school where his friends might witness it. Helen found that quite upsetting, but Tom was more sanguine about it. The male culture of emotional repression, of wanting to belong to the gang, started early.

On the main road below the school, Tom and Helen caught the bus into the city together, Tom getting off a few stops before his wife. The university History Department was in a collection of buildings opposite the Royal Hallamshire Hospital. The core of the complex was a large, rather shabby Victorian red-brick house, but Tom's office was in the more modern — but equally shabby — annexe at the rear of the house. Bruce Kelly, one of his fellow lecturers, was in the communal kitchen on the ground floor of the annexe, making a pot of tea.

Tom joined him for a few minutes, chatting inconsequentially while he filled a mug for himself, then both men went upstairs to the first floor.

Tom's office wasn't large. The original dimensions of the room had not been over-generous, but the addition of a desk and chair, filing cabinets and shelving on three walls had shrunk the available work space to an area little bigger than a broom cupboard. Tom put his tea down on the desk, switched on his computer and started to unpack his briefcase. He was logging on to check his emails, gazing distractedly out of his window at the ugly grey edifice of the hospital across the road, when the telephone rang. He picked up the receiver.

'Yes?'

'Dr Whitehead?' It was the departmental secretary in the main building.

'Good morning, Sylvia.'

'Dr Whitehead . . . ' The secretary paused. 'There are two police officers here. They'd like a word with you.'

★ ★ ★

Police officers? *Police officers?* The words kept repeating themselves inside Tom's head as he strode across the car park. Police officers? Something must have happened. His first thought was for the children. Something must have happened to Ben or Hannah. And for the police to be here, it must be something serious. Dear God, what was it? An accident? Had they

12

been knocked down by a car? But no, they were at school. What could have happened to them at school?

Helen then? Yet she was at work. An accident at work? What could happen in an architect's office? His imagination went into overdrive. Perhaps she'd had a stroke, collapsed, been taken to hospital. But Helen was fit, healthy. He wasn't thinking clearly. He'd never had any dealings with the police. Maybe it was something else. A break-in at their house, a burglary. That could be it. He started to feel almost relieved at the thought. Or something completely trivial, a parking offence perhaps, some insignificant transgression that had slipped his mind. He felt his throbbing pulse ease a little. That was it. It was probably nothing to worry about.

The police officers were standing by the window in the departmental office. They were big, imposing men, one in plain clothes, one in uniform. Seeing them revived Tom's state of agitation.

'What is it?' he asked quickly. 'My children? My wife? What is it?'

'Dr Whitehead?' the plainclothes officer said. He had a soft, reassuring voice, but Tom found his calm demeanour perturbing.

'What's happened? Has something happened?'

'This isn't about your wife, or children,' the officer said.

'It isn't? Then what . . . ?'

'Do you have an office?'

'Yes. In the other building.'

'Perhaps we could talk there.'

13

'Talk? Talk about what?'

'Let's go to your office, Dr Whitehead.'

They walked in silence across to the annexe. Tom's fears for his family had subsided, but in their place had come a different, less defined anxiety. What did these men want? Their very reticence, their reluctance to explain the purpose of their visit, was disquieting. Why couldn't they just come out and tell him?

There was barely room for all three of them in Tom's office. Tom pushed a box of books out of the way under his desk to clear some space and offered the police officers a couple of moulded plastic chairs from the stack in the corner that were used by his students in tutorials. The policemen declined the offer. The plainclothes officer took out a slim black wallet and flipped it open. In one half of the wallet Tom saw a photo ID card inside a protective transparent sleeve, in the other half the silver shield of the South Yorkshire Police Force.

'I'm Detective Constable Jack Parramore, of Hammerton Road CID,' the officer said. 'This is Police Constable Keith Skinner from the Telecommunication and Internet Crime Unit.'

Telecommunication and Internet Crime Unit? Tom had never heard of it. What was going on?

'How can I help you?' Tom asked.

'We have two search warrants here, Dr Whitehead,' Parramore replied. 'One for your office, and one for your home.'

Tom stared at him. 'Search warrants? You want to search my office?'

'Yes, sir. Then your home. Then we'd like you

to accompany us to the station.'

The phrase seemed to reverberate around the office like a distant but familiar echo. It was a cliché of every television police series Tom had ever seen. It seemed so surreal that for an instant it crossed Tom's mind that these two men were actors, put up to this as a joke — like a strippagram for someone's birthday. Only it wasn't his birthday, and these two certainly didn't look like strippers.

'What are you searching for?' Tom asked.

'We have reason to believe that there may be indecent images of children on your computer and elsewhere in your office and home.'

Tom blinked, wondering if he'd misheard.

'I'm sorry? Indecent images of children? On my computer?'

'Yes, sir.'

'Put there by whom?'

Parramore didn't reply. Tom realised with horror the implications.

'By *me*? You think *I've* been downloading indecent pictures? Of children?' The thought revolted him. 'There must be some mistake. You must have come to the wrong place.'

'You *are* Dr Thomas Whitehead?'

'Yes. But perhaps there's another Thomas Whitehead.'

'Of 98 St John's Close, Fulwood?'

'Yes, that's my address.'

'There's no mistake, sir,' Parramore said. Then his voice took on a more formal tone, reciting something he knew by heart. 'You do not have to say anything. But it may harm your defence if

15

you do not mention, when questioned, something which you later rely on in court. Anything you do say may be given in evidence.'

'Am I being arrested?' Tom said.

'No, sir. Just cautioned.'

Parramore glanced at his uniformed colleague.

'I'll bring the van round,' Skinner said.

'What's this all about?' Tom said. He felt sick. He sensed the beginnings of a cold sweat on his face and sat down heavily in his chair, wondering if he was going to faint.

'This is the warrant for you to read, sir.'

Parramore handed him a sheet of paper. Tom looked down at the paper, expecting some impressive document with seals and stamps on it. What he saw was a single, innocuous-looking sheet of white A4, photocopied so badly that the royal coat of arms at the top was an indistinct blur of ink. Below the coat of arms were the words 'Sheffield Magistrates' Court', then a few typed lines listing the premises to be searched and the items to be seized — 'all computer and associated equipment, and any photographs or documents relating to the possession or distribution of indecent images of children.'

Tom read the words in a daze, numb with shock. *Indecent images, children, possession or distribution.* This was all wrong. They couldn't mean him. He'd never had any indecent images of children on his computer, or anywhere else.

'I don't understand,' he said, looking back up at the police officer. 'What makes you think I have anything like that on my computer? Is this someone's idea of a prank? I assure you, there are no indecent images of children on that computer.'

Parramore nodded expressionlessly. 'That's what we're going to check, sir.'

Tom looked out of the window. A police van was reversing up to the main entrance of the building. Everyone will see it, he thought. The whole department will know I'm under suspicion — or was it investigation? — for this . . . He couldn't bear to think about the offence, it was so abhorrent.

His eyes flickered across to his computer screen. His email inbox was displayed, showing twelve new messages had arrived overnight. His hand reached automatically for the mouse.

'Don't touch that!' Parramore said sharply. Then again, less ferociously, 'Don't touch any part of your computer, please, sir.'

'I was only . . . ' Tom stopped. 'No, of course.'

He pulled his hands away and sat with his arms crossed while the two officers went methodically through the office. The uniformed constable dealt with the computer, closing it down and separating the parts — monitor, system unit, keyboard, mouse — before carrying them out to the van. Parramore took care of the papers, removing files from the shelves and the cabinet and sifting through their contents. One or two he put back, but most went into piles on the floor which PC Skinner — when he'd finished with the computer — started to remove from the office.

'Those are my work papers,' Tom said. 'My

lecture notes, my research. Why do you need those?'

'Anything not relevant to our inquiry will be returned, sir,' Parramore said, without looking up from the file he was studying.

'But you can see there are no indecent images of children in there,' Tom persisted. 'They're history notes. You can't possibly need them.'

'We'll be the judge of that,' Parramore said.

Tom pushed his chair away from the desk, feeling suddenly claustrophobic. The office was too cramped, there was no room to breathe. He needed some air. He stood up and moved towards the door.

'You going somewhere, sir?' Parramore asked.

'To the toilet. Is that a problem?' Tom replied. He was starting to get annoyed with these intruders. His initial shock had waned a little. His anxiety was giving way to indignation. What the hell was going on here? He'd done nothing wrong, yet he was being treated like a criminal.

He went down the corridor and closed the toilet door behind him. Leaning over the basin, he splashed cold water on his face, then rubbed it dry with a paper towel. He realised he was out of his depth. He knew he had rights, but he had no idea what they were. He needed advice, proper legal advice.

He went back to his office. Bruce Kelly had come out into the corridor, disturbed by the noise, all the comings and goings. No doubt he'd also seen the police van from his own office window.

'What's going on?' he said.

18

'I don't know, Bruce,' Tom replied with a weary sigh. 'I don't know what's going on.'

'You OK?'

'Yes, I'm fine.'

Tom went into his office. Parramore was handing another pile of files to Skinner.

'Explain again to me what's happening,' Tom said. 'You're going to finish here, then search my house?'

'Yes, sir.'

'With me present?'

'We have the right to use force to effect an entry, sir, but I'm sure you'd rather unlock the door for us.'

'Then you want me to go to the police station with you?'

'You're under no obligation to attend, sir, but it would help us in our inquiries if you did so.'

'But I'm not under arrest?'

'No, sir.'

'I'm entitled to consult a solicitor, I assume?'

'Yes, sir. If you don't have one of your own, we can contact the duty solicitor for you.'

'That won't be necessary,' Tom replied.

He dug out his address book and went to the phone. Michael Russell wasn't really his solicitor. Tom didn't actually *have* a solicitor, unless you counted the one who'd drafted his will, or the one who'd handled the conveyancing on his house. But they weren't criminal lawyers, they weren't experienced in this kind of thing. Michael was a friend, and Tom was reluctant to use him in his professional capacity, but at least he'd know what to do.

Tom rang the number. Russell was in court all morning, the solicitor's secretary told him.

'Can I get a message to him?' Tom said. 'My name's Tom Whitehead. Can you tell him I'm being questioned by the police at . . . ' He broke off and looked at Parramore. 'Which police station are we going to?'

'Ecclesfield, sir,' Parramore replied.

'I thought you said you were from Hammerton Road?'

'The Sheffield North custody suite is at Ecclesfield.'

That gave Tom a jolt. Custody suite? They made it sound like a hotel, but he knew it was just a euphemism for cell block. Was he going to be locked up?

He passed on the information to Russell's secretary and rang off, feeling a little better. He hadn't done much to ease his predicament, but the very act of doing something, *anything*, was therapeutic. It helped reduce the debilitating feeling of impotence that had overwhelmed him.

He still felt sick. Still felt utterly bewildered. His mind was seething with a ferment of emotions — anxiety, anger, confusion. He was accused of being a paedophile, there was no other way to describe it. And though he was confident of clearing his name, sure that the police would find nothing incriminating either in his papers or on his computer, nevertheless he still had a nagging sense of unease. Why me? he wondered. Why had they come here, why had they singled him out if there was no evidence against him?

The interview room at Ecclesfield police station was a drab little box with nothing in it except a table with a bench on either side, all bolted to the floor. At one end of the table, next to the wall, was a tape recorder, also bolted down as if they feared someone might attempt to steal it — a sensible precaution, perhaps, given the clientele.

Tom waited there alone for half an hour, nursing a strong cup of tea a uniformed WPC had brought him, until Michael Russell arrived.

The solicitor was tall and lean, rimless glasses perched on a thin, bony nose. He was wearing a smart dark-grey suit, brilliant white shirt and gleaming black shoes and looked every inch a typical conservative provincial lawyer — a deceptive appearance that gave no true indication of his political philosophy. The outfit was a sort of sartorial Trojan Horse. If you wanted to eat away at the Establishment from the inside, you had to dress like them, you had to look as if you belonged. But no one belonged less to the British Establishment than Michael Russell. Tom had first met him twenty years earlier, during the farcical trial of the Orgreave pickets, and had been struck then by Russell's quiet radicalism, his fervent belief in the essential, and malign, corruption of the state.

'What on *earth* is going on?' Russell said, sitting down on the other side of the table and adjusting his tie. He had a vast collection of ties, many discreet and sober, but many more intended to be deliberately provocative. He had a Greenpeace tie, a Friends of the Earth tie, a CND tie and even — when he really wanted to irritate the Bench at the Magistrates' Court — a Socialist Workers' Party tie. Not that the SWP actually *had* an official tie — that would have been too much like joining the enemy — but Russell simply put a SWP badge on one of his stock of plain ties. In the old days, he'd occasionally sported a Labour Party tie, but he rarely wore it now for fear of being mistaken for a Tory. Today, in a less overtly political vein, he had on a navy-blue WWF tie with a striking picture of a giant panda on the front.

'I don't know,' Tom said. 'I wish I did.'

'You're the last person I'd ever have expected to see here. Have they questioned you yet?'

'No, we were waiting for you.'

'Good. I had a word with the DC who brought you in, but he's a cagey bastard. What exactly have they told you?'

'Not much. They searched my office, my house. Took away my computers and loads of papers. All my work stuff, I don't know why.'

'Papers?'

'My research papers, even my lecture notes.'

'How many computers did they seize?'

'Two. My office one and my home PC.'

'Looking for indecent images of children?'

'That's what they said. It's all a mistake, it has to be.'

'Did they tell you that you don't have to be here? You're what they call a PACE 9, voluntary attendance at a police station. You have the same

22

rights as an arrested person, only you can walk out any time you choose.'

'I want to get this cleared up, Michael. If I help, maybe it can all be sorted out quickly. I'm sorry to get you involved.'

'Don't be silly. It's my job. You're my friend.'

'That's what I meant. You might find it tricky, representing a friend.'

'You'd prefer a total stranger to handle it?'

'No, I wouldn't.'

'Then it's settled, I'm your man. You don't want to end up with one of the sozzled old shysters I see down at court every day. You want a top pro. And failing that, me.'

Russell stood up and headed for the door.

'Right, let's see what they have to say, shall we?'

★ ★ ★

Parramore and Skinner were both present during the interview, though only Parramore asked the questions. Skinner didn't sit at the table, but kept at a distance, leaning back on the plain grey wall next to the door. Parramore's bulk, his broad shoulders and bulging chest — the product of some serious iron pumping in the police gym — seemed to fill the entire bench on which he was seated. Tom found his manner, the atmosphere in the room, intimidating. Without Russell's relaxed, familiar presence beside him, he knew he would have been absolutely terrified.

Parramore took his time, unwrapping two brand-new ninety-minute cassette tapes and inserting them into the tape recorder, then switching the recorder on, both tapes running simultaneously, and noting the date, time and persons present. He cautioned Tom again, for the tape, and scribbled a few details down on the notepad in front of him. When he looked up, his face was blank, devoid of expression, like an experienced poker player giving away nothing about his hand.

'Thank you for coming in today, Dr Whitehead,' he said politely. 'I hope this won't take long. Before we go on, I want you to know that you are under no obligation to remain here. You may leave the police station at any time. Do you understand?'

Tom nodded. 'Yes, I understand.'

'Do you have a credit card?'

'A credit card?' The question took Tom by surprise. 'Well, yes I — '

Michael Russell put a restraining hand on Tom's arm. 'Don't answer that.' Russell looked across the table at the detective. 'My client is attending voluntarily,' he said. 'He hasn't been arrested, there are no charges against him. I think you should tell him first why he has been asked to come here. What grounds do you have for making any allegations — let alone allegations of this nature — against him?'

Parramore's eyes met Russell's. Tom wondered whether the two had met before. They didn't appear to know each other, but the police officer would certainly have been aware of Russell's reputation as a tenacious, awkward-school defence solicitor. Parramore gave a conciliatory

24

nod. Now was not the moment for confrontation.

'The American FBI has been conducting a widespread investigation into a number of websites,' he said. 'Websites based in the US which display indecent images of children.'

'Like Operation Ore, you mean?' Russell said.

'Yes, very similar. Only these are different websites. The FBI has provided us with a list of UK residents who have accessed these sites. Dr Whitehead's name is on the list.'

'That's impossible,' Tom interjected swiftly. 'I've never been near a website displaying that kind of material. Never.'

The protestation seemed to make no impact on the detective. Without acknowledging Tom's reply, Parramore went on, 'These websites can't be accessed accidentally. The user has to authorise a credit card payment first.'

'This is ridiculous,' Tom said. 'I've never used my credit card to access any such website. Good God, what do you think I am? I have children of my own. The very idea is utterly offensive.'

'All the same,' Parramore said calmly. 'Your name and credit card details are on the list supplied to NCIS — the National Criminal Intelligence Service — by the FBI and forwarded by NCIS to us. Which is why I asked if you had a credit card.'

'Yes, I have a credit card,' Tom admitted. 'But it has never been used to pay for child pornography.'

'Do you keep the card in a secure place?' Parramore asked. 'You haven't lost it recently, or lent it to anyone?'

'No, it's here in my wallet, where it always is.'

'Could I see it, please?'

Tom glanced at Russell, who held up a warning finger.

'Just one moment. Detective Constable, perhaps you would give us the number of the card you have on your list first.'

Parramore hesitated, reluctant to give ground. Then he shrugged and searched through the cardboard file he'd brought in with him. He found a piece of paper and read out a Visa card number.

'Is that yours?' he asked Tom.

Tom pulled out his wallet and slid his credit card out of its leather pocket. He felt the knot of anxiety in his stomach tighten.

'Yes, that's my number.'

'Expiry date, o-four, o-six?'

'Yes.'

'Could I see the card, please?'

Tom looked at Russell. The solicitor nodded.

'You're sure no one else has had access to this?' Parramore said, examining the card.

If only they had, Tom thought. That might make some sense of this whole ludicrous business.

'Not that I'm aware of,' he said. 'But you don't need to physically possess the card to use the number. Particularly on the internet. It could have been someone else.'

'That's quite possible. Credit card fraud is very common. Does anyone else know your number? Friends, colleagues?'

'I don't think so. But I can't be sure. In any case, it could be a complete stranger. A waiter in a restaurant where I've used my card, a petrol station attendant, a supermarket checkout girl.'

Listing the people who had had access to his card number made Tom feel more comfortable. There must have been dozens of people who could have had the opportunity to note down his card details. That had to be the answer. A simple — if worrying — case of credit card fraud.

'My client is right,' Russell said. 'Any number of people might have used his number to access these websites.'

'That's why we've brought in your computers, Dr Whitehead,' Parramore said. 'To see if there's anything on the hard drives.'

'You're going to check the hard drives?' Tom said. 'There are personal things on there. Letters, financial records, all sorts of private documents. Not just belonging to me, but to my wife too.'

Parramore looked across at Skinner, who stepped away from the wall and came nearer the table.

'We're not interested in your private files,' Skinner said. 'What we do is make mirror copies of the C drives. We bag the original system units up, fasten them with a forensic seal and put them away in a secure store. We only work on the mirror copies, and we don't look at anything that doesn't appear relevant to the investigation. We don't have the time to trawl through every file. Nor do we want to.'

'How long will that process take?' Russell enquired.

'A few days, perhaps. Maybe less.'

'We'd be grateful if you could do it as quickly as possible,' Russell said. 'The sooner this cloud is removed from over my client's head the better.'

The solicitor stood up. Taking his cue, Tom also rose to his feet.

'And, Detective Constable,' Russell said to Parramore, as if it were an afterthought, 'the academic papers and files you took from Dr Whitehead's office and home, they can't possibly have any bearing on your investigation. I want them returned tomorrow, or I'll be in court the day after to obtain an order for their return.'

Outside, walking to their cars, Tom said to Russell, 'What happens now?'

'We wait and see what the police find,' the solicitor replied.

'They won't find anything. I've never viewed or downloaded any indecent images of children.'

Russell nodded. 'Then you've absolutely nothing to worry about.'

2

For once, it wasn't the beep of the alarm that woke Tom, but something more distant, less expected. A ringing sound, followed by a loud hammering. It took him a moment to realise there was someone at the front door. He looked at the clock — 6.46. Who the hell could it be? The postman sometimes rang the bell when he had a package too big to fit through the letter box, but he was never this early.

Tom struggled into his dressing gown and slippers, fumbling awkwardly in the darkness, and went downstairs. Parramore was outside at the front of the house, standing a little to one side, so Tom was fully exposed as he opened the door. There was a sudden flash of dazzling light from the garden wall, then another. Tom blinked. In the yellowish glow of the street lamps he could see figures on the pavement. There was another flash. A camera. There were photographers out on the street.

Parramore stepped in front of the door. It was cold, but he wasn't wearing an overcoat. The folds of his suit jacket were flapping in the breeze.

'Thomas Whitehead,' he said sombrely. 'I'm arresting you on suspicion of downloading and possessing indecent images of children.' Tom barely took in the rest of the detective's words, though he was aware he was being cautioned again. All he could think of was the phrase 'downloading and possessing indecent images of children'. No, that wasn't him. That wasn't something he could ever conceive of doing.

'You're arresting me?' he said confusedly, his senses still half asleep, his mind drifting, wondering what was happening, what the cameras were doing there.

'Those people,' he said. 'Out on the street. Who are they?'

'I don't know,' Parramore said. 'Press, maybe.'

Tom looked at the detective's face. There was something in Parramore's eyes, in the curl of his mouth, that seemed malicious, mocking. He's enjoying this, Tom thought. He wants to see me humiliated.

'You'd better come in.' Tom's brain suddenly cleared, as if it had been doused in water. He moved out of sight behind the door, concealing himself from the prying lenses on the pavement, waiting for Parramore to enter the hall, then closing the door quickly behind him.

Helen was on the stairs, fastening the cord of her dressing gown. Her eyes flickered towards Parramore, then back to Tom.

'What's going on?'

'I'm being arrested,' Tom said.

'*Arrested*? Oh, my God, you mean for the . . . Now? They're taking you away *now*?'

'Can I put some clothes on?' Tom asked Parramore.

The detective nodded phlegmatically. 'Yes, you can get dressed.'

Tom went up the stairs. He could feel his legs

shaking, the nausea taking hold in his belly. He was being arrested. This was way outside his experience. Arrested with the press there to record his shame. They would relish the opportunity to pillory him. A middle-class professional — 'boffin', that was the ridiculous term the tabloids always used for academics — hauled out of bed at dawn to face charges of paedophilia. Jesus Christ, he'd be ruined.

'Tom, Tom,' Helen's voice was urgent, agitated. 'What's happening? Why? Did they find something on the computers? Is that it?'

'I don't know.' Tom put on a shirt, rummaged for underwear and socks in a drawer.

'What did he say, the policeman? He must have said something.'

'Nothing. I don't know any more.'

'What will happen? Where are they taking you? Tom, I don't know what — '

'Helen.' Tom gripped her arm, silencing her. 'Calm down. I want you to call Michael for me. Tell him what's happened.'

'Are they going to detain you? Keep you in custody?'

'I don't know.' Tom slipped on his jacket. 'Just call Michael.'

Hannah was out of her bedroom, standing on the landing in her pyjamas.

'There's a police car outside the house, people with cameras,' she said. 'What's going on?'

'It's nothing to worry about,' Tom said. He kissed his daughter. 'Have a good day at school. I'll see you tonight.'

The words tumbled out automatically, but as

31

he spoke, it occurred to Tom that he might not see her tonight. The thought was chilling. Perhaps he wouldn't see any of them for a while.

He had to see Ben. See his son, just in case. He went into the smaller front bedroom. Ben was stirring, emerging from sleep in his fuzzy, disorientated way. Tom leant over the bed and cuddled him, feeling him small and warm in his arms.

Ben murmured drowsily, 'Is it morning?'

'Not yet,' Tom said, kissing his son on the cheek. 'Go back to sleep.'

'Dr Whitehead . . . ' Parramore was calling from downstairs.

Tom hurried out. Helen was waiting on the landing. Tom gave her a hug. He could see she was close to tears, but holding them back. Not wanting to get emotional.

'Things will be OK,' he said, trying to sound optimistic. 'I'll call you if I can, let you know what's happening.'

Helen nodded. She was staring at him, her eyes moist, frightened.

'It'll be OK,' Tom repeated and headed downstairs.

The photographers were still outside at the front. Their flashguns exploded in Tom's face as he climbed into the back of the police car. He caught a glimpse of the faces behind the cameras — the leering, triumphant faces bearing witness to his downfall.

'Where did they come from?' Tom asked foolishly.

Parramore twisted round in the front seat, almost smirking.

'Can't think,' he replied.

⋆ ⋆ ⋆

There was no hot cup of tea this time. Everything at the police station felt different. Tom didn't know if the sensation of hostility he detected was due to the real attitude of the police officers concerned or to his own distorted perceptions. Was it the way the officers viewed him, or the way he viewed himself that made him feel so dirty, so loathsome?

The custody sergeant who processed his arrival at the station was calm, matter-of-fact, going through the paperwork with a solid, methodical precision. There was nothing in his manner, or his speech, to indicate that he had any particular feelings — negative or positive — about this latest prisoner. But Tom, over-sensitive to every nuance, was sure he saw contempt, repugnance in the sergeant's eyes. I revolt him, he thought. He despises me. He despises me more than a thief or a robber, maybe even more than a killer, for what I'm accused of doing is something no decent man could ever excuse. Theft, murder had their rationalisations, but paedophilia? That was beyond the pale.

Michael Russell arrived while Tom was still in the charging area of the custody suite. He was freshly shaven, dark suit immaculate despite the early hour. His face was taut with anger.

'This is outrageous,' he said furiously to the

sergeant. 'Who's the arresting officer? This could easily have been done quietly, in a civilised manner. My client would have surrendered himself at any time of your choosing. Why was he arrested at seven in the morning, with the press tipped off about what was happening?'

The sergeant made a few placatory murmurs, but Russell was not going to be fobbed off so easily.

'I want to see the duty inspector. *Now*. I intend to make a formal complaint.' Russell turned to Tom. 'Are you all right?'

'Yes, I'm fine,' Tom said. 'A bit shaken, that's all.'

'I'll be right back. This won't take a minute.'

The solicitor had calmed down a little by the time he returned. He had a brief conference with Tom, the two of them alone in the interview room, then Parramore came in. Once again the detective unwrapped two tapes and went through the preliminary legal formalities before he was finally ready to start the interview. Tom waited tensely, trying not to show his impatience. But the ordeal was excruciating. He wanted to *know*. He wanted to know what the evidence against him was.

'We've now had an opportunity to examine your computers, Dr Whitehead,' Parramore said eventually. 'On the hard drive of one of them — your office computer — we found fifty-six indecent images of children, all of them downloaded from the same internet website on three separate occasions.'

Tom gazed in alarm at the detective.

'No, no, no. That's impossible,' he said. 'Utterly impossible.'

'Nevertheless, the images are there.'

'No, I don't believe it.'

'The images are on *your* computer, Dr Whitehead, paid for with *your* credit card. The dates the card was used and the dates the images were downloaded correlate exactly.'

Tom shook his head. 'No, I've never *ever* accessed any website like that. And I've never used my credit card to pay to download indecent images of children.'

'The payments were made,' Parramore said. 'We have the documentation to prove it.'

'What documentation?' Tom countered. 'To my knowledge, I've never paid any Visa bill with a child pornography website transaction on it. I check my statement every month and I'm sure I would have noticed something like that.'

'What are the dates of these alleged transactions?' Russell asked.

Parramore referred to the file on the table.

'February 8th, February 10th and February 14th.'

'That was — what? — three weeks ago, a bit less?'

'That's correct.'

Russell looked at Tom. 'Have you had a statement covering that period yet?'

'I don't think so, it's too recent.'

'So, technically,' Russell said to Parramore, 'whatever your documentation shows, my client has not actually made any payment.'

'That's irrelevant,' Parramore replied. 'His

credit card was used, the fee for downloading was paid to the website operators and the indecent images are there on Dr Whitehead's computer. How do you explain that?'

He was looking at Tom now. Tom lifted his hands in a gesture of complete bewilderment.

'I can't explain it. All I know is that *I* didn't download them.'

'You're saying someone else did?'

'They must have.'

'Who?'

'I don't know.'

'Let me put it to you, Dr Whitehead,' Parramore said. 'That it was you who accessed this website, it was you who used your credit card to pay for that access and you who downloaded the indecent images of children we found on your computer.'

Tom shook his head. 'That's wrong. None of it is true. I deny absolutely every part of those allegations.'

'You're sure about that?'

For an instant, Tom flared. 'For God's sake, yes. I'm not a paedophile, I don't look at pornographic images of children. How many times do I have to tell you that?'

Tom ran a hand over his face, trying to rub away some of the tension. His fingers were trembling. He felt short of breath.

Russell stepped in, giving Tom time to compose himself.

'What was the name of this website you allege my client accessed?' he asked.

'Nymphs4you.com,' Parramore replied.

Nymphs4you? Tom thought. What a sick, disgusting name. But then it was a sick, disgusting business.

'And just let me confirm what you told us yesterday,' Russell continued. 'That Dr White-head's name was on a list compiled by the FBI and forwarded to the South Yorkshire police by NCIS?'

'That's correct. As part of Operation Gold Dust, an international investigation into internet child pornography.'

Tom stared down at the table. He felt drained. He'd denied the charges. There seemed little point in protesting further. The evidence against him was strong — more than strong. To an impartial observer it might have appeared conclusive. Yet Tom knew it was wrong. He knew he was innocent. But he knew also that, in the criminal process, innocence was not always enough.

'My client has nothing further to say,' Russell said. 'I think you'd better charge him, or release him.'

There was never any question that he wouldn't be charged. Tom submitted to the procedure in a semi-trance — going through the fingerprinting, the photographing, the taking of a DNA sample from the saliva in his mouth, like an automaton. His thoughts were elsewhere, wondering how he was going to tell Helen, the children, his colleagues. There was no way of concealing what was happening — the press already had the story. That was another thing to contend with. How would he endure the publicity, the stigma of being labelled a paedophile? The allegations were false, but the mere fact that they were being made would persuade some people — maybe most people — that they were true. What were the clichés? No smoke without fire. Mud sticks.

The only light in the whole dark, harrowing experience was the fact that he wasn't going to be kept in custody. Being locked up in a cell would have been more than Tom could have endured. The custody sergeant bailed him to appear before the magistrates the following day, then released him.

Russell gave Tom a lift into town. Tom slumped despondently in the passenger seat, staring out at the passing scenery as they drove south from Ecclesfield.

'Don't let it get you down,' Russell said. 'You have to keep your spirits up.'

'Oh, yes? And how am I supposed to do that?' Tom regretted the remark immediately. 'I'm sorry, Michael, that was rude of me. I apologise.'

'That's OK. It's a stressful time. And it won't go away quickly, that's what I'm saying. If you're going to get through it, you have to be resilient.'

'Helen is going to be devastated.'

'She'll support you, I'm sure.'

'What do I tell Ben and Hannah?'

'As little as possible. Try to keep them in the dark. They're too young to really understand what's going on.'

'What happens tomorrow? In court.' Tom shut out the thoughts of his family, they were too distressing. Better to concentrate on the practical issues.

'You'll appear before the Bench, either a panel of three lay magistrates or the District Judge,' Russell said. 'It won't take long. The charge will be read out, we'll indicate our intention to plead not guilty. The Bench will then decide whether to hear the case themselves or commit it to the Crown Court — the offence you're charged with is triable either summarily or on indictment.'

'In the Crown Court there'll be a jury, won't there?'

Russell nodded. 'They'll almost certainly commit you. The Crown Court has much greater powers of sentencing.'

Tom looked at him. 'You mean they can impose longer prison sentences?'

'Yes.'

'Will I be jailed — if I'm convicted?'

'That's not something you need to worry about now.'

'Will I?'

Russell slowed, coming to a halt at traffic lights.

'Yes,' he said. 'You could expect a custodial sentence. At least twelve months, I'd guess, maybe more.'

Tom shuddered. A year in jail. A year in jail branded a child sex offender, the most reviled category in the prison system. It didn't bear thinking about.

'But I'll be on bail until the trial?' he said.

'Almost certainly. There's no reason for you not to be granted bail. There may be conditions attached, but you'll be a free man.'

'Conditions?'

Russell seemed reluctant to answer. The lights turned to green and he pulled away, moving up through the gears, overtaking an elderly cyclist who was wobbling along next to the kerb.

'What conditions?' Tom asked.

'I'm not saying they *will* be attached, but in cases like these — '

'Paedophilia, you mean.' Tom almost spat the word out, overemphasising it as if he were flagellating himself. 'A paedophile. That's what they think I am. That's what everyone will call me.'

' . . . they do what they call a 'risk assessment'. It's possible they may restrict your contact with your children.'

Tom went cold. 'With Ben and Hannah? Stop me seeing them, you mean?'

'In extreme cases they can make children wards of court. But I don't think any of that is likely here. There's no allegation that you've been abusing your children.'

'Jesus, I should hope not.' Tom let out a deep breath. 'This is a fucking nightmare.'

They were in Hillsborough now, driving past the Sheffield Wednesday football ground. High on the valley side to their left, refuse lorries were moving in and out of the landfill tip, seagulls circling above them. Further on, Tom could see the white strips of the dry ski slope at Parkwood Springs. Tiny figures were zigzagging down the runs.

'It looks pretty bad, doesn't it?' Tom said. 'The case against me.'

'Yes, I'm afraid it does,' Russell conceded. 'If it

40

were just the credit card payments, we might be able to prove it was fraud, that someone else used your card number. But the images on your computer are going to be harder to explain away.'

Tom glanced at the solicitor. Was that a note of doubt he heard in Russell's voice? He thinks I did it, Tom thought. And who can blame him?

'I never downloaded those images,' Tom said. 'I swear it.'

Russell nodded. Then he said gently, 'Don't infer anything from this, I'd do it with any client. But I have to tell you, if you did it, it may be better to admit it now, plead guilty and get this all over with. The sentence may well be lighter if you do.'

'I didn't do it, Michael,' Tom said vehemently. 'You've known me for twenty years. Do you think it sounds like me? Do you really think I'm capable of something like that?'

The car turned into West Bar Green, heading up the hill past the central police station. Russell waited until they were almost at his office before he replied. He pulled over to the side of the road and applied the handbrake, swivelling in his seat so he could look Tom directly in the face.

'I believe you,' he said.

'And you'll help me?'

'Yes. I don't know what's going on here, but whatever it is, we're going to fight it.'

★ ★ ★

'You've got to appear in court? They're putting you on trial?'

Helen stared at Tom incredulously. She shook her head, momentarily lost for words.

'It's not going to be pleasant,' Tom said. 'It'll be in the newspapers, people will know.'

'What about the children? They're bound to find out.'

'We'll shelter them as much as we can,' Tom said.

'I don't understand. How did these . . . these images get on your computer?'

'I don't know. I certainly didn't put them there.'

'Then who did? They'd have to have access to your computer. You have a password, don't you? They'd have to know your password.'

Helen looked down at her cup of coffee. She'd barely drunk any of it since Tom had broken the news to her. She glanced around the café. There were people at the other tables, people engrossed in their own conversations, their own problems. They were taking no notice of anyone else.

'Maybe some of your students did it as a sick joke?' Helen said. 'You know, sneaked into your office and accessed this website. Or even one of your colleagues. Would anyone do that?'

'I don't know. I'm as baffled as you are.'

'Maybe they'll come clean and admit it now it's all blown up. Tell the police and clear you.'

Tom forced a feeble smile. It was tempting to go along with that optimistic scenario. It might ease their anxiety for a time, give them something to hope for. But it wasn't a realistic picture. The reality was, he'd been charged with a serious criminal offence, and proving his innocence was not going to be easy.

Helen lifted a finger to the corner of her eye, wiping away a tear. Only the presence of the other people in the café, her determination not to draw attention to themselves, prevented her from weeping openly.

'This is awful,' she said quietly. 'Awful. You're sure it's not just some dreadful mistake? It can't have been your computer. You'd never do anything like that.' She gazed at him, blinking away another tear. 'I know you didn't do it.'

Tom took her hand and squeezed it. That reassured him more than anything. At least Helen had faith in him.

* * *

Telling Douglas Kemp, head of the History Department, was less of an emotional ordeal for Tom than Helen had been. There was never any likelihood that the professor would break down in tears, but that didn't mean it was a straightforward interview. If anything, there were aspects of it that Tom found even more daunting than his earlier conversation with his wife. Helen and he had the physical and emotional ties of their marriage to bond them together. Too shocked by events to think with any great clarity, and sensitive to her husband's obvious distress, Helen had not pried very deeply into the details of the case, but Tom knew that Kemp would have no such reservations.

The professor — his face framed by a shock of grey hair and large, shaggy beard — gave the impression of a benign, rather woolly academic, but his mind was as sharp as a stiletto. He regarded Tom with a look of bemusement, the steely blue tint of his eyes softened by the thick lenses of his glasses.

'What do you mean, the police have made certain allegations against you?'

Tom shifted uncomfortably in his seat. Kemp was in his early sixties, only fifteen years older than Tom, but Tom looked on him as a different generation. He felt as if he were a boy again, confessing some terrible transgression to his father.

'Well . . . ' Faltering a little, trying to play down the more repugnant aspects, Tom explained what had happened.

Kemp frowned at him. 'Indecent images? You mean pornography, pictures of little girls naked or something?'

'I don't know what the images were,' Tom admitted. 'I didn't ask.'

'Good God! I'm shocked. This is astonishing. You of all people. And these images are on your office computer, here in the department?'

The professor wasn't going to pass over the details of this any more than he passed over the details of the medieval manuscripts he analysed for his work.

'So the police say,' Tom replied. 'I've got to appear in court tomorrow. I thought you should know.'

'Yes, yes, that was absolutely the right thing to do,' Kemp agreed.

'I'll be pleading not guilty, of course. There's no truth in the allegations.'

'Quite, I should hope not.'

Kemp eased himself out of his chair and walked to the bay window of his office. He slid his hands into the pockets of his baggy trousers and stared out across the car park.

'I assume I can count on your support?' Tom said.

'What?' Kemp turned round. 'Support? Yes, of course.'

The professor paused. Tom knew there was a 'but' coming.

'Naturally, you have our full support,' Kemp reaffirmed. 'You're a valued, long-serving member of the department. However . . . ' He struggled for the words. 'This is all very awkward, Tom. It puts us in a very difficult position.'

What about *my* position? Tom thought. How do you think *I* feel?

'I'll have to talk to the Vice-Chancellor. He has to be told. In the meantime, I think it would be best if you took a leave of absence until this matter is cleared up.'

'What about my classes, my students?'

'Someone else will have to cover for you. Between us we'll manage.'

'You're suspending me?' Tom said, though he'd known it was inevitable. The university couldn't possibly allow a lecturer to continue working with a criminal charge hanging over him.

'Yes, I suppose I am,' Kemp said. 'It wouldn't be appropriate, given the circumstances, to do otherwise. I'm sorry.'

'I understand.'

'You're quite sure there's no truth in the allegations?'

Tom was going to have to get used to that question. An angry denial was halfway to his lips, but he bit it back. That kind of response seemed futile, wasteful.

'None whatsoever,' he said quietly.

The interview concluded, Tom went across to the annexe. He was relieved not to encounter any of his colleagues or students on the way. His office seemed very bare, his computer gone, the shelves stripped of their files. He took down a couple of books and tucked them under his arm, then had a final, bleak look around, wondering when — if ever — he would be coming back.

3

Tom had never been in the Magistrates' Court before. He'd expected something rather grand and imposing, but was struck by how bland and functional the place was. There was none of the theatre of the Crown or High Court — no barristers in wigs and gowns, no robed judges, no 'your honours' and 'm'luds' flying about between counsel and bench. It was quiet, civilised, curiously low-key for such an important forum, where decisions on guilt or innocence, freedom or incarceration were made on a daily basis.

He'd arrived promptly at half past nine, as Michael Russell had instructed — only to find that his case wasn't likely to be called for at least an hour. The solicitor — tied up with other clients who were also appearing that day — suggested Tom go downstairs to the coffee bar in the meantime. Helen was with him. She'd taken the morning off work to give him some moral support. They sat together at a table in the far corner of the coffee bar. Tom had chosen it for its isolation, its distance from the counter and other customers. Instinctively, he wanted to segregate himself from anyone else — from decent people — to hide his shame in the darkest recesses of the room.

He knew he wasn't the only — what was the word they used? Defendant? — in the coffee bar.

The others were easy to spot. You could tell from their clothes, from the relatives and friends accompanying them. But Tom felt no affinity with them. In background and appearance — he'd put on his best suit for the hearing — he had more in common with the lawyers in the building than the defendants, yet he was accused of probably the most revolting crime of any of them.

The time didn't pass easily, or quickly. Helen was as tense as he was and could think of nothing to say. She wanted to help, to reassure her husband, but was finding it difficult. They were there. They had to go through with it. There was nothing she could do to lessen the ordeal for either Tom or herself. Unnerved by the silence, by Tom's brooding distraction, she tried the occasional remark, attempting to divert his mind from his predicament, but ordinary conversation seemed trivial. Everything beyond the court seemed utterly irrelevant.

It was a relief to go back upstairs to the long, open concourse outside the courtrooms. They had to wait for a while there too, but at least it was a step nearer to the hearing than the coffee bar had been. When, finally, the usher came out of Court One and called Tom's name, he got to his feet with a grim determination, wanting only to get the business over with as quickly as possible.

Helen followed him into the courtroom. The usher directed her to the two rows of public seats at the back of the room, then escorted Tom to the defendants' box — a long, narrow enclosure with toughened-glass walls. There were slits in the glass to enable prisoners to talk to their solicitors. Tom was locked into the box, a prison officer sitting just behind him. He glanced across at Helen. She gave him a smile that he knew was intended to be encouraging but came across as scared and worried.

Russell arrived moments later, a pile of files under his arm. As he came past Helen he touched her arm sympathetically and said, 'Keep your chin up, not long now.' Helen nodded and watched the solicitor walk over to Tom and exchange a few words before he took his place in the centre of the courtroom. There was another man in a suit near him. Helen guessed he was probably the lawyer from the Crown Prosecution Service.

On the left-hand side of the room, facing the defendants' box, were two rows of seats with narrow ledges in front of them for writing on. The front row, occupied by a lone woman in a skirt and blouse, was marked 'Probation Officers'. The rear row was for the press. There were four reporters slouching in the seats, chatting to one another. One of them glanced in Helen's direction. She looked away, not wanting to make eye contact. Of all the people in the courtroom, she loathed the journalists the most. Tom had bought the local evening paper, *The Star*, the previous day. Helen had advised him against it, but he was determined to see what, if anything, they'd printed about him. There'd been a short piece on an inside page, accompanied by a photograph of Tom, looking pale and startled in the flashlight, being loaded into the police car outside their house. The exposure made Helen angry. It seemed so callous, so deliberately hurtful. Everyone else in the room was a necessary part of the criminal justice system, but the reporters were simply there to gloat and wallow in her husband's disgrace — vultures waiting to pick over his carcass for the entertainment of their readers and the profits of their proprietors.

A man came into the courtroom and squeezed past Helen's legs, taking a seat at the other end of the row. He was wearing a shabby brown suit and brown suede shoes. His face was raddled, his nose red, his cheeks blotchy and pock-marked. His grizzled hair had the texture of wire wool. He stared intently at Tom for a moment, then sniffed and turned his gaze on Helen. He had dark, furtive eyes that made her feel uncomfortable. She turned her head and studied the dreary grey walls of the room, wondering what the man was doing there, what possible interest any ordinary member of the public could have in the case.

The District Judge came in a few minutes later. Bespectacled, clad in a dark suit and tie, he looked just like all the other middle-aged lawyers in the room. Tom had to give his name and address, but said nothing else throughout the hearing. It was over very quickly. Russell indicated their intention to deny the charges and the District Judge, with barely a moment's consideration, made the decision to send the case to the Crown Court. A date for the committal proceedings was fixed for eight weeks later.

That left only the question of bail, or custody. Tom waited nervously for the District Judge's ruling. Russell had said that a custody order was unlikely, but Tom had prepared himself mentally for the worst: prison or, perhaps more unbearable, freedom but forbidden to see his children. The District Judge looked across at him from his raised dais at the front of the court.

'Stand up, please, Dr Whitehead.'

Tom rose to his feet, his hands clasped tight behind him to stop them trembling.

'I see no reason not to extend your bail,' the judge said. He looked down at the prosecution solicitor. 'I take it there are no objections from the police or CPS?'

'No, sir, there are no objections,' the solicitor replied.

'In the circumstances, I don't feel it necessary to impose any conditions on the bail. You must be back here in eight weeks' time, Dr Whitehead. You are free to go.'

Tom closed his eyes and exhaled deeply, feeling his shoulders relax a little. In the overall context of the case nothing really significant had occurred — his status as an accused man free on bail had not changed — but to Tom the judge's decision was crucial. The committal and trial were still to come, but until then the court had officially recognised that Tom was still an innocent man.

There were seats in the concourse immediately outside the courtroom. Tom slumped down heavily on to one of them. Helen sat down next to him.

'Thank God that's over.'

Tom nodded. He felt exhausted. Russell joined them, waiting a moment for the newspaper reporters to file out of the courtroom and leave the precincts. Tom watched the four journalists head towards the exit, their departure confirming what he'd feared during the hearing. He was their target. There was no other case that had brought them there this morning.

'You know those men?' Tom asked Russell. The solicitor nodded. 'What are they, local reporters?'

'One's an agency reporter.'

'Working for the nationals?'

'He'll send the story to the nationals, yes. It doesn't mean they'll print it, of course.'

'No,' Tom said, though he knew they would. The tabloids wouldn't pass up an opportunity like this.

'The good news is that they're severely restricted as to what they can report,' Russell said. 'Just basic facts, like your name and address, the charge, your occupation. No background to the alleged offences, that isn't allowed.'

'It's still enough,' Tom said. 'Everyone will know.'

'Don't think about it too much. What we have to concentrate on now is your defence. The CPS will be sending me their file, but that might take a couple of weeks — probably will, they're so inefficient. But we can get a few things moving before then. Can you come in to my office tomorrow afternoon?'

'I can come in any time you like. I've been suspended from work.'

Russell wasn't surprised. 'Look on it as only temporary. Half past two. I'll see you then.'

There were more media people waiting outside. Tom and Helen had left the court building before they saw them. The Magistrates' Court was set on a steep hill. To get to and from it you had to cross a bridge. At the far end of the bridge — beyond the court precincts, where photography was prohibited — were two press photographers and a camera crew accompanied by one of the journalists who'd been inside the court. Tom hesitated, knowing he was already being taped by the camera crew. He could have turned around, gone back into the courthouse and found another exit, but he didn't know if there was another exit. And to do so would make him look shifty. It was better to brazen it out. Tom took hold of Helen's hand and walked calmly across the bridge. It was a still morning. He could hear the click of the photographers' cameras as they snapped off half a dozen shots each. The video camera lens followed him, tracking him as he walked past. Tom braced himself for questions from the reporter, had 'no comment' ready in reply, but no questions came. The group watched him in silence. The pictures were all they wanted. Tom had seen shots like that many times on the television news — and no matter what the facts of the case, that person, simply because the cameras were there at all, always seemed guilty.

They were parked in the multi-storey car park across the road from the Crucible Theatre. Tom handed the car keys to Helen.

'Would you mind driving? I don't think I'm up to it.'

'Of course,' Helen replied, though she wasn't sure she could concentrate either.

They were out of the car park, heading up Surrey Street past the Town Hall, before Tom said. 'Thank you for coming with me. It made a big difference having you there.'

'Of course I came with you. I'm your wife.'

'I know it was an ordeal for you.'

'Not as much as it was for you. I was just a spectator.'

'Sometimes that can be worse than taking part.'

'Not in this case.' Helen braked for a junction. 'What are we going to do, Tom? I'm so worried. I know you're innocent, but how do you prove it?'

'I don't know,' Tom replied. 'I don't know how I prove it.'

The court appearance out of the way, Tom was expecting to feel a little less anxious than before. But once the immediate sense of relief that he'd come through the hearing had subsided, the anxiety returned with renewed force. What had he really thought would happen in court? That the charges against him might miraculously be dropped? That the police would suddenly concede that they had the wrong man? There was another Tom Whitehead, they'd made a mistake over the computers and it wasn't his that contained indecent images of children? That was never going to happen. He had to face up to the facts. He was going on trial and the evidence against him was damning.

They had a cup of tea and a ham sandwich in the kitchen when they got home. They were both subdued. Tom picked at his sandwich, not feeling like eating. Helen made an attempt to draw him out of himself, but her heart wasn't in it. They'd gone over the morning's proceedings in the car and there seemed little to add to the discussion.

'I have to get back to work,' Helen said when she'd finished her sandwich.

'Do you?'

'I said I'd pop back in for an hour or so. I'll be home in time to get the children. Will you be all right?'

'Yes.'

'You're sure?'

'Yes, I'll be fine.'

She left him there at the kitchen table. She was relieved to get away, to find a distraction to take her mind off her worries.

After she'd gone, Tom sat for a while, going over and over the events of the previous few days until he could bear it no longer. He stood up and paced restlessly around the house, wandering from room to room, looking for something to blot out his melancholy thoughts. He didn't feel like reading. He couldn't face daytime television, some cheap quiz programme or chat show that would depress him even more. He could have gone for a walk, but he was reluctant to leave the house. He didn't want to show his face in public.

Upstairs, he went into the spare bedroom that served as his study, wondering if there was any work he could get on with. It was the sight of the empty shelves that reminded him. The police still had all his files. And besides, he'd been suspended. What was the point of work?

Never, in all his life, had he felt so unsettled, so uncertain of his future. Even if he managed to clear his name — and right now he wasn't confident of succeeding — people would remember the allegations and wonder whether, perhaps, they had been true. Accusations lingered longer in people's minds than vindication. He was tarnished, unsafe. The university would never allow him to return, to teach young people again. Whatever the outcome of the case, Tom knew his career was over.

★　★　★

Helen picked Ben and Hannah up from school at 3.30. She worked three days a week — a partner in a small firm of architects — but school hours only. It was important to her that she should be able to take the children to school and pick them up every day. There was an after-school club for the children of working parents. It had a good reputation, but Helen would have contemplated using it only in dire emergency. She saw it as an abdication from her parental responsibility. Ben and Hannah were *her* children. It was her job to look after them.

56

Most days she tried to get to the school a few minutes before home time, to have a chance to chat to her friends outside the gates, but today she was running late. Ben and Hannah were out in the playground waiting impatiently for her. Helen's friends had already left with their own children. For once, she was glad. They might well have seen Tom's picture in the local paper. Helen didn't know how she'd cope if they mentioned it to her.

The children were surprised, and pleased, to find their father at home. Tom got them a drink and a biscuit and sat with them in the kitchen while they told him about their day. Ben, as a general rule, was reticent about school, answering most questions with, 'I can't remember' or, 'It was boring', but today he'd been to the lunchtime chess club and beaten a boy from Year Four, the year above him.

'You got him in checkmate?' Tom said. 'Wow, that was good.'

'Not checkmate, there wasn't time. But I'd taken his queen, both his knights and one of his bishops, so Mr Parkinson said I'd won.'

'And he was in Year Four? Well done.'

'I have to play him again next week. If I win, I move up a place on the ladder.'

'What was his name?' Hannah asked.

'Kieran Walker,' Ben replied.

'That's Trish Walker's little brother. She's a cow.'

'Hannah,' Helen growled.

'Well, she is. She's always trying to boss everyone around, telling us what to do. We always have to play *her* games and they're *so* boring.'

Hannah came round the table and sat on Tom's knee, recounting some long, involved story about what had happened at playtime, who had fallen out with whom and why.

'Have you got homework to do?' Helen interrupted.

'Literacy. I'll do it later,' Hannah said.

'Is there much?'

'I have to finish a story — a fable. You know, like, who is it again?'

'Aesop?' Tom said.

'Yes, Aesop. But it won't take me long.'

'Do it now,' Helen said firmly. 'Then it's out of the way before tea.'

Tom glanced at his wife. Helen was looking at him strangely. Well, maybe not just him. She was looking at him *and* Hannah. Hannah perched on his knee.

'Now, Hannah,' Helen said firmly.

Was he imagining it? Was that a look of wariness, of suspicion, in Helen's face? She's not sure about me, Tom thought. My ten-year-old daughter is sitting on my lap, something she does all the time, but suddenly you don't want her there. You want her away from me.

Tom eased Hannah off his knee. 'You get your fable, I'll help you finish it.'

For a moment, his eyes met Helen's. He knew he was right. The realisation was like a blow. Even my wife has doubts about me, he thought. She's beginning to wonder, *did he?* Helen couldn't hold his gaze. She turned away, hiding her face, filling the kettle with water to cover her discomfort.

Later, when Hannah and Ben were settled in front of the television, Tom went out to the newsagents and bought a copy of *The Star*. His court appearance was given prominent place on page three — not much text, but a big photograph of Helen and him leaving the courthouse. The headline read, 'University Lecturer on Child Porn Charges'.

Tom put the paper down, feeling sick. That was it. It was all official. He'd been arraigned in court, been formally accused of a sex offence. All their friends in the city would know now. By morning all his colleagues at the university, all his students — probably every student in the entire university — would know about it. He'd be the subject of speculation, of lurid gossip. And who, among all those people, would truly believe in his innocence?

It was on the local television news too — the BBC's *Look North*, from Leeds. Tom didn't want to watch it, but he needed to know what was being reported. He watched the programme by himself in the sitting room. Helen was in the kitchen, the children upstairs. Ten minutes in, there he was, walking across the bridge from the Magistrates' Court, hand in hand with Helen. It wasn't a long video clip, but enough for him to notice how pale and strained his wife looked.

'Daddy, that looks like you.'

Tom twisted round, his finger automatically changing the channel on the remote control.

Hannah was by the door. He wondered how much she'd seen.

'Pardon?'

'On the television. That was you and Mummy, wasn't it?'

He couldn't bring himself to lie directly.

'I don't know, I wasn't paying attention,' he said vaguely.

'Was it?' Hannah persisted. 'Have you been on television?'

'It was nothing,' Tom said.

He switched off the television and walked across to his daughter. He was going to have to tell the children some time — it was unavoidable. But for how long could he put it off?

'Let's get you ready for bed. I'll read you a story.'

Tom often went to his study to work after the children had gone to bed, but this evening he stayed downstairs with Helen. They watched television. There was nothing on that interested them, but they watched all the same — some house makeover programme that was like a sedative, dulling the senses. It was what they both needed at that moment.

The end credits were rolling when the telephone rang out in the hall. Helen got up from the settee and answered it. There was a man's voice at the other end.

'Is that Mrs Whitehead?' he said.

'Yes, it is.'

'What's it like, being married to a pervert?'

She wasn't thinking clearly. She didn't take in

60

the words, didn't react.

'I'm sorry . . . '

'I bet he likes to give it you up the arse, doesn't he? Or does he just fuck the kids?'

Helen put the phone down quickly. She was startled, shocked. Even now she couldn't quite believe what she'd heard. She swallowed, waiting a few seconds before she felt up to returning to the sitting room.

'Who was it?' Tom asked.

She couldn't tell him. It would distress him even more than it had her.

'No one,' she said. 'There was no one there.'

She sat down, gazing at the television screen. A gardening programme was just starting.

'You OK?' Tom said.

'Yes.'

He reached out and touched her shoulder affectionately. She pulled away from him.

'I'll make us a cup of tea.'

It was the same later in bed. Over the years they'd established a routine. No matter how late it was, how tired they were, they'd always have a cuddle and talk for a while before they went to sleep. Helen lying against Tom's chest, his arm around her. But tonight she didn't want to be touched.

'It's been a long day, I'm worn out.'

She kissed him lightly and rolled over on to her own side of the bed. Tom lay on his back, staring up at the ceiling. Feeling hurt, isolated in the darkness.

4

'They can't do this, surely? Look at it.'

Tom flung the newspaper down on Russell's desk. The solicitor slid the paper towards him and studied the open page. The article was short, only four paragraphs in total, tucked away in an obscure corner, but he could see immediately what it was that had upset Tom. The headline read, ' 'Pervert' on child sex charge.'

'How can they call me a pervert? I haven't been convicted of anything. And calling it a sex charge, that's grossly misleading. It makes it sound as if I've been abusing children.'

Russell sighed. 'Sit down.'

'They're prejudicing my case. Isn't that contempt of court?'

'Tom, sit down, please,' Russell said calmly. 'Do you want a cup of tea or anything?'

Tom shook his head. 'I nearly rang you this morning, when I first saw it. It's in all the papers — well, the tabloids anyway. But this is the worst. How can you call that fair and unbiased reporting?'

'It's the *Sun*,' Russell said. 'They're not renowned for their fair and unbiased reporting.'

'But this is going too far. I'm an innocent man and they're labelling me a pervert.'

'In inverted commas.'

'That makes a difference?'

'To the *Sun*, yes. They would claim they're not

actually calling you that, it's just a convenient headline writer's shorthand.'

'But that's nonsense. They're prejudging the outcome of the case.'

'The law of contempt is a big mess, Tom. Newspapers print this kind of stuff all the time and they're almost never prosecuted.'

'You mean they can get away with it?'

'I'm afraid they can.'

Russell pushed the newspaper to one side and looked at Tom sympathetically.

'This is going to be very unpleasant, for you and your family,' he said gently. 'All I can advise is that you try to inure yourself to it. Don't look at the papers. And if you do, try not to let their distortions upset you. The offence you're charged with arouses strong emotions. The press are going to milk those emotions for all they're worth.'

Tom gave a resigned nod. 'I'm sorry, it was just a bit much for me. After everything that's happened in the last few days, to see that in print . . . Well, you know, it really got to me.'

'How's Helen?'

'She's finding it hard.'

'You'll need her with you during this.'

'I know.'

'And the kids?'

'It's too soon to say. I haven't said anything to them, but Hannah's bright, observant. She'll notice I'm not at work, sense something's not right. I'll have to tell her before long.'

Tom glanced away pensively across the office, past the shelves of leather-bound law reports to the window, which looked out over a small Georgian cobbled square, one of the very few in the city that had managed to survive the attentions of the Luftwaffe and the city council planners.

'But that's not your concern,' he said wearily. 'I'm taking up your time. Where do we stand?'

Russell had a file on the desk in front of him. He opened the cover and checked over the notes he'd made inside.

'Well, let's just review the position. The two key areas for us to concentrate on are, obviously, the credit card transactions and the images on your computer.'

'What are these images?' Tom said. 'What am I supposed to have been looking at?'

'We won't know until we get the CPS file. They don't have to be hard-core pornography for them to be classed as indecent, but many of these child porn websites do display very disturbing images. The nature of the ones found on your computer might have a mitigating effect on sentence, if they're relatively innocuous — and I use that word advisedly. But it won't make any difference to whether you're convicted or not.'

'Even if I never looked at them? If I had no idea there was anything like that on my computer?'

'It would be very difficult for us to prove that you never looked at them. In any case, the prosecution don't have to show intent to view indecent images. The fact that the images are there is *prima facie* evidence that the offence has been committed. Even if they'd been down-loaded accidentally, that would still be enough for a conviction.'

'So what defence can I possibly have? The police say the images are there, ergo I'm guilty.'

'That's our problem.' Russell turned his head away, running his forefinger over his jawline. The silence weighed heavily on Tom.

'We've lost before we even start, haven't we?' he said despondently.

Russell looked back. 'Certainly not,' he said firmly. 'That's not an attitude I ever take. Nothing is lost until it's lost. A blindingly obvious statement, I know, but it's been my guiding principle since the day I first started to practise.'

'So where do we go from here?'

'If *you* didn't download the images on to your computer, then there must be an explanation as to how they got there. We have to find that explanation. Let's look at the website issue first. It's possible that the site might have been accessed accidentally, but it's not remotely plausible that the images were then downloaded on to your hard drive accidentally. As the police said, the images had to be paid for first. And your credit card was used for that.'

'But not by me,' Tom said.

'Let's assume someone else did it. Who else, apart from you, has a key to your office?'

'The departmental secretary has a pass key. There may be spares too, I don't know.'

'Do you know where the pass key is kept?'

'In the main office. In a drawer of her desk.'

'So one of your colleagues might have access to it?'

'Yes. I've used it myself in the past. I forgot my own key once. I borrowed the pass key to get into my office.'

'But, in theory, you could have used it to gain entry to one of your colleagues' offices?'

'Yes, I suppose I could.'

'How are your relations with your colleagues? Are there any who dislike you, who might want to discredit you?'

'Well, there are the usual tensions you get in any work place. Academics are competitive, envious people, always comparing themselves with rivals in their field. How much they publish, in what journals, that kind of thing. But it would be pretty extreme for anyone to do something like this to get at me. You think a colleague might have set me up?'

'I'm just exploring possibilities. Could anyone in the department hate you that much?'

Tom pondered the question. *Could* they? It was a fairly small department. Tom had been there for twenty years. He knew all his colleagues reasonably well, thought his relations with most of them were amicable. Did any of them harbour a grudge against him? Were there seething resentments of which he was unaware?

'I don't think it's likely,' he said.

'Students? Any students who might want to discredit you, take revenge for some perceived wrong?'

'I can't think of any. Helen wondered if a student might have done it as a prank.'

'That's something for us to bear in mind. What's the set-up at the university. Are you on a network?'

'Yes. I have a PC in my office, with its own hard drive, but I have internet access, and access to the university network.'

'Could someone have hacked into your computer from outside, through the network?'

'I don't know. I'm not technical enough to know if that's possible.'

'And what about your credit card? Have any of your colleagues seen it? Maybe in a restaurant or somewhere. You leave it on the table, they take a look at the number and memorise it.'

'I couldn't say that was impossible,' Tom replied. 'I've certainly used my card with colleagues in the past. But why would any of them want to do this to me? To ruin me?'

'I want you to check your diary for the dates in question,' Russell said. 'February 8th, 10th and 14th. Try to recall what you did, where you were on those dates.'

'I've already been trying to remember. But the police took my office diary — it's the only one I have.'

'I'll get on to them. They should have returned your papers by now.'

'The dates alone aren't enough, Michael. If someone went into my office when I wasn't there, they'd only need a few minutes to access the net. I need to know the exact times the police claim the images were downloaded.'

Russell scribbled a note on his memo pad. 'I'll see what the CPS have got. In the meantime, call

Visa. You must be due a statement fairly soon. Get them to send you one immediately, and ask them to include the times of the transactions as well as the dates. They can give you that kind of information.'

Tom nodded. 'I'll do that.'

'Let me know when it arrives.'

Russell pushed back his chair and stood up.

'Is that it?' Tom said.

'For the time being, yes.'

Tom hauled himself reluctantly to his feet. He didn't want to leave the comforting environment of Russell's office. In here he had a friend, an ally who was going to help him fight his corner. Out there were only adversaries.

He shook Russell's hand. 'Thank you, Michael. I can't tell you how much it means to me, having you on my side. You think we have a chance?'

'Of course we have a chance,' the solicitor replied.

The words, the tone, were confident enough, but looking into Russell's eyes, Tom thought he detected a flicker of doubt that flared momentarily and was then extinguished.

★   ★   ★

Helen began to notice the change in her friends almost immediately. It was subtle, covert, but she could detect it nonetheless. A group of mums talking outside the school, animated, laughing, but falling suddenly silent the moment Helen approached. Other friends looking at her in a certain way, pity, puzzlement in their eyes. She caught snippets of conversation, subjects hastily changed as they saw her coming. No one mentioned Tom, though Helen was certain that everyone knew. How could they possibly not know?

She felt hurt by the reactions. Did they think she was contagious? Did they think she'd caught something from her husband that could be spread to them and their partners? The beginning and the end of the school day, which had always been such a welcome, sociable time, suddenly became an ordeal for Helen. No one was openly rude, but their distant politeness was worse than outright hostility. The awkward shufflings, the sly, fearful glances as people repositioned themselves to avoid direct contact with her, cut her to the bone. She knew what it felt like to be a pariah.

Only her closest friend, Liz, who had a daughter in the same class as Hannah, seemed immune to this spreading rash of rejection.

'I don't believe a word of it,' Liz said to Helen. 'I know Tom. I know he wouldn't do anything like that. You want to talk, just give me a call.'

That people could be mean and indifferent was no surprise to Helen, but that they could change so abruptly, so unjustifiably, was more of a shock. Yet the mothers, for all their wary circumspection, were nothing like as cruel as their children.

Two days after the court hearing, Hannah came out of school in floods of tears. For the first few hundred yards of the walk home, she was inconsolable, refusing to talk. Only when they were well away from the school, no other people within earshot, did it all come pouring out.

'They say Daddy's a pervert,' she sobbed, her cheeks wet with tears. 'What's a pervert? They say he does horrible, nasty things to little children.'

Helen's blood turned to ice. 'Who do? Who's saying that?'

'Everyone. In my class, in the playground. They asked what he did to me. They danced around me chanting, 'Your daddy's sick, your daddy's a pervert.' What's a pervert?'

'Take no notice of them, Hannah. Try to ignore what they say.'

'They won't play with me. They say that Daddy's going to go to prison. Has he done something wrong?'

'He's done nothing wrong. Children make up things, they call each other names, you know that.'

'But why are they saying it? What's happened?' Hannah gulped for air, her body shaking.

'None of it's true. You know it isn't true. Daddy's a very good, loving daddy. He'd never do anything like that.'

Helen hugged her daughter tight, her own eyes filling with tears. This had all come from the other parents. How could they poison their children's minds like this? How could they incite this kind of malicious victimisation of another child? But she was aware also that humans were

70

fundamentally tribal animals. When someone broke the rules of the tribe, other members — not all, but some — could react with an unpredictable, terrifying hatred.

Helen thought she was resilient, but she wasn't prepared for the level of malevolence, the sheer nastiness, that began to manifest itself. One morning, when Tom had gone out, she returned home from the supermarket and was distressed to find a note pinned to the front door, reading, 'Piss off pervert'. The letter box and glass pane of the door were smeared with what looked like mud. It was only when she got closer and the sour aroma hit her, that she realised it was dog shit.

Another morning there was a letter for her in the post, typewritten address, plain manilla envelope. She opened it to discover a photograph of a naked young Filipino girl in a disgusting pose, with a note stapled to one corner that read, 'This is what your sick husband likes to look at.' Helen couldn't bring herself to throw the photograph away — the thought of it being accidentally discovered in the bin was too awful to contemplate — so she put it in the sink and set fire to it, flushing the ashes away down the plughole.

Tom, too, was struggling to come to terms with his situation. He moped around the house, unable to concentrate on anything for long, then started going for long walks in the countryside to fill his days — driving out to some remote spot where he hoped he wouldn't encounter anyone else. He felt unclean. He felt an outcast. He withdrew into himself. He pulled out of his weekly game of badminton with colleagues from work, he refused to contact any of his friends for fear they would reject him. The ostracism he believed was his rightful punishment became a self-inflicted reality.

Worst of all, he stopped engaging with his family. The affectionate, physical relationship he'd always had with his children ended abruptly. He didn't feel he could touch them — particularly Hannah. He analysed every move he made towards them to ensure they could never be misinterpreted, kept out of their way, especially at bath and bed times. He rarely exchanged more than a few words with them. Hannah and Ben were confused, hurt by his distant, taciturn manner.

Helen did her best to maintain some semblance of a family life, but her own mind was in too much turmoil for her to deal effectively with the pressures of disturbed children and an uncommunicative husband.

She brooded long and hard on the facts of the court case. The evidence against Tom was pretty incontrovertible. The images were there on his computer. How did you explain them away? They'd been married for twelve years, but she wondered now how well she knew him. Did any wife *really* know her husband? He seemed a normal man, but what was a normal man? She didn't know his thoughts. Did he have another side to him, a weird, perverted side?

The kind of men who accessed these

paedophile websites weren't necessarily freaks who lived in seedy bedsits. They were often apparently stable family men with careers and mortgages and children of their own. Helen had always considered their relationship to be open and strong. They had what she regarded as a normal, healthy sex life, but what did that mean? Did Tom harbour other base desires, peculiar fantasies about which she knew nothing? Jesus, was it possible that the allegations against him were true? She was standing by her man, but did he deserve her support?

★   ★   ★

One evening, the week after Tom had appeared in court, he and Helen were in the sitting room — mindlessly watching television to avoid the effort of having to talk to each other — when Hannah came in in her pyjamas.

'I can't sleep, Mummy,' she said, sitting down next to Helen on the settee.

'What is it?' Helen asked. 'Is something bothering you?'

Hannah hadn't been sleeping well since the incident at school — an incident that, thankfully, hadn't been repeated, largely because Helen had been in to see the headteacher to ensure that neither Hannah nor Ben was ever picked on again like that.

'There are some people outside my bedroom window,' Hannah said. 'On the street.'

'There are often people walking past. Just

close your eyes and think of something else.'

'They're not walking past. They're just standing there.'

'Doing what?'

'Nothing really. Their voices are keeping me awake.'

'They'll move on. It's probably some of the local kids meeting up. Now go back to bed, it's late.'

Helen took Hannah out into the hall and watched while her daughter went back upstairs. Then she went into the front room, without switching on the light, and pulled back the curtains a fraction to peer out. It was dark outside, but she could see the group on the pavement in the light from the street lamps. It wasn't unusual for youngsters to gather nearby, aimless teenagers looking for something to do away from the prying eyes of their parents. But they were generally local kids — Helen usually recognised a few of them. But this group weren't kids — they were men, five or six of them in their twenties — and she recognised none of them. As she watched, two more men arrived. A similar age to the others, they had the short hair and swaggering gait that Helen always associated with football hooligans or other yobs. Their presence made her uneasy.

'There's a group of lads hanging around at the front,' she said, going back through into the sitting room.

Tom didn't even glance up from the television.

'Tom,' Helen said. 'There's seven or eight of them, outside the house.'

Tom turned his head. 'It's nothing to worry about.'

'Why are they there? I think we should call the police.'

'What for? A group of kids on the street? The police wouldn't want to know.'

Helen sat back down, gazing at the television — some execrable sitcom. What were they doing? They *never* watched sitcoms.

The chanting began.

At first Helen thought it was on the television. But the screen showed only a young girl in a shop. It was coming from outside. The group of yobs.

'Tom.'

He'd heard it too. He got up and went out into the hall. He listened to what they were chanting. 'Paedophiles out. Out, out, OUT.' Loud, rhythmic, repeated over and over.

Oh, Christ, what the hell was going on? Helen was next to him now, one hand on his arm.

'Call the police, Tom.'

Hannah appeared on the stairs.

'I'm scared. What are they doing?' she asked anxiously. 'Making all that noise.'

'It's OK,' Helen said. 'Why don't you go into our bed? It'll be quieter there.'

There was a crash of breaking glass from upstairs.

'Ben!'

Tom took the stairs two at a time, reached the top, crossed the landing and flung open his son's bedroom door. Ben was sitting up, cowering in a corner of his bed, speechless with fright. The curtains had contained most of the force of the impact, but there were fragments of glass on the carpet, a half brick among them. Tom scooped Ben up in his arms.

'Are you all right? Are you hurt? Ben, are you hurt?'

Ben shook his head and began to cry. Tom carried him out. Helen and Hannah were on the landing.

'Is he — ' Helen began.

'He's OK. Here.' Tom passed Ben to his wife. 'Take him downstairs.'

Tom stepped into his study, picked up the telephone extension and dialled 999. As he spoke to the operator, then the police, he could hear the group out at the front still chanting. The noise sent a shiver through him.

There was another crash — this time from downstairs. Tom heard Helen cry out, Hannah scream.

'Hurry, this is urgent,' he said into the phone, then slammed down the receiver and raced out of the room.

'Helen!' he shouted.

'Here.'

'You OK?'

Tom hurtled down the stairs. Helen, still holding Ben, was rooted to the spot in the hall. Hannah was clinging to her mother's arm, sobbing hysterically.

'You OK?' Tom repeated.

Helen nodded. She was pale, staring wide-eyed at the front door as if she expected it to be smashed open any moment.

'The crash I heard?' Tom said.

'The front room.'

'Get in the kitchen.'

Tom picked Hannah up and carried her to the back of the house. She clung tight to him, shaking violently as she wept.

'They can't do this,' Tom said angrily. 'I'm not putting up with this.'

He lowered Hannah to the floor and looked around the kitchen. He snatched up Ben's cricket bat, which was squeezed into the gap next to the fridge.

'Don't go out,' Helen yelled. She grasped hold of his arm. 'Don't be stupid. They're a mob, they'll kill you.'

He saw her terrified face.

'Don't go out. That's what they want.'

Helen pushed the kitchen door to and sat down at the table, Ben curled up on her lap, crying uncontrollably. Tom sat down. Hannah came into his arms, so small and vulnerable. He held her, her face pressed tight against his neck. He could feel her tears warm on his skin. Where were the police?

A loud hammering on the kitchen window gave him a jolt. Helen screamed. Tom twisted round. A leering face was pressed to the glass. A young man with cropped hair and wild eyes, his features contorted with loathing. He jabbed an accusatory finger at Tom.

'Fucking pervert!' he shouted. 'Chop your balls off. Lock you up and throw away the key.'

The man's fists hammered on the window again so violently it seemed it might break.

'Fuck off out of here,' he screamed viciously. 'We don't want people like you round here.'

Tom eased Hannah off his knee and whipped the kitchen blind down, shutting out the man's snarling visage. Where the hell were the police?

The hammering continued for a few seconds, then stopped as abruptly as it had begun. Tom heard running footsteps on the path around the side of the house, getting fainter, then gone. Helen was crying now too. Tom drew Hannah to him and crouched down beside his wife, putting his other arm around both her and Ben, wanting to hold the whole family close and protect them.

A long ring of the front doorbell made him look up.

'Don't go, Tom,' Helen said in a panic, tears streaming down her face. 'Don't answer it.'

'It might be the police.'

Tom swung open the kitchen door. Across the hall, through the glass of the front door, he could see a figure outside, a flashing blue light in the background.

'I think it is. It's the police.'

Tom opened the front door to let them in.

⋆　⋆　⋆

It was gone midnight by the time Tom got to bed. The police had driven around the neighbourhood immediately after their arrival, but there was no sign of the yobs — they appeared to have melted away into the night. Then there were the children to calm and comfort, statements to be made, an emergency

78

glazier called out to board up the two broken windows.

Ben and Hannah were too scared to go back to their own rooms so they went in the double bed with Helen. Tom took Hannah's bed, but he didn't go to sleep for a long time. Those yobs hadn't been local. 'We don't want people like you round here,' the face at the kitchen window had yelled. But *he* hadn't been from round here. He was an outsider, like the others. They were a rent-a-mob. Tom lay awake, wondering who had organised them. And why.

5

Next morning Tom's emotions were still running high. The sheer terror he'd felt the previous evening had gone, but in its place had come a fierce sense of outrage, an anger that had driven out the despondency that had afflicted him since his court appearance. The threat to his family had jolted him out of his lethargy. He knew now that he had to take action.

He waited until the glazier had finished replacing the glass in the broken windows and all the mess had been cleared up before he went into his study and called Michael Russell. He told the solicitor what had happened.

'My God!' Russell exclaimed. 'Are you all right? What about Ben and Hannah?'

'They seem OK now,' Tom said. 'But it was terrifying at the time. For all of us. I'm worried, Michael. Particularly for Helen and the kids. What if it happens again? What if those yobs come back?'

'What did the police say?'

'I talked to one of the officers who came out, asked him about protection. He said they didn't have the manpower to put a twenty-four-hour guard on the house.'

'They'd have to find it, if we asked for it,' Russell said.

'I was thinking, maybe it would be better if I moved out.'

'That's a tough decision.'

'What would you advise?'

Russell was silent for a time. Then he said, 'That's not something I can really help you with, Tom. Have you talked to Helen?'

'Not yet.'

'Discuss it with her, see what she thinks.'

'Someone is orchestrating all this,' Tom said. 'Someone who must really hate me. Who wants to see me ruined, in jail. I don't know why, but I'm not going to sit back and let it happen. I'm innocent, I've done nothing wrong. I want to know who's behind it, but I need help, I've never dealt with anything like this before. The police are no use, they've already decided I'm guilty, but what about a private investigator? Do you know any?'

'We use one from time to time, yes. He's good, but he's not cheap.'

'I don't care about the money. I just want to get to the bottom of this. Can you give me his number?'

'Leave it with me. Let me talk to him. See if he can help us.'

Helen was in the kitchen, making a pot of coffee, when Tom went downstairs. He sat with her at the table and broached the subject of his moving out. Helen frowned at him.

'What do you mean?'

'That after last night maybe I should find somewhere else to live for a while.'

'Do you think that's a good idea?'

He studied her face, trying to guess what she was feeling. He'd told himself that his decision would ultimately depend on Helen's first reaction. If she rejected the suggestion out of hand, he would stay. If she embraced it, then he would go. Her equivocal reply disappointed him. He'd wanted a clearer sign that he was still welcome in the family home.

'It might be better if I weren't around,' he said.

'Better for you, you mean?'

'Better for all of us. I know things haven't been easy for you this past week. Or for the children. But I never thought it would come to this, to people throwing bricks through our windows.'

Helen hadn't told him about the other incidents — the dog shit on the door, the obscene photograph in the post. They'd shocked her at the time, but they seemed comparatively mild now next to the physical assault on their home.

'You'd leave us here alone?' she said.

'They weren't after you, or the children. *I* was their target. If I'm not here, they won't come back. You don't need to worry about that.'

'Are you sure?'

'They were making a point. A mindless, primitive point. They wanted to scare us, to intimidate us. They could have broken in easily if they'd really wanted to harm me.'

'That didn't make it any less frightening.'

'I know. That's why I don't want it to happen again. I don't want to put you or the children through anything like that again.'

'Where would you go?'

'I don't know. I thought I'd ask Bruce. He's

got a spare bedroom. Failing that a hotel or guest house. It'll only be for a few months.' Until the trial, he almost added, but didn't. That was not something he wanted to dwell on.

Helen screwed up her features, biting her thumbnail. 'Tom, I don't know. I don't know what we should do.'

'Do you want me to stay?'

What was she to say to that? Did she? She felt more secure with him in the house, but maybe that was an illusion. Maybe he was right. With him gone, she and the children would be safer. And it might make other things easier. She and Tom weren't getting on — there were too many doubts in the air for their relationship to be the same as it had been before. But was a separation the answer? Would it not simply make the rifts wider, more unbridgeable?

Her hesitation gave him his answer.

'You'd like me to go, wouldn't you?' he said.

'I haven't said that.'

'You haven't said anything. Either way.'

'That's because I don't know what to do.'

'If you want me to go, I will.'

'Don't put the decision on to me. Do *you* want to move out? Is that it? You want to go, but you don't want the guilt of doing it?'

'No, that's not it.' He saw it as a sign of how far things had deteriorated that she could even think such a thing. 'Look, I don't want this to turn into an argument. I only suggested it because I'm frightened for you and the children. Hannah and Ben were terrified out of their wits last night. I want to be here. I can't bear the thought of you all being alone in the house. But *I'm* the problem. With me gone, the problem is solved.'

Helen rubbed her eyes with the tips of her fingers, then put her palms together in front of her, almost as if she were praying. Her expression was troubled.

'I don't know, Tom. I just don't know.'

Tom looked at her. He'd never asked her this directly, but he felt he had to now.

'Helen, do you think I did it? Do you think I downloaded those pictures?'

She turned her head away, avoiding his gaze.

'Do you?' he asked again.

'Tom . . . I don't know . . . I don't know what to think.'

'You think I could do something like that?'

'No, no.' She hesitated. 'But the internet is a strange thing. It corrupts, it changes people. The guys at the office, I know they surf the net looking for porn, or titillation at least. They do it quite openly. They aren't ashamed, or embarrassed by it. It's like a joke to them. The internet has made some things acceptable that weren't before. They'd never read porn magazines in the office, but they think nothing of looking at it on the web.'

'But this is *child* pornography. That's different.'

'I know.'

The trust had gone from their marriage, Tom realised, eaten away by the allegations hanging over him. They were becoming estranged. They no longer talked, they no longer touched — not even a brief kiss or a fleeting embrace. Tom knew he was going to have to make the decision. He loathed the idea of moving out, of giving in to a bunch of violent thugs. It made him feel hounded. It made him feel he was surrendering, running away and going into hiding like a guilty man. Yet what alternative did he have? If he made enough noise, the police would probably have to provide protection, but did he really want a guard outside his front door, a uniformed watchdog emphasising his status as a reviled outcast? Could he even rely on the police, in the circumstances? They were hardly likely to be very sympathetic to an alleged paedophile, and they certainly couldn't protect all the family, day and night. Why rely on other people when the simplest, and perhaps best, solution — to distance himself from his family — was entirely within his own hands?

'Let's try it,' he said. 'For a few days, a week. See how it works out.'

★   ★   ★

Bruce Kelly, Tom's colleague from the History Department, lived in a two-bedroomed flat in a large block near the city centre, one of many such apartment complexes that were gradually taking over the inner core of Sheffield. Almost every available building plot within a mile radius of the Town Hall was being developed for residential occupation by young urban professionals — a process of gentrification that fascinated Tom. His specialist subject was twentieth-century industrial history and he took a close interest in the changing character of the city centre. The areas that had been devastated by the slum clearances of the 1960s — their small shops and businesses lost, their populations forced out to soulless estates on the periphery of the city — were now being repopulated by the affluent middle classes, whose main preoccupations, if the new developments were anything to go by, seemed to be en-suite bathrooms and tapas bars.

It amused Tom that the banks of the River Don, for years one of the filthiest waterways in England, had suddenly become a desirable place to live. Apartments in an old brewery only yards from the inner ring road were being sold for a quarter of a million — luxurious, beautifully appointed flats with balconies on which the owners could sit out with their orange juice and croissants, enjoying the heady aroma of exhaust fumes from the stationary traffic below.

Bruce's apartment building suffered from a similar juxtaposition of opulence and squalor. The flats were expensive, reasonably well built given the rock-bottom standards of the British construction industry. There were shops on the ground floor that reflected the interests of the well-heeled residents: a Chinese noodle bar, an up-market estate agency, a ski and surf equipment shop, a *cachacaria* — whatever one of those was — and, lowering the tone a little, a Budgens supermarket that had somehow sneaked past the developers' chic pretensions. But a quarter of a mile away there were prostitutes loitering on the street corners and out at the front of the building, near a skateboard park daubed with obscene graffiti, you could hardly move without bumping into a crack cocaine dealer.

Bruce had been happy for Tom to move in with him, relaxed about the nature of the arrangement.

'Stay as long as you like,' he'd said. 'Come and go as you please, I'll give you some keys. Cook what you like too. I tend to eat out quite a lot, but the kitchen's got everything you might need.'

Tom was in the kitchen now. He'd come over with his suitcase by taxi earlier, leaving the car for Helen. Bruce had been there to greet him, to show him his bedroom, but he'd since gone out to friends for the evening. Tom had the place to himself. It seemed strange, unsettling. He was used to the noise and activity of a family house, the children's clutter constantly under his feet. Their kitchen was the centre of the home, a place of dirty footprints on the lino, of lingering smells, of food and happy chatter. Bruce's kitchen was like the galley of an expensive cabin cruiser. Cunningly laid out to maximise the space, it contained every gadget you might wish to have, but only the microwave and espresso machine looked as if they were ever used. The stainless-steel oven hood gleamed, the granite work-tops were pristine and polished, devoid of any objects. There was a sterility about the room that also characterised the rest of the flat. It wasn't in keeping with the Bruce Tom knew. But Bruce had changed since his divorce nine months earlier, since he'd moved out of the marital home and acquired this swish new apartment. It was as if in parting with his wife he'd also shed most of his other worldly goods and reverted to a minimalist bachelor existence.

There didn't seem to be any food in the flat, apart from milk and cheese in the fridge and a packet of muesli in a cupboard. Tom found some tea bags and brewed a pot of tea, taking his mug out into the living area and settling himself into an armchair that had 'designer catalogue' written all over it. He was depressed. The surroundings were not conducive to a warm, homely feeling, but he'd have been down wherever he was. Moving out had not been pleasant. The children had not taken it well and Tom had mixed feelings about that, pained to see them so upset, but glad that they didn't want him to go. Hannah and Ben had both been in tears.

'Why, Daddy?' Hannah had kept saying. 'Don't you want to be with us? Don't you love us any more?'

'Of course I do,' Tom had said, kneeling down and embracing both his children, close to tears himself. 'But I don't want any harm to come to you. You and Ben matter more to me than anything. I don't want those nasty men to come back and frighten you again.'

'But we need you here to protect us.'

'It won't be for long. I'll call you every evening to see how you are. You look after Mummy for me.'

He'd held on to the children for as long as he could, the taxi driver waiting impatiently out on the street. Then he'd kissed them one last time and gone to the door. He and Helen had looked at each other. She'd seemed uncertain, cool even.

'Well, I'll see you,' he'd said.

'Yes,' Helen had replied.

She'd made no move. Nor had he. They hadn't kissed, hadn't hugged. All the way over to Bruce's flat in the taxi, Tom had wondered bleakly whether this separation might prove to be more than just temporary.

★ ★ ★

The day after the move Tom went back home. Helen had called him early that morning, before she left for work, to say that the police — complying with a court order obtained by Russell — had finally returned his files and papers. Twelve large cardboard boxes contained all the material they'd seized from both his office and his study.

Tom let himself into the house, picking up the mail on the doormat and riffling through it. He recognised one item — the statement from Visa that he'd been awaiting impatiently for several days. He ripped open the envelope and scanned the list of transactions, hoping, praying, that they wouldn't be there. But they were. Three payments to nymphs4you.com, on three separate dates in February. Tom studied the entries, as bewildered now by their appearance in print as he had been when the police first told him of their existence. Where did they come from? he

89

asked himself again. Where the hell did they come from?

The exact times of the transactions — information that Russell had so far been unable to obtain from the Crown Prosecution Service — were recorded next to the dates. At last! All he needed now was his diary. He turned to the boxes of files that the police — with characteristic lack of consideration — had simply dumped in the hall, half blocking the dining room door. Tom could see that they were going to be too heavy for Helen to move, so he took them upstairs to the study, one box at a time. Breaking open the seals, he sorted through the contents. His office desk diary was in the fourth box he checked. He tucked the diary under his arm and went out of the study. The Visa statement was in his pocket, but he couldn't bring himself to take it out. That name alone — nymphs4you.com — conjured up such ghastly images in his mind that it seemed disgusting to even look at it in this, his family home, his children's home.

He glanced into the bedrooms as he crossed the landing. The duvet of their double bed was pulled back, Helen's nightdress crumpled on the pillow, a blouse on the sheet where she'd discarded it. He imagined her there, sleeping alone, waking up alone. Had she missed him as much as he'd missed her?

Hannah's room was tidier. She'd made her bed, placed her favourite teddies against the wooden headboard. Ben's room was a bombsite. There was Lego strewn all over the carpet, a half-completed jigsaw poking out from under the bed, along with his pyjamas, slippers and a whole collection of cuddly toys. Tom looked around the room, feeling a sudden pang of loss, wondering whether he'd done the right thing.

Dispirited now, he went back downstairs, scribbled a brief note for Helen, then left the house.

He waited until he was back at Bruce's apartment before he took out his Visa statement and studied it again. There was a whole page of entries. Tom glanced down the list, noting payments to Sainsbury's, to Waterstone's book shop, to Texaco, the local petrol station, to Toys Я Us and to Pizza Hut, where they'd all gone for a meal one Friday after school. Every entry seemed legitimate — except the three website transactions. Tom found a piece of paper and wrote down the details of the payments to nymphs4you.com: February 8th, 12.47 p.m., £16.04; February 10th, 12.43 p.m., £15.62; February 14th, 1.15 p.m., £15.84.

The amounts seemed strange, but according to the information on the statement they were all the sterling equivalent of $25, slight fluctuations in the exchange rate accounting for the different sums charged to Tom's card.

Tom got out his office diary and checked the dates: February 8th had been a Tuesday, a normal working day. He had no unusual entries for that particular day. He'd had a tutorial until noon, then a Third Year seminar at 2 p.m. In the evening he'd gone to a meeting of the South Yorkshire Industrial Society. What had he been doing at 12.47 p.m.? Lunchtime. There was no record in his diary, and he couldn't remember specifically where he might have been at that time on that day. He had no set routine for his lunch break. Sometimes he had a sandwich at his desk, sometimes he left his office to go to the bank or the shops, occasionally he went to the university staff club and ate there.

He turned to the next date — February 10th. That was a Thursday. The time 12.43 p.m. Lunchtime again. He couldn't recall what he'd done for lunch that day either and his diary was no help. Unless he had a prearranged appointment with someone else, he never made a note of his lunchtimes in his diary. Who did? It was beginning to look as if someone had been waiting for him to go out to lunch, and had then somehow gained access to his office and used his computer. Did that make sense? He could think of no other rational explanation. Yet it seemed a bizarre conclusion to come to. Had someone really been watching him, monitoring his movements?

He flipped over a page of his diary to get to February 14th — a Monday. He'd had a lecture at 9 a.m., a tutorial at 11. No indication of what he might have been doing at 1.15 p.m.

Tom went still.

One-fifteen? That couldn't be right.

He reached for the Visa statement, staring at one of the entries. Of course. There it was. He thought back to that particular day, working out the times in his head, feeling a mounting sense of elation.

He went to the phone and called Michael Russell.

★   ★   ★

Tom put the Visa statement down on the desk, turning it around so that the solicitor could read it clearly.

'These are the three entries,' Tom said. 'I've marked them with asterisks. This is the first one, February 8th. According to this statement, the credit card payment to nymphs4you.com was made at 12.47 p.m., which was presumably the time at which the images from the website were downloaded on to my computer. So at that moment someone must have been using my computer.'

'Yes, that would seem to be an accurate assessment of the information,' Russell said in his cautious, lawyerly way.

'I can't prove where I was at that time,' Tom went on. 'The same applies to the second transaction, on February 10th. I can't prove one way or the other whether I was in my office at that time. But the third entry.' Tom put a finger on the statement, underlining the time of the transaction. 'On the 14th, at 1.15 p.m., I can prove that I was not in my office.'

Tom looked at Russell. The solicitor was gazing at him intently.

'The proof is here,' Tom said. 'The very next entry on the statement. See? A payment of £59.99 to Toys Я Us. Made on the same day, at 1.23 p.m. It was Ben's birthday the following week. I went out to Toys Я Us on the Supertram and bought him a Scalextric set. Toys Я Us is three or four miles from my office, down in the Don Valley. It's a good fifteen or twenty-minute journey, longer if you have to wait for a tram. If I bought a Scalextric in Toys Я Us at 1.23 p.m., there is no way I could have been in my office eight minutes earlier at 1.15. It's just not possible.'

Russell picked up the Visa statement and scrutinised it closely. Tom watched him impatiently. The solicitor's restraint was infuriating.

'It can't have been me,' Tom said. 'At 1.15 p.m. I was in Toys Я Us.'

Russell put down the statement. His brow furrowed. 'This gets odder and odder.'

'But it puts me in the clear, doesn't it? I have an alibi for the time they allege I was at my computer.'

'It would appear so,' Russell replied. 'But let's not be too hasty. There may be an error on the Visa bill. They may have got the date or the time wrong.'

'Oh, come on,' Tom said incredulously. 'They might have got my card number wrong too, charged these transactions to the wrong account. Why would they have got the date wrong?'

'I'm only thinking ahead to what the prosecution might say. Perhaps there's a time delay at Visa. Perhaps that time, 1.15 p.m., isn't the time any indecent images were being downloaded, but the time at which Visa recorded the transaction.'

'They record it instantly, don't they?' Tom

said. 'It's all electronic. Why would there be a delay?'

Russell acknowledged the point. 'I don't know. I'm trying not to get too excited too soon.'

'Well, you're succeeding there.'

'On the surface this would seem to be good news, very good news. But I've had good news in the past that has turned out to be not quite so good. It pays to be careful.'

'But isn't this conclusive evidence that someone else must have used my computer?' Tom said.

'Perhaps,' Russell admitted. 'But it's only one instance out of three. What if the police allege you were part of a paedophile ring, that one of your fellow members used your computer on that day with your acquiescence. We're not out of the woods yet.'

Tom leaned over the desk. 'Michael, I'm being set up here. Someone has been watching me, breaking into my office and using my computer when I wasn't there. I want to know what's going on. Did you get in touch with the private investigator we discussed?'

'I've spoken to him. Given him the background.'

'What's his name?'

'Moran. Dave Moran. He wants to meet you tomorrow afternoon. Are you free?'

Tom gave a sardonic laugh. 'What else am I going to be doing?'

'You were right. We need professional help. Moran has skills, contacts we don't have. There are too many things about this case that just don't add up.'

Russell paused, pulling a cardboard boxfile across the desk and opening the lid.

'I've been making enquiries myself. About Operation Gold Dust.'

'The international paedophile investigation the police mentioned?'

Russell nodded. 'The FBI handled the American end of the investigation. The websites at the centre of it — including nymphs4you.com — were all based in the US. The FBI obtained the names of all the people who'd used the websites and compiled lists according to where in the world the users lived. They then sent the lists to the Department of Justice, which forwarded them to the appropriate authorities in the countries concerned — in our case, the National Criminal Intelligence Service.'

Russell produced a piece of notepaper from the file.

'I had a chat with a very helpful fellow at the Department of Justice in Washington. The Americans have such a refreshingly open legal system. He told me that the preliminary FBI list of suspects from the UK was sent to the Justice Department on February 3rd and forwarded by the Justice Department to the UK on February 5th.'

Tom squinted at him. 'On February 5th? But then — '

'Exactly. Your name can't possibly have been on that list.'

'Then why did the police — ?'

'Let me finish,' Russell broke in again. 'Now

96

that wasn't the end of the investigation. It continued for a couple more weeks — the FBI, so I gather, were letting the websites keep operating in the hope of apprehending more users — but the sites were eventually shut down on the orders of the US Attorney General on February 20th. There's another list, apparently, relating to the users who were identified during that final period.'

'And my name is on that list?' Tom said.

'It might be,' Russell replied. 'Only there's one problem. The FBI has yet to deliver the list to the Justice Department. So how is it possible for NCIS to already have a copy of the list?'

6

Tom went downstairs just before 2 p.m. and waited on the pavement in front of the apartment building. It was a warm, sunny spring day. Office workers were sitting out on the green across the road, eating sandwiches. A group of noisy youths in T-shirts was clattering around the concrete curves of the skateboard park. The Chinese noodle bar was crowded with business executives and smartly dressed women. No one gave him a second glance. Tom relished his anonymity. A week ago he would have hidden his head in shame, convinced that everyone knew who he was, what he was supposed to have done. He had a better perspective on things now. His photograph had been in the papers, but notoriety — like celebrity — was short-lived. No one around here cared who he was.

A silver Jaguar pulled up next to him and the big, beefy man in the driver's seat leaned across and opened the passenger door.

'Dr Whitehead?'

Tom slid into the car. The beefy man held out his hand.

'Dave Moran. Pleased to meet you.'

'You too,' Tom said.

Moran's hand was large and fleshy. The skin was soft and slightly clammy, like a toad's belly, but there was nothing yielding about his grip.

'Which floor are you on?' he asked, easing the

Jaguar out into the line of traffic.

'Pardon?'

'In there.' Moran nodded back towards the apartment complex.

'Oh, the fourth.'

'Nice view?'

'Not bad.'

'I went in there once. Didn't think much to it. No character. They're all the same, these new apartment blocks. Red brick and that tacky blue trim all over them. Horrible. And the prices . . . ' Moran let out a long sigh. 'Two hundred thou for a glorified rabbit hutch. Who'd pay that? They sold most of them before they'd even been built, you know. People buying to let, for an investment, renting them out to yuppies. But what happens when the yuppies all get hitched, have kids? Who's going to live in 'em then?'

Moran glanced in his rear-view mirror and accelerated past the van in front. Tom studied him. The private investigator had black, slicked-back hair and a plump, ruddy face. He was wearing a dove grey suit, pale pink shirt and a psychedelic green and yellow tie. There was an aroma of aftershave about him — sweet and pungent. Tom put his age at somewhere in his late forties.

'Michael Russell tells me you're a history lecturer,' Moran said.

'That's right.'

'Big subject, history. You cover it all?'

'Mostly the nineteenth and twentieth centuries. Post-Industrial Revolution.'

'I hated history at school. Nothing but dull

99

facts and dates. We had this twat of a teacher, old fart who'd read out the same notes for forty-odd years, never changed them. Jesus, it was boring. I've got more interested in it since. You do, don't you? Education, it's wasted on kids. You should start school at thirty, when you're interested in learning.'

Moran paused, but only to draw breath. 'You see that programme on the telly the other week? History programme, looking back at the kings and queens of England. Seems that Henry VII came from illegitimate stock, so did his wife, so Liz and Charlie and all the other tossers in the House of Windsor are bastards. We knew that already, of course.'

'I don't think I saw the programme,' Tom said.

'It was good. Well researched. They traced the real line of accession from Henry the something, the last legitimate king. Turns out the true king of England lives in Australia. Some shitty little dump in the outback. Wagga Wagga or somewhere, you know what these Australian names are like. Nice bloke, got kids and grandchildren, likes a few beers on a Saturday night. And he's the rightful king. Would you believe it? Give him the job, I say. He couldn't be any worse than the lot we've got.'

'Where are we going?' Tom asked, hoping it wasn't far.

'Your house,' Russell replied.

'My house? Why?'

'I want to take a look around.'

'For what?'

'Anything I can find,' Moran said ambiguously. 'Maybe nothing, maybe something. St John's Close, Fulwood, Michael said.'

'That's correct. Number 98.'

'When we go in, I don't want you to say anything. Absolute silence. Find a chair somewhere and sit down. Try not to make any noise at all. OK?'

Tom nodded. What was going on? There were questions he wanted to ask, but he sensed it wasn't the right moment. Better to wait and see what happened.

Moran turned into St John's Close and stopped the car outside Tom's house. Reaching over on to the back seat, he grasped hold of a black attaché case and climbed out. Tom went first up the drive, unlocking the door to let them into the house. It was one of Helen's work days, so the place was deserted.

Tom led them into the sitting room. Moran gestured at an armchair and, while Tom sat down, opened his case on the settee. Inside were various tools in pouches and an assortment of boxes and gadgets whose exact purpose was unclear. Tom had never seen anything like them before. Moran picked out one of the gadgets, a slim, black device about the size of a television remote control, and slipped a pair of headphones over his ears. He adjusted the controls on the device and began to walk slowly around the room, pausing occasionally as if he were listening to something through the headphones. When he got to the alcove to the right of the chimney breast he stopped, then crouched down and held the device close to the electric socket on the wall. Removing the headphones, he went back to his case and took out a screwdriver. He had the electric socket unscrewed in seconds. He eased the plastic cover away from the wall and peered behind it. Then, silently, he screwed the cover back in place.

Tom watched Moran continue his circuit of the room, then waited patiently while he did the same in every other part of the house. The whole operation took almost half an hour. When Moran returned his face was inscrutable. He put a finger to his lips, reminding Tom to be silent, and packed away his equipment in his case.

Even outside on the drive and getting into the car, Moran held his peace. He waited until they were several streets away from the house before he pulled into the kerb and turned off the engine.

'Interesting,' he said. 'There was one in the socket in the sitting room, one behind a cupboard in the kitchen and one upstairs in the bedroom — *your* bedroom.'

'One what?' Tom said.

'Listening device,' Moran replied. 'A bug.'

Tom gaped at him. 'A bug? My house is bugged? Bugged by whom?'

'Now that,' Moran said, 'is the question.'

★ ★ ★

Moran's office was in a block behind the cathedral, on the hillside sloping down to the Law Courts, where many of the city's legal firms

102

had their headquarters. A discreet brass plaque beside the door read, 'Moran Associates — Private Investigators and Security Consultants.' Inside the front door was a brightly lit reception area with walls and carpet in different shades of grey, shiny metallic light fittings and, beneath a framed Mondrian-like geometrically patterned picture, a large black leather settee with a glass and steel coffee table in front of it.

The room had a clean, sophisticated feel, an effect spoilt slightly by the elderly, grey-haired woman behind the reception desk who looked at Moran over her reading glasses and said, 'Hello, love, you want a cuppa?'

'Tom,' Moran said. 'Meet my mother. Mum, this is Dr Tom Whitehead. And before you ask him about your varicose veins, he's a doctor of philosophy, not medicine.'

'Hello, love,' Mrs Moran said. 'How do you like your tea?'

'Milk, no sugar. Thank you,' Tom replied.

'We'll be in the box,' Moran said, heading upstairs.

'The box' turned out to be a room in the centre of the first floor, a strange, rectangular space which had been constructed by removing slices off all the adjoining rooms. It had no windows and was big enough for just a table and four chairs. There was no other furniture. The surface of the table was clean, save for a telephone, a pad of white paper and a pen.

'Make yourself comfortable,' Moran said, easing his large frame down on to one of the chairs. He'd been uncharacteristically quiet on the car journey back into town. Tom had attempted to probe him further about his discoveries in the house, but Moran had deflected the questions by saying simply. 'Let's wait till we get to my office.'

Tom had already detected a trace of the showman in Moran, begun to suspect that he had a fondness for some of the more cloak-and-dagger elements of his trade, but the air of mystery Moran was creating was genuinely worrying to Tom. Someone had installed listening devices in his house. Apart from the question who? there were other unanswered queries — why? for how long? and where else had his privacy been violated? Someone had been monitoring his private conversations, listening in on his life. It puzzled Tom, made him indignant, angry. But it was also very disturbing.

'We can talk freely in here,' Moran said. 'I sweep this room every day for bugs. The walls, ceiling and floor are completely soundproof — lined with copper mesh to distort electronic surveillance — and there are no windows for bouncers to home in on.'

Tom had no idea what he was talking about. 'Bouncers?'

'Window bouncers. You aim a laser beam at a window. It picks up the vibrations in the glass created by the sounds inside the room. The sounds are then translated, amplified and clarified — and listened to.'

'They can do that?' Tom said.

'That and a lot more.'

Tom looked around the room. The blank

walls, the low ceiling gave him a feeling of claustrophobia.

'Is this really necessary?'

'It pays to be careful,' Moran replied. 'Just because you're paranoid . . . and all that.' He reached out and swung the door wider to let his mother in. She was carrying a tray bearing two mugs of tea and a plate of cakes.

'Here you are, love,' she said, putting a mug down in front of Tom. 'Have some parkin. I made it myself.'

'Thank you.'

'Mum's parkin is legendary,' Moran said. 'I've had some of the toughest characters in here, real hard men, but give them a slice of my mum's parkin and they're practically weeping.'

Mrs Moran rolled her eyes. 'Take no notice of him,' she said to Tom. 'He doesn't deserve me. The things I have to put up with, working here. And the pay's rubbish.'

'Any messages?' Moran asked.

'I put them on your desk. Your suit's ready. I'll pop out and pick it up now. Oh, and Janice rang. She said she'd meet you at Ricky's at eleven.' Mrs Moran clicked her tongue disapprovingly. 'I don't know, going out clubbing at your age, it's ridiculous.'

'You should come with us,' Moran said. 'They allow zimmers on the dance floor, you know. You might score.'

'Cheeky bugger,' Mrs Moran said.

'Go on, get out, you old bat. Go and fetch my suit,' Moran said, shooing his mother out and closing the door behind her.

'Now,' he said, resuming his seat. 'Down to business. Let's look at what we've got. Bugs in three different locations in your home — kitchen, sitting room, bedroom — the locations where most conversations in a house take place. But your phone was clean. That's significant. I'll come back to that. The bugs are state of the art. Very sensitive, very reliable. They'll be linked to recording apparatus, probably voice-activated. That could be anywhere — they have a range of several miles.'

'My conversations have been recorded, as well as listened to?' Tom said.

'That's right.'

'For how long?'

'That's impossible to tell.'

'And you left these bugs in place?'

'Best course of action. Remove them and they know we're on to them. They might put some other surveillance in place, something we might not pick up on.'

'Who are 'they'?' Tom asked.

'Well, these bugs are available on the open market. Anyone can buy them, it's not illegal. It's possible this could be a private job. I've come across embittered husbands, in the throes of divorce, who've hired someone to bug their wife's house, to collect dirt on her. Or they're used by business people to spy on rivals, suspect employees. You know, industrial espionage. But you're not in business. And the lack of a bug in your phone is suspicious. They wouldn't overlook the phone unless they were monitoring your calls in some other way.'

'What do you mean?'

'Tapping them at the exchange,' Moran said. 'That requires a warrant. Which, I'm afraid, means this isn't a private job. It's the Big Boys.'

'The state?' Tom said.

'Either the police, NCIS, Customs and Excise or Five.'

'Five? You mean MI5?' Tom said. He sat back heavily in his chair. 'MI5 are spying on me? Good God, what for?'

'It's not necessarily Five,' Moran said cautiously. 'It could be any of them, they all have the power. Maybe the police have been monitoring you. Maybe they suspect you're part of some paedophile ring and they want to catch the others. Or they might have some other reason.'

'What other reason?'

Moran paused to take a mouthful of his mother's parkin.

'Try it,' he said.

Tom nibbled at his own slice, though he didn't feel like eating. There was a heaviness in his stomach that hadn't been there a few minutes earlier.

'I'm a law abiding person,' he said. 'Why would the state want to spy on me?'

'Let's take a look at your life,' Moran said. 'You're a university lecturer. Married. How many kids?'

'Two.'

'A middle-aged, middle-class academic with a wife and two kids. It's not the most obvious profile of a subversive. You political in any way?

You know, an activist?'

'Not now.'

'But you were?'

'In my student days, yes.'

'In what way?'

'The way lots of young, idealistic people are. I was in CND, wrote pieces for the student paper, sat around in bars talking about how I was going to change the world. I did a lot of drinking, but the world remained sadly unchanged.'

'You were a communist?' Moran said.

'I was a socialist. Back then that had some meaning.'

'What about more recently?'

'Well, I write articles still. For periodicals, the national press. Mostly on industrial history, industrial relations. That's my specialist field. But I've written more political stuff too.'

'What sort of political stuff?'

'Current affairs. Opinion pieces on various subjects — university tuition fees, the education system, reform of the House of Lords, the war in Iraq. A pretty broad range of subjects, really.'

'From a left-wing perspective?'

'I try to be objective, but you could say that my sympathies are inclined that way.'

'You written any articles in the last few months that might have upset the security services?'

'No.'

'You think they might have a file on you?'

'They have a file on just about everyone, don't they?'

'It's a serious question.'

'I don't know.'

'What about your friends? Are any of *them* activists, would any of them be considered subversives by the state?'

'I don't think so.'

'You mixed up in any crime?'

'No.'

'What about drugs?'

'No.'

'Smuggling? Anything that might interest Customs and Excise?'

'No.'

'You're not making this easy. What about your work? You lecture, you do research, I suppose?'

'Yes.'

'Anything in particular at the moment?'

'I'm writing a book — on the industrial unrest of the 1970s and '80s.'

'What, strikes, that sort of thing?'

'Yes.'

'Anything controversial?'

'Controversial? No, I don't think . . . ' Tom stopped. 'Well, maybe . . . I don't know.'

'Try me.'

'There is one thing that might possibly be controversial. I'm looking at the miners' strike of '84 – '85, both the strike itself and its aftermath. You know, the decline of the South Yorkshire pit communities. There was an incident during the strike — the mysterious death of a miner named Danny Shields — that caused a lot of bad feeling. I'm intending to take a closer look at that. But I haven't started yet.'

'Danny Shields?' Moran said. 'Rings a bell.

109

Remind me of the facts.'

'There's not much to say. Shields was a young man — early twenties — worked at Clayton Main colliery, up in the Dearne Valley. One night during the strike he went for a drink at the social club in the village — in Clayton Woods — but he never came home. His body was discovered next morning on some wasteland. He'd been badly beaten about the head, died from the injuries. His killer was never found.'

Moran sat back. He put his hands behind his head and stretched, pulling his shirt taut over his broad chest. He was running to fat, his stomach bulging over his trousers, but the muscles of his shoulders and arms were impressively hard.

'I remember the case,' he said.

'The locals were convinced the police did it.'

'Bollocks.'

'That's what they believed at the time.'

'Was Shields a scab?'

'No. Far from it. He was a committed striker, on the picket lines every day of the strike until his death.'

'Because there was that other death, wasn't there? In South Wales. The taxi driver taking the strikebreaker to work. And there it was the miners who did it. Dropped a concrete block through his car window from a bridge.'

'This is a sensitive issue, isn't it? Personal.'

Tom knew from Michael Russell that Moran was a former copper, twenty years' service with the South Yorkshire force.

'Were you involved in the policing?'

'Maybe,' Moran said evasively.

110

Of course he would have been. Officers from half the police forces in England had been drafted in to handle the pickets. It was unthinkable that a local officer wouldn't have played a role.

'I've touched a nerve, I'm sorry,' Tom said.

Moran waved his hand dismissively. 'Christ, I'm not that thin-skinned. It was a bad time, that's all. A lot of things happened that I'm not proud of. But it was twenty years ago. I'm not a copper any more.'

'You changing your mind about my case?'

'I never let personal feelings cloud my professional judgement. You talk to anyone recently about the Shields incident? Told them what you're doing.'

'I mentioned it to my head of department, Douglas Kemp.'

'Face to face, or on the phone?'

'Face to face, in his office. I think I probably sent him an email about it too.'

'An internal email? Just within your department, I mean.'

'I think I may have sent it from my home computer, in the evening. Does it matter?'

'Can you get me a copy of it?'

'The police took away both my work and home computers. But I can access my emails from another terminal. You think that could be at the root of all this? An obscure, twenty-year-old unsolved murder case?'

'I don't know, but it's worth checking out.'

Moran concentrated on his parkin for a time. Tom asked him the question that had been

111

troubling him since Moran had discovered the bugs in his house.

'What made you suspicious? What made you think I might be under surveillance?'

'A hunch,' Moran replied. 'These things that have happened to you aren't isolated incidents. They must have a rationale behind them. The images on your computer, downloaded when you weren't there, the use of your credit card, your name on an NCIS list that can't exist. They all point to a concerted plan to discredit you. And the people with the resources and influence to do that cover all the bases. They watch you, they monitor your phones. They don't leave anything to chance.'

'They can get hold of my credit card details?'

Moran snorted. 'Dead easy. You give me someone's name and address, I could have their credit card numbers, bank account details, a whole list of financial information about them within twenty-four hours.'

'What about my office? Getting access to my computer, my password. No one knows my password except me.'

Moran gave him an amused look, as if he couldn't quite believe his naivety.

'An office? That's hardly much of an obstacle to a pro. And as for your password, well, discovering someone's password is the simplest thing in the world to do. Forget all that crap you see in films, people guessing your password, typing in your date of birth or your wife's middle name. You'll never guess a password in a million years. You use keystroke logging.'

'What's that?'

'Computer software. You break into someone's office and add a new program to their hard drive, hidden inside something innocent like their word processing package. It intercepts their keystrokes, logging everything they type, then sends it automatically to the eavesdroppers when the target next connects to the net. This is the twenty-first century. Nothing you do is secure.'

Tom licked his lips. 'So these people — whoever they are — have monitored everything I've been writing on my computer. My work, letters, emails?'

'The lot,' Moran replied.

'And the images, the indecent images . . . they'd do something revolting like that? Put child porn on my computer?'

'If I wanted to discredit someone, frame them for something they didn't do,' Moran said, 'what offence would I choose? Theft? That's easy to set up. Plant something stolen in their house, slip an extra tin of beans into their shopping bag. But with theft you have to prove intent to steal — *mens rea*, the lawyers call it. It has to be in bloody Latin, of course.

'That might not be easy with a bloke like you — respectable professional, no previous convictions. Sexual harassment, now that's a possibility for a lecturer, teaching all those attractive young women. You'd need some student to cooperate in making the allegations, but that shouldn't be too much of a problem. They're all so in debt they'd do anything for a bit of cash. But it would be her word against yours and you'd probably have

113

good character witnesses to vouch for you. Even if it succeeded, it wouldn't really blacken your name. I mean, a bit of harassment between teacher and student, it's normal, isn't it? Those gorgeous twenty-year-olds in their low-cut crop tops, how do you keep your hands off them?'

Tom eyed Moran coolly, unsure whether he was being serious. If it was a joke, it was in very bad taste.

'No,' Moran went on, 'harassment's a bit dodgy. But child porn, that's perfect. It's not an offence that requires witnesses to prove it, or even guilty intent. All it needs is the indecent pictures there on your computer and you're guilty. It doesn't matter how they came to be there. We trust computers, they rule our lives, but they're only as honest, or as accurate, as the people controlling them want them to be. You know, they did an audit of the Police National Computer a couple of years back. The government didn't publicise the results very widely, and you can see why when I tell you that 65 per cent of the entries were found to be inaccurate. That's nearly two-thirds of the entries on the Police National Computer that were wrong. But you try proving you're innocent when the police arrest you, check the computer and it tells them you've got previous. If it's on the computer, it's bloody gospel.'

Moran finished off his slice of parkin and washed it down with a swig of tea.

'They've stitched you up good and proper,' he said. 'Child porn. It's the one offence that's guaranteed to make everyone loathe you, get you sacked, discredit you so that no decent person will ever want anything to do with you again. If I wanted to ruin a respectable family man like you, I'd go for child porn.'

Moran licked his finger and ran it around his plate, chasing the last few crumbs of parkin.

'Why?' Tom said. 'Why would anyone want to do this to me?'

'Maybe it's something to do with Danny Shields, maybe not,' Moran replied. 'That case was two decades ago. That's a long time. Why should it bother anyone now? But you've done something, that's for certain. It might have been accidental, you might not have been aware of it, but somewhere you've done something to put the wind up them.'

Tom held out his arms, a gesture of helplessness.

'I have absolutely no idea why anyone — let alone the state — should want to ruin me.'

'Here's what I want you to do,' Moran said. 'Go away and think about everything you've done over the past couple of months. Check your diary, your phone bill, try to get hold of any emails you've sent or received. Make a list of everyone you've met or spoken to, particularly people you don't usually encounter. Take your life apart and try to discover if there's something that's happened to you that might have brought all this about. When you've done that, give me a call. But not from the phone in your friend's apartment.'

'I have a mobile.'

'Don't use it. Find a payphone.'

115

'They can monitor my mobile?'

'You bet your life they can. They can listen in to your conversations, and they can use it to pinpoint your location as well, even when you're not using it. If the phone's switched on, it's sending a signal to the nearest base station that can be picked up. That tells them where you are to within a few metres.'

'I didn't know that.'

'You're learning,' Moran said.

He looked across the table at Tom's barely touched slice of parkin.

'Didn't you like it?'

'It was very nice,' Tom said. 'But I wasn't hungry.'

'No sense in wasting good food,' Moran said.

He reached across the table, picked up the parkin and shovelled it into his mouth in one go.

7

'How are things?' Tom asked.

'We're coping,' Helen replied. 'You?'

'I miss you all. It's depressing living apart.'

'I thought you'd be enjoying yourself. Eating out, going to the pub with Bruce, doing all those things you used to do before we were married.'

'*Enjoying myself*? After everything that's happened, you think I might be enjoying myself?'

Helen looked down at the table, her cup of coffee and toasted cheese sandwich. They were in the café near her office — the one in which they'd met the day Tom had been charged by the police. It was crowded with lunchtime customers, the noise of conversation making it hard to hear. The windows were spattered with rain, beginning to steam up. Helen's dark hair was damp from the walk to the café. Tom wanted to reach out and brush away the droplets, but restrained himself. She still seemed distant, unsure about him.

'There've been some developments,' he said.

Helen looked up, her eyes narrowing anxiously, fearing more bad news.

'What do you mean?' she asked quickly.

'Good developments,' Tom replied, then immediately qualified the remark. 'Well, I *think* they're good. Some of them, at least.'

He told her about the pictures being

downloaded on the day he'd been at Toys Я Us. Helen's face brightened, a spark returning to her eyes.

'Then you can't have done it. Doesn't that prove it wasn't you?'

'It's helpful,' Tom said cautiously. 'There are still the other two occasions to deal with, but it's certainly in my favour.'

'But it must undermine the police case against you, make the charges unsustainable. Surely they can't go ahead with a trial now?'

Her hands were on the table. She was leaning forward, suddenly animated.

'They can't proceed, can they? Not now,' she went on. 'You weren't there. Doesn't that make the other two times suspicious?'

Tom touched her hand tentatively with his fingertips, half expecting her to pull away. But she turned her palm over, entwining her fingers in his, squeezing tight. It seemed the first time they'd touched each other since all this had begun.

'There are other things, too,' Tom said.

'What other things?'

'The list of suspected paedophiles from America that the police claim my name was on — the US authorities haven't yet compiled the list for February, for the dates the police say I was downloading indecent images.'

'Haven't compiled it? I don't understand.'

'Operation Gold Dust. It's an international child porn investigation, but the only list of suspects the Americans have so far drawn up stops at the end of January. There's no way the

118

police could have been given my name by the Americans.'

'Then how . . . ?' Helen stopped. 'What are you saying?'

'That the police added my name to the earlier list, the one they'd already been sent. Or someone else added my name and referred it to the police.'

' 'Someone else'?'

'I've been under surveillance. Michael put me in touch with a security expert, a guy named Moran. He's checked our house. He found three bugs — listening devices.'

'In our house? You're not serious?'

'I'm afraid I am.'

'Where?'

'The kitchen, sitting room and bedroom.'

'The bedroom? Someone's been listening to us in the bedroom? Jesus, I don't believe it. Who?'

'I don't know.'

Helen's eyes were fixed on his. Tom could feel her fingers gripping his hand.

'This is more than I can take in,' she said. 'What the hell is going on? We're being bugged? Why? By the police? They can do that?'

'Or the security services.'

'That's even worse. What are we supposed to have done?'

'Not we, me. It's me they're after,' Tom said.

'Why?'

'I don't know that either.'

Helen let go of his hand and sat back in her chair, still staring at him. She'd turned pale. The feeling of relief that had swept through her earlier, when it seemed clear that Tom was innocent of the child porn charges, had been replaced by a dark sensation of dread and foreboding.

'They're watching you, listening to you,' she said. 'They're framing you for something you didn't do. Have I got that right?'

'That's how it looks to me.'

'Dear God. That scares me.' She leant forward again. 'Tom, that scares the shit out of me.'

He took her hand once more. 'Me too.'

'What does Michael say? Can't he do anything?'

'He's holding fire. He wants to find out more before he makes a noise. The bugs are still there, so be careful what you say around the house. The phone's almost certainly tapped too.'

'I want you to come back, Tom.'

'I don't want to do anything to put you or the children at risk.'

'I don't care. I want you with us. I'll feel safer if you're with us. Hannah and Ben are missing you terribly.'

'You thought I might have actually done it, didn't you? Downloaded those images.'

Helen hesitated. 'I didn't know what to think. Yes, maybe I did. I'm sorry. It didn't look good, though, did it? But I don't now. Come back, we shouldn't be apart.'

Tom was tempted. He hated being away from home. The liberation from domesticity that — like most parents — he occasionally pined for, was much less appealing now it had been forced on him in such painful circumstances. He wanted more than anything to be back with Helen and the children. The fact that Helen wanted him back was enough to lift his spirits. But there were other considerations. Maybe this wasn't a good time to return.

'Give it a few more days,' he said. 'Moran doesn't want to tip off the watchers that we're on to them in case they change tack, or cover their tracks. We'd never manage to act naturally if I came home.'

'Then when?' Helen said.

'Soon. Very soon.'

★   ★   ★

There were more than 250 of them, all printed out on separate sheets of paper. Tom placed them on the table in front of Moran — a daunting pile as thick as a phone book.

'All the emails I've sent and received over the past few weeks,' Tom said.

Moran eyed the pile. 'I hope you're not expecting me to read them all.'

'It looks worse than it is. Most of them are very short.'

'You've checked through them?'

Tom nodded. It had taken him the best part of a day to print the emails out, then study them all carefully. The vast majority of them were of no interest whatsoever — routine emails to students about assignments and other coursework, inconsequential replies to colleagues, all the dull administrative chores and memos that at one

121

time had been done on paper but were now carried out electronically. Tom slid one of the sheets across the table to Moran.

'This is the only one that seemed to me of any significance. The email I sent my head of department, on February 4th.'

Moran picked up the piece of paper and read out the text.

''Douglas, *Re my research — as we discussed last week — I intend to take a closer look at the Danny Shields case. I want to see if I can discover exactly what happened the night he died. The circumstances were highly suspicious and my gut feeling is that there was much more to the whole affair than was revealed at the time. I suspect, in fact, that there may have been an organised cover-up by the authorities.*

''*This might be a controversial line of research. Some people won't want me reopening such a sensitive case. I'll need to talk to Danny's relatives, and the police — see if I can get them to disclose their file on the case, though I'm not optimistic about succeeding.*

''*I wanted to clear this with you in advance as it might potentially cause problems for the department. Best, Tom.*''

Underneath the message was Kemp's reply: ''*Your concerns have been noted. I see no reason why you should not pursue this investigation.*''

Moran put the paper back down on the table.

'Interesting. Is this the only email you sent on the subject?'

'Yes.'

'There's nothing in the rest of the pile?'

'Not about Danny Shields.'

'What about other things? You see anything else that struck you as worthy of a closer look?'

Tom shook his head. 'I'm afraid not.'

'OK, what else did you bring in? What about your phone bill?'

Tom spread his quarterly phone bill out on the table. Moran examined the itemised list of calls.

'You know who all these numbers are?' Tom nodded. 'Let's start at the top then. This one?'

Tom referred to the notes he'd brought with him, the phone numbers and names he'd collated from both his own and Helen's address books.

'That's my wife's mother in Norfolk.'

'Only thirty-six minutes?' Moran said dryly. 'Not bad. You must have her well trained. My old lady — ex old lady — hell, she was on for bloody hours to her mother. I wouldn't have minded but the old trout only lived around the corner. You could've gone in the garden and shouted to her. This one?'

'Our dentist.'

'We can probably rule him out. This?'

'My brother.'

'And this?'

'My wife's sister.'

'Let's cross off the family numbers. You must have been calling them for years without anything like this happening. What we want is something out of the ordinary, something that you don't do every month of the year. What's this one here, Locall? The same number repeated, what, must be a dozen times or more.'

'That's our internet connection.'

'You not on broadband then? Must cost you a fortune, paying every time you go on.'

'We don't use it that often at home. I do most of my net searching at work.'

'What about your kids? Don't they go on the net?'

'Only infrequently. Under supervision.'

Moran gave him an incredulous look. 'Yeah? Shit, how do you manage that? Mine are never off it. They come round weekends and I hardly see them — they're stuck in front of the computer all the bloody time.'

'You have children?'

'Two boys. Fifteen and thirteen. Live with their mum out at Mosborough. What's this one here, the mobile number?'

'My brother again.'

'This?'

'A friend of my wife's. One of the other mums at school.'

One by one they went through the items on the list. Except for a couple of brief local calls which Tom had been unable to identify, every entry was accounted for.

'Nothing very encouraging there,' Moran said gloomily. 'They all seem to be regular numbers, people you've contacted before. Do you remember anything odd about any of the calls? Any surprises, any pieces of news or information that seemed out of the ordinary?'

Tom shook his head. 'Sorry.'

'What about phone calls from work, from your office?'

'I don't have a record of those. They'd only be business calls. Mostly internal. You know, within the university.'

'Yeah?' Moran's tone was sceptical. 'You never make personal calls from work then?'

Tom grinned. 'Occasionally. But I can't think of any that might be significant.'

Moran sniffed and loosened his tie. 'The box' had no air conditioning or even ventilation grills — Moran regarded them as potential security risks, a way in for eavesdroppers. The atmosphere was stuffy, uncomfortable.

'What about your diary?' he said. 'Let's go through it day by day for the past month.'

It was slow, tedious work. Even with his diary to prompt him, Tom was surprised how little detail he remembered about the previous four weeks. The truth was that he hadn't done anything particularly unusual during that time. His work had a regular pattern of lectures, seminars and tutorials, and his home life tended to revolve around the activities of his children — swimming lessons, Ben's football club, Hannah's gymnastics.

'I'm sorry, this isn't being very helpful, is it?' Tom said. 'I have a pretty unexciting existence. My work, my family, a few social activities, that's about all I do.'

Moran picked up the diary and leafed slowly through the pages again. Then he went back to the phone bill and studied the list of calls. He shook his head.

'The email, that seems to be all we've got.'

He picked up the printout and read through it again.

'I'd like to run this past a contact of mine. There'll be an expense involved.'

'How much?' Tom said.

'Five hundred pounds. Cash.'

Tom winced. He was suspended from work on full pay at the moment, but he didn't know how long that would continue.

'That's a lot of money.'

'It's a tricky job. You ever heard of Echelon?'

'No, what is it?'

'It's a top-secret global eavesdropping network run by the US National Security Agency, GCHQ here in Britain and their sister services in Australia, New Zealand and Canada. Basically, what it does is intercept communications — satellite communications, but also wire communications, phone calls, faxes, emails. It can listen in to them all, millions and millions of calls every hour. But because there's so much raw material flying around the world, the system has to filter out the rubbish and focus only on stuff that may be of interest to the client organisations, customers, if you like — in America, the CIA and FBI, in the UK, MI5 and MI6. So they program in keywords that the eavesdropping computers search for. You know, like 'Al Qaeda', or 'uranium enrichment', anything that looks like a threat to national security. The computers pick up those keywords and listen in to the communications containing them. I'd like to see if anything in this email you sent your boss is an Echelon keyword.'

'You think I've somehow inadvertently triggered off the surveillance with the email?'

'It's possible.'

'You can do that? Get access to a top-secret spying network?'

'Well, it's not actually that top-secret. It's well documented in books and newspaper articles. Type 'Echelon keywords' into Google and it'll give you a list as long as your arm. Unfortunately, most of them have been put there by conspiracy theorists and other assorted nutters, so they're not very reliable. I have a better source.'

'And that's what the five hundred quid's for?'

Moran gave a twisted smile. 'We live in a surveillance society. Big Brother has the power and the means to monitor everything we do. But what I love about human nature is that our greed is always one step ahead of the technology. The computers do the work, process the data, but ultimately it has no use until it's passed on to a person. And where you have someone with access to that information, you always have someone who can be bribed to disclose it. Moran's First Law of Palm Greasing, I call it.'

8

Annie O'Brien had worked for Moran for just under three years — not as a staff employee but as a freelance operative whom Moran could call on for specific jobs. Moran knew his business, could move easily in certain circles, blend anonymously with certain groups of people, but no matter how good he was, he couldn't escape the fact that he was an overweight middle-aged male with the unmistakable stamp of an ex-copper.

Annie, by contrast, was nineteen, stick-thin, silver studs in her ears, nose and tongue, jet-black hair and a wardrobe that was eclectic and flexible enough to cover a wide range of assignments. Her natural territory was the twilight world of pubs and clubs, of petty crime and casual sex — the youth environment into which Moran would never be accepted. But a change of clothes, of hair style, the removal of jewellery from her more obvious piercings, and she could pass muster in just about any company. She had a chameleon-like ability to change her appearance, the way she spoke, according to her surroundings. Junkies and pimps and prostitutes in their dark, squalid haunts; students and secretaries in the bars and neon-lit diners of the urban sprawl; the more refined, sheltered daughters of the leafy suburbs — she could blend in convincingly with them all, which was why Moran found her so invaluable. And why she was now on her way to Cheltenham for him.

It was mid-morning, but the M5 was still choked with vehicles — far too many for Annie's liking. Her natural temperament was impatient, reckless. When she drove she liked an open road in front of her, the freedom to put her foot down. But today there was too much traffic for her to indulge her fondness for speed. In any case, she was trying to be careful. Sticking to the limit, watching her rear-view mirror. The last thing she wanted was for the police to stop her.

The Filth were a pain in the arse. She could handle them all right, but there was no sense in courting trouble, especially when she didn't actually have a driving licence. Never had. She'd been driving since she was fourteen — joyriding for the most part — but she'd never bothered to take her test. What was the point? Another piece of paper, another piece of documentation for the authorities — the Faceless Ones, she called them — to put on their computers. She'd give a false name and address, of course, if she was pulled over. Act all waifish and innocent — she was good at that — and promise to take her licence to her local police station when she got home. They'd never trace her, or the car. It was Moran's vehicle — *one* of his vehicles. He had a big, shiny Jag he cruised around in, but he also had a couple of clapped-out old Ford Fiestas he lent out to his operatives for certain jobs. They were registered to some untraceable shell company he'd set up. She liked that side to him.

Secretive, devious. Like her. Moran was OK, considering he'd been a copper. He paid well — always cash in hand — didn't patronise her like most blokes his age did, and had never — so far — tried to screw her.

This was Annie's third trip to Cheltenham — her third meeting with 'the Geek'. She didn't like Cheltenham much. It wasn't her kind of place. It was one of those Heritage Britain towns that, like Stratford or Bath, seemed designed more for tourists than residents. It was all so genteel and picturesque: the streets of white-washed Regency terraces with their gleaming black wrought-iron balconies; the grand porti-coed buildings; the beautiful parks whose colour-coordinated floral displays and mani-cured lawns might have been laid out by the art director of an expensive period arthouse film. Even the public toilets were spotless and fragrant, as if Chanel were the contract cleaners.

Why it had been chosen as the location for GCHQ, the government's electronic eavesdrop-ping agency, was a mystery to Annie. There didn't seem to be any particular reason, yet it seemed an appropriate choice. Annie always thought of Cheltenham as a town of busybodies and net curtain twitchers, populated by people with an unhealthy interest in their neighbours' affairs. And GCHQ was the nation's biggest net curtain twitcher — charged with the task of prying into and monitoring its citizens' private communications.

The rendezvous was a café on the western fringes of the town centre. Annie had never been there before. Their previous two meetings had been at different locations close to the GCHQ offices in Oakley, but since their last encounter the agency had relocated to a brand-new, purpose-built £330-million headquarters in the suburb of Benhall — a vast, circular building nicknamed 'the Doughnut'. Annie had never set foot in it, but the Geek had told her all about it, even shown her a glossy brochure which described in detail the attractions of the new HQ — its open-plan offices 'the size of seventeen football pitches', its internal glass-covered 'street' where employees could eat and drink, the open-air garden in the middle, the gym and 'prayer room' for use by staff. Annie couldn't believe it. This ultra-secret spying agency, whose existence had been denied by successive governments for decades, had a sodding brochure. It made the place sound like Disneyworld.

Annie arrived early at the café. She bought herself a coffee and a chicken sandwich and waited for the Geek. Her contact's name was Craig Hanbury, but Annie always thought of him as the Geek — a name she'd bestowed on him sight unseen when Moran first told her she was to meet him. That's what GCHQ analysts were, weren't they? Anoraks with beards and buck teeth and dandruff, who lived with their mothers and collected beer mats. Their first meeting, Annie had been pleasantly surprised to find that the Geek was actually nothing like that. He was in his late twenties, clean shaven, good teeth, not a trace of dandruff on his grey suit — not

Annie's type, but not totally repugnant either.

He was wearing the same grey suit again today. He'd worn it to all their meetings, so maybe it was the only one he had, though Annie didn't think so. Hanbury gave her the impression of a fashion-conscious guy, someone who fancied himself as a bit of a dresser, a bit of a ladies' man, in fact. Those were the words he'd probably use himself — she'd never heard him use the word 'women'; it was always 'the laydeez' or 'females'. He was the kind of guy who said things like, 'I'm a great believer in feminism, but . . . '

'Hi, Craig.'

She nodded at him as he sat down at the table. Hanbury glanced around the café, noting who was there. He was always cautious, Annie had noticed, but never nervous. That had surprised her at first, then she'd realised that he didn't regard what he was doing as particularly serious — a technical breach of the Official Secrets Act, true, but nothing really heinous.

'Hello, Lucy,' he said. 'How are you?'

The name gave her a momentary start, reminding her to get in character. She never used her real name on jobs — not that Annie O'Brien was her real name. She'd lost track of how many false names she'd used over the years — since the day she'd first been caught shoplifting in Manchester's Trafford Centre. Thirteen years old, nicking a pair of jeans from Top Shop, then haring it down the concourse pursued by two out-of-condition security guards. She'd have got away too, only the bastards had radios and there were two more waiting to collar her outside Debenhams. She'd told them she was called Mary Pearce — the name of a girl she hated at school, when she could be bothered to attend school — then given them the slip and escaped through a service door before the police arrived.

'I'm OK,' Annie said. 'You?'

'Fine. You're looking well.'

He gave her an appraising glance. She'd toned down her appearance for the occasion. Gone easy on the eye make-up, put on a tight black top and smart trousers, taken out her tongue stud though she knew Hanbury found it fascinating. She'd been wearing it the first time they'd met and he'd eyed her up with a lascivious leer and said, 'Where else are you pierced?'

'Guess,' she'd replied.

'You want a coffee?' she asked now.

'No, thanks,' Hanbury said. 'I can't stay.'

Annie took a folded piece of paper out of her trouser pocket and slid it across the table. Hanbury picked the paper up and slipped it smoothly away inside his jacket.

'The usual time and place tonight?' Annie said.

Hanbury nodded. 'Look forward to it.'

He stood up from the table and strolled casually out of the café. Annie finished her sandwich, then ordered another cappuccino. This was the bit she hated most: the waiting around, killing time until the evening. Cheltenham, for all its undoubted merits, was not a place in which she would have chosen to spend a damp spring afternoon.

She lingered a while in the café, then walked into the town centre through Montpellier, the Regency suburb where the cream of Georgian society had once come to drink the waters. The Rotunda Pump Room spa, with its green copper-covered cupola, was now a bank, but the surrounding streets — home to bistros, pavement cafés, jewellers and chic boutiques — still attracted the rich and affluent.

Annie's route took her past the French-Gothic frontage of the exclusive Cheltenham Ladies' College. On her first visit to the town she'd rather hoped that the girls of the college would have had hockey sticks and straw boaters like the Belles of St Trinian's and was disappointed to find that they wore black trousers and drab green pullovers like comprehensive school kids. She saw a cluster of pupils in the courtyard of the college now, stone-mullioned windows and ivy-clad walls all around them, and paused for a moment to watch them. She didn't envy them their privileged existence — it wasn't a life she coveted in any way — but she couldn't help wondering how she might have turned out if she'd had their opportunities.

The pedestrian precincts in the middle of the town had flowers hanging from baskets on posts and streets uncontaminated by litter or unsightly vagrants. It was the cleanest town centre Annie had ever seen. The people, too, all seemed slim and beautifully dressed. There were no fat people, no louts eating burgers, no pasty-faced women with fags in their mouths yelling at their anti-social brats. It was as if all the undesirables

— and there must surely have been some — had been rounded up and sent to a health farm, only being allowed back when they'd lost twenty pounds and acquired some designer labels.

Annie went into the Regent Arcade, a covered mall with two storeys of shops and a high arched glass roof, and spent the next few hours wandering in and out of stores, trying on clothes she had no intention of buying. There was some nice stuff, expensive and classy. Though she'd given up the serial shoplifting that had been such a feature of her adolescence, she still occasionally kept her hand in — for the thrill of it rather than anything else. She was tempted by some of the shops in the Arcade, but resisted. She was being paid to stay out of trouble today.

As the shops started to close at the end of the afternoon, she drifted slowly across to her rendezvous at the Royal Oak, taking her time so she would arrive late. She wanted Hanbury to be there first. Sitting alone in a pub held no fears for her, but a woman on her own was more likely to attract attention and Annie didn't want anyone to notice her tonight.

Hanbury was waiting at his usual booth in the corner of the lounge bar, a pint on the table in front of him. Annie squeezed on to the banquette opposite and let her eyes stray casually around the room. It was only six o'clock. The place was pretty empty — a group of men in suits near the bar, a couple of women in one of the other booths. No one Annie recognised. No one suspicious. She knew she hadn't been followed, but Hanbury was a GCHQ employee.

It paid to be very careful when meeting him.

'You want a drink?' Hanbury said.

'Just an orange juice.'

'You sure? Nothing stronger?'

'I'm driving.'

'Why don't you stay on for a bit? You always dash off. We could go for something to eat.'

'I don't think that's a good idea. For either of us.'

Hanbury gave her a look. 'OK.' He stood up and went to the bar.

Annie knew he'd try it on again. He was that type. Saying no wasn't the end of the matter to him, it was only the opening round of the game — a game he wanted to pursue whether Annie did or not. She sighed. It was tiresome, but not altogether unexpected. Hanbury no doubt fancied his chances. He was smooth, not unattractive. He probably had a smart flat somewhere, a flashy car — a GTi of some sort, she guessed — the kind of material acquisition that he probably thought impressed women, but which left her cold. His salary wouldn't have been particularly high, but he'd push it to the limit, run an overdraft, mortgage himself to the hilt, buy on HP. And make a bit of cash on the side wherever he could. Greedy, overstretched, unscrupulous, he was the perfect partner for Moran, maybe for others too, for Annie didn't think Hanbury was a monogamous informer, faithful to only one paymaster.

He was coming back from the bar now, swaggering a little, something predatory in his movements. Annie carefully erased any trace of contempt from her face. This was part of the job. Moran never said anything, but Annie knew that was one of the reasons he sent her on trips like this. A bit of honey never went amiss where men were concerned.

'Here's your *orange juice*,' Hanbury said, his lip curling as he emphasised the words. 'You should have a proper drink. You want to try some of this?' He held up his pint.

'What is it?'

'Well Stewed Stoat. They make it not far from here. Little place out in Gloucestershire. That's why I like this pub, they know their ales.'

Annie nodded, trying to show some interest. Was there anything more boring than a guy who talked about beer? She must have kept her face inscrutable, for Hanbury proceeded to lecture her on the finer points of bitter for the next five minutes. Annie wondered how soon she could take her leave. Moran wanted her to keep Hanbury happy, to string him along a bit, but there were limits.

'So what've you been up to this afternoon?' Hanbury asked when he'd exhausted his real ale data.

'Nothing much. Wandered around town a bit.'

'Shopping, eh?' Hanbury gave a superior smile. He knew women. 'Shoes, I'll bet.'

'What else does a girl buy?' Annie said, as sweetly as she could manage.

'Well, there's lingerie.'

Oh, *please*. Annie steered the conversation on to more grown-up territory. 'Did you do the check?'

137

But Hanbury wasn't going to be rushed.

'All in good time, Lucy,' he said. He took a gulp of beer and licked his lips. 'You know, you don't look like a Lucy.'

'Don't I? What do Lucys look like?'

'I don't know.'

What would you prefer? Annie thought. How about Pussy Galore? That would suit him, add to his fantasy that he was some kind of James Bond character, that some day he'd get to lay her. Fantasy was the right word. Annie knew that Hanbury's job was predominantly tedious drudgery — sitting at a desk sifting through the mounds of crap GCHQ picked up from their listening station. Snooping on their own population, panning through phone calls and emails in the hope of picking out a nugget of golden information. The whole thing was laughable. They'd probably get more 'intelligence' from a two-year-old copy of *Hello* magazine, but who cared? The government gave them £800 million a year to maintain this farce. It kept a lot of people in work and it kept the Americans happy — Annie knew that 95 per cent of the analysis at Cheltenham was done for the NSA.

There was nothing glamorous about Hanbury's job. He was a bureaucrat, a deskman as far removed from active espionage as it was possible to get. A suburban milkman had a more exciting life than a GCHQ analyst. Hanbury would work there for forty years, retire on a modest pension and sit in his garden wondering whether what he'd done for all those years had made a difference. Who could blame him for livening up his existence by doing a little trading on the side?

'You sure you don't fancy going for dinner?' he said. 'I know this great place. Mexican. You ever had Mexican food?'

'Yes.'

'Or a Chinese. You fancy a Chinese?'

'It's nice of you to ask, Craig. But I really have to get off.'

'Go later. There'll be less traffic.'

This was becoming a pain.

'Do you want your money now?' Annie asked.

That focused his mind.

'Assuming you've earned it, that is.'

He looked at her sharply. He didn't like that.

'Of course I've fucking earned it.'

Annie regretted the remark. He was scowling now. Christ, I hope he's not going to sulk, Annie thought. She forced herself to smile apologetically.

'Sorry, I didn't mean that,' she said soothingly. 'I know you've earned it. You always do.'

'Yeah, well,' Hanbury said. 'OK.'

'We appreciate your help,' Annie continued. 'You always deliver.'

She waited. That's as far as I'm going, she thought. Who the hell do you think you are? You're selling classified information, for God's sake. Do you want a fucking medal?

Hanbury took a folded slip of paper out of his pocket — the one Annie had given him at lunchtime — and passed it across the table. Annie covered the slip with her hand, but didn't pick it up. She left it there for a moment, watching the other people in the lounge, her eyes checking the doors. Waiting, just in case. Only when she was sure that no one was showing any interest did she slide the piece of paper off the table and into her pocket.

She paused again, sipping her orange juice, before taking an envelope out of her jacket and passing it under the table to Hanbury. Their fingers touched. For one horrible instant Annie thought he was trying to hold her hand. But it was the envelope he was interested in. First things first.

She didn't see him stash the money away. He was slick, practised. It confirmed her guess that he was dealing with other people too.

'Don't spend it all at once,' she said dryly.

Hanbury grinned. 'Why not? It's what it's for, isn't it?' He looked at his watch. 'If you can't stay for a meal, how about a coffee? I don't live far away.'

'No, thanks.' She'd got what she'd come for. She didn't want to hang around.

'Sure? We could watch a film. I've got a home cinema system.'

That figured.

'Yeah?'

'More than a hundred movies on DVD. You should see the quality. I've got a plasma screen.'

That was a new one on her. Come up and see my plasma screen. She wasn't tempted.

'Honest, Craig, I have to go. Maybe next time I'm down.'

They parted outside on the pavement in front

of the pub. Annie kept it brief, a few feet of space between them. Not giving him any excuses. Then she walked back through the town centre to her car. Clicking on the overhead light, she unfolded the piece of paper. It was a photocopy of an email that someone called Tom Whitehead — his name and email address were at the top of the message — had sent to a Douglas Kemp. Annie didn't know who they were. Didn't care. The message was three or four paragraphs long. Annie didn't bother reading it. All she was interested in was the mark that Hanbury had made in the text. Ringed in red were the two words 'Danny Shields'.

9

Over the few days since Moran had discovered the bugs in his house, Tom had developed a heightened sense of awareness, of sensitivity to his surroundings. He looked carefully at every vehicle he saw, every pedestrian behind him on the street, registering their details and filing them away in case he encountered them again. If his house and phone were being monitored, it seemed reasonable to assume that he was too. Was there a team of trained watchers on his tail? Even in his present state of increased alertness he had not managed to spot any. But that didn't mean they weren't there. Moran had told him that surveillance was no longer a 'shoe leather' job. The days of men in raincoats following suspects around the streets were over. This was the hi-tech age. With directional microphones that could pick up voices from a mile away, cameras that could read your lips from even further, it wasn't necessary for the watchers to reveal their presence. They were spectres. Unseen, unheard, unnoticed.

Moran had impressed on Tom the need to be cautious in all his movements, to conceal what he was doing from inquisitive eyes. So the morning Tom went out to Clayton Woods he did so not in his own car but in one Moran had lent him, taking a circuitous route through Sheffield before heading north to Barnsley, then doubling back on himself twice to ensure that he wasn't being followed.

He'd been out many times before into what had once been the heart of the South Yorkshire coalfield — the great triangular swath of collieries between Rotherham, Doncaster and Barnsley. The first time he'd visited the area, back in the early 1980s — just before the miners' strike — the pits had been thriving, probably the most productive and efficient in the country. The adjacent villages, their fabric and well-being inextricably linked to the fortunes of the mines, had also been prosperous. Money had flowed freely, shops and pubs had done good business, there'd been an atmosphere of security and optimism in the communities.

The strike and the subsequent pit closures had destroyed that prosperity, that security and optimism. In one short, devastating blitz the work of a century and more had been wiped away. Over a period of months rather than years, the pits had been shut, the miners laid off and the collieries razed to the ground as if the Coal Board had been desperate to eliminate all trace of their very existence. The collieries might never have been — but for the inescapable evidence of the shattered communities left in their wake.

In the years since, the tradition of work, of hard graft underground, that had built and nourished the pit villages, from one generation to the next, had been replaced by a culture of despair and dependency — unemployment, drugs and crime. The heart had been ripped out of the area, and with it the lifeblood that had sustained the villages and their inhabitants.

The air was probably cleaner now, the surrounding countryside more aesthetically pleasing, though Tom had always found there was something powerful and evocative about the pit buildings, the skeletal winding gear and louring spoil heaps — manmade structures that had a strange beauty of their own. But the villages hadn't recovered. Tom doubted they ever would. With the mines gone, these communities had no real reason for being there.

Clayton Woods was typical of the area. One of the smaller pit villages, it had an older part which predated the coal-mining industry, but most of the houses had been built in the early and mid-twentieth century to provide homes for miners and their families. There were one or two streets of red-brick terraces, their walls blackened by grime, and a more extensive 1950s council estate on the hillside. It was on this estate that Mick Shields, Danny Shields's older brother, lived.

Tom drove slowly through the streets, looking for the address he'd been given. The area had a bleak, rundown feel to it. Many of the houses — ugly semis with small windows and grey pebble-dashed frontages — were boarded up. A few had been vandalised, their roofs had been stripped of tiles, fires started in their decaying shells. There was graffiti on walls, mounds of rubbish in front gardens. A burnt-out car sitting on a patch of wasteland had been there so long it had shrubs growing out through its charred orifices.

Tom pulled in outside one of the occupied houses and climbed out of his car. The breeze plucked at his jacket. Below him in the valley he could see the expanse of open land where Clayton Main Colliery had once stood. It was astonishing how quickly nature had reclaimed the terrain. There was no obvious indication that the pit had ever been there. To the experienced eye there were one or two telltale signs: the hillock to the west of the village — the colliery slag heap — was just a little too smooth and symmetrical to be entirely natural. The grass covering it was perhaps a shade yellower than the fields across the other side of the valley. But it was supporting life. There were bushes and silver birch saplings on it as well as the grass. The patch of disintegrating tarmac, its surface broken up by weeds, that occupied one tiny part of the valley bottom was another indication that some kind of building had once been there. The area around the tarmac had been colonised by more vegetation, but it still had the underlying look of former industrial land. A new block of workshops and warehouse space had been erected in a corner of the site — an attempt at regeneration that was well intentioned but ultimately just a drop in the ocean. It would provide only a handful of jobs to replace the hundreds lost in the pit.

Mick Shields wasn't a big man. Tom was always surprised by how slight were many of the former miners he encountered. But considering the narrow seams and tight corners in which they'd had to work, it made perfect sense for them to be on the small side. Shields was probably only five feet six or seven, several inches shorter than Tom, but he had a lean, wiry build — the kind of whipcord muscles that made him stronger than he looked. His handshake was iron hard, his palm like old leather.

'Come and sit down,' he said.

The house had a through lounge, windows at both ends, a big television set in one corner. It smelt of fried eggs and bacon.

'I dug out some photos for you,' Shields said, handing Tom a stack of prints.

They were typical family snaps. Poorly composed, some out of focus or overexposed, a lot of red eyes from the flash. Tom recognised Shields in a few. He was twenty years younger, but it was him all right. In most of the pictures he was with another young man with the same build and facial features — unmistakably a brother.

'Is this Danny?' Tom asked.

'Aye, that's 'im.'

'He looks like you.'

'No way. I were much better-looking than 'im,' Shields said, grinning. 'You ask the girls.'

'When was this taken?'

''Eighty-three maybe.'

'Before the strike.'

'Aye.'

'Was he working at the pit then?'

'Oh, aye. We both were. There's a couple of the lads.' Shields picked up the photographs. 'There, that's one. That's me there. That's Danny just behind.'

He pointed to two indistinct faces in the group of miners, maybe twenty men, their faces black with coal dust, just coming off shift.

'And that's us outside Welbeck Colliery, picketing.' Shields handed Tom another photograph.

Tom studied the print. It showed a cluster of men huddled together at the side of a road. In the background, dominating the skyline, was the winding wheel of a colliery. There was frost on the ground.

'You look cold,' Tom said.

'We bloody well were. Up at two, three in the morning to get to Nottinghamshire before the police set up their roadblocks. Then standing around on a picket line for ten hours. It were no picnic, I can tell you.'

Danny Shields was easy to spot. He was in the middle of the group. Shoulders hunched, hands in pockets, the collar of his donkey jacket pulled up around his neck. He was grinning for the camera. He looked a nice lad. They all did, in fact. Young, clean-faced, something naive and innocent in their expressions. Not at all the violent thugs they'd been portrayed as.

'This was early on in the strike?' Tom said.

'Aye. Before things started to get nasty. The coppers were OK then. We'd chat to them, even share a cigarette on the picket line. There'd be no trouble. Then someone up 'igh decided it were all a bit too cosy. The coppers were told to take an 'arder line, you know, push us around a bit. It turned into a war, them against us. That's when they brought in the riot police with shields.

147

Mean bastards, they were. They had steel-capped boots they liked to smash into your shins, batons and gloves reinforced with steel strips. I got 'it once. A fist in the face — out of the blue. I 'adn't done nowt. It bloody 'urt. The Met, they were the worst. Nasty buggers. They 'ated us, couldn't wait to get stuck in and beat the shit out of us.'

Shields picked out another photograph and handed it to Tom. It showed a line of uniformed police officers blocking the entrance to a colliery. Standing in front of the line was a senior officer with a swagger stick tucked under his arm.

'See 'im,' Shields said. 'Chief Superintendent Something-or-other. He used to march up and down like a duck, shouting out orders as if he were a fucking general. We'd all sing the Laurel and Hardy tune. You know, dum di dum, dum di dum. I remember one morning, when it had snowed, the lads built a snowman in the middle of the pit lane and they put a hat and Chief Super's pips on it, stuck a stick under one arm. When he arrived, the General, he were bloody furious. Drove his police Landrover straight at it. What he didn't know were that we'd built the snowman around a concrete bollard.'

Shields laughed, enjoying the memory. 'You should've seen 'is face.'

'How old were you then?' Tom asked.

'Twenty-three. Danny were twenty-one. He were still living at 'ome, but I were not long married. We 'ad a nipper, just a couple of months old when the strike began.'

'That must have been hard.'

'It were. My wife didn't work. The government

148

gave us nowt, no benefit, no social. We got a bit of strike pay, but that 'ardly covered the costs of picketing. Most of it went on petrol, getting down to Nottinghamshire every day. We struggled. My mother-in-law used to send us food parcels — meat balls every bloody week. There were a soup kitchen in the village too, run by the wives. We used that sometimes — when we'd swallowed us pride enough. The winter were the worst. We couldn't pay the electric. They cut us off. We'd sit there with candles, 'uddled around a fire I'd made from picking coal out of the spoil tip. But, you know, that's not what I remember most. I've forgotten the 'ardship, all the miserable stuff. What I remember is the comradeship, how we stuck together and got through it. Looking back, it were an exciting time.'

Tom had heard other former miners say the same thing — about the camaraderie of the picket lines, the adrenalin rush of the conflict, pushing against the police lines, running from the charging horses. He remembered one former picket saying to him, 'There's nowt so fucking exciting as being chased by 'alf a ton of 'orse wi' a copper on top trying to knock your bloody block off.' Mick Shields had been a young man in 1984. Tom could understand how his experiences during the strike — for all their adversity — might have given him a buzz, a heightened, more intense sense of being alive.

'Tell me about the day Danny died,' Tom said.

'June 18th 1984,' Shields replied.

'The day the trouble flared at Orgreave?'

'Aye. The so-called riot. Well, it were a riot, only it weren't the pickets what did the rioting, it were the police.'

'You were there?'

Shields nodded. 'We didn't intend to be. We were on us way to Nottinghamshire, four of us in a car. Me, Danny, two others from Clayton Main. We got stopped by the police. They turned us back, so we went to Orgreave instead. There'd been pickets there before, but it were the first time for us. We got there early. There were a load of other pickets there already. The police were helping them park their cars in the Asda car park, then escorting them over to the coking plant. We couldn't believe it. What were going on? Every other picket I'd been on, the coppers had done everything they could to stop us, yet here they were being nice and friendly, falling over themselves to get us to the coking plant. We found out later, of course, what they were up to — when we got to the plant and they herded us all into a field, the 'orses and the dog 'andlers and the four thousand riot police waiting for us. It were a fucking set-up. Whatever we did that day, they were going to give us a good 'iding. And they did.'

Tom had talked to other former miners — the sad fact about the coal industry was that virtually all miners *were* former — about Orgreave. As a young research student, just finishing his PhD, he'd sat through a lot of the trial of the Orgreave pickets. That was where he'd first met Michael Russell, who'd been a junior solicitor for the defence. Tom knew in detail what had happened that day, had heard both sides of the story, but was still interested to hear what Mick Shields had to say.

'There must've been a couple of 'undred of us in the field. The police were down the bottom, by the coking plant — all lined up with their riot shields and crash 'elmets and truncheons. I've got a picture of it somewhere.'

Shields leafed through the photographs on the coffee table and selected one.

'Here. You see them? They were like an army. Some of them *were* Army. Squaddies they'd dressed up in black boiler suits, no numbers on them, nothing to identify them. Drafted in by Maggie to teach us a lesson.'

Tom took the photograph from Shields's outstretched hand. The police lines were a dense black strip across the full width of the picture. Behind the lines, waiting ominously, the mounted police cavalry were clearly visible.

'Bloody terrifying they were,' Shields said. 'You ever 'eard four thousand coppers banging on their riot shields with their truncheons? I remember when the first lorries came up the road towards the plant, belting along with no regard for safety or speed limits. We did a push against the police lines — I mean, that's why we were there, weren't it? But it were more for show than anything else. We knew we were never going to get through. Then, when we'd pulled back, the police lines opened up down the middle and the 'orses came out. Shit, you should 'ave seen us run. It would've been funny, if it 'adn't been so fucking scary. The coppers on the 'orses 'ad their batons out, swinging at anything that got in their way. I saw miners go down, dozens of them knocked unconscious, blood pouring from their 'eads.'

'Were you attacked?' Tom asked.

'Not that first time. We got out of the way sharpish. Then the 'orses retreated and things quietened down. A lot of the lads — the smart ones — started to leave. The rest of us 'ung around. I remember we played football, ate us sandwiches. Here, look at this.'

Shields held out another photograph.

'I took this one, that's why I'm not in it.'

In the foreground of the picture were five or six young men, including Danny Shields. They were lounging back on the ground, stripped to the waist. One was eating a banana, another was drinking from a bottle of Coca-Cola.

'Only summer I ever got a suntan,' Shields said. 'Normally I were all white and pasty from working underground. Look at us. Do we look like thugs who'd gone spoiling for a fight? The police said we'd come armed with axes and knives and iron bars. You see any signs of any weapons? We were in trainers and T-shirts. You think the police would have let us get to the coking plant if we'd been carrying iron bars? We spent most of the morning sunbathing, then the 'orses came out again. No warning. This time they were followed by PSUs — the Police Support Units — coppers with round shields and truncheons. They were picking people off all over. Didn't matter what you were doing. They'd club you over the 'ead and drag you back

152

through the police lines. We scattered. Danny and I just ran for it. But there weren't many places to run. On one side were the 'orses, on the other the police dogs, so we went down to the railway line. There were pickets everywhere, sliding down the embankment, scarpering across the tracks. If a train 'ad come along, it'd've been a bloodbath.'

Shields shook his head and winced. 'I were on the top of the embankment when this 'orse comes out of nowhere. I remember Danny yelling at me, then I felt this pain in the back of me 'ead and I went down. Lucky for me I rolled down the embankment or the 'orse would've trampled me. I think I must've blacked out for a moment. When I came round, I were lying next to the railway tracks with Danny bending over me, picking me up. There were blood all over me T-shirt, me trousers. There were ambulances there, but they were all behind the police lines. Anyone seeking medical attention were arrested, so Danny took me over the railway line and along the road to Asda. He bought some cotton wool and a bandage and fixed me up 'isself. I were one of the fortunate ones. There were other lads injured much worse than me. And then there were all the ones what were lifted by the coppers. Put on trial for riot. It were a fucking joke.'

For the first time, Tom noticed a bitter note in Shields's voice.

'Did you know any of the men on trial?' Tom asked.

'One. Not from Clayton, but from Wath Main.

We met 'im on the picket lines a few times. We used to kid 'im on about 'is age, call 'im an old man, should be pensioned off. He were probably only the same age as what I am now. Lovely bloke, regular churchgoer, wouldn't 'arm a fly. They picked 'im off, same as they did all the others, then fitted 'im up.'

Tom nodded. He'd spent enough time in the courtroom during the trial to have made an objective assessment of the evidence against the arrested pickets. The miners' behaviour had not been entirely above reproach, but it had been clear from the very beginning of the case that almost every police witness had been lying about what happened that morning at Orgreave. The sight of senior police officers sticking resolutely to their version of events, despite the fact that their own video footage — called by the defence — contradicted that version in almost every detail, had made Tom ashamed of the English legal system. The whole trial had been a farce from start to finish. Little wonder that after forty-eight days — in the face of incontrovertible evidence that the police had run amok that day — the prosecution had withdrawn all charges against the miners.

'I spent a couple of days in court,' Shields said. 'You know, watching from the public gallery. You 'ad to laugh really. All them coppers admitting that some senior officer 'ad dictated their evidence for them, told them what to put in their notebooks. All them coppers saying 'ow scared they'd been by the pickets' violence when the only copper who was injured that day was 'it by one of 'is own mates' riot shields. Yet there were dozens of miners with 'ead wounds from truncheons, concussion, fractured skulls.'

Shields chuckled. 'The bit I remember most. There were this one copper, said a picket had thrown a brick at 'im. He claimed the brick 'ad bounced up under 'is riot shield, hit 'im in the balls and knocked 'im over.'

Tom smiled. 'I was there that day too.'

'You were? You remember it? After the dinner break, that defence barrister coming back in wi' a brick, saying 'e'd been in the car park but try as 'e might 'e couldn't get it to bounce. I loved that bit. The bouncing brick.'

Shields started to laugh, but broke off into a fit of coughing, leaning forward, his shoulders shaking with each violent spasm.

'You OK?' Tom said.

Shields nodded. 'I'm fine,' he said breathlessly. 'Too many cigarettes.'

Tom waited for him to recover, to get his breathing fully back to normal, before he said, 'When did you stop being a miner?'

'Eighty-nine. When they closed the pit. Just as we'd said they would.'

'What do you do now?'

'Drive a delivery van for a firm in Wath. The money's not much, but it's a job, isn't it? Round 'ere that makes me a celebrity.'

'What about Danny? I know the basic facts, but not the details of how he died.'

'It were that night,' Shields said. 'We got back from Orgreave in the early afternoon. I were OK, but groggy, you know. I 'ad this gash on the back

155

of me 'ead, couple of inches long. Danny took me to Casualty in Barnsley and they stitched it up. When I got 'ome I went to bed and 'ad a lie down. In the evening Danny called round, said 'e were going over to the social for a drink. I weren't up to going wi' 'im — not that I would've anyway. We didn't 'ave the money to spare on beer. But Danny went. Then about midnight, me mum rang, said Danny 'adn't come 'ome. Well, that weren't unusual — you know, Danny were a bit of a lad. I said he'd probably gone to a mate's 'ouse, but I thought more likely 'e were with some bird. I told me mum not to worry and I didn't think no more about it until the morning when me dad rang to say the police 'ad been round. Danny's body 'ad been found on the wasteland not far from the social.'

'He had head injuries, didn't he?'

'Aye. Someone 'ad beaten 'im up bad. At the inquest they said it were some blunt instrument what did it. You know, like an iron bar or a piece of wood. Or a truncheon.'

'You think the police did it?'

'I did at the time. Everyone did.'

'On what grounds?'

Shields shrugged. 'It were just 'ow things were back then. We'd always got on all right with the police, but the strike changed all that. Not just what 'appened on the picket lines, but they'd come around the village in their vans, looking for trouble. You know, waving fistfuls of tenners in us faces, rubbing in the amount of money they were making in overtime when we 'ad nowt.

156

That really pissed us off.'

'But there was no specific evidence that pointed to police involvement in Danny's death?'

'No. There were no evidence at all. That's why they never caught whoever it were what done it.'

'Did anything happen at the social club that evening? Was there any trouble?'

Shields shook his head. 'Danny just 'ad a drink with a few of 'is mates, the mates 'e'd always drunk with. Nothing 'appened. No arguments, no fights.'

'And he walked home alone?'

'As far as anyone knows. 'E always took a short cut over the wasteland, it were quicker that way.'

'Did other people know that was the way he went home?'

'Aye, I suppose they did.'

'They could have followed him, or lain in wait for him?'

'Aye. The police looked into all that at the time. They couldn't find any witnesses. No one saw or 'eard a thing.'

'Did Danny have enemies?'

'That's 'ard to say. There were people who didn't take to 'im. You know, like there always are. Who can honestly say that everyone likes them? You'd 'ave to be a bit funny if people did, wouldn't you?'

'There was no one who particularly disliked him?'

'No. Certainly no one who'd 'ave wanted to kill 'im.'

'Do you still think the police did it?'

Shields looked down pensively.

'I dunno. He 'ad a lip on 'im, our Danny. A quick temper when 'e were provoked. The coppers didn't like 'im. But to do that? They could've lifted 'im any time they liked, roughed 'im up. That were 'ow it were then. If you were a miner you were fair game, the coppers could get away with owt. Orgreave showed that. But to kill 'im? I dunno. I don't know any more now than I did then.'

Tom put his empty mug down on the coffee table and gathered the photographs into a pile.

'Thanks for your time, I appreciate it.'

He glanced again at the top photograph — the group of pickets sunbathing at Orgreave — noticing something for the first time. The figure at the right-hand side of the picture, partially concealed by the others in the group, looked familiar.

'That's not Geoff Ibbotson, is it?'

Shields leaned over the table. 'Aye, that's 'im.'

'He was at Orgreave with you?'

'We met 'im there, aye. We were on a lot of picket lines together. Well, we would've been, wouldn't we?'

Tom didn't know why he was surprised. He knew that Geoffrey Ibbotson had been a miner at Clayton Main. It was probably just the incongruity of it. Seeing a man with such a high profile, a man who appeared so regularly on television or in parliament wearing immaculate suits, stripped to the waist in a South Yorkshire cornfield. But it wasn't just the physical appearance of the man that struck Tom — there

158

was something else too, something more visceral, that gave him a jolt. It was a shock to be reminded that a man who'd become one of the most notoriously illiberal government ministers in political history had once been a striking miner.

'Do you still know him?' Tom asked.

Shields gave a snort of laughter. 'What, me and Geoff Ibbotson? You kidding?'

'He doesn't come back here much then?'

Shields's lip curled. 'Only for photo opportunities. You know, coming back to 'is roots. In 'is ministerial Jag, surrounded by minders. The working-class boy made good. 'E needs the fucking minders 'n' all.'

'You don't like him?'

'No one round here likes 'im. He's a traitor to his class, isn't 'e? A turncoat.'

'What about during the strike?'

''E were all right then. Pulled his weight underground, then on the picket lines. 'E were on the NUM branch committee. 'E were a good bloke.'

'What happened?'

''E smelt power, didn't 'e? Lost all 'is principles to further 'is own career. Like all the rest of them. I've got no time for people like Geoff Ibbotson. What've politicians ever done for anybody except themselves?'

Tom smiled wryly. He took a final look at the photograph and stood up.

'I'd better be going.'

Shields came to the front door with him and stood on the steps, looking down into the valley

159

at the site where the colliery had once been.

'It used to make me angry at the beginning,' Shields said. 'When they closed it down. But I quite like the view now. There's foxes down there, you know. Badgers too. I've seen peregrine falcons 'unting mice where the main shaft used to be. I don't miss it. It were a 'ard job. There's still twenty-plus years of coal reserves down there. In workable seams. It's the same in most of the pits round 'ere they closed. When the oil and the gas run out — and they will — they'll regret what they did to us.'

Shields held out his hand.

'But by then it'll be too late.'

10

Tom met Moran in the café of the Millennium Galleries, one of the showpiece attractions of the new Sheffield. The coffee and sandwiches there were good, so were many of the exhibitions, but the building itself was a monstrosity. Like most of the renaissance developments in the city, it was regarded by Tom as a Missed Opportunity. For all the time and money the council had expended on the project, they'd managed to construct an edifice with all the architectural distinction of a B&Q warehouse.

Moran arrived five minutes late, one hand brushing back his hair, which had been blown about by the breeze outside. He sat down at Tom's table and gazed around, noting the other people in the café. No one he knew. And no one who looked as if they knew him. That was a start. He checked the menu, propped up against a slim vase of flowers in the centre of the table. Espresso, cappuccino, macchiato, latte — shit, not another of those places where you had to speak Italian to get a coffee.

'Are we eating?' he said.

'Not if you don't want to,' Tom replied. 'I thought we might, it's nearly lunchtime.'

'Yeah? OK, let's see.' Moran glanced down the menu, marvelling at the things you could put between two slices of bread and call a sandwich.

'Tandoori chicken with coriander and lime

161

yoghurt on ciabatta?' he said scathingly. 'Whatever happened to cheese and pickle?'

'You should try it,' Tom said. 'You like curry, don't you?'

'Only on a Saturday night, after a skinful of lager and an onion bhaji. What's this one here? 'Rosemary and garlic-flavoured Tuscan bread with a tomato, bacon and rarebit topping, oven baked and accompanied by a compote of fruit chutney.' That's cheese on bleeding toast. Three quid seventy-five for cheese on toast?'

'Maybe we should skip the food?' Tom suggested.

'No, I'm hungry. I'll have this one. 'Fresh bap with tuna mayonnaise.' At least I can pronounce the ingredients.'

Tom gave the waitress their order.

'You haven't been here before then?' he said.

Moran gave him an up-and-under look. 'What, an art gallery? Me?'

'There's some good stuff in it.'

'I'm sure there is. Pity they had to put it in a tacky shed. How many millions did it cost? Fifteen, was it? Is corrugated plastic really that expensive?'

Moran slipped off his jacket and hung it on the back of his chair. It was warm in the café, the huge floor-to-ceiling glass walls radiating heat from the sun outside.

'It doesn't surprise me, of course,' Moran went on. 'Given that the council makes the Muppets look like the Nobel Prize committee. Look at the Winter Gardens. The one thing they've built in this city that absolutely everyone likes and what do Kermit and Co do? They give the OK for a seven-storey hotel next to it so no one can see the bloody thing any more. And over there, Park Hill flats.' He pointed. In the distance, on the hill behind the station, the concrete walkways of the flats were just visible. 'The ugliest buildings in Britain, probably the world. Even the old Soviet Union would have considered them unfit for human habitation. And what's the council doing? Spending forty mill or something on tarting them up. What for? You couldn't pay people to live in them.'

He glanced up, smiling at the waitress as she brought their coffees.

'Thanks, love. Sandwiches on the way, are they?'

'They'll be a few minutes,' the waitress replied.

Moran watched the waitress head back towards the kitchen.

'I wish they wouldn't do that,' he said. 'Bring your coffee, then ten minutes later your sandwich arrives, by which time you've either drunk your coffee or it's stone cold. I like 'em both together.'

'Having a bad day?' Tom asked.

'What? Oh.' Moran grinned sheepishly. 'Am I going on a bit? I could gripe for England, that's what my mum says. I'm a bit tired, that's all. I was out late last night. Bin job. You know, going through someone's dustbin, checking their rubbish for useful information — receipts, letters, credit card slips. The glamour of being a PI.'

'You do things like that?' Tom found it hard to picture him, in his snappy suits and ties, sifting through household waste.

'Well, I have a young lad I usually get to do it. But he was on another job. So how did you get on out in the wilds of darkest South Yorkshire? Where was it again?'

'Clayton Woods.'

'Never been there.'

'It's near Wath.'

'Now Wath I do know. What a bloody dump. Most of those pit towns are. You ever been to Grimethorpe? Jesus, it's a hole. Ugliest place I've ever been. Bleak and windswept. I went there one winter. Place was deserted. There was a gale blowing. You could imagine tumbleweed rolling down the streets like you see in westerns. Horrible houses, this huge black pit surrounded by mounds of coal and slag. No wonder everyone worked underground. The view was better.'

'It's different now,' Tom said. 'Grimethorpe's still pretty grim, that's true, but Clayton Woods isn't at all bad. The Dearne Valley's quite picturesque there.'

'Yeah?'

'There's hardly a trace of the pit left. It's all grass and trees now.'

'You'll be telling me next the National Trust's bought it, set up a tea shop. All these ex-miners selling pot-pourri and plum bloody chutney.'

'It's bad out there,' Tom said. 'But not *that* bad.'

The waitress arrived with their food. Moran

164

inspected his sandwich, lifting off the top and peering suspiciously at the contents. Satisfied that there was nothing too exotic lurking in among the tuna, he took a bite and chewed it slowly.

'Pretty good,' he said with his mouth full. 'Mind, for the price . . . ' He swallowed. 'You find the brother?'

Tom nodded.

'And?'

'Nothing much.'

Tom told him what Mick Shields had said. Moran pulled a face.

'Doesn't sound a lot of help.'

'That's all he knew,' Tom said. 'There were no witnesses, no obvious suspects. Just a body on a bit of wasteland.'

'There's probably a very simple explanation,' Moran said. 'Dig deeper and you'll find some local feud was behind it. Some bloke who didn't like Danny Shields — bore a grudge against him. Maybe Shields shagged some other bloke's girlfriend and the bloke went after him with a pit prop. Those villages, they all know each other. They all have histories together. Their dads and granddads knew each other, they all went to the same schools, all went down the pit, all chased the same women.'

'Maybe,' Tom said. 'But that doesn't explain why Danny Shields's name is an Echelon keyword.'

Moran nodded, acknowledging the point. 'True. There must be something else.'

'There has to be a national security angle,'

Tom said. 'For Shields's name to be on Echelon, for the security services to have bugged my home, set me up like this. There has to be something sensitive, something political about the case. But what? Shields was just a miner. It was twenty years ago. One thing I learnt, though. Both the Shields brothers knew Geoffrey Ibbotson.'

Moran gave a start and lowered his sandwich to the table.

'*The* Geoffrey Ibbotson? Secretary of State for — what is he now?'

'Trade and Industry,' Tom said. 'Ibbotson worked at Clayton Main too. I saw a picture of them all together. At Orgreave.'

'On the picket line?'

'They were sunbathing, eating sandwiches.'

'Having a break from throwing missiles,' Moran said sardonically.

'Were you there?'

'No, but I was on plenty of other jobs where they threw stuff at us.'

Tom let the remark pass. He didn't want to reopen old wounds with Moran.

'Do you still know people on the force?' Tom asked.

'Of course. I wouldn't be in business if I didn't.'

'Anyone who might know a bit more about Danny Shields's death? The police must have a file on it.'

Moran took his time replying, eating a bit more of his sandwich, then drinking some of his coffee.

'There may be someone,' he said. 'But wheels will have to be oiled.'

'How much this time?'

'Another five. Is that a problem?'

Tom shook his head. 'The more I think about all this, the angrier I get. My life has been blown apart. My wife, my children are suffering, my career has disappeared down the toilet, I could end up in prison. I don't care what it takes, I just want this over with.'

★　★　★

For the second time in less than four days, Tom went to the Leopold Street branch of the Yorkshire Building Society, where they kept their savings, and withdrew £500 in cash. He asked for it in tens and twenties and watched nervously while the cashier counted out the notes and put them in a white envelope. The envelope was barely a centimetre thick, but Tom was acutely conscious of it tucked into the pocket of his jacket as he walked the quarter of a mile to Moran's office.

The private investigator wasn't there. He'd been delayed on another job, apparently, but his mother made Tom a cup of tea and directed him to the black leather settee in the reception area.

'Make yourself at home, love. Dave won't be long.'

Tom picked up some glossy colour brochures from the coffee table and flicked through them while he drank his tea. They were trade brochures, page after page of photographs and descriptions of different kinds of surveillance equipment — bugs, eavesdropping devices, cameras. For £400 you could buy a 'bug vibrator', a small box like a pager that would vibrate in your pocket whenever it detected a hidden transmitter in a room. For £900 you could buy a pair of sunglasses with a tiny camera concealed in the nose bridge that could relay pictures to a remote video recorder and monitor. Other cameras could be hidden in pens or wristwatches or briefcases. Directional microphones were available, disguised as packets of cigarettes or wallets. One brochure focused entirely on lie detectors, sophisticated portable machines that measured 'subaudible micro tremors in the vocal cords', and could be used over the phone or in an office without the target being aware of it.

Tom was astonished by the range of equipment that was on the market. All the ridiculous gadgets he associated with spy films — and had always assumed were either the exclusive province of state security services or too far-fetched to be real — were available by mail order or over the counter from a retailer, if you knew where to go. Big Brother was yours for the asking — all you needed was a credit card.

Fifteen minutes later Moran walked in.

'Sorry,' he said breathlessly. 'Accident on the Parkway, held me up. You OK?'

Tom nodded. 'Your mother's been looking after me very well.'

'She's good at that. Aren't you, Mum?'

Mrs Moran gave a dismissive snort.

'It's been a pleasure, love,' she said to Tom. Then to Moran, 'You want a cuppa? I can make a fresh pot.'

'I'll wait till Brian gets here. Did you call him?'

'I put back the appointment to eleven. He said that was fine. I'll put the kettle on, cut a few slices of apple cake.'

'Thanks.'

Moran smiled affectionately at his mother, then nodded to Tom.

'Let's go upstairs.'

'Has your mother always been in the business?' Tom asked when they were settled in Moran's office.

'Only since my dad died. I took her on initially to give her something to do — my previous secretary had just left. It was the best bloody move I've ever made. Don't be fooled by that 'little old lady' act she puts on. She's as sharp as a knife. Does outside jobs for me too. I send her to snoop around, to interview people. You wouldn't believe how much information she can find out. Difficult cases, sensitive cases, she's perfect. She goes in, pretends to bumble around a bit, lose her reading glasses, that kind of thing — you should see her perform, worth an Oscar any day — and in just a few minutes they're pouring their hearts out to her. Did you get the cash?'

Tom passed the envelope across the desk. Moran flipped it open and riffled through the notes inside.

'It's all there,' Tom said. 'I watched the cashier count it.'

'Just making sure,' Moran said. 'Brian Slater will go through every note, checking the watermarks, the metal strips, feeling the paper. If I gave him a magnifying glass, he'd use it.'

'Doesn't he trust you?'

'It's not that. Let me explain. Brian is ex-Special Branch. Retired now. Special Branch officers, they're not like other coppers. Most police officers like rules. You wouldn't join the force unless you liked discipline and order. But Special Branch blokes are obsessive — all the ones I've met, anyway. They're repressed, unimaginative people. That's what comes of being poodles for MI5. Most ordinary coppers think there's something underhand about Special Branch, listening in on people's private conversations, spying on trade unionists and politicians. I've got an open mind — after all, nosing into what doesn't concern me is how I make a living — but Brian Slater is too much of an old woman even for me.'

Moran pushed the envelope of cash to one side of his desk and looked at Tom.

'I'll tell you the kind of bloke he is. His wife told me this years ago, swore she'd kill me if I ever let on I knew. Brian had a routine every night he came home from work. He'd go upstairs to get changed, take off his work clothes. He'd remove all the loose change from his trouser pockets and stick it on top of the chest of drawers in neat little piles — one pile for each denomination, pennies, two pences, fives, tens, twenties and so on. Then he'd fold his trousers and put them in a heated trouser press, hang up his jacket and tie and get out his underwear and socks for the next day — a fresh set every day. He had separate drawers for his socks and underpants. His socks always had to be ironed, given knife-edge creases and then stored in individual polythene bags. Can you imagine it? His wife said it just about drove her crazy. That's Special Branch for you.'

'If he's so particular, how come you can bribe him to provide information?' Tom said.

Moran looked aghast. 'God, don't let him hear you call it a bribe — even though it is, of course. He'd be out the door and scuttling home to iron his socks before you could say 'anally retentive'. He's doing me a favour, for an old colleague, and I, in turn, am showing my appreciation for our friendship by giving him an envelope of cash. It's a fine distinction, but an important one. When you're living on a pension like Brian, and you like a winter break in the Canaries, your principles tend to become rather more elastic.'

The intercom on Moran's desk buzzed.

'Yes?'

'Brian's here,' Mrs Moran said.

'Tell him to come up. We'll be in the box.'

Moran picked up the white envelope and pushed back his chair. Tom followed him through into the secure chamber. Brian Slater, when he walked in, was everything Tom had expected from Moran's description. He was perhaps a little younger than he'd anticipated — only in his mid-fifties — but then he'd forgotten how early police officers retired. He

171

was tall and thin with a small, tight mouth, greying hair brushed back from a high forehead and a neatly clipped moustache. He had the air of an Army NCO or a pernickety town hall clerk. Tom resisted the temptation to lean down and sneak a look at his socks.

'Good morning, David,' Slater said. He was carrying a shiny black leather briefcase, which he placed carefully on the table.

'Hello, Brian. This is Tom. He's going to be helping me this morning.'

'Tom.'

Slater held out a red, bony hand. Tom took it. It was like shaking the fingers of a skeleton.

'The weather is very inclement this morning,' Slater said. 'A nasty north wind. A damp chill in the air. Most unpleasant.'

He hitched up the knees of his impeccably pressed trousers and sat down.

'Perhaps before we commence we could tidy up our arrangement.'

Moran handed Slater the envelope of cash. Slater took out the £500 and divided it up into piles of tens and twenties. Then he went through the notes, holding each one up to the light, rubbing the paper between his thumb and forefinger. Tom avoided Moran's eye.

'That all seems to be in order,' Slater said eventually.

The money went back into the envelope, then swiftly away into the inside pocket of Slater's jacket. He opened his briefcase and took out a bulging cardboard file.

'You have two hours,' he said.

Moran took in the thickness of the file. 'Is that all?'

'My contact has to have it back by the early afternoon. That was the best he could do. He's taking a big enough risk as it is. You can make notes, but nothing must be photocopied. Is that understood?'

'That's fine, Brian.'

The door swung open and Mrs Moran came in with a tray of tea things.

'Milk, Brian?' she asked, pouring him a cup.

'Just a dash, thank you, Mrs M,' Slater replied.

'Sugar?'

'I have my own sweetener with me, thank you.'

Slater delved into his pocket and pulled out a small pewter case about the size of a cigarette lighter. He flipped open the lid and dropped a couple of tiny pills of sweetener into his tea.

'Have some apple cake, I made it myself,' Mrs Moran said.

'I shouldn't,' Slater said, pursing his lips and patting his stomach. 'Well, perhaps a small slice.'

Slater took the plate from Mrs Moran and unfolded a paper napkin on his knee, spreading it out to protect his trousers from crumbs. Not that he was likely to produce many crumbs, given that he held the plate up so that it was almost underneath his chin as he ate the apple cake.

'Very good, Mrs M. Very good indeed,' he said, licking his lips.

Moran had pulled the cardboard file across the desk and was glancing through the contents.

He waited for his mother to leave the room and the door was firmly closed before he said, 'What have we got here?'

'That's the Special Branch file on Clayton Main for 1984–5.'

'You had a file on just that one colliery?'

'We kept files on every pit in South Yorkshire.'

'And Danny Shields? Is he mentioned in here?'

'I haven't looked,' Slater said. 'I don't want to know. What you take from the file is your business.'

'What about the separate case file?'

'On Shields? I asked my contact. He checked. He couldn't find a file.'

'An open file? The case was never solved.'

Slater shrugged. 'It was twenty years ago. Who's interested in it now?'

'I am.'

'The file's gone, David. My contact could find no trace of it. He looked very thoroughly.'

'Did Special Branch play any role in the murder inquiry?'

'Not directly, obviously. CID would have handled it. But they may have had some input. I remember the case, but Clayton Main wasn't my area. You'll have to check the file.'

The papers inside the file were loosely bound together in bundles. Moran passed a couple of sections across to Tom.

'So we're looking for any mention of Danny Shields,' Tom said.

'That's about it,' Moran replied. 'I know it's very vague, but we're fishing. We don't know what we're going to catch until it tugs on the line.'

Tom leafed through the documents he'd been given. Some were handwritten, some were typed. The paper sizes varied: sheets of A4, of foolscap. Some were little more than scraps — pages torn from notebooks and stapled together or tied with faded green treasury tags. All were dog-eared and yellowing, their print fading with age. They smelt of dust, the scent reminding Tom of airless attics or the shelves of an antiquarian bookshop.

One section in particular caught his attention — a collection of papers bound together with string. They bore all the hallmarks of the pre-word-processing era, their text clearly banged out on some old manual typewriter. The lines weren't always straight, the density of the ink was inconsistent, dark in places, difficult to read in others. Occasionally a key had hammered right through the paper, leaving a tiny hole behind. Greyish smudges marked the places where mistakes had been Tippexed out and corrected.

They appeared to be profiles of individuals, information on National Union of Mineworkers activists at Clayton Main, starting with the NUM branch committee members. The president of the branch got a couple of sheets to himself, as did the secretary and treasurer. Tom read through the first few profiles. Apart from the basic facts that were presumably accurate — dates of birth, addresses, national insurance numbers and so on — there seemed to be surprisingly little substantiated information in them. Phrases like 'sources say', 'it is suspected' and 'we believe' cropped up several times in each report. They seemed flimsy documents to Tom, more speculation and gossip than confirmed fact.

He flicked forwards through the collection, glancing at the names at the tops of the sheets: Harry Osborn, Jim Gillespie, Billy Harding, Geoffrey Ibbotson . . .

Tom scanned the profile of Ibbotson. It seemed particularly low on the kind of corroboration and proof he would have expected of a police file. Ibbotson's character assessment was less than flattering. He was described variously as a 'scheming communist agitator', a 'violent thug' and a 'dangerous militant', apparently on the say-so of various 'sources' and 'informers'. A passage on his alleged relationship with a married woman in the village seemed little more than salacious tittle-tattle.

'Geoff Ibbotson doesn't get a very good write-up,' Tom said.

'He was a troublemaker,' Slater replied. 'Bad news.'

'If the press got hold of this, they'd have a field day. A Cabinet minister described as a thug and an agitator. Where did the information in these profiles come from?'

'All over,' Slater said. He put down his tea cup and wiped his lips with his napkin. 'The sources would be wide and varied. Police officers who knew the person. Other local people. The pit managers, probably. Neighbours, shopkeepers, publicans.'

176

'You used to write reports like these?'

'Not about Clayton Main, but about other pits, yes.'

'Do you think they were accurate?'

'Well, as accurate as we could make them,' Slater said defensively. 'You have to understand, we were fighting a war back then. The miners were trying to undermine our democracy, to overthrow the elected government. We needed information on these people. We needed to know who the ringleaders were, who were the people we had to watch.'

'You kept them under surveillance?'

'We monitored them, yes,' Slater said.

'Tapped their phones, you mean?'

Slater hesitated. He glanced at Moran.

'Come on,' Tom said. 'Everyone knows you tapped the phones of senior NUM officials — Scargill, Heathfield, Taylor, people like that. But what about a branch committee member like Geoff Ibbotson? Would you have tapped his phone too?'

Slater shifted uncomfortably in his seat.

'Possibly,' he said. 'But unlikely. Unless we had good reason to consider him a particular threat.'

'Threat?'

'There were police officers on the front line every day of the strike. Many of them got injured. If we could nip any possible violence in the bud, stop pickets getting to the Nottingham-shire pits, then we would. Committee members were obvious targets for surveillance. They were the ones organising the flying pickets. But we didn't have the manpower or resources to tap all their phones as a matter of course.'

Tom leafed through the rest of the profiles, spotting Danny Shields's name near the end.

'Danny Shields was a branch committee member too,' he said. 'Would you have been monitoring him?'

'I couldn't say,' Slater said. 'You'll have to check the file.'

Tom read through Danny Shields's profile. It was shorter than the others, only half a page of single-spaced text. It, too, seemed to be rather thin on substantiated facts. Shields was described as a 'heavy drinker', 'prone to arguments', 'promiscuous' and 'subject to possible violent tendencies'. No information was recorded to support the descriptions. Shields had, apparently, never been in trouble with the police. He had no criminal record. There was no mention of what incidents or observed behaviour had led to this critical character assessment.

Tom scribbled down a few notes on his pad of paper, feeling a degree of empathy with both Danny Shields and Geoff Ibbotson. He knew what it felt like to have your private life scrutinised by the state.

He read on through the pile of documents. It was a difficult job. Much of the material seemed trivial and irrelevant, yet he felt he ought to examine it all just in case it contained something significant. But what exactly, in this case, constituted a significant fact?

An hour passed before he came across anything further that struck him as worthy of detailed note. Moran had given him a thick wad of brownish, curling papers. They were all identical printed sheets of pro forma South Yorkshire Police stationery. Each one was headed 'Telephone Record'. The information on the papers was all handwritten — not always by the same person. As the official heading indicated, they were records of phone conversations conducted by Special Branch officers during the strike. Many of the conversations were not very revealing — just dull administrative matters that had been routinely filed — but some seemed to warrant a closer inspection.

Tom separated the sheets into piles according to the handwriting on them. At the bottom of each page was the signature of the officer who had made the notes. One particular pile was very much larger than the others. The signature on them read, 'DC Harkis'. Tom studied the notes Harkis had written down.

Most were very brief, and there was a striking similarity between them, the majority simply a short message consisting of a date and a place name: March 14th, 1984 — Ollerton; March 26th, 1984 — Thoresby; April 6th, 1984 — Welbeck. Tom examined the sheets more minutely. There must have been thirty or forty of them. The times the messages were taken were recorded at the top, next to the date, and on nearly all of them the word 'Spike' had been written next to the sub-heading 'From'.

Tom showed the papers to Moran.

'Take a look at these. Ollerton, Thoresby, Welbeck — those are the names of collieries in Nottinghamshire. Ones that kept working during

179

the strike and so were picketed. See the dates? There's one in each of the messages. But then look at the tops of the forms. There's another date written in there, the date the message was taken. The dates are always a day apart. They're tip-offs. Someone's phoning in. Giving Special Branch the location of the following day's picketing.'

'What do you think, Brian?'

Moran passed the papers across the table to Slater, who picked them up and examined them, one finger stroking his sleek moustache.

'Looks that way to me,' Slater said. 'The times on the messages are very similar: 9.53 p.m., 9.56, 9.48. Probably just after the branch meetings had ended.'

Slater handed the papers back to Moran.

'All the NUM branches had regular evening meetings at which the targets for the next day's picketing were discussed,' he continued. 'Most of the operations were coordinated from NUM headquarters in Sheffield. Someone from HQ would call the branches, telling them where they were to go. They'd use payphones sometimes, use a code system that kept changing so it was hard for us to keep tabs on which pits were being targeted. This kind of tip-off would have been invaluable to Special Branch, who'd have passed it on immediately to the uniforms. That was half the battle, knowing which pits were going to be hit so you could close the roads, stop the pickets before they got there.'

'You're saying someone from the branch, one

of the miners, was informing on his colleagues?' Tom said.

'Not necessarily someone from the branch,' Slater replied. 'Though it looks the most likely explanation to me. We got information from all sorts of people: neighbours of miners, bitter estranged wives, people with old scores to settle. But from the regular nature of these calls I'd say it was someone on the inside. It has to have been a miner.'

'Spike?' Tom said. 'I assume that's a code name?'

'That's correct,' Slater said. 'Neither the informer nor his handler at Special Branch would ever have used the man's real name.'

Tom spread the telephone records out on the table. 'Danny Shields was killed on June 18th, 1984.' He checked the dates on the records. 'June 14th, that's the last one. Whoever Spike was, he was phoning in throughout March, April and May, but in the middle of June he suddenly stopped. Why? The strike went on until the following year.'

'You think Shields was Spike?' Moran said.

'It adds up.'

'And what? Someone found out he was working for Special Branch so they killed him?'

'It's quite possible,' Tom said. 'The way things were back then in the pit communities, if they found out you were a nark for the police they'd have lynched you, no question. It fits the facts.'

Moran turned to Slater. 'The officer who wrote these reports, DC Harkis. Is he still around?'

Slater shook his head. 'Colin Harkis. He died a few years back. The Big C.'

'Would anyone else have known the identity of Spike?'

Slater shrugged. 'Depends. Harkis would have played his cards close to his chest, guarded his contact jealously. Certainly none of his immediate colleagues, people like me, would have known Spike's true identity. Our guv'nor might possibly have been in the know, but I wouldn't bet on it. It's academic anyway, because Ray Stoddart — our super back then — is no longer around either. Heart attack.'

'Stoddart?' Moran said. 'I've seen his name somewhere.'

Moran rummaged through the stack of papers on his side of the table and extricated a number of small slips.

'Petty-cash payments,' he said. 'Five of them, all for £100. One in March 1984, two in April, then another two in May. All of them authorised by Ray Stoddart.'

'Payments to Spike?' Tom said.

'Or someone. The recipient isn't recorded. All untraceable, unfortunately, so we'll never know.'

Slater looked at his watch.

'I'm going to have to hurry you, it's nearly one o'clock.'

'We need more time, Brian,' Moran said.

'Sorry, that was the deal.'

Moran turned to Tom. 'Skim through what you can. See if there are any more references to Spike, or to Shields.'

Tom took another pile of documents from the

cardboard file and flipped through them, his eyes scanning each page, not reading the text but simply looking for those two key names. He was nowhere close to finishing when Slater said, 'Time's up' and began collecting in the documents.

'Anything?' Moran said.

Tom smiled ruefully. 'No.'

They watched Slater slip the papers back into the cardboard file and return the file to his briefcase.

'Thanks, Brian,' Moran said.

Slater nodded, already on his feet, anxious to be off. Moran accompanied him downstairs to the exit, then came back up to the box. He glanced at the notepad on the table in front of Tom.

'I know,' Tom said. 'It's not much to show. How about you?'

'Same. A lot of documents, not many notes. But we're progressing.'

'You think so?'

'These things take time. Piecing together information is a slow process. What've you got on Shields?'

'A few notes from the police profile. Nothing at all about his death. If Shields was an informer, and that's why he was killed, wouldn't Special Branch have taken more of an interest in his murder?'

'They might,' Moran said. 'But there again, they might not.'

'Meaning?'

'Well, Special Branch isn't like the rest of the

police force. They're political. They're effectively the foot soldiers, the public face, of MI5. Their loyalties, their allegiances are complicated. They're police officers, but in many ways they're more accountable to the security services than they are to their chief constables. That was certainly true during the miners' strike. South Yorkshire was crawling with Special Branch officers, not just local but a lot imported from the Met. They ran their own operations — dirty tricks, agents provocateurs planted in picket lines to incite violence, that kind of thing. I was there, I saw it. My Super, in the regular uniformed branch, had no idea what these characters were up to. They were answerable to nobody round here. Somebody in London was calling the shots. And there were others on the scene in direct day-to-day control of their activities — shadowy people from MI5. Spooks.

'Shields's death could have caused them a lot of problems. Let's say Shields was an informer for Special Branch. And someone found out about him, or at the very least began to get suspicious of him. This person — maybe a fellow striking miner — confronted Shields, they argued, got in a fight and Shields was killed. It fits what happened. Shields was beaten to death. Somebody really didn't like him. Now Special Branch would not have been very keen on their role in all that being revealed. It was one can of worms they would not have wanted opening. Shields's work for them resulted in his death. They would have kept well out of it, maybe taken subtle steps to have the whole thing brushed under the carpet.'

'You think that's what this is all about?' Tom said. 'MI5 covering up their involvement in Danny Shields's death? They think I'm prying into the case and they're frightened what I might uncover.'

'Maybe,' Moran said. 'But I want to check something out before jumping to conclusions.'

He lifted up the pad on which he'd written his notes. Underneath was a single small sheet of paper.

'I borrowed this when Brian wasn't looking,' he said. 'I like to have the original document.'

'What original document?'

'You remember those petty-cash slips I found — a hundred quid a time, all authorised by Ray Stoddart? This was with them.'

He turned the piece of paper around so Tom could read it.

'This is another petty-cash payment?' Tom said.

'A payment. But not petty cash. This is bigger — see the amount, £1000. Also authorised by Ray Stoddart, on May 25th, 1984. It's too big for an anonymous cash transaction, a bung under the table in a pub somewhere. Stoddart would have had to account for a sum that size, show where it was going, produce some paperwork. So it went into a bank account.'

Moran pointed to the numbers at the top of the paper.

'It's a credit transfer. From South Yorkshire Police to this account.'

'You can find out whose account it was?'

Moran gave him a pained look.

'Come on. I've got the account number, the sort code of the branch. What do you take me for?'

11

The lounge bar of the Red Lion was crowded with people, many more than Tom had expected on a Wednesday evening. He looked around, scanning the unfamiliar faces, and saw Moran sitting with a woman in a corner of the room. Tom manoeuvred his way across to them, threading a path through the tightly packed tables. There was a fug of cigarette smoke hanging in the air, thick and acrid.

Moran looked up and nodded at Tom as he reached the table. Then he introduced him to his companion.

'Tom, Janice. Janice, Tom.' He pronounced her name Janeece, as if it were French.

Tom shook the woman's hand. She was in her thirties, tall and slim with silky, dark hair and smooth, tanned skin. She had diamond studs in her ears, a gold chain around her neck and an expensive gold watch on her left wrist.

'What'll you have?' Moran said, stubbing out his cigarette in the ash tray on the table.

'My round,' Tom said.

'All right. A pint of bitter then, thanks.'

'Janice?'

'Could I have another red wine?'

It was ten minutes before Tom returned with the drinks, having had to fight his way to the bar and wait to be served.

'Is it always this busy?' he asked.

'Quiz night,' Moran said. 'Very popular.'

He took a sip of his beer, leaving a smear of froth along his top lip which he licked away with his tongue.

'They pull a good pint too. You're on our team, by the way. For the quiz. And don't piss me off by saying you've got to go. I'm depending on you.'

'I've never taken part in a pub quiz in my life, you know,' Tom said.

'Doesn't matter. You've got to be better than her.'

'Hey!' Janice lifted her hand and slapped Moran on the arm.

'Well, you've got to admit you're not much bloody good, are you?' Moran said.

Janice sniffed and turned her head away.

'At least I'm not a fact fanatic like you.' She leaned towards Tom and said confidentially, 'You should see him. Spends his weekends memorising facts. Useless stuff you'd never need in a million years. The other Saturday he spent the afternoon and half the evening learning the periodic table. I mean, what's that all about?'

'Take no notice of her,' Moran said. 'I'm in training for *Mastermind*.'

'*Mastermind*!' Janice said scornfully. 'Have you ever heard anything so daft?'

'Give me any element in the periodic table. Go on. Any.'

Tom reflected for a moment. 'Potassium.'

'One of the alkali metals,' Moran said. 'The others being lithium, sodium, rubidium, caesium and francium. Symbol K, atomic number 19. Correct?'

'I haven't a clue,' Tom said. 'I'm a historian. What do *I* know about the periodic table?'

'See, you could tell us anything and we wouldn't know if it was right or not, would we?' Janice said.

'You're going on *Mastermind*?' Tom said.

'No, he's not,' Janice replied.

'I am,' Moran said indignantly. 'Well, I'm applying anyway.'

'What's your specialist subject?' Tom asked.

'You need two. One I'm still thinking about, the other's the Life and Films of Humphrey Bogart. Go on, ask me anything you like about Bogart.'

'Leave him alone, poor man,' Janice said in disgust, pursing her lips and blowing a cloud of smoke across the table.

'Go on,' Moran repeated. 'Try me.'

'When and where was he born?'

'Too easy. December 26th, 1899, New York City. Another.'

'What was the name of the boat in *The African Queen*?'

'Now you're trying to wind me up. Come on, think of a hard one.'

'How many wives did he have?'

'Four. Lauren Bacall, she was the last. Before her was Mayo Methot. And the first was Helen Menken.' Moran paused. 'Shit! Who was number two?' Moran glanced at Janice.

'Don't look at me,' she said. 'I can't even remember who *I've* been married to, never mind

Humphrey Bogart. Excuse me a second.'

Janice stood up, her bag clutched under her arm, and headed across the room towards the Ladies. Moran lit up another cigarette and sucked on it. He was still in his work clothes — a double-breasted charcoal suit and a wide kipper tie that looked out of date to Tom's eye but had probably come back into fashion without him noticing.

'I checked out that bank account,' Moran said. 'We were wrong about Spike.'

'Yes?' Tom didn't take his eyes off Moran's face.

'The account is no longer active. It was closed twelve years ago. NatWest branch in Barnsley. But I found out whose it was in 1984 — Geoffrey Ibbotson.'

'Ibbotson?' Tom said in disbelief. 'Ibbotson was a paid informer for Special Branch? Not Danny Shields?'

'We got it the wrong way round,' Moran said. 'You know what I think? Shields wasn't killed because someone found out he was an informer. He was killed because *he* discovered Ibbotson was working for Special Branch and someone didn't want that fact to come out.'

'Ibbotson himself?' Tom said. 'You're saying he murdered Danny Shields to cover up his own links with Special Branch?'

'Or Special Branch did it to protect their source.'

Tom sat back in his chair and stared at Moran.

'Jesus,' he breathed. 'No wonder they're out to get me.'

'It would explain a lot,' Moran said.

'What about the dates on the phone records? The calls from Spike appeared to stop about the time of Shields's murder.'

'The records stopped. That doesn't mean the tip-offs stopped. Maybe Ibbotson lay low for a while after Shields was killed. Maybe he continued informing, but his calls weren't recorded in the file. Or if they were, the notes have been lost. There are several possibilities.'

Tom licked his lips. His mouth had gone suddenly dry.

'What now?' he said. 'Do we go public? Go to the police? The press?'

'Let's not jump the gun,' Moran said. 'If we're going to accuse a Cabinet minister of involvement — either directly or indirectly — in a murder, we'd better be damn sure we've got our facts right. We don't have a case at the moment. A bank account isn't proof of anything. We've got to dig deeper, see what else we can find.'

★   ★   ★

They stayed in the pub until closing time. They only came third in the quiz, much to Moran's annoyance, but Tom felt he'd acquitted himself well, answering a number of questions that had stumped Moran. On the pavement outside they shook hands.

'I've got my car,' Tom said. 'You want a lift?'

'Thanks for the offer, but Janice only lives around the corner.'

Tom walked away down the street. His car was

191

parked on a side road a hundred yards from the pub. He was tired, his eyes stung from the lounge bar smoke, but he felt up to driving. He'd only had a couple of pints of bitter, switching to orange juice when it had become clear that it was going to be a long evening.

He was fifty yards from his car, passing a gateway that led into a small yard, when it happened.

Later, when he tried to recall the exact sequence of events, his memory was hazy about the details. He remembered a figure emerging suddenly from the yard. A man's figure. Moving fast, coming for him. Tom stopped, turning away instinctively to avoid a collision. It was that one small movement that saved his life.

He felt the man's hand brush against his jacket, then a burning pain across his side as if the skin had been ripped open. Tom staggered, clutching himself, feeling a tear in his shirt, a warm stickiness beneath it. The man backed away a little. His face was in shadow, a cap pulled low over his eyes. Tom saw a glint of something metallic in the man's hand. A knife.

The knife came up in a vicious arc, aiming for Tom's chest. Tom lashed out with his left arm, knocking the knife sideways. He felt another blaze of pain on the back of his forearm, cried out in agony. He felt his vision blur, a dizziness overcome him. He couldn't see clearly, couldn't think. Even the pain in his side and arm was no longer so excruciating. He was aware of a voice shouting in the distance — Moran's voice — but couldn't make out the words. Then he heard footsteps running towards him. Tom fell. He toppled sideways, hit his head on the edge of the gatepost and blacked out.

*   *   *

Helen was in bed, just drifting off to sleep, when the telephone rang. She roused herself quickly, before the noise woke the children, and padded barefoot across to the extension in the study.

It was Moran. Helen had to pause to think when he gave his name. *Moran?* Yes, Tom had mentioned him. The private investigator. 'There's been an accident,' he said. 'Your husband.'

The drowsiness fell away from her, her mind cleared abruptly. 'Accident?' She listened to Moran explaining, certain words registering more than others: *knife, hospital, intensive care.*

'He's in the Royal Hallamshire,' Moran said. 'You'd better come over.'

'Yes, yes, of course.' Then she remembered. The children. 'What time is it?'

'Ten past midnight.'

'I have children. I'll have to make some arrangements.'

'I'll pick you up in twenty minutes.'

Helen put down the phone. She was agitated. What to do? Get Hannah and Ben out of bed and take them with her? Not a good idea. They'd be half asleep, irritable, and in any case she didn't want them to see their father in a hospital intensive care unit. Taking them was a last resort only. A friend then? It was the middle of the

193

night, but she knew Liz wouldn't mind. She called her, explained what had happened. Liz, cool and efficient even at this hour, didn't balk. She came straight over, was there a few minutes before Moran's silver Jaguar pulled up in front of the house. Helen went out to the car, breathing deeply to try to control the feeling of nausea in her stomach.

She knew Moran's name, but almost nothing else about him. She was struck by how big he was, the sheer bulk of him squeezed into the Jaguar's deep leather seats. She looked at him uncertainly. He smelt of beer and cigarettes.

'Everything OK?' he said, his voice low, unexcitable. 'The kids, I mean.'

Helen nodded. 'A friend's looking after them.'

The Jaguar purred away. On the drive to the hospital, the Jaguar moving fast through the darkened streets, Moran told her again what had happened.

'Lucky I turned round when I did,' he said. 'Saw the bloke going for him.'

'A knife, you say?' Helen said, still trying to take everything in. 'How badly hurt is he?'

'Couple of nasty gashes, I think. They were still seeing to him when I phoned you.' Moran looked at her. 'I don't think it's life-threatening.'

'You don't?' A weight came off her shoulders. 'Are you sure?'

'I got the ambulance there quick. The paramedics knew what they were doing. He's lost some blood, he was unconscious.'

'Unconscious?' Suddenly her anxiety flooded back.

'He banged his head. Don't think the worst. Let's see what the doctor says.'

'What about his attacker?'

'He got away,' Moran said. 'I could've chased him, but it was more important I looked after your husband.'

'Thank you.'

Moran glanced at her sympathetically. 'That's OK.'

The doctor on duty in the intensive care unit was a young house officer, mid-twenties, unshaven, eyes hollow from lack of sleep.

'Your husband is still unconscious, Mrs Whitehead,' he said. 'But he's breathing unaided. He took a nasty knock to the head.'

'How serious is it? You're saying he's in a coma?'

'He's unconscious.' The doctor chose his words carefully.

'But he'll recover consciousness?'

'There's no reason at the moment to think he won't.'

'How badly was he stabbed?'

'The wounds he incurred were incisions — gashes. One to the waist, one to the left forearm. Neither is very deep.'

'So his life isn't in danger?'

'Not from the knife wounds, no. They affected no vital organs, no significant blood vessels. He's lost some blood, but nothing to get alarmed about. We've stitched up the incisions. They should heal well.'

'Can I see him?'

Tom was in a room all by himself. He had a

drip in his arm and wires connecting him to a heart monitor. His bandaged left arm was out on top of the sheet, but the wound to his abdomen was hidden beneath the covers.

Helen sat down next to the bed. She was alone. Moran and the doctor had remained outside. She gazed at Tom. He looked as if he were asleep. His face was relaxed. He was breathing peacefully.

'It's me,' she said softly, wondering if he could hear her. 'You're going to be OK. You're going to be just fine.'

She watched his face. Open your eyes, Tom. Please open your eyes. He didn't stir. What if he never recovered consciousness? she thought.

'It's me, Tom. Helen. I'm here.'

She took his hand and held it. Come back to me, she thought. Come back into the light, into the living world. Please. She gripped his fingers in her own, holding on tight. Staring at his face, feeling the tears trickling down her cheeks.

12

It was the middle of the following morning when the hospital rang Helen to say that Tom had recovered consciousness. The relief was so overwhelming that she sank to her knees in the hall, leaning back against the wall as she listened to the nurse at the other end of the line.

'He's asked for you,' the nurse said.

'I'll be there as soon as I can. How is he?'

'He seems fine. He's been talking. He's had a cup of tea and something to eat.'

Helen's eyes filled with tears. She wanted to sob, to release some of the tension that had built up inside her, but she waited until the call was over before she allowed herself a quiet weep. He was back. Thank God. All her fears, those wild, exaggerated fears that he might remain in a coma indefinitely, had proved groundless. She couldn't wait to see him.

Every minute of the journey to the hospital was a frustration. The other vehicles on the road, the traffic lights, the queue to get into the Royal Hallamshire's car park all seemed to be conspiring to delay her arrival. The lifts in the main foyer — notoriously inefficient — were another obstacle she had to endure. She waited impatiently for what seemed an eternity but was probably less than half a minute, sorely tempted to take the stairs. But the intensive care unit was on R Floor, the seventeenth storey of the building — a few more steps than she felt up to tackling just now.

The ICU nurse assigned to Tom was on the phone at the nurses' station. She put her hand over the receiver when she saw Helen and said, 'Go on down, he's waiting for you.'

Tom's room was at the far end of the corridor. Helen glanced in through the glass panel in the door, registering the presence of a white-coated figure standing by Tom's bed, then she walked in. The noise of the door opening made the doctor turn round. No, not turn. He *spun* round, spun round almost violently, his sudden movement implying surprise, nervousness and — the first impression that Helen got — a furtive guilt. An object he was holding in his hand slipped from his fingers and skittered away under the bed.

'I'm sorry,' Helen said. 'Am I interrupting?'

The doctor — she assumed he was a doctor from his white coat, the stethoscope around his neck — was looking directly at her. He wasn't the house officer she'd met during the night. This man was older, his face red and blotchy. Something about him seemed familiar.

'Mrs Whitehead,' the man said coolly. He seemed to have recovered his composure.

'Please, don't let me get in the way,' Helen said.

She smiled at Tom. He was half sitting up in bed. He was pale, sickly-looking, but his eyes were bright, delighted to see her.

The doctor moved towards the door. 'It's all right, I was just leaving.'

198

His face, I've seen it somewhere before, Helen thought. She took in the rest of his appearance, unconsciously noting the details — the brown suit beneath his coat, his brown suede shoes. She searched for a name badge, for the photo identity card all the hospital staff wore clipped to their uniforms. He didn't have one. And he knew my name, Helen thought. An educated guess? Was she being silly? Then it came to her. The Magistrates' Court. He'd been there in the public seats for Tom's hearing. Why would a doctor have been in court?

'Excuse me,' Helen said. But she never finished the sentence. The man was coming for her, pushing her roughly aside. He threw open the door. Helen reached out, trying to grab him. He swung his fist, knocking her to the floor. She heard Tom cry out in alarm, felt her head spinning. The door slammed shut.

'Helen, Helen, are you OK?' Tom's voice.

She pulled herself to her feet, saw him struggling to get out of bed.

'No, don't,' she said urgently. 'I'm fine.'

'What the hell was all that about? The doctor, why did he — ?'

'He wasn't a doctor,' Helen broke in.

She whipped open the door, eyes scanning the corridor in both directions. The man had vanished. Helen ran towards the nurses' station.

★ ★ ★

There were two police officers, both in plain clothes. They arrived about ten minutes after

199

Helen had alerted the nurses, called in immediately by the hospital's internal security department, which had also launched its own thorough search of the building.

Helen was in with Tom, sitting beside his bed, when the two officers entered the room. They were accompanied by a uniformed hospital security guard whose radio, clutched in his hand, was switched to 'receive', crackling with intermittent reports from other security guards as they attempted to track down the bogus doctor.

One of the police officers flashed his warrant card.

'You see which way he went?' he asked Helen, wasting no time on preliminaries.

Helen shook her head. 'The nurses said they didn't see him leave through the main exit. He must have got out some other way.'

'There's another exit?' the officer said to the security guard.

'At this end of the corridor. It takes you out into the central lobby,' the guard replied.

'Where the lifts are?'

'That's right.'

'What about the stairs?'

'They're through a door at the back of the lobby.'

'They're covered by the CCTV cameras?'

'All the public areas are covered.'

'We'll want the tapes. Maybe you could show my colleague where they are.'

The security guard gave a nod and left the room with the other police officer. The first detective looked carefully around. He was in his forties, on the short side for a police officer, Helen thought. He had a plump face and dark, almost black, eyes.

'This doctor,' he said to Tom. 'What did he say to you?'

'Just that he was going to give me an injection. That it wouldn't hurt,' Tom replied.

'He dropped the hypodermic needle when I came in,' Helen said.

The detective crouched down, looking under the bed. He slipped on a pair of gloves and picked up the hypodermic needle where it had fallen.

'Anyone touch this?'

'The security guard who arrived first — after I'd told the nurses — said to leave it where it was,' Helen explained.

'A wise precaution. We'll need a description of the man. You get a good look at him?'

Helen nodded. 'I'd seen him before.'

'Did he drop anything else?'

'Not that I noticed.'

The detective held up the hypodermic needle in his gloved hand. It contained some kind of clear liquid.

'Excuse me a minute. I'll just find a bag for this.'

The detective went out of the room. Helen looked at Tom and tried to smile.

'This goes from bad to worse, doesn't it?' she said, the flippancy disguising her anxiety. She had no idea what was in the hypodermic needle, but she knew it had not been intended to do

Tom any good. It seemed extreme, even melodramatic, to assume that the bogus doctor had come to kill Tom, but why else had he been there? They'd tried once with a knife, and when that had failed, they'd resorted to other, less violent but no less effective methods. The more Helen thought about it, the more frightening it became.

'How are you feeling?' she said. With all the unexpected activity it was the first opportunity she'd had to ask.

'I'm doing OK,' Tom said. 'I've got a bruise and a lump on the side of my head, but they'll mend.'

'And the knife wounds?'

'Uncomfortable, that's all. One of the nurses gave me some pills to take away the real pain.'

'You were lucky.'

'I know.'

'Twice. The man — the doctor — he didn't do anything else to you?'

'No. He'd only just arrived when you walked in.'

'Me today, Moran last night, we're cutting it fine,' Helen said.

'I must remember to thank Moran.'

'I thanked him for you. Oh, Tom.' A tear trickled down her face.

'Hey, it's OK,' Tom said. He reached out to take her hand.

'I'm sorry. I'm just so worried. And scared.'

'I know.'

'I don't want you in here. It's not safe.'

'It won't be for long.'

Helen heard the door open and turned her head. Two uniformed police officers were walking into the room. One of them unbuttoned his tunic pocket and pulled out his notebook and pen.

'Sorry for the delay in getting here,' he said politely.

'That's all right,' Helen replied. 'We've already spoken to your plainclothes colleagues.'

The police officer frowned at her quizzically.

'What plainclothes colleagues?'

* * *

For the first few minutes it seemed as though it might have been a simple case of poor communications — hardly an unknown phenomenon in a bureaucratic organisation like the police. The call from the Royal Hallamshire's internal security department must have somehow resulted in both the CID and the uniformed branch being alerted to the incident at the hospital. It was only as questions were asked, radio and phone calls made, that it became apparent that something rather more alarming had occurred.

'Plainclothes?' the first uniformed police officer said. 'They're here already?' He seemed surprised. 'From where? Which station?'

Nobody knew.

'Ask them yourself,' Helen said. 'They were here only a few minutes ago. One of them went to find a bag to put the hypodermic needle in.'

'A bag? Needle?'

203

'Yes, he can't be far away.'

'What was his name?'

'He didn't give a name,' Helen said, and it was at that moment that the first dark inklings began to seep into her mind. 'There were two of them. The other went off to find the CCTV tapes.'

Oh, Jesus! The tapes.

'Call hospital security,' Helen said urgently.

The police officer looked at her blankly. 'What?'

'Call security. Something's not right.'

Helen cursed herself for her trusting nature. She should have been suspicious earlier, but she'd been so relieved to see the detectives that she hadn't picked up on the signs. The speed with which they'd shown up — if she'd given it any thought — should have been the first indication. In retrospect, it seemed incredible that the detectives could have got there so quickly. How long had it taken? Ten minutes from the time the nurses had called security. Ten minutes for security to assess the situation, to phone police headquarters, for a message to be relayed and for officers to be dispatched — through the city centre traffic — to the hospital. That was far too short.

Then the men themselves. They'd carefully given no names. They'd flashed warrant cards, but Helen hadn't thought to examine them more closely, to check their identities. She'd just accepted what they'd said; so had the hospital security guards, but that was no consolation. And now they'd disappeared — she had no doubts about that. With the hypodermic needle, with the CCTV tapes that would have helped identify the bogus doctor. They'd been close to hand throughout — the backup team — maybe waiting in a car outside the hospital, ready to step in if anything went wrong.

Each subsequent event confirmed Helen's fears. The uniformed officers radioed back to base and were told that no detectives from either Hammerton Road — which covered the Royal Hallamshire — or West Bar, the city centre police station, had gone to the hospital. The head of hospital security himself came over to the intensive care unit. His men were called up on the radio, questioned. The CCTV control room officer verified that the master tapes had all been handed over to one of the detectives. They'd been signed for but — on closer examination — the signature turned out to be illegible. The uniformed police officers were out of their depth, unsure what to do next, so they did the sensible thing and passed the buck — radioed for reinforcements.

Helen waited by the nurses' station. Tom had been left alone in his room. He was still weak. He needed to rest. How could I have been so stupid? Helen thought, berating herself for her gullibility. Yet it was only hindsight that made her so hard on herself. At the time, who but the most certified paranoiac would have suspected that a bogus doctor would be followed by two bogus policemen? That's what we have to become, she thought. Paranoid. We have to learn to trust no one.

She recognised one of the genuine detectives

who arrived shortly afterwards. It was the man who'd come to the house to arrest Tom, though it was only now that she learnt his name. Detective Constable Jack Parramore, it said on his warrant card, a card she made sure to examine in minute detail. He talked to his uniformed colleagues first, then the hospital security guards, before he turned his attention to Helen.

'Take me through it, step by step,' he said, pulling up a chair and taking out his notebook. The notebook looked very small in his hands, his pen almost hidden by his fat, fleshy fingers.

Helen told him what had happened.

'You say you'd seen him before?' Parramore recapitulated at the end, flicking back through the notes he'd made.

'When my husband appeared in court. He watched the hearing from the public seats.'

'OK, let's get a description. The doctor first, then the men who said they were police officers.'

Parramore wrote down the details in a slow, laborious longhand, then they went along the corridor to Tom's room. Tom appeared to be dozing, but he opened his eyes when they entered, his expression surprised — and not pleasantly so — as he recognised the detective.

Parramore looked around the room.

'The man posing as the doctor, was he wearing gloves?' he asked.

'No,' Tom said.

'Did he touch anything, apart from the door handle and the hypodermic needle?'

'Not that I can remember.'

'We'll have to dust the place, see if we can get any prints.'

'One of the police officers put on gloves,' Helen said. She could picture him now, picking up the hypodermic needle, leaving the room . . . rubbing the door handle as he left — suddenly that apparently inconsequential action made sense. Helen felt her hopes subside. They were merely going through the motions here. Fingerprints, descriptions, statements — she knew that none of them would lead the police to the three men. Whoever they were, they would never be traced.

'I'm going to seal the room, bring in a scene of crime team,' Parramore said. 'Just let me talk to the nurses.'

Tom was moved to the adjoining empty room, a straightforward procedure which involved little more than disconnecting him from his monitoring machines and wheeling his bed out. Helen stayed in the room while the nurses carried out the move. She watched Tom's heavy, steel-framed bed being manoeuvred through the door, preparing herself to follow. She glanced around, making sure nothing had been forgotten. Tom's clothes, the possessions he'd had on him when he was attacked, had all been transferred to the secure locker in his new room, but Helen wanted to make sure no items had been missed.

It was then that she saw it.

On the floor where the bed had been.

It was small, easy to overlook. If the light hadn't been shining in a particular way, hitting the lino tiles at just the right angle, she might not have noticed it — a thin tube of opaque plastic.

Helen bent down. She was alone in the room. The nurses had gone, Parramore was down the corridor making phone calls. She looked more closely at the plastic tube. It was about three inches long and less than half an inch in diameter. She reached out to pick it up . . . and stopped herself. She was in a hospital. Things left lying around on floors were more than likely to be medical waste, perhaps contaminated waste. It was better to let the nurses clear it up.

She'd straightened up and was heading for the door when she realised suddenly what the plastic tube was — the protective sheath from a hypodermic needle. It must have fallen under Tom's bed when the bogus doctor was preparing to give him the injection, then not been seen by the bogus detective.

Helen's first thought was to call for Parramore, to have the police take the sheath away for examination, but she hesitated. Was that the best course of action? *We have to learn to trust no one*, she thought again. How compromised were the police? Did she trust them?

She took a paper tissue out of her handbag and crouched down, wrapping the tissue carefully around the plastic sheath, then transferring it to her bag. She'd think about what she did with it.

Parramore was outside in the corridor.

'We'll need to take your fingerprints,' he said brusquely. 'You must have touched the door, the chair, maybe other things when you first

208

arrived. We're doing all the nurses too, eliminating them from the picture.'

'And my husband?' Helen said.

'We have his fingerprints on record,' Parramore replied.

There was something in his tone, something contemptuous, arrogant, that Helen didn't like. He was passing judgement on Tom, declaring him guilty simply because his prints were on file. Yet if anyone was an innocent victim of a crime, it was Tom.

'I meant, what are you going to do about him?' Helen said.

'Do? How do you mean?'

'How are you going to protect him? Someone is trying to kill him. First last night in the knife attack — '

'You don't know that,' Parramore interjected. 'You don't know what the assailant intended to do.'

'I know he intended to harm my husband.'

Parramore shrugged. 'These kinds of crimes can make some people very angry.'

'Crimes?'

'Downloading child porn. I hear you've already had a few problems with vigilantes.'

Helen couldn't believe it. Was that a trace of a smirk on the detective's face? She tried to stay calm.

'Perhaps I'd better remind you that my husband has been convicted of nothing,' she said icily. 'He was attacked last night, and then this afternoon someone posing as a doctor tried to poison him. Don't you think that deserves to be taken seriously?'

'What makes you think it was poison in the hypodermic needle?'

'I know it was something harmful. Why else was the man there? Are you saying he was just a vigilante too?'

'Maybe he was, maybe he wasn't,' Parramore said indifferently. 'The facts are going to be difficult to establish. It's easy to get over-emotional about things like this, start to imagine things that aren't there.'

Helen stared at him. 'You're not suggesting I imagined it, are you? That I imagined the man knocking me over and fleeing? That I imagined the two detectives who showed up, removed the evidence and then conveniently disappeared? You've spoken to the nurses, the security men. Did they imagine it all too?'

Parramore turned and started to walk away.

'I'll give you time to calm down a bit, Mrs Whitehead,' he said over his shoulder.

Helen grabbed hold of his arm.

'I haven't finished,' she said, so angry now that she had to make a real effort not to slap him across the face. 'I want to know how you're going to protect my husband?'

'I don't know. You got any suggestions?' Parramore replied insolently.

'Yes, as a matter of fact I have,' Helen said. 'But I'll make them to someone more senior than you. When I also tell him how unhelpful you've been.'

The threat didn't seem to bother him.

'You do whatever you like, I've work to do,'

Parramore said coolly and sauntered away down the corridor.

★ ★ ★

Helen phoned Michael Russell on her mobile, then sat beside Tom's bed, keeping watch over him until the solicitor arrived. The police forensic team showed up while she was waiting. Helen could hear them next door and in the corridor, going about their business.

Tom was only half awake. He had his eyes closed, dozing off intermittently. Russell looked at him with concern when he came into the room.

'Is he — ?'

'He's fine,' Helen said. 'He's sleeping, that's all.' She checked her watch. 'I haven't got long, Michael. I have to get the children from school.'

'I'll take over now,' Russell replied reassuringly.

Helen nodded her thanks. Russell always seemed calm, in control. It was immensely comforting to have him around.

'I don't want to leave Tom here,' Helen said. 'Not without some kind of protection.'

'I'll speak to the police.'

'I mentioned it to one of the detectives — Parramore. He didn't seem overkeen to do anything.'

'It won't be up to him. I know people I can talk to, put pressure on. Don't worry, I'll get something in place before I leave. If the police need a bit of time to get the manpower sorted out, I'll get the hospital to put a security guard outside the door in the meantime. Either way, Tom won't be left alone.'

'Thanks, Michael. That's put my mind at rest.'

Helen felt inside her handbag and lifted out the hypodermic needle sheath wrapped in tissue paper, taking care not to squeeze the tiny package. She held it out to Russell.

'This is for you.'

13

There were ways. It was one of the fundamental tenets of Moran's professional faith. There were always ways. No matter how difficult the challenge, it was always possible to complete it if you had money and knew the right people: the two Cs, cash and contacts, the most important assets in the private investigation business, probably in any business.

The cash was rarely Moran's — and if it was, it was soon billed back to a client — but the contacts were his. He'd spent his working life cultivating them. Twenty years in the police force, the last ten as a detective sergeant, then another ten in the PI game, you met a lot of people. A lot of useful people. Moran was never too blatant or pushy about utilising his contacts — that was a guaranteed way of losing them — but he recognised that the business he was in was all about symbiosis — about nurturing mutually beneficial partnerships with other people.

He was a gregarious man. He enjoyed company, enjoyed drinking — the two occupations, preoccupations perhaps, that had been the primary cause of his marital breakdown — and he wasn't too particular about whom he socialised with. He had an easy manner, he could talk to anyone, make them feel comfortable, get them to open up and share confidences with him. The circles he moved in were broad and varied. He had a large number of acquaintances in the criminal underworld, but the source of much of his information was police officers — both colleagues from his days on the force and other officers he'd met since his early retirement. He avoided dealing with seriously bent coppers, not through any moral scruples but because truly corrupt officers were dangerous and more likely to get caught, bringing down anyone rash enough to have been associated with them. But there were plenty of people in the criminal justice system — not just police officers but civilians connected to other institutions — who had a pragmatic, flexible approach to the ethics of their calling. You had to take them individually, know what they would and would not do, and be careful not to push them beyond the parameters they had set themselves. Moran knew police officers who considered themselves honest men — who would never have dreamt of planting evidence or fitting up a suspect, but who had no qualms about supplying information for money.

It was to one of these 'flexible friends' that Moran turned when Russell presented him with the hypodermic needle sheath Helen had found in her husband's room at the hospital. It wasn't an exceptional undertaking for Moran — he'd done similar things before — but it was slightly out of the ordinary and required delicate handling. His contact was a fingerprint expert with the South Yorkshire force, a police officer, not one of the civilians who worked in the forensic branch. And that was crucially important to the task, for Moran needed someone who could not only dust and lift a print from an item, but could then get access to the Police National Computer to try to identify the print.

They met in a café-bar near the City Hall — another tarted-up coffee shop, in Moran's view, selling overpriced cappuccino and washy continental bottled lager. But it had been the contact's choice to meet there as it was far enough away from his work-place to limit the risk of meeting anyone he knew.

Moran ordered a couple of German Pils — weren't they things you took for a headache? — and joined his contact at a table at one end of the room. The table was low, surrounded by four squashy settees. Settees? Moran thought. In a bar? Whatever next? They chatted about work, about football, about nothing really, for a while. Moran had noticed this with some of his contacts. They liked to prevaricate, to pretend that their encounters had some purer social purpose before they got down to the grubby business of trading information. It assuaged their feelings of guilt, Moran guessed, though he'd noticed they were quick enough to pocket the cash when he handed it over.

They were still chatting — Moran beginning to fear that he'd have to buy two more bottles of German dishwater — when the contact suddenly said, 'You're in luck. He's got form.'

Moran took a moment to realise what the contact meant.

'Yeah?' Moran was surprised. The hypodermic

needle sheath was very narrow, not much surface area for a finger to mark. He hadn't been optimistic that they would actually find a usable print at all.

'A string of petty burglaries and an ABH,' the contact said. 'Small-time stuff.'

'What's his name?'

'Miller. Gary Miller.'

'Address?'

'London.'

The contact looked around the bar, then casually handed Moran a plain white envelope. A second envelope, containing £250 in cash, was passed in the other direction. The contact didn't hang around afterwards. They never did. Moran likened it to a client and a whore doing the business then parting quickly, both feeling cheapened by the transaction — though he could never be sure which of them was the tart and which the punter.

Alone now, he opened the envelope. On the piece of paper inside were a few lines of information about Gary Miller, extracted from the Police National Computer. Not an official printout — that would have left an incriminating record on the system — but some handwritten notes the contact had made. Moran read through them: *Gary James Miller. Born, London, June 14*th*, 1957. Address, Basement Flat, 62 Shackleton Avenue, London N1.*

Then came the criminal record: a long list of burglaries — fifteen in total — for which he'd received prison sentences of varying lengths, then the ABH, eighteen months inside. All of the offences had been committed when Miller was in his twenties. Since 1986 his sheet had been clean. It was possible that he'd gone straight. It wasn't an entirely unknown phenomenon. Maybe he'd settled down, got a proper job and a family, but Moran was sceptical. He'd seen too many kids like Miller when he was on the force. There was a pattern to their lives — offending, prison, reoffending — that very few of them managed to break away from. Besides, what had he been doing in Sheffield? A Londoner coming up north to impersonate a doctor and attempt to kill a hospital patient? That was hardly the mark of a reformed criminal. Nor was it something he'd done of his own volition. Miller's record — multiple petty offences that stopped abruptly — bore all the hallmarks of a criminal who'd found himself a protector. Who'd not necessarily stopped offending, but had simply not been caught. Or if he'd been caught, he'd not been charged. The classic profile of a nark, or a hired hand.

But a hired hand for whom?

Moran put the paper back in the envelope and slid it into his pocket. This was a job for someone else.

* * *

Annie had been sixteen when she'd first met Moran. She'd been in Sheffield for only a couple of days at the time, sleeping rough down near the railway station. Manchester, her home town, had finally got too hot for her. The police knew her.

Every shop assistant and security guard in the city centre had her photograph. She couldn't even step into a store without some uniformed heavy asking her to leave, threatening her with the law. So she'd got on a train and headed east. To start all over in a city where no one knew who she was or what she did.

She'd liked Sheffield at once. Walking out of the station that first morning she'd been struck by the light, by the spacious feel of the city. Manchester had always felt oppressive to her. The overcast skies, the flat terrain, the dark, imposing architecture had all contributed to a gloomy, stifling atmosphere. But Sheffield was built on hills and river valleys. The buildings and streets were smaller, more intimate. From its reputation, Annie had expected a dirty industrial hole, but her first impression was of a bright, clean modern metropolis.

Standing outside the station she'd seen crowds of young people across the road, students not much older than she was going in and out of the Hallam University union building. She'd walked across and mingled with them, had a drink inside the union, watching the people around her, eavesdropping on their conversations. She'd started to feel at home immediately. This was a place where she felt she could be happy.

She'd checked out the city centre, spent the day wandering around the shops, noting the security cameras, the guards, getting a feel for the territory before she started work. Shoplifting was still her main interest, but her experiences in Manchester had prompted her to develop a second string to her bow — picking pockets and bag dipping. She'd tried it a few times and found it surprisingly easy. People were careless. They left their possessions unattended, they kept wallets in their exposed back pockets, the tops of their handbags unzipped, so a quick-fingered opportunist could be in and out in seconds. Annie was slick and fast. Fast on the dip, and then fast in getting clear of the area.

But not fast enough for Moran.

She'd spotted him on the second day, walking towards her along Chapel Walk, a narrow, shop-lined alley just off the main city centre pedestrian precinct. She'd studied the alley well in advance. It was always busy — plenty of people to shield her approach — but not so choked with crowds that her getaway would be impeded. Moran had looked a perfect mark. A middle-aged fat guy in a smart suit. Prosperous and slow, the way she liked them. She'd examined the line of his trousers, the material smooth and tight over his thighs. No telltale bulge of a wallet. It must be in his jacket, the inside breast pocket. Left or right? She couldn't tell. Most guys were right-handed. She went for the left side. Moved in quickly, swerving deliberately to avoid another pedestrian, colliding briefly with the guy, her hand sliding inside his jacket, pulling out his wallet. Then she was away before he even knew what had happened. Round the corner and in through the rear entrance of Marks & Spencer.

She'd gone upstairs to the Ladies and sat in a cubicle going through the wallet. She'd struck lucky. There'd been a clutch of credit cards with the name David T. Moran on them, and a wad of cash. A lot of cash. Nearly £300 in fifties and twenties. She'd waited fifteen minutes, then gone back downstairs and out of the front entrance of the store, not hurrying, playing it cool. A little way up the street she'd felt a hand like a vice on her arm and a voice in her ear saying softly, 'I think it's time we had a little chat.'

He'd taken her to the Peace Gardens next to the Town Hall and sat on a bench with her. He'd let go of her arm, but she could still feel the ache where his fingers had gripped her flesh.

'I'll have my wallet back, please,' he'd said. Polite, no trace of anger in his voice.

Annie hadn't argued. She knew when she was in a tight corner.

'You take anything from it?' Moran had asked.

'No.'

'What's your name?'

'None of your fucking business.'

He'd smiled at that.

'That wasn't bad, back there. I'm impressed. No one's ever picked my pocket before. You're good.'

Annie hadn't said anything. She was gauging her chances of getting away, making a break for it across the gardens. But the guy was watching her closely. She sensed he was faster than he looked. What did he want? Most people would have called the police by now. She took in his appearance again. Shit, maybe he *was* the police. Just her fucking luck. Her first mark and he turns out to be a copper.

'I have a proposition for you.'

Annie had smiled cynically. So that was it. He was just a dirty old man who wanted to screw her. Who wanted a blow job in return for letting her go. Like some of the security guards she'd encountered in Manchester. Nasty bastards who'd touch her up, cop a feel when they caught her, then offer her a deal.

'What kind of proposition?'

'Not what you think.'

He'd opened his wallet and taken out a twenty.

'This is in advance. There's another for you when you complete the job.'

The 'job' had turned out to be simple. Watching a guy in a suit — looked like a businessman or a lawyer — then snatching his briefcase from his hand as he walked from his office to his car. The easiest forty quid Annie had ever earned. There'd been more jobs since. Some legal, others on the edge or well over it. She'd got to like Moran, his no-bullshit pragmatism. He'd found her a cheap room at the beginning, lent her some money, put in a word with a mate to get her some bar work. He hadn't needed to do any of it. Annie wasn't used to people doing her favours. Not without a pay-off in return, anyway. But Moran never took advantage. He gave her work every now and again, but asked no questions, didn't pry into her life. She was grateful for his help, though she knew it wasn't entirely altruistic, grateful for his discretion, but grateful most of all to him for introducing her to Zac: the best thing that had ever happened to her.

She glanced across at the passenger seat. Zac turned his head, sensing her gaze.

'What?'

'Nothing,' Annie said.

'You want to swap?'

'Not yet.'

'We could stop, have a coffee.'

'I'd rather just get there.'

'We don't want to be too early.' Zac peered at the speedometer. 'Careful. No need to rush.'

Annie pressed down on the accelerator, watching the needle creep over eighty. The Ford Fiesta started to judder. She grinned at Zac. He didn't rise. He never did. That was the most annoying thing about him. He turned his head away and looked out of the window. The cassette player was on loud — some weird esoteric rock tape Zac had brought along — but it was almost impossible to hear it over the engine noise of the car.

'I wish Moran would lend us his Jag for once,' Annie said. 'All we ever get is this piece of shit.'

'He's seen you drive,' Zac replied dryly, and left it at that.

It was evening when they got to London. They found Shackleton Avenue on the A – Z. It was in the area just north of King's Cross station, a seedy enclave of low-rise flats and terraced houses that had seen better days. They drove slowly past number 62, a four-storey terrace built of muddy, yellowish brick. The white paint on the stone lintels and windowsills was peeling off, as it was on all the other houses along the street. Black bin liners bulging with rubbish were dumped on the pavement at the front, their contents seeping out across the paving slabs — empty tin cans, blackened banana skins and potato peelings, bits of old meat chewed over by scavenging neighbourhood dogs. Everything seemed grubby, neglected.

Annie turned the corner at the end of the street and pulled in to the kerb. It was beginning to get dark. There was a dusky haze over the rooftops. The shadows of the buildings were growing more intense, merging into the night.

'You take a look at the front,' Zac said. 'I'll check the back.'

Annie walked down the street to number 62. There were steps up to the front door and another flight leading down to the basement flat, which had its own separate entrance. Annie could see it in the well below her, a solid wooden door with a window beside it. There was a light on inside the flat. Annie kept walking, circling round the block to return to the car. After a few minutes Zac rejoined her.

'He's in,' Annie said.

'The door?'

'Pretty sturdy-looking. And it's very exposed. Not promising.'

'The back it is then.'

'You get round to it?'

'No, but I took a look from the end of the row. Shinned up a wall. There's a small garden. Another door and a window.'

'Possible?'

'Hard to tell from a distance. But I'm

223

optimistic. Provided he goes out, of course.'

They turned the car around and drove back into Shackleton Avenue, parking at the top end, about fifty yards from the house. Close enough to see if Miller went out, but not so close that he might spot them. Annie put the cassette player on softly and they waited, listening to the music, talking desultorily. Annie hated surveillance jobs, sitting around doing nothing. After half an hour she was restless, an hour or more and she was ready to scream with frustration. Zac, however, seemed to enjoy the inactivity. Annie found that odd in a guy who could be so energetic, so alert when required. But he seemed to have the ability to shut down part of himself — like a hibernating animal slowing its metabolism. Annie looked across at him. His eyes were open, but from his posture, the quiet rhythm of his breathing, he might well have been asleep.

'I'm hungry,' she said. 'You want something to eat?'

'Sure,' Zac murmured.

'I'll see what I can find.'

She climbed out of the car and wandered off to explore the neighbourhood. She was in no particular hurry. Walking the streets was better than staying in the car. They'd been there almost two hours already. It was starting to look as if Miller was going to remain in his flat for the entire evening and they'd have to come back the next day to resume their watch. The thought was too depressing to consider.

The other streets in the area were as shabby

as Shackleton Avenue. The houses were dilapidated, most converted into flats and bedsits. Litter drifted in the gutters, blown by the wind that funnelled between the buildings. A woman in a short skirt and skimpy top was standing by a junction. As Annie walked past on the opposite side of the road, a car pulled up by the woman and Annie heard the driver negotiating a price. The woman climbed into the passenger seat and the car sped away.

There was a row of shops a few streets further on: a laundrette, a pawnbroker's, an off-licence and grocery store and a café — closed for the night — whose neon-lit frontage seemed to ooze grease. Annie went into the grocery store and bought some biscuits, a couple of chocolate-chip muffins and two cans of larger.

Zac was in exactly the same position she'd left him, slouched back in his seat, his half-closed eyes fixed on the house.

'Anything happening?' Annie asked.

'No.'

She gave him a muffin and a can of lager.

'It's all there was,' she said apologetically. 'Unless you fancied one of those plastic-wrapped sausage rolls that look like they're stuffed with dog meat.'

'A muffin's fine,' Zac said.

Annie checked her watch. It was gone 9.30. She chewed on her muffin.

'We could always have a shag to pass the time,' she said.

'Yeah, why not?' Zac agreed, but he didn't move. He allowed half a minute to pass then said, 'How was it for you?'

'Good.'

At 9.50 a figure came up the steps from the basement flat. He paused on the pavement, then turned and walked away down the street. They gave him fifteen minutes, just in case he'd only nipped out for a pint of milk or something, then got out of the car. Zac removed a small rucksack from the boot and slipped it over his shoulders.

Number 62 was four or five houses from the end of the row. Zac and Annie walked past it. The basement flat was in darkness. They rounded the corner by the last house on the street and continued walking for a few yards until they were level with the gardens behind the houses. There was a brick wall next to them, just above head height.

'This the one you climbed earlier?' Annie said.

Zac nodded. 'Watch how you go. The garden on the other side's crammed with junk.'

They checked no one was watching and scrambled nimbly over the wall, dropping to the ground in the garden and pausing to listen, making sure they hadn't been seen. Then they picked their way through the mounds of rubbish — a pile of building rubble, rotting planks and an old settee and a washing machine someone had dumped.

A further four walls scaled and they were in the back garden of number 62. Like the others they'd traversed, it wasn't really much of a garden. There didn't seem to be any plants in it, just a patch of grass which in daylight might have resembled a lawn but at night seemed more like a dark rectangle of mud. A few concrete slabs adjacent to the house formed a crude patio for sitting out in fine weather. The back door of the basement flat was half glazed, the paint peeling off the woodwork. Zac took out a pencil torch and carefully examined the lock.

'Three-lever mortice. No problem.'

He could have forced the door, but they didn't want Miller to know they'd been inside. Picking the lock was trickier, more time-consuming, but it still only took him a couple of minutes.

The room immediately inside was the kitchen-diner. Zac's torch beam lanced around, picking out the worktops, the fridge, the cooker. No phone. They went through into the rest of the flat. There was one bedroom, a bathroom and a sitting room at the front. The phone was on a table by the front door.

'Hold the torch for me.'

Zac searched inside his rucksack and pulled out a screwdriver. He removed the front of the telephone handset and inserted a tiny adhesive bug about the size of a five-pence piece into the cavity inside. He screwed the plastic casing back on and replaced the handset.

The electric sockets were next. One in the sitting room, one in the bedroom and one in the kitchen. 'Let's give 'em a taste of their own medicine,' Moran had said. 'See how they like it.'

Zac was in the kitchen, just finishing off, when Annie came through from the sitting room where she'd been keeping watch.

'He's back,' she whispered urgently.

Zac paused, tilting his head. They could both

hear it now — footsteps coming down the steps from the street.

'Hurry.'

But Zac never hurried. He put the last screw into the socket above the worktop and tightened it. At the front of the house a key was inserted into the lock.

Annie already had the back door open.

'Come on,' she hissed. Her pulse was racing. She could feel the exhilarating surge of adrenalin in her system. 'Zac, come on.'

Zac picked up his rucksack, pulled a tool out of it and strolled across to her. Mr Cool. The front door clicked open. The living room light snapped on.

Annie took hold of Zac and bundled him out through the back door, closing it quietly behind them. Zac knelt down to see to the lock.

'There's no time,' Annie whispered. 'Let's go. He's coming.'

'He can't know we've been in. It'll blow the whole thing.'

'Well, get a move on, for Christ's sake.'

Annie crouched down beside him, both hidden behind the solid lower panel of the door. Zac manipulated the levers of the lock. To Annie, the noise seemed deafening. Come on, Zac, she thought. Do it. Just *do* it.

The kitchen light came on. A bright fluorescent wave burst out through the glass pane of the door and the adjacent kitchen window. Annie and Zac instinctively ducked lower, curling up on the ground. The paving slabs behind them were bathed in light. Annie held her breath, Zac motionless beside her.

They heard footsteps on the floor tiles inside. Miller was crossing the room. If he tried the door, that was it. Everything blown. He was getting closer. His footsteps were louder. His shadow flickered over them. He had only to reach out for the door handle.

The sink tap was turned on. They heard the sound of a kettle being filled. Miller was only feet away from them. Then suddenly a block of light was blotted out. He'd pulled down the window blind. He moved to the door. He was right over them. His shadow stretched out across the garden. If he glanced down . . . Zac and Annie pressed themselves against the paving slabs. Through the thin panel of the door, they could hear Miller shuffling his feet. Annie's muscles began to tighten up. She felt a twinge of cramp in one of her legs, resisted the urge to stretch. Her leg muscle began to knot. She couldn't hold it much longer. Then — thank God — she heard Miller's shoes scuff the tiles. He was moving away. Heading out of the kitchen.

Annie slid her legs out from underneath her, easing the pain in the muscles. Zac was back on his knees, a thin metal tool inserted into the keyhole of the door. The lock engaged with a sharp click. They didn't wait around to see if Miller had heard. They snaked away beneath the kitchen window, then over the wall into the adjoining garden.

★ ★ ★

It was too late to drive all the way back to Sheffield, so they found a hotel off the M1, paying cash for a room with the expenses money Moran had given them. They gave their names as Mr and Mrs Gary Miller of 62 Shackleton Avenue, London N1. The room was a standard chain-hotel clone — big double bed, television, en-suite bathroom with soft white towels that Annie made a mental note to remove before they left in the morning. There was even a minibar. Annie opened a couple of miniature whiskies and poured them into the plastic tumblers provided.

'I'm going to take a shower,' she said. 'You want to join me?'

Zac was on the bed, lying back on the pillows, his thumb on the TV remote control, flicking through the channels.

'No, you go ahead,' he said indifferently.

There was soap and shampoo in the bathroom, and plenty of hot water. Annie took her time, making the most of the unfamiliar luxury. To stand naked in a bathroom without feeling cold, that was a rare experience for her. She washed her hair, thinking about Zac, annoyed that he'd turned down her offer. She knew it was silly to make too much of the rejection. Zac was unpredictable in everything he did. Sometimes he was up for it, sometimes he wasn't. But it pissed her off, nevertheless. Didn't he fancy her any more?

They'd known each other for eighteen months, been sleeping together on and off for more than a year, but she didn't really feel she knew him. He was Moran's technical man, the guy who handled all the equipment, took care of the electronic surveillance and covert ops side of the business. The first time Annie had met him she'd been intrigued by his self-contained manner — not unfriendly, just so relaxed and spaced out she'd thought he must be on drugs. They'd done a job together at a factory down in the East End — some kind of industrial espionage, Annie had guessed, though she'd known better than to ask. Annie had stood guard outside with a walkie-talkie while Zac broke into one of the offices. He'd said barely a word to her, picked her up in a car then dropped her off afterwards without even telling her his name. She'd found out later — on another job — that Zac wasn't actually his real name in any case. 'What does it matter? It'll do for the time being,' he'd said when she'd pressed him to tell her more.

That had been the start, the discovery that Zac — like her — was living under a false name. It gave them something in common, prompted Annie to want to know more about him. He wasn't an easy guy to fathom. She had to make all the running, initiate everything. That was a novelty for her. She was used to men coming on to her, used to turning them down. But Zac seemed so oblivious to her as a woman that she wondered at first whether he was gay, or whether he had a live-in girlfriend. Wrong on both counts, as it turned out when she finally got an invitation back to his place — a room in a rented house in Pitsmoor, Zac just about the only white guy in the neighbourhood — to find he lived alone and, once she'd got him in the sack, was anything but gay.

She'd never met anyone quite like him. Anyone so self-reliant, so determined to have no part in what he called 'the oppressive totalitarianism of the modern state'. It wasn't just the false name he'd adopted: he seemed intent in all ways on providing no evidence of his true identity, or even his very existence. He was at pains to ensure that there was no record of him anywhere. He had no passport, no driving licence, no National Insurance number. He had no bank account or credit cards. He paid no income tax or council tax, his name appeared on no electoral register, no databases. He was a non-person. He worked for cash only — for Moran and occasionally others who asked no questions — and paid cash for everything. He lived in a world which, in his words, was 'below the radar of the Faceless Ones'. Annie had picked up the term from him, adopted it into her own vocabulary. The Faceless Ones, the unseen powers that sought to control and restrict the freedom of the individual for their own malign purposes. To Zac, they were the enemy who had to be resisted at all costs.

Annie rubbed her hair dry with a towel, looking at herself in the long bathroom mirror. Her skin was damp and glowing from the shower. She felt revitalised, horny. Sod you, Zac, she thought. Look at me. Aren't I attractive? Aren't I desirable?

She went out into the room, stark naked. Zac

232

had turned the lights off, but the television was still on. He was lying back on the bed, his face hidden in shadow.

Annie walked around the end of the bed and stood in front of the television screen, blocking his view.

'What do you say to a late-night porno show?' she said, thrusting her hips forward provocatively. 'Full audience participation . . . Zac?'

She walked to the head of the bed and looked down at him. His eyes were closed. She could hear the steady murmur of his breathing as he slept.

Annie swore. Then she went to the minibar and poured herself another whisky.

14

No one seemed to know exactly how long Tom was going to have to remain in hospital. A few days, a week, perhaps longer — the estimates varied according to whom Tom asked. Everything was dependent on how well he progressed, how quickly he recovered from his knife wounds.

His condition had improved markedly over the few days he'd been in the intensive care unit. He felt less tired, there was more colour in his face. His wounds were healing well. They were still bandaged up, but the pain was easing.

Helen and the children came in to see him every day and those visits too were doing their bit to aid his recovery. His spirits lifted whenever his family was there, Helen sitting beside the bed, the children next to her, chattering away to him about their days, about what they'd been doing. After their initial horror at finding their father badly injured in hospital, Ben and Hannah had quickly come to accept the situation, even to find it quite exciting. Daddy had been attacked and stabbed. That wasn't something that happened every day. Sheltered from the disturbing details of what had occurred, from the life-threatening implications of the attack, they could indulge their childish fascination with the macabre. It was like being taken to see a horror film at the cinema, enjoying the thrill of being scared, but knowing that there was no real danger, that when the lights went up their secure, protected world would still be the same.

Tom was impatient to get out of hospital. Now he had more energy, now his injuries were troubling him less, he wanted to return to the fray, to hit back at the people who had done this to him. He felt isolated, vulnerable in the ICU — despite the twenty-four-hour police guard outside his room. He had a terrifying sense of foreboding that something else was going to happen.

On the Sunday, four days after his admission to the Royal Hallamshire, it did.

Helen had been in to visit, as usual — in the evening with the children. Tom had been out of bed, sitting in an armchair. He'd even been up to reading Ben and Hannah a story, something he hadn't done since he'd moved out to stay at Bruce's apartment. Later on, nearing ten o'clock, the night nurse — a cheerful young black woman named Grace — came in to check that he was all right for the night. She adjusted his pillow, refilled the tumbler of water on the bedside locker, then stayed a while to chat to him.

'You've made a good recovery,' she said. 'I'm going to miss you when you move.'

Tom gave a start. 'What do you mean, when I move?'

'From the ICU. Didn't they tell you?'

'Tell me what?' Tom's stomach knotted.

'You're well enough now to be moved to an ordinary medical ward.'

'When?'

235

'Tomorrow morning. It's nothing to worry about. Everything should be — '

'Grace,' Tom interrupted. 'I wasn't told anything about this. When was the decision made? Who made it?'

'One of the doctors, I guess. You're just fine, Dr Whitehead. You don't need to be in intensive care any longer.'

'And the police guard?' Tom said. 'Is he moving too?'

'No, he's gone.'

'*Gone?*'

'Yes, he said he was no longer needed.'

Tom felt a wave of nausea sweep over him. He tried to remain calm.

'When?' he asked urgently. 'When did he go?'

'Oh, about ten minutes ago. He said he'd had a call on his radio, telling him to return to the police station.'

No, *no*, Tom thought. This isn't what I think. His legs were trembling, he was short of breath.

'So there's no guard outside the door?' he said.

'No.'

'Did the policeman — the one who left — say anyone was coming to take his place?'

'Well, no, he didn't. But I don't think you're in any danger, you know.'

'Grace, will you do something for me? Get me a phone, then call hospital security. Ask them to send someone to watch my room until I find out what's going on.'

'I'm not sure I can do that,' Grace said hesitantly. 'I don't have the authority.'

'Who does have the authority?'

'I don't know. I think you're worrying about nothing, Dr Whitehead. Honestly, I can assure you that . . . What're you doing?'

Tom threw back the covers and climbed awkwardly out of bed.

'Dr Whitehead, you shouldn't be — '

'The phone, Grace. *Now.* This is important.'

★   ★   ★

The security guard in the cubicle on B Floor — the main entrance to the tower section of the Royal Hallamshire Hospital — looked up as the man walked into the foyer. The guard took in the visitor's appearance in a single experienced glance — late forties, big, broad-chested, smartly dressed in a suit and tie, not someone who looked like trouble.

Moran loomed up outside the cubicle, his body large enough to cover the tiny opening in the glass pane. He put his business card down on the counter.

'I've come to collect a patient from intensive care,' he said.

The security guard picked up the card and read it, then peered quizzically at Moran.

'You what?'

'A patient. I've come to take him home,' Moran explained with quiet forbearance.

'At this hour?'

'Check with the ICU. They're expecting me.'

'It's half ten, mate,' the security guard said. 'I've never known anyone be discharged this late.'

Moran sighed. He'd known this would take a long time. These jobsworths were all the same.

'Just phone the ICU, will you?'

He glanced round behind him while the security guard was picking up the phone. Where was the kid? He was quick. Was he already inside?

★ ★ ★

Zac ran around the corner at the back of the foyer and paused for a second, getting his bearings. He knew he was in a blind spot — out of sight of the CCTV cameras that covered the main hospital entrance and the area in front of the lifts. He'd have been picked up when he entered the building, of course, but a security camera was only effective if someone was watching the pictures it produced, and the guard in the cubicle was too busy dealing with Moran to pay much heed to the monitors on the wall behind him.

Zac studied the doors along the corridor: male and female toilets with a door in between marked 'Staff Only'. Zac tried the middle door. It was unlocked. He stepped through and closed the door behind him. He was in a big walk-in store cupboard, shelves of supplies around the walls, a cleaning trolley parked to one side. Zac lifted a mop and bucket off the trolley, then donned a khaki cleaner's coat which was hanging from a peg. Going back out into the corridor, he took the stairs up to D Floor, emerging into the wide central lobby where the lifts were located.

He pressed the call button for the lift and waited, mop and bucket in his hand, his back to the CCTV camera on the wall. Moran should still have been keeping the security guard downstairs busy, but even if Zac was seen on the monitor, the security guard was unlikely to be concerned by a cleaner going about his duties.

Once inside the lift, Zac relaxed until he reached R. Walking out into the lobby outside the intensive care unit, he was aware of being on camera again for just a few seconds before he ducked into the side corridor. He slipped off his work coat, dumped the mop and bucket and walked back round to the main doors of the unit. Moran should have finished downstairs by now, be on his way up. Zac knew they didn't have much time. The Faceless Ones would be on their way. Maybe they were here already. The thought sent a shiver down Zac's spine. Let's hope we're not too late, he thought.

There was a nurse behind the desk inside the ICU, a good-looking black girl in a mauve uniform. Zac smiled at her.

'Moran. I've come for Dr Whitehead,' he said.

The black girl looked surprised. 'That was quick. I've only just got off the phone to security.'

'Lift came straight away. Where do I find him?'

'I'll show you.'

The black nurse walked away along the corridor.

'This really isn't necessary, you know,' she said. 'I think Dr Whitehead is panicking, overreacting.'

Zac gave a non-committal nod. 'Well, you can't be too sure, can you?'

'You'll have to sign some paperwork. The hospital won't take responsibility if anything happens to him.'

'No problem.'

Tom was on his feet, fully dressed, waiting anxiously just inside his room.

'I'll get the forms for you to sign,' the nurse said to Zac and headed back along the corridor.

Zac looked at Tom.

'Are you up to walking?'

Tom nodded.

'Then let's go.'

Zac held the door open. Tom hesitated. He'd suddenly realised he had no idea who this young man was.

'We have to hurry, Dr Whitehead,' Zac said, trying to sound calm while his brain and pulse were racing. The Faceless Ones couldn't be far away. Time was short. Where was Moran? He should've been here by now.

'Who are you?' Tom said.

Christ, this wasn't the moment for questions.

'I'll tell you on the way,' Zac said.

'No.'

'We can't afford to delay. I work for Moran, OK?'

Tom thought of the bogus doctor with the hypodermic needle, the two bogus detectives. He had to be on his guard.

'Moran? Prove it.'

'Jesus, you want a contract of employment, or something?' Zac said in exasperation. 'Why

240

else would I be here?'

'What's Moran's girlfriend's name?'

'Janice.'

'His receptionist?'

'Edith. She's his mother. Satisfied? Now, please, we have to leave.'

Zac stepped out of the room, glancing both ways along the corridor. He could just see the black nurse at the nurses' station near the exit. She was half hidden around the corner, only one arm and shoulder visible. She was talking to someone. On the phone? Zac listened. He heard a man's voice now, but couldn't see who it was. A doctor? A male nurse? Zac knew it was neither. They were here.

'Quickly,' he whispered to Tom, taking his arm and guiding him the other way along the corridor, towards the back doors of the ICU. Zac could hear the nurse's voice. Louder now. Angry. She sounded as if she were arguing with someone. Then she cried out suddenly. A cry of what? Alarm? Pain? Zac pulled Tom into the alcove by the back doors. There was a catch on the inside of the doors. Zac turned the catch and the lock clicked open. He cocked an eye back around the corner. There were two of them. Coming along the corridor towards Tom's room. Zac ducked back, pushing open the doors and dragging Tom out into the lobby.

There were six lifts, three on either side of the lobby. Zac pressed the button. How long did he have? A few seconds, no more. Come on, come *on*. Where *was* the lift? The two men would be inside Tom's room now, discovering he

241

was gone. The illuminated display above the lift doors on the other side of the lobby registered R Floor. Zac pulled Tom across, gripping his uninjured right arm tight. The two men would be back out in the corridor, heading for the exit. Any second they'd burst out into the lobby.

The lift doors slid open. Very slowly. There was someone inside, stepping out. Thank God! It was Moran. Zac heard footsteps behind him. He turned. The two men were running across the lobby. Zac hauled Tom into the lift. Moran gave him a nod. He knew. Zac punched the button for B, the ground floor. The doors started to close. He caught a glimpse of Moran outside, shoulders hunched, legs splayed, blocking the men's path, then the doors snapped shut. The lift began to descend.

★ ★ ★

Moran took one look at the two men and knew that this was going to hurt. They were pros, he could sense that immediately — as mean and nasty a pair of thugs as he'd ever encountered. But he was a pro too. And he had more to lose than they did.

He didn't give them any moment to reflect. He was bigger than them, knew how to handle himself in a fight. But he was outnumbered, and they'd hit him hard if he gave them the chance. He went for the one on the right, the taller of the two. Not trying anything subtle, not thinking for a moment about tactics, just going for brute force. Getting in close, using his weight, his

242

power, like the prop forward he'd been in his rugby days. The man grunted as Moran slammed into him. His arms flailed, his fists hammering into the solid bulk of Moran's back and shoulders. He had no room to move, no space to throw a proper punch. Moran kept his head tucked low, driving the man back. Hoping to take him out before the second man could join in. One at a time, that was his best shot. Moran's fists were down at waist level. He pulled back his right and let it rip. His knuckles sank deep into the man's stomach. He heard the man gasp, gave him no time to recover. His left went in hard to the solar plexus. The man toppled backwards, falling to the floor.

Moran sensed the movement behind him. Took a gamble on which way to duck. And lost. Something heavy caught him on the side of the head. Not a fist or a foot. A club, a cosh, maybe a pistol butt. The pain jarred through his skull. He felt his legs give way. He tumbled forwards, saw the lino tiles rushing up to meet him. Everything hazy. The lobby spinning, the pain all over his head now. His shoulder hit the floor. He heard a voice, one of the men talking into a radio. Talking to someone downstairs. The words were just a blur of sound. Moran felt the darkness closing in. Play it smart, Zac. For me. It was his last thought before he blacked out.

★　★　★

Zac watched the glowing red light on the control panel beside him, counting off the floors as the

lift went down. Q . . . P . . . O . . . N . . . Only
the button for B was illuminated. It was a clear
run to the bottom. Provided no one in between
wanted to get on. M . . . L . . . K . . . How many
more to go? Seventeen floors in total. Eight
down, nine left. He wondered how long Moran
could hold them off. How much time did Zac
have? Two on to one. Even for a guy like Moran
the odds weren't optimistic. *Two?* Zac felt a
sudden stab of ice in his guts. Only two? No way.
No fucking way. There'd be others. There'd be
backup.

H . . . G . . . The floors were flashing past. Zac
reached out on impulse and jabbed his thumb
into the button marked C. He watched the
indicator light.

'Can you run?' he said to Tom.

'I don't know.'

'Try.'

E . . . D . . .

'Get ready,' Zac said.

C . . .

The doors slid open. Zac took hold of Tom's
arm. There was someone waiting outside. Zac
braced himself, ready to hold them off, to give
Tom a chance to escape. Then he saw the
uniform. It was a woman. A night nurse or an
auxiliary. Zac stepped round her, his eyes
scanning the lobby. No one else in sight. But if
they were below, they'd have seen the lift stop at
C Floor, be on their way up the stairs.

Zac turned left into the corridor at the front of
the lobby. The hospital was vast. Seventeen
storeys in the tower section, then a much

broader two-storey complex around the base of the tower. At the far end of the two-storey section was Casualty. Zac reached into his pocket, took out a mobile phone and punched in a number with his thumb.

'I'm heading for Casualty,' he said and hit the 'off' button. No time for anything more. Annie would know what to do.

Tom was struggling to match Zac's pace. His wounded arm was fine. It was his side that was the problem. The wound was throbbing. Every pace he took sent a spasm of pain across his stomach and up his chest. He was finding it difficult to breathe.

'Try to keep going,' Zac said.

Tom gritted his teeth. 'I *am* trying.'

'Not far now. We can do it.'

Zac flung open a set of doors and plunged into another featureless corridor. The building appeared to be deserted. Their footsteps echoed eerily off the bare walls and ceiling. Tom was slowing. The wound felt as if it were splitting open again. He put his hand over the surgical dressing, trying to ease the pain, but it made no difference.

'Nearly there,' Zac said encouragingly. 'Just hold on.'

He saw a sign for the stairs, pushed through more doors, then descended a dog-leg flight of stairs to the ground floor. He paused to check their position, then saw the sign on the wall: 'Accident and Emergency'.

'This way.'

Zac put his arm around Tom's shoulders,

holding him, supporting him as they limped along the corridor. They reached more doors. Through the small glass windows in the doors Zac could see an open treatment area, a few patients waiting on chairs. Beyond that was the exit, the ambulance pulling-in area outside the hospital. Zac pushed one of the doors. It wouldn't open. Shit! He tried again, then saw the numbered keypad on the wall beside the doors. He punched in a few numbers at random, hoping for a lucky break. The doors stayed locked.

The heavy thud of footsteps made him turn his head. Two men were sprinting along the corridor towards them. He'd never seen either of them before. He hammered on the doors, yelling at the top of his voice. The two men drew nearer. Zac's fists pounded on the door. A face appeared at one of the windows. A nurse.

'This is an emergency,' Zac shouted. 'Open the door.'

He glanced round. The two men were fifteen yards away.

The lock snapped back. The men were nearly on them. Zac thrust the door open with his shoulder, dragged Tom through and slammed the door shut. The nurse was staring at him.

'Call security,' Zac said. 'Those men are intruders. Don't let them through.'

'I beg your — '

'Call security!' Zac said again.

He put his arm around Tom and assisted him across the waiting area. Behind them, he could hear the men banging furiously on the locked

246

door. Annie was waiting for them outside, parked in an ambulances-only zone, the engine of her car running. Zac tore open the rear door and helped Tom inside, then threw himself in next to him. He barely had time to close the door before the car was pulling off, turning out of the hospital forecourt and away down the street.

15

Tom was aware of two things as he emerged
from his troubled sleep. The ache in his side
— no, more a pain than an ache, the wound not
just throbbing but feeling as if it were on fire.
And the smell. A strange smell — a mixture of
damp and hot, spicy cooking, the latter so
pronounced he could pick out the individual
ingredients: garlic, ginger, onions, chillies.

He opened his eyes, remembering suddenly
where he was. Remembering the room, at least,
his immediate surroundings. Exactly where he
was, in a geographical sense, he had no idea. He
didn't even know whether he was still in
Sheffield. The journey from the hospital had
been a haze of confusing sensations. The car
moving rapidly through the streets, turning
— always turning — street lamps flashing by,
buildings Tom didn't recognise. Seeing darkened
shapes, shadows, headlights, neon signs. Hearing
voices — the young man talking intermittently to
the woman who was driving. All of it
experienced through a fog of pain, the wound
hurting so much that he had been unable to
concentrate on anything much around him.
Most of the time he'd been slumped in the
corner of the seat with his eyes closed. He
recalled vaguely being helped out of the car and
into a house, though he had no memory of what
its exterior looked like. They'd carried him

upstairs between them, brought him into the room and laid him down on the bed. The young man had given him a couple of tablets, only paracetamol but they'd taken away some of the pain. Enough to enable him to sleep. After that he remembered nothing.

Tom stared up at the ceiling. He wondered what time it was. He had a watch on, but it never occurred to him to look at it. The curtains were closed, but the material was only thin. He could see it was daylight outside. The wallpaper — a ghastly dirty green colour with splashes of yellow — was peeling off below the plaster cornice. The dark, spreading stains and flecks of black mould explained the odour of damp in the room.

'Hello?' Tom was surprised how weak his voice sounded. He tried again, louder.

'Hello?'

He turned his head, looking around the room. The door was shut, a Yale lock halfway up it. There was a desk with a computer on it beside the window, a plain wooden chair drawn up in front. The walls were bare. No pictures, no posters. The carpet was a hideous purple remnant of the 1970s. Tom was reminded of the bedsit he'd rented near the university when he'd been doing his PhD — a single room in a converted Victorian house, furnished just like this place only with a small kitchen area in one corner complete with fridge, sink and two-ring Baby Belling. The bedsit had always reeked of the previous night's meal — like this room, though there was no cooker here. The kitchen must have been somewhere else in the house.

A key turned in the lock. The young man entered, careful to close and lock the door behind him.

'How're you feeling?'

'Rough,' Tom said. 'My side hurts.'

'Let's take a look at it.'

Zac knelt down by the bed and pulled back the covers. Tom was still in his day clothes. They'd put him straight to bed without undressing him the night before.

'Where am I?' Tom said.

'Pitsmoor.'

'Why Pitsmoor?'

'Why not?'

'Whose room is this?'

'Mine.'

Zac rolled back Tom's shirt to expose the surgical dressing over his wound.

'This might hurt a bit.'

Tom gritted his teeth as Zac pulled away the adhesive tape and removed the dressing.

'Could be worse,' Zac said phlegmatically. 'I don't think you've done any serious damage. The wound's seeping a bit. I'll clean it up, put a new dressing on.'

He went out of the room for a few minutes and returned with a bowl of warm water, some cotton wool and a fresh sterile dressing.

'Ouch!' Tom winced as Zac dabbed at the wound with the damp cotton wool.

'Stitches look OK,' Zac said. 'It's healing up nicely. We'll leave it open to air for a bit, help dry it out.'

'What time is it?'

'Half nine. You want some breakfast?'

Tom nodded. 'My wife, does she know where I am?'

'No, but she knows you're safe. Moran's spoken to her. Told her everything's under control.'

'And is it?' Tom asked. 'Under control?'

Zac gave a short, sceptical laugh. 'Who knows?'

'Those men last night, who were they?'

'Faceless Ones,' Zac replied.

'Faceless Ones?'

'Don't worry about them. They'll never find you here.'

Zac headed for the door.

'I don't know your name,' Tom said.

'It's Zac.'

'Thanks, Zac. For last night.'

Zac shrugged, embarrassed by the show of gratitude.

'Toast and tea OK?' he said.

* * *

'How are you?' Moran said, sitting down on the end of the bed.

'Not too bad,' Tom replied stoically. He looked at the livid bruising on the side of Moran's head, just above the right ear. 'You've taken a knock yourself.'

'If you're going to get hit over the head, where better than in a hospital?' Moran said dryly.

He fingered the lump on his temple. It felt very tender. He'd been out cold for about twenty

251

minutes the previous night, woken up to find himself lying on a bed in the intensive care unit, a nurse watching over him. By then the police had arrived. Moran had made a statement and gone home — against the wishes of the doctor who'd been called to treat him. Needless to say, the men who'd come for Tom had disappeared without trace.

'Didn't they want to keep you in? For observation,' Tom said.

'To observe what, exactly? The lump on my head getting bigger?'

'You might have concussion.'

'I have a thick skull. I've had worse over the years. An icepack, a few aspirin, that's all I need.'

'What's happening?' Tom said. 'I can tell you, I'm scared witless by all this. Isn't discrediting me, ruining my career, enough for them? Why do they want me dead?'

'Because you're not going quietly, you're not rolling over and letting them crush you. They don't like that. They're scared, panicking. And frightened men don't always act rationally. Believe me, headless chickens have got nothing on these people.'

'Zac calls them Faceless Ones. Who the hell are they?'

Moran opened the briefcase he'd brought with him and took out a small digital recording machine. He plugged the machine into the socket by the bed.

'I'd like you to listen to this. A bit of background first. The bloke with the hypodermic needle in your hospital room, the fake doctor

— his name's Miller. Gary Miller. Lives in London. I had a word with an old mate on the South Yorkshire force, tipped him the wink that it might be worth having a closer look at Miller. Checking him out to see if they got a reaction. They didn't send anyone down — too bloody tight to pay the train fare — but they got the Met to go round to Miller's flat. Have a listen.'

Moran pressed a button on the recording machine. 'This is the edited version, a compilation of all the source material.'

There was a slight hiss, a bit of background noise that sounded as if someone was moving around a room, then the sudden ring of a doorbell. They heard footsteps. Someone going to the door. The noise of a key being turned in the lock was clearly audible. A man's voice said, '*Mr Miller? Mr Gary Miller?*'

Another voice replied. '*Yes. What do you want?*' His tone sharp, unfriendly.

'*DC Connors, Metropolitan Police.*'

A pause. Some indistinct shuffling noises.

'He's checking his ID card,' Moran said. 'A careful bloke, our Mr Miller.'

'*Can I come in?*' Connors asked.

'*What for?*'

'*I'd like a word.*'

'*What about?*'

'*It would be easier if I could come in.*'

More shuffling. The sound of the door closing. Then Connors's voice again.

'*Where were you last Thursday?*'

'*Why d'you want to know?*'

'*Just answer the question, please.*'

253

'Not until you tell me what's going on.'

'Do you have something to hide, Mr Miller?'

'Look, what the fuck is this about?'

'South Yorkshire police have asked us to talk to you. Were you in Sheffield?'

'Why would I have been in Sheffield? I don't even know where Sheffield is.'

'They have reliable information that you were in Sheffield at that time. Do you deny that?'

'This is fucking ridiculous. One phone call will sort this all out.'

'No phone calls.'

'Piss off. This is my home. I can make as many fucking calls as I like.'

A soft scraping sound — shoes on carpet — then a low clatter. Moran paused the recording.

'He's picking up the phone — a cordless one — and taking it through into the kitchen,' he explained. 'The next bit is the call he made.'

Moran pressed the 'play' button again. They heard a series of beeps, then a ringing tone.

'We know the number he called,' Moran said.

Someone picked up the phone at the other end. A man's voice said curtly, '*Templeman.*'

'*What the fuck are you playing at?*' Miller said, his voice low, but sizzling with anger. '*Sending the coppers round. You trying to fit me up too?*'

'*Not on the phone,*' Templeman said quickly.

'*He's here now. If you're setting me up, you prick, I'm going to take you down with me.*'

'*Not on the phone,*' Templeman repeated.

'*I don't give a fuck. He's asking me if I was in*

Sheffield. Someone's tipped the bastards off. I'm telling you — '

'*Shut up!*' Templeman interrupted. '*Who is he?*'

'*Some DC. Name's Connors.*'

'*Calm down. This is nothing to do with me. Stall him. Someone will call you back in two minutes.*'

'*What am I supposed to do? Who fucking told them?*'

'*Two minutes.*' The line went dead.

Moran paused the recording again.

'I've edited out the next bit — it's just Miller bullshitting Connors, telling him to wait a moment, everything will be taken care of. Then two minutes later — almost exactly two minutes, this bloke Templeman knows how to pull strings — we get this incoming call.'

Moran restarted the recording.

'*Miller?*' Another man's voice, a deep growl.

'*Yes.*'

'*Put Connors on.*'

Miller's voice, fainter now. '*It's for you.*'

'*What?*' Connors in the background.

'*Take it.*'

Then Connors's voice on the line. '*Who is this?*'

'*Chief Superintendent Ross, New Scotland Yard. There's been a mistake. You shouldn't be there.*'

'*A mistake?*'

'*Yes, you've been misinformed. Who's your Super?*'

'*Andy Carlisle.*'

255

'I'll have a word with him.'

'I'm sorry, sir, do I know you?'

'No, but you will if you don't get the fuck out of there. Now. Do you understand me?'

Moran pressed the 'stop' button on the machine.

'That's all you need to hear.'

'That was a phone tap. How did you get hold of it?' Tom asked incredulously.

Moran gave him a look. 'Let's just say, if you can't beat 'em . . . '

'And the two men on the phone?' Tom said. 'You know who they are?'

Moran nodded. 'Ross. Ian Ross. He's a chief superintendent with Special Branch.'

'And the other one? Templeman?'

'He was trickier. Took a bit more work to find out. John Templeman. He's an assistant director of MI5.'

'This goes to the top?'

'Oh, yes,' Moran said. 'Right the way to the top.'

16

The image on the screen was grainy, the words difficult to read. Moran adjusted the focus control, bringing the picture up sharper. He scrolled down, checking the dates at the top of each microfilmed page: June 10th 1984, June 11th . . . He increased the speed. The screen dissolved into a blur of flashing black and white dots. He eased back on the control lever, saw the date June 23rd. He'd gone too far. Reversing the lever, he went back a few days. There it was. June 18th, 1984, the day of the so-called Battle of Orgreave.

The front page lead of the Sheffield *Star* had the headline, '*Scargill Hurt in Orgreave Riot.*' The intro read, '*Miners' leader Arthur Scargill was injured today as thousands of pickets clashed with police at the Orgreave coking plant near Sheffield.*'

Next to the text was a photograph of a visibly shaken Scargill being helped by two ambulancemen. He'd been knocked unconscious by a police riot shield, according to witnesses, though the police denied the allegation, claiming that the union leader had slipped and hit his head on a railway sleeper. Another story on the front page reported that the casualty unit at Rotherham District General Hospital had been at full stretch dealing with injured miners and police officers brought in from Orgreave.

Moran scrolled down the microfilm. On pages six and seven of the same June 18th edition there was more on the day's clashes at the coking plant, accompanied by graphic pictures of injured pickets, blood running down their faces and bare chests, and a photograph of a wounded policeman receiving medical attention.

Moran moved on to the next day, June 19th. Danny Shields's death was the front page splash. Beneath the headline, '*Miner Murdered*', the story read:

'*Police are hunting the killer of a South Yorkshire miner who was brutally beaten to death in his home village late yesterday evening.*

'*Danny Shields, aged 21, of Kirkby Lane, Clayton Woods, near Barnsley, was found dead on wasteland early this morning by a man out walking his dog. Mr Shields, a striking miner from Clayton Main Colliery, had been battered about the head and left for dead.*

'*The police officer leading the inquiry, Detective Chief Supt Bill Jordan, said today: 'This was a vicious attack on an unarmed young man. We are anxious to speak to anyone who might have seen Mr Shields walking home at around 11.30pm last night.*''

The report — a blurred photograph of Danny Shields inserted into the text — continued for several more paragraphs, describing how Shields had been out drinking with friends at the miners' welfare club in Clayton Woods. There were quotes from a couple of the companions he'd been with and from the manager of the welfare club. Moran read through to the end. There was

258

nothing in the story that he didn't already know.

At the foot of the report was a line reading, '*See Tribute, page 3.*' Moran scrolled down and found the article, headed, '*Friends and family pay tribute to slain miner.*' There was very little substantive information in the piece. It was mostly a series of quotes from relatives and people who'd known Danny Shields, some very well, like his parents and brother, Mick, others not so well. The reporter had obviously covered the ground thoroughly, for even the assistant in the local newsagents, where Shields had picked up his *Daily Mirror* every morning, had given her banal verdict on the dead miner: '*Always smiling, a lovely young man. We're going to miss him here.*'

Elsewhere on the page were stories on the aftermath of the confrontation at Orgreave. Nearly a hundred picketing miners had been arrested at the coking plant and taken away to police stations in Sheffield and Rotherham. Magistrates in both cities had sat late into the night on the 18th, processing the prisoners and making decisions on whether to remand in custody or release on bail. Because of the large number of pickets held, many had not had their cases heard that evening, but had been detained in the cells overnight and brought before the magistrates on the morning of June 19th. Moran skimmed down through the text. At the bottom of the page something attracted his attention. He stopped the microfilm and adjusted the image to make it clearer.

There was a photograph.

Moran peered at it. There were two men in the picture. Two men emerging from the front entrance of Sheffield Magistrates' Court. One of them was unfamiliar to Moran, but the other he knew. He read the caption underneath the photograph and stiffened as the implications struck home.

He'd come to the Local Studies Library without any great hopes of finding anything. It just seemed to make sense to check through the newspaper microfilms, to see what there was on Danny Shields's death. He stared at the photograph again, then reread the caption to make sure. He hadn't expected to find much. Certainly nothing like this.

★   ★   ★

Tom stayed in bed all that first day, getting up only to go to the toilet in the bathroom at the end of the landing — a grubby room with an old cast-iron enamelled bath and dirt thickly coated on the lino around the skirting boards. A communal bathroom shared by men, Tom guessed — young men. There were razors and cans of shaving foam on the windowsill, soap, deodorant and hair gel and at least four different varieties of aftershave. The men obviously cleaned themselves but not the room.

Zac brought him a cheese and tomato sandwich and a mug of tea for lunch, then in the evening a plate of chicken curry and rice. In between, Tom rested, dozing on and off, the time passing without his being aware of it. His

260

wounds — particularly the one to his abdomen, the more serious of the two — began to ache less, but he still felt lethargic. He was surprised at how much the exertions of the previous night had drained him.

The curtains remained closed on Zac's orders, but Tom had sneaked a glance out through a crack, taking in the red-brick Victorian villas across the road, the rows of parked cars. It was a quiet residential street, not much through traffic. Tom could lie with his eyes closed for long periods without hearing a sound from outside. The house too was silent most of the time. Zac kept the door locked, taking Tom out to the bathroom at set intervals, standing guard on the landing while Tom relieved himself, then escorting him back to bed. Tom saw no sign of the other occupants of the house, heard nothing until the evening, when the faint sound of voices, of footsteps, the occasional flush of the lavatory, drifted in through the door.

It was a frustrating experience. His confinement in the hospital had been bad enough. To have that isolation extended further only added to his feeling of impotence. He wanted to know what Moran was doing, wanted to press on with their investigation, bring it to some kind of resolution.

On the second morning Moran accompanied Zac into the room. The private investigator was carrying a black zip-up holdall that Tom recognised as his own.

'I picked it up from your wife,' Moran said. 'It's got your wash stuff in it, and clean clothes

261

— shirts, socks, underwear. Enough for a few days.'

'How long am I going to be here?' Tom asked.

'You leave this morning,' Moran said. 'Zac's taking you over to Wales.'

'To *Wales*?'

'Snowdonia. I have a cottage there — a safe house.'

'You don't think I'm safe here?'

'It's just a precaution. You'll like it. Pitsmoor has many attractions, but fresh air and mountain scenery aren't two of them.'

Tom shook his head.

'No, I'm staying here. I can't afford to go away, to go into hiding. I need to be here, on the spot, trying to find out what's going on.'

Tom swung his legs out of bed. A stab of pain knifed through his side. He clutched at it, stifling a cry.

'You're in no fit state to do anything except rest,' Moran said.

Tom waited for the pain to subside.

'I'm OK. I don't want to rest,' he said breathlessly. 'I want to nail those bastards.'

'They're trying to kill you,' Moran said. 'They're looking for you as we speak. If they find you, you're in no condition to even run, much less fight back.'

'I can't just do nothing.'

'That's why you've got me. Let me do the work.'

'Doesn't that put you at risk too?'

Moran shrugged. 'I can look after myself.'

Tom sagged back on to his pillow. He knew

Moran was right. He needed to rest, to let his wounds heal.

'I went to the Local Studies Library,' Moran said. 'Take a look at this. It's a photocopy of a page from *The Star* for Tuesday, June 19th, 1984, the day after Danny Shields was killed.'

He handed Tom the sheet of paper.

'Look at the photograph at the bottom of the page, the two men coming out of the Magistrates' Court. See the caption?'

Tom read out the words beneath the photograph: ''*Arrested Orgreave pickets Jack Scammell and Geoff Ibbotson leaving court after spending the night in the cells.*''

'Spoils one of our theories a bit, doesn't it?' Moran said. 'Puts Ibbotson in the clear. Shame, really. I liked the idea of Ibbotson as the killer. But it's a pretty watertight alibi. Being under lock and key at Sheffield Magistrates' Court when Shields was murdered.'

'So that leaves Special Branch in the frame,' Tom said. 'Ibbotson didn't do it, but Special Branch did, to protect him. But we know the case file's disappeared, probably all the evidence too. We're never going to be able to prove Special Branch had anything to do with it.'

'I want to check out the Echelon listing again,' Moran said. 'Find out more about it, if possible.'

'You'll want more money, I suppose.'

'Another five hundred.'

'How do I get that if I'm in Wales?'

'I'll take care of it, put it on your account.'

Tom sighed. 'I feel I should be doing more.'

'You're injured. There's nothing you *can* do.

263

Now get dressed. Zac's going to drive you to the cottage, then stay with you.'

'Does Helen know where I'm going?'

'She knows you're going away, but not where.'

'She'll worry.'

'I'll keep her fully informed, OK? Of everything, including any progress I make in the investigation. You'll only be away for a few days, until the heat's off.'

The car was parked outside the house — a rusting green Fiesta, its back seat packed with cardboard boxes of provisions: rice, pasta, bread, tinned meat and vegetables. Moran helped Tom into the front passenger seat next to Zac.

'You're going to a lot of trouble to look after me,' Tom said. 'I appreciate it.'

Moran flashed him a sardonic smile. 'You wait till you see my bill.'

They drove west out of the city, across the Peak District to Buxton and then up over the bleak moorland plateau, the surrounding countryside smothered in heavy mist, drizzle spattering the windscreen of the car. On the long descent into Congleton, the weather cleared. The sun came out. Zac pulled off the main road on to a rutted forest track and followed it for a hundred yards or so until he was well out of sight of any passing traffic. He turned into a narrow gap between trees, the branches above hiding them from the air, and brought the car to a stop. He opened his door.

'This won't take long.'

He went round to the back of the car and opened the boot. Tom heard him remove something, then heard a faint metallic scratching sound as if Zac were adjusting some part of the vehicle. Tom twisted round in his seat, but Zac was hidden behind the car, crouching down below the boot. It was only when Zac came round to the front of the car that Tom saw that he was carrying a screwdriver and a new front number plate. Zac knelt down on the ground and switched the plate. The whole operation took only a few minutes.

After dumping the old number plates in the boot, Zac reversed the car out on to the track and drove back through the forest to the main road.

'You think someone has the car number?' Tom said. 'They're looking out for us?'

'Maybe.'

'Following us, you mean?' Tom glanced back automatically, but the road behind was clear.

'They don't need to follow us,' Zac replied. 'At least not physically. You know those blue cameras you see at the side of the road? On top of blue poles.'

'Yes, I've seen them. They're for traffic management, aren't they? To identify bottle-necks, accidents, that kind of thing.'

'That's what they say.'

'You don't believe it?'

'Well, that's certainly one of their functions,' Zac said cautiously. 'But if that's all they're intended for — keeping an eye on traffic conditions — why is it that they're all fitted with number plate recognition software?'

Tom looked at him. 'What's that?'

'Sophisticated electronic gear that can photograph and record the number plates of cars passing — up to three thousand an hour. The cameras are all linked together in a network that the Faceless Ones can tap into any time they like. They can programme in a particular registration number and ask the cameras to look out for it.'

'Really?'

Zac nodded. 'You could leave your house in Sheffield, or anywhere, and each time you pass one of the cameras — and they're all over the country, new ones being installed every week — it will note your number plate and pinpoint your exact location. They can follow you around England without even leaving their control room.'

'My God, I never knew,' Tom said. 'I suppose I'm very naive.'

'Step outside your house, you're on camera,' Zac said. 'On a normal day you're caught on CCTV probably fifty times or more. Every shopping street you walk down there's a camera somewhere watching you. Almost every shop you go into. The bank, filling stations, supermarkets, they've all got cameras.'

'But those kinds of cameras aren't linked together, are they?'

'Not yet,' Zac said. 'But give them time.'

★ ★ ★

The weather stayed fine as they drove across the plain to Chester, but once over the Welsh border black clusters of cloud began to sweep ominously overhead. By the time they reached the hills it was raining heavily, the road glazed with running water. Just before Betws-y-Coed, Zac pulled off again into a copse and changed the number plates a second time. A mile further on, as if reminding them of the need to be vigilant, they passed a blue traffic camera high on a pole beside the road. Tom ducked his head as they drove past it, thinking how easy it was to live in ignorance of the true nature of the state — until you challenged it and the mask came off.

They were deep into the Cambrian Mountains now, though the summits were all hidden in dense fog. A long glacial lake passed by on one side of the road. On the far side of the lake, a rocky crag jutted out into the water. There were patches of oak forest just above the shoreline and higher up, fading away into the mist, steep, grass-covered slopes dotted with specks of white that Tom realised were grazing sheep.

'You know this area?' Zac asked.

'Not well. I've passed through it — going to Anglesey for a holiday years ago — but I've never really explored it.'

'Over there, beyond the lake, tucked away behind that mountain, is Snowdon. Yr Wyddfa, they call it round here.'

Zac eased on the brakes and turned off the main road. They went over a humpback bridge, a broad, boulder-strewn river below them, then began to ascend. The road was narrow, wide enough for only one vehicle. There were stone walls on either side, fields of grazing sheep. A dark line of coniferous forest cut across the slope of the hill, a ridge of bare rock just visible above it, the craggy edge coming in and out of focus in the drifting mist. The road got steeper. Tom caught a glimpse of a farmhouse in a hollow below the road. That was the last building, the last real sign of human habitation, he saw before they veered off on to an even narrower unmade track and drove higher up the mountain.

Moran's cottage was tucked away in a sheltered depression beneath an outcrop of rock. It was enclosed on three sides, a high sheer sandstone wall at the back and two spurs curving round to right and left, leaving only a narrow opening at the front for access. The cottage — a low, one-storey stone building with a slate roof — blended in perfectly with its surroundings. Not surprising given that it had once been part of the hillside, the blocks used to construct it having been quarried from the ground on which it stood.

Zac reversed the car into the opening and cut the engine. The rain was lashing down, pounding against the windscreen. The mist was so thick that the track they'd just left was almost invisible. Tom could see the near edge of its stony surface, the track continuing on past the cottage, but beyond that was a curtain of grey haze, obliterating everything behind it.

'Give me a minute to open up,' Zac said. 'You don't want to hang around in this.'

He took a key from his pocket and scrambled out of the car, pulling his jacket up over his head to protect himself from the rain. When he

268

returned he had an umbrella open above him. He helped Tom out and sheltered him as they walked across to the cottage. Inside it was cold and damp, the air tainted by the scent of stale wood smoke.

'It's pretty basic,' Zac said. 'No gas or telephone or mains sewerage. But it's got electricity and water. You make yourself comfortable while I unload the car.'

Tom eased himself down into an armchair by the hearth. Despite the umbrella, he'd been splashed with rain on the short walk from the car. His trousers, shoes and sleeves were all slightly wet. He shivered. The cold seemed to make his wounds ache more. He pulled his jacket tight around him and watched Zac bring in their luggage. Tom's holdall went into a room across the tiny hall which appeared to be the only bedroom. The boxes of groceries were carried through to the kitchen at the rear of the cottage.

Zac brought his own bag in last, dropping it on the floor in the living room.

'I'll sleep on the sofa bed,' he said.

He pulled a mobile phone out of his jacket pocket and punched in a number.

'We're here,' he said into the phone. 'Yeah, no problems. I'll check in every day. OK.' He switched off his phone and put it back in his pocket, then noticed Tom hunched over in his chair.

'You cold?' Zac knelt down by the hearth. 'We'll soon get a fire lit.'

He took some old newspapers from a basket,

then a handful of kindling and coaxed a fire into life in the grate, adding bigger logs as the flames took hold. Tom felt the warmth seeping out across the room.

'Is this place used much?' he asked.

'Not much,' Zac replied. 'I've stayed here a few times. It's a good base for walking, or just a place to chill out, do nothing for a while.'

'Does Moran come here? For holidays, I mean.'

Zac seemed amused at the idea.

'Moran? Here? Well, it's a thought, but I can't see it. Moran likes his comforts. Ibiza is more up his street, or one of the Costas. A pool, a bar, a lot of women in bikinis — that's his idea of paradise.'

'Who else knows about it?'

'You worried we'll be found? It's owned by a company, one of Moran's fronts. You've seen how isolated it is. I'd say you'll be as safe here as anywhere in the country.'

Zac went out into the kitchen. Tom huddled down into his armchair. He stared at the flickering flames of the fire, thinking about what Zac had said — 'as safe here as anywhere in the country' — and hoping that those words didn't come back to haunt them.

17

For the first couple of days the weather was mixed. Occasional torrential downpours gave way to heavy showers. The heavy showers became lighter showers. The lighter showers, in turn, were followed by periods — long periods — of drizzle. In between, to vary the diet, there was sleet, hail and even, for one brief moment — as if it couldn't bear to be excluded from the menu — snow. The Inuit supposedly had twenty — or was it forty? — words for snow. Tom began to wonder whether the Welsh had forty words for rain.

The cottage, high on the hillside, was permanently shrouded in damp fog, sometimes mist, sometimes low cloud. Zac had assured Tom that the views of Snowdon on a fine day were stunning, but Tom — who had yet to see further than the bonnet of their car parked outside — was inclined to be sceptical.

'Has anyone actually *ever* seen the top of Snowdon?' he asked Zac, as the rain was once again battering at the window panes, the mist creeping under the doors.

'Yes, I believe someone once did,' Zac said dryly. 'A bloke named Jones. Some Sunday afternoon back in 1926, I think it was. They made it a national holiday.'

Tom was standing by the front window, gazing out at the grey nothingness, the skeins of mist twisting and turning hypnotically in the wind. He turned to look at Zac, who was crouching down by the hearth, putting more logs on the fire.

'This is driving me mad,' Tom said. 'Being cooped up like this.'

Zac nodded sympathetically. 'I know, the weather can get to you round here. There's a fellow down in the valley — bit of a nutter really — who's written pamphlets claiming that Noah — as in the Bible — was Welsh.'

'Well, I can see his point,' Tom said sourly.

'He spends his weekends scouring Snowdon, searching for the remains of the ark. But he hasn't found anything yet.'

'I'm not surprised, in this mist,' Tom said. He looked back out of the window. 'How long are we going to be here?'

'That depends on Moran,' Zac said.

'Is he getting anywhere?'

'I don't know.'

'Why don't you phone him and find out?'

'Not safe.'

'Why not? You call in every day.'

'Not to Moran. I call a secure number. Moran picks up the messages later.'

'That works? The calls can't be monitored?'

Zac shrugged. 'I've a pay-as-you-go phone. It can't be traced to me. I'm careful what I say. Avoid anything that Echelon might pick up. It's as secure as we can make it.'

'Can I get a message to my wife? Letting her know I'm OK.'

'She knows you're OK. Moran will have told her.'

Zac prodded at the fire with a poker, getting a good blaze going.

'I'm nipping out to the shops this morning,' he said. 'Get some milk, bread, a few other provisions. You want anything?'

'Why don't I come with you?'

Zac shook his head. 'Uh-uh.'

'We could find a pub somewhere. Have lunch.'

'Sorry.'

'Oh, come on, what's the problem?'

'Moran's orders. You stay here.'

'I'm going crazy here. What's the risk? We're in the middle of Wales. Who's going to know who I am?'

'No deal.'

'Why not?' Tom persisted. 'At least let me come with you. I could sit in the car. It would make a change from this place.'

Zac shook his head again. 'You go nowhere, that's what Moran said.'

'I don't care what Moran says. Who's he to tell me what I can and can't do?'

'Someone is trying to kill you, Dr Whitehead,' Zac said. 'Have you taken that in? Without Moran you wouldn't be here now.'

That brought Tom to his senses. 'Yes . . . OK,' he said shame-facedly.

'You're not a prisoner. You're free to walk out of the door any time you like.'

'Yes . . . I'm sorry, you're right. I owe Moran — you too — my thanks.'

'It won't be for much longer,' Zac said gently. 'I'm sure of that. Now, do you want anything from the shops?'

'You could get me a paper.' There was no television in the cottage, not even a radio. Tom had lost touch with what was going on in the outside world.

'The *Guardian*, right?' Zac said.

Tom smiled. 'Is it that obvious?'

'Anything else?'

'How about some fresh meat and vegetables? I'll cook something for us tonight. You want some money?'

'I have money. I won't be long. Lock the door behind me.'

After Zac had left, Tom settled himself down in the armchair by the hearth. The open fire was the best thing about the cottage, which, in other respects, was rather basic and uncomfortable. The furniture was old and tatty, even by holiday cottage standards. The double bed in Tom's room, from its iron frame and mahogany headboard, had to be pre-war at the very least. And the mattress on it — poorly sprung with a deep hollow down the centre — wasn't much newer. The armchairs and sofa bed in the living room all sagged and were in urgent need of reupholstering, and the kitchen, with no fire or radiator, was as cold and unwelcoming as a butcher's fridge. The chair by the living room hearth was the most congenial spot in the house, but even the log fire could not entirely dispel the dampness in the atmosphere.

Tom stretched out his legs, letting the heat of the flames warm them. At least his injuries were less of a problem now. Zac was changing the dressings regularly and the enforced period of rest — frustrating though it was — was aiding the path to full recovery. Tom picked up the book he'd left tucked down the side of the chair: *The Murder on the Links*, the second Agatha Christie he'd read since their arrival. The cottage, fortunately, had a good supply of books. On the shelves in the alcove there were twenty or thirty, mostly popular fiction, which Tom assumed reflected Moran's tastes in literature. Crime novels by Ed McBain and Elmore Leonard, well-thumbed Hammond Innes and Alistair MacLean adventure stories, books by Deighton, Lyall, Le Carré and others. Tom had attempted an old Robert Ludlum thriller, but given up halfway through, unsettled and confused by the convoluted strands of con-spiracy and paranoia which seemed too close to his own predicament for comfort. He'd turned instead to the reassuring homeliness, the unreal intricacies of Hercule Poirot and Miss Marple.

But now he struggled to concentrate on the book. He was restless. He stood up and wandered around the room. There wasn't much space — a couple of paces was all he could manage before he had to change direction to avoid the furniture. He contemplated going out. Walking down the track to the road. What danger could there be in that? He was highly unlikely to encounter anyone, and in the thick mist there was even less chance of his being spotted from a distance. It was the weather that stopped him doing it. The rain was bucketing down and he had no proper waterproofs to wear. He would get drenched and Zac would certainly notice his wet clothes when he returned from the shops. That reminded him: he'd forgotten to lock the front door. He went out into the hall and turned the key in the lock. Not that it was much protection — a thin panel of wood, a fragile pane of glass; they wouldn't be much of an obstacle if the men Zac called the Faceless Ones came to get him.

But would they? Tom still found it incredible that anyone might want to kill him. It seemed so absurd. Him, a law abiding, middle-class professional. What threat was he to anyone? There were moments when he still thought that they were after the wrong man. They had to be. Surely they couldn't mean *him*. It had to be a case of mistaken identity. Yet the memories of the knife attack, of the bogus doctor with the hypodermic needle, then his nocturnal flight from the hospital, were still fresh and vivid. His side and arm still ached. They can't all have been mistakes. Surreal though it seemed, Tom knew he was undoubtedly their target.

It was an hour and a half later that Zac returned. Tom unlocked the front door for him and helped him carry the bags of groceries into the kitchen. They unpacked the tins, the bread, the cartons of milk together and stored them away in the cupboards and the tiny fridge. Tom was pleased to note the bags of onions, of courgettes, carrots, green beans and peppers. And the pack of four fresh chicken breasts. Up till now Zac had done all the cooking — everything out of a tin. Tinned meat, tinned vegetables, tinned soup. If it didn't come in a tin, it wasn't food.

'Where did you go?' Tom said.

'Beddgelert.'

'Is that far?'

'A few miles. Nearest shops. They didn't have any *Guardians*. Plenty of *Daily Telegraphs*, but I couldn't see you reading the *Telegraph* so I got you the *Independent*.'

'That's fine, thanks.'

They made a couple of mugs of coffee and went back into the living room to sit by the fire. Tom opened the newspaper and scanned the front page.

'You want some of this?' he asked Zac. 'The inside pages?'

Zac shook his head. 'I don't read papers.'

'Never?'

'Not if I can help it.'

'You're not interested in the news?'

'Not really. It's all depressing, isn't it? Wars and famines and tosspot politicians.'

'You don't like politicians?'

'Does anyone? They're all wankers, aren't they? Lining their own pockets, promising one thing, doing another. Bunch of arrogant liars, the lot of 'em.'

'Which way do you vote?'

'I don't. What's the point? It's just window dressing, isn't it? To give us the illusion that our opinions count. You get the same thing whoever you vote for.'

Zac inserted a compact disc into his portable CD Walkman and slipped the headphones over his ears. He wasn't the most garrulous of companions. Tom had tried several times to engage him in conversation, but without much success. Zac was in his early twenties, about the age of most of Tom's students, but unlike the students, some of whom had an irritating fondness for the sound of their own voices, Zac seemed reluctant to talk at all. He spent a lot of the time listening to his Walkman, shut away in his own world. When he wasn't doing that, he was out in the woods down the hill collecting logs, then chopping them up for the fire in the small garden at the back of the cottage. He didn't read much. They'd played a few games of chess together, but Zac didn't give the impression that he enjoyed it much: it was simply another way of passing the time.

Tom suppressed a sigh and turned back to his newspaper. He could hear the rain drumming on the window, feel the draught biting his ankles. He hoped his stay in Wales was not going to be a long one.

★ ★ ★

The Geek seemed uncharacteristically nervous. He came into the café as if he were in a hurry, his movements urgent, fingers fumbling to close the door behind him. Annie watched him walk across to her table. The cool, self-possessed swagger had gone, replaced by a quick, anxious furtiveness. He didn't want to be there, and he most certainly didn't want to linger.

'What the hell do you want now?' he said in a low whisper as he sat down.

His eyes flickered towards the other tables. A couple of women in their fifties were having tea and scones near the window. An elderly man and a younger woman — from her features, almost certainly his daughter — were engrossed in conversation at the table in the corner. At the table by the door a woman sat alone with a cafetière, her long pink nails turning the pages of a glossy magazine. From concealed speakers came the soft sound of classical music. Genteel and soothing. Mozart, Annie guessed.

'You OK?' she asked Hanbury.

'Yes, I'm OK.'

'What's the matter?'

'Nothing's the fucking matter.' He glanced around suddenly, as if fearing that the expletive might have been overheard.

'Have a coffee,' Annie said.

'I don't want a coffee. This is too soon, you know that.' His voice became even lower. 'What *is* it?'

Annie saw the proprietress heading for their table and gave Hanbury a slight shake of her head. The proprietress — a permed matron whose pink and white striped dress seemed to have been chosen to match the wallpaper — smiled at them.

'Can I get you anything?'

'Thank you,' Annie said before Hanbury could reply. 'Another coffee for me, and one for my friend.'

'I said I didn't want a fucking coffee,' Hanbury

hissed when the proprietress had disappeared into the kitchen.

'You're drawing attention to yourself,' Annie said sharply. 'Has something happened?'

'Yes, your boss called. That's what's happened. It's too soon after the last time. Have you any idea of the risks I'm taking?'

'Calm down,' Annie said soothingly.

'Don't tell me to calm down. I'm the one at the sharp end here. I'm the one who could end up in jail.'

You knew that at the beginning, Annie thought. You've known it all along, but you're too greedy to stop. You like the money too much. So quit whining, you're hardly an innocent virgin.

'Are you blown?' she said.

'Course I'm not blown.'

'You sure? You picked up signs?'

'No.'

'You absolutely sure?'

'I wouldn't be here if I wasn't.'

'If you're compromised, we can stop now.'

'I've told you, I'm not compromised. I just don't like meeting again so soon. It's dangerous.'

'You think *I* like it? Were you followed?'

'No.'

'How do you know?'

'I *know*. Now, what do you want? I haven't got much — '

He broke off as the proprietress brought their coffees to the table.

'Thank you,' Annie said.

The coffee was pale brown, filter, served in

delicate, floral-pattern porcelain cups with a small biscuit resting in each saucer.

'The keywords from last time,' Annie said, adding milk to her coffee. 'We need to know more about them. You remember the words, the name?'

'Yes, I remember.'

'Drink some of your coffee, the woman's watching us from the kitchen. Don't look, you cretin.'

He was making *her* nervous now. Annie turned her head to look out of the window. She could see nothing that struck her as out of the ordinary. Just a plain suburban shopping street, a hairdressing salon and a bakery in the row immediately opposite, a steady flow of traffic passing by. No pedestrians loitering suspiciously, no parked cars with people inside.

'What do you mean, 'know more'?' Hanbury said, his tone petulant. He hadn't liked being called a cretin.

'Anything you can get. When the keywords were programmed into Echelon would be useful. Who, why would be good too.'

'I can tell you when now. All the keywords have a date. I remember it from last time. February 2003. I don't recall the exact day. It had a Menwith Hill source code, I remember that too.'

'Menwith Hill? You sure?'

'No question.'

'The NSA listed it?'

'They programmed the keywords. That doesn't mean GCHQ wasn't involved.'

'We'd like to know why as well.'

'You don't want much, do you?' he said sarcastically.

Annie gave him a smile. The last thing she needed was him going off in a sulk, taking his cricket bat home.

'I'm sure you can do it, Craig. You're smart, you're cunning. You've always delivered in the past.'

'It won't be easy.'

'There must be a file, a reference somewhere on the computer system. You have access to that.'

'Only within limits.'

'See what you can do.'

Hanbury shook his head. 'This is different.'

'You've done it before for us.'

'It's risky. It's outside my area. If I do a search, there'll be a record of it. I'll leave a footprint behind on the system.'

'You can cover your tracks, can't you?'

'How would *you* know?'

Annie guessed what was coming. Flattery, complicity in previous joint operations, were not going to be enough this time.

'I'll want more money,' he said.

Annie didn't argue. 'How much?'

'Seven-fifty.'

'I'll talk to my boss.' Hanbury didn't know Moran's name, knew nothing about him. And Annie was always careful to keep it that way.

'You do that.'

Hanbury pushed himself up from his chair.

'The usual place?' Annie said.

He nodded. 'Six o'clock.'

He leant towards her, his customary cockiness resurfacing. It was a seller's market, and he knew it.

'Seven-fifty, remember. Cash. Or your boss can go screw himself.'

★　★　★

'You want a game of chess?' Tom asked.

Zac shrugged. 'If you like, why not?' He didn't sound over-enthusiastic.

'You don't have to, you know,' Tom said.

'It's OK.'

Tom set the pieces out on the board. He'd been reading for several hours. Finished his Agatha Christie and then started Alistair MacLean's *Where Eagles Dare*. He'd read the book when he was a teenager, seen the film at least three times on television. He was enjoying revisiting it, but his eyes were tired. He wanted a break. Not that chess with Zac was much of a break. Every game they'd played Zac had won with effortless ease.

'White or black?' Tom said.

'Don't care.'

'It's my turn for white, I think.'

'Whatever.'

Zac played chess the way he did almost everything. With a sort of laid-back indifference that Tom, living in close and enforced proximity to him, was beginning to find irritating. Zac was an amiable enough companion. That was one of the problems. He was *too* amiable, too happy to go along with anything Tom suggested

283

— with the exception of letting him venture out of the cottage. That was one thing he was not prepared to countenance. But this good-natured acquiescence, this willingness to accommodate Tom, was becoming wearing. Zac simply didn't seem to care what they did, didn't have an opinion one way or the other. His stock response to every question seemed to be, 'Yeah, why not?' or, 'If you like' or, 'I don't mind'. He agreed to just about everything Tom requested, but agreed with such an air of boredom that it made Tom feel bad about asking him in the first place.

'You play a lot?' Tom asked, moving one of his pawns.

'Not really.'

'You're good. Where did you learn?'

'Just picked it up. Playing with mates. A bit at school.'

'My son's in a chess club at school. He really enjoys it.'

'Yeah?'

'He's getting good. Keeps me on my toes. Give him a year and he'll be able to beat me.'

'As much as a year?' Zac's mouth twitched.

'Don't rub it in,' Tom said. He moved one of his bishops.

'You sure you want to do that?' Zac said.

He said something similar every game. 'You might want to think again about that', 'Did you intend to do that?' or even just a cryptic, 'Interesting' — as if he were trying to give himself more of a challenge, make it more of a match. Tom found it patronising.

'What's wrong with it?' Tom said.

'Nothing.'

'Is it a stupid move?'

'No, it's fine.'

Zac moved one of his knights, then six moves later took Tom's queen, effectively closing out the game. Tom stared at the board, seeing now how that one careless move early on had allowed Zac to get the upper hand. Only it hadn't seemed careless at the time. That was Tom's problem. He didn't have a chess player's mind. He never had a strategy. He simply fumbled from one move to the next. Zac, however, thought ahead, laying the groundwork for his inevitable victory by planning his attack, by anticipating and neutralising his opponent's defences.

'How did you do that?' Tom said, thinking out loud.

'Lucky fluke,' Zac replied offhandedly.

'I'm not much of an opponent, I know. I'm sorry.'

'No, it's OK.'

'You're a natural. I bet you were good at maths at school, weren't you?'

Zac shrugged. 'I was OK.'

'Good at most things, I'd guess. Have you been to university?'

'Why would I want to go to university?'

The question surprised Tom. It wasn't something he was used to hearing. In his world, among the young people he encountered, it was an undisputed assumption that school was followed by further education.

'You're obviously bright. Did you not want to?'

'What for?'

'The learning experience. The chance to develop your mind. To explore new interests.'

'To acquire massive debts, get pissed on a Saturday night? I can do that without going to university.'

'There's more to it than that,' Tom said, realising he was in danger of metamorphosing into Zac's personal tutor. 'The social experience is important. It can be fun. But learning can also be fun.'

Zac gave him a look. 'Yeah? That's what they said at school, but I was bored out of my mind. Couldn't wait to get out, find a job. Actually *do* something.'

'Is that when you started working for Moran?'

'Not at first. That came later.'

'What exactly do you do for him? Besides look after people like me — which, I hope, isn't a very common experience.'

'Technical stuff,' Zac said.

'Technical stuff?'

'Yeah.'

'Like what?'

'You really want to know?'

'That's why I asked.'

'You know, surveillance, that kind of thing.'

'What, watching people, bugging their homes?'

'I can do that, yeah. We have the gear.'

'Isn't it illegal?'

'Yeah.'

'That doesn't bother you?'

'The government does it all the time. That's their hypocrisy. They make laws, but they never apply them to their own activities. They watch us, monitor us. Their ultimate aim is to know absolutely everything about everyone.'

'You think that's possible?' Tom said.

'Oh, yes, it's possible.'

Zac gazed at him intently. At last, a subject that really animates him, Tom thought.

'You look at the information they hold on us,' Zac went on. 'Or the information that's available to the state from other sources. They know when we were born, where we live, who we live with, how much we earn, what we buy at the supermarket, where we go on holiday. They eavesdrop on our phone calls, open our post, monitor our emails. They want to know everything. Privacy is a thing of the past. You can't escape their prying eyes. You encrypt your emails so they can't read them, what do they do? They give themselves the power to demand the key to your code. You withhold it, you go to jail. If you tell anyone that the police have asked for your key, that's also an offence.

'They want us all to have smart cards so all that information they have on us is readily available to them. The police take fingerprints and DNA samples from everyone they charge. If you're acquitted, those records aren't deleted. They stay on the computer. The databases are getting bigger and bigger. Next they'll be telling us all we have to put our fingerprints and DNA profiles on to ID cards before we're entitled to anything. Those electronic tags they use for offenders released from prison. They've got the technology now to implant a microchip under a person's skin instead — tells them where you are every second of the day. How long do you think it'll be before they decide that the entire population has to have a microchip under their skin? All for our own good, of course.'

Zac gave a snort of disgust. It was the most he'd said in all their time at the cottage. He lapsed back in his chair as if the effort had exhausted him.

'That seems a pretty extreme view,' Tom said, wanting to prolong the conversation.

'Look what they've done to you,' Zac said simply.

Tom had no answer to that. He stared pensively at Zac for a moment, then gathered in the chess pieces and started to set them out on the board.

'You want another game?'

Zac yawned. 'Don't mind.'

★   ★   ★

Annie spent the afternoon drifting aimlessly around Cheltenham town centre — window shopping, browsing in bookstores, sitting on a bench in the High Street just watching the people passing by.

Shortly before five to six, she set off for the Royal Oak, pacing herself to arrive at the pub no later than ten past — giving the Geek enough time to settle in with his pint of real ale, but not so long that he got pissed off and left. In her

288

jacket pocket, sealed in an envelope, she had the £500 in cash she'd brought with her. She'd called Moran during the afternoon to see about the extra two-fifty Hanbury had demanded, but Moran was out on a job and unavailable, something sensitive which necessitated him switching off his mobile. The Geek would have to wait for his bonus. He wouldn't like it, but Annie was confident she could handle him. Maybe she'd agree to stay on this time, have a meal with him, perhaps even take a look at his plasma screen — no, that was too much. She wouldn't go back to his place, even for Moran.

There were cars parked by the kerb outside the Royal Oak. A woman in a Burberry overcoat was climbing out of the front of a dark-green Toyota 4×4. She reached back in for a cat box and carried it into the vet's surgery a couple of doors up the street. Behind the Toyota was a white Transit van. It had no markings on it, but in the thick dirt caked on to its rear doors someone had used their finger to write, 'My other van's a Porsche.'

Annie went into the pub. There was a small vestibule immediately inside, a door to the left for the saloon bar, one on the right for the lounge. She pulled open the lounge door and stepped through, pausing automatically just beyond the threshold. It was something she did out of habit, almost a reflex action, when she entered bars. See who was there, taste the atmosphere before committing herself to going in. The lounge seemed pretty much the way it always was. Not many customers at this time of day. Just the usual scattering of office workers having a quick one on their way home.

A man and woman were sitting in one of the booths over by the wall, a couple of men in suits were nursing pints at a table in the middle of the room. A lone man, dark-grey suit and pale-blue shirt, was occupying a table closer to the door. Another lone man in a suit was perched on a stool at the bar, a half-pint glass on the counter in front of him. He took a sip of his drink. The level didn't seem to go down by much. Then he turned to look at Annie, sizing her up the way guys do when a woman walks into a bar on her own. She gave him a hard stare and he looked away. There was a row of bright spotlights on the ceiling above the bar. Annie caught a fleeting flash of silver on the man's ear as he turned his head. A metallic stud of some kind. Annie looked into the far corner of the lounge. Hanbury was there in the booth. He was half turned away from her, tapping a beer mat impatiently on the table. He hadn't seen her yet. Annie started across the room.

That was when it hit her.

Nothing physical, but it had the same impact as a blow. A sudden split-second realisation that gave her stomach a jolt, as if she'd been punched.

The guy at the bar. The flash of silver. The stud. It hadn't been *on* his ear, pierced through the lobe. It had been *in* his ear, in the orifice. A hearing aid? No way, not a young guy like him. He was wearing an earpiece — a radio receiver. Suddenly the other signs came together with a

290

sickening clarity. The van outside, the other guys in the lounge. All in suits. Too many suits. This was a real ale pub, for Christ's sake.

Annie kept walking. Hanbury started to turn his head. Shit! Don't look. Don't *look*. You prick, she thought. They're on to you. You're blown sky fucking high. Don't look at me. She kept her gaze fixed on the door at the rear of the lounge, the exit sign above it. But she still caught the movement out of the corner of her eye. Hanbury's head turning. She knew he was looking at her. She couldn't see his face. Or his expression. Had the other guys noticed? Was there anything in Hanbury's face to alert them?

She tried not to hurry. The exit was right there in front of her. She noticed the brass strip screwed to the wall beside it — 'Toilets'. Maybe Hanbury would assume she was going to the Ladies. Maybe that's what they'd all assume. Annie pushed open the door and walked out of the lounge.

She was a little breathless. Her stomach was knotted. She tried to relax, to clear her mind. Think through her next move. She was in the vestibule at the back of the pub, a rectangular hallway with a dirty lino floor and four doors opening off it: the Gents and Ladies, another door marked 'Staff Only', which Annie guessed led behind the bar, and the rear exit to the street. Annie walked towards the exit. Get out of the pub and well away from the area, that was her primary objective.

She paused as she reached the door, peering cautiously out through the small glass panels, some of them clear but a square panel in the centre embellished with a mixture of green and red stained glass. She saw a car parked on the street outside. A man was getting out of the car, coming across the pavement. His left hand was raised, his head tilted forwards towards it like a woman testing a scent on her wrist. Annie saw the man's lips move. He was talking into a mike concealed up his sleeve. He hadn't looked up yet, hadn't seen her. Annie pulled back from the door and ducked into the Ladies.

It was an instinctive action, the only move available to her. But she knew it had its hazards, was at best only a temporary solution. Were they on to her too? Had they been waiting for her to arrive and make contact, had they been watching her earlier? Or had something in Hanbury's face, his demeanour just now in the lounge, suddenly aroused their suspicions? Either way, she was in trouble, and the Ladies was no refuge. They wouldn't wait for her to emerge, they'd come right in after her. She had maybe a minute, certainly no more.

There was a small window high up on the wall behind the row of cubicles. Annie stood on the seat of one of the toilet bowls and pushed the window open, looking out into the yard behind the saloon bar, a cramped little courtyard enclosed on three sides. The window opening was narrow, too tiny for a mature woman. But Annie was skinny. Her small breasts and boyish hips would just squeeze through the gap. She pulled herself up the wall and manoeuvred her shoulders through the window. Behind her, the door to the toilets banged open. She heard footsteps, a man's voice gabbling urgently into his radio.

She wriggled forwards. Her waist was through now, her hips following. She was tipping downwards, falling head first into the yard. She felt a hand grab her ankle. She kicked out hard with her other foot, felt it connect. A man yelped in pain and let go. Annie tumbled down on to the lid of the industrial refuse bin that was pushed up against the wall below the window. Her shoulder hit first, sending a shuddering jar through her whole body. She rolled over, twisting off the bin in a single supple movement and landed on her feet on the ground. She caught a brief glimpse of a man's face peering out of the toilet window, but she was already turning away, sprinting across the yard.

There were wooden gates blocking the exit. Annie lifted the catch, swung one of the gates wide and darted through. She was out on the street now. Which way to go? Didn't matter. Get the hell out. That was all that counted. Annie went left, haring down the street. She was fast. Always had been. She had the build of a sprinter, an explosive, whippet-like speed. They'd come after her, she knew that. How many were there? A couple inside the pub, the others watching the outside, plus the ones in the van. There could be half a dozen of them, maybe more. Fuck! And they had vehicles. They could head her off, block her lines of escape. So get off the streets. Find somewhere vehicles couldn't go — the pedestrian precinct in the centre of town.

How far was that? Half a mile? Maybe more. She could run half a mile. She came to a crossroads and was forced to stop. The traffic was speeding across her path, two unbroken lines of fast-moving vehicles. Annie looked round. There were cars behind her too, slowing for the red light at the junction. One in particular caught her attention — a dark-blue Rover saloon eight or nine cars back. It came up rapidly to the end of the queue and braked hard. A man jumped out of the passenger seat and came running towards her.

Annie turned left, heading along the main road. But she was on the wrong side. The town centre, the car park where she'd left her car, were both across the main road. She twisted her head round without reducing her pace. The man was coming around the corner. He was wearing a grey suit and a purple tie. He looked young, fit, not the type to give up easily. Annie knew she was nippy, agile. Over a short distance she probably had the edge, but did she have the stamina to outlast her pursuer over a longer haul?

The lights still hadn't changed. The traffic on the main road was still solid, still moving dangerously fast. The man was narrowing the gap between them. Annie knew she had to take the chance. She glanced back, gauging the speed of the oncoming vehicles, assessing the distances between cars. Not this one . . . nor this . . . yes, go for it. She veered out suddenly into the road, accelerating. She heard a screech of brakes, then an angry blast from a car horn, but didn't pause even for a second. She was in the middle of the carriageway, running parallel to the traffic for a few yards before she plunged across the second lane and on to the pavement at the far side.

She looked back. The man in the grey suit had stopped on the other side of the road, waiting for a safe moment to cross. He had his wrist raised to his mouth, talking into his mike. Annie turned right into a side street. Her lungs and legs were starting to hurt. The street was lined with big white Regency mansions. It was a good hundred yards long — too far for her to get to the end before her pursuer made it across the main road. She knew she had to get out of sight. The third house along, she ducked into the drive which curved around in front of the impressive Georgian edifice — white-painted ashlar stone, black wrought-iron balconies on the upper storeys, the whole building so large it had been converted into a luxury hotel. She ran along the side of the building, past the kitchen entrance and out on to a York-stone terrace at the rear, pausing to draw breath. The back garden of the hotel consisted mainly of a smooth, velvet lawn fringed with trees and mature shrubs. The boundary was a brick wall a couple of metres high. Annie ran out across the lawn, pushed through a gap in the undergrowth and scrambled over the wall.

The garden on the other side of the wall was slightly smaller than the hotel's, again mostly lawn, with shrub-filled borders around the edges. Annie ran across it and climbed over another brick wall into a third garden. She crouched down, leaning back on the wall, panting for breath. The Faceless Ones would be out on the street — not just the man who'd chased her, but his backup car, maybe other members of the team. They'd figure out pretty quickly that she'd taken refuge in one of the gardens. They wouldn't know which one, but there weren't many to choose from. She had to keep moving.

She took her bearings. Looking diagonally through the trees, she could see more houses running at right angles to the street she'd just left. That was where she had to head. She couldn't remain in the gardens; she needed to keep going towards the town centre, to find her car. She straightened up and followed the wall around to the rear boundary, clambering over into the garden beyond, which belonged to one of the houses on the other street. She traversed that garden, then two more before she approached the back of one of the houses, crossing a patio and climbing over a locked wooden gate to get round to the front. She waited for a moment, pressed up close to the side of the house while she scanned the street. She could see no pedestrians, no cars.

Running down the gravel drive, she paused one more time at the gateway to check the street. It was still clear. She darted out and raced away along the pavement. It was a quiet residential street, cars parked by the kerb but not much moving traffic. Horse chestnut and lime trees lined the edges. She began to think she'd made it. At the next junction she had to stop to take her bearings again, then turned left. She was in unfamiliar territory, but her sense of direction told her that was the right way to go.

Moments later she heard the noise of an engine behind her. She turned her head. Saw the Rover saloon. She kept running, looking for an escape route. She knew she couldn't outrun the car. The houses were smaller here — Victorian red-brick villas on both sides of the street. No gaps between them.

Or were there?

She almost ran past it. A narrow footpath next to one of the houses, its entrance partially blocked by a chicane of low fencing intended to force cyclists to dismount. Annie skidded to a halt, grabbed hold of the fence and swung herself round through the chicane, sprinting away along the footpath.

At the far end she looked back. No sign of the Faceless Ones. Yet. What would they do? Leave their car and come after her on foot? Maybe. Drive round the block to cut her off? That was what she would have done.

And there they were. The Rover coming round the corner and down the street towards her now. Annie ducked back into the mouth of the footpath, intending to run back the way she'd come, but they'd thought of that too. There was a man standing at the other end, waiting for her. Annie stepped back out on to the pavement. The Rover was nearly on her. She wasn't going to give up. If they wanted her, they were going to have to come and get her. She took a deep breath and ran across the road — straight up the drive of the house opposite. The passage along the side of the house was blocked by a gate — a locked gate. Annie leapt up and grabbed the top of the gate, then swung her legs up and over, dropping lightly to the ground on the other side. Through the wooden slats, she saw the Rover stop, the driver get out and run into the drive. He was small, overweight. The gate would slow him up, perhaps even block him altogether, Annie thought, as she dashed across the garden, scrambled over the perimeter fence and through another garden to the street beyond.

Immediately across the road she saw the entrance to a park. A pair of high green iron gates, padlocked in the middle, filled almost the full width of the entrance, leaving only a narrow pedestrian gateway to one side. Annie sprinted across the road and through the gateway. The park wasn't large. It was just a green oasis in the urban desert, a patch of grass and a few flower beds surrounded by houses. She reached the far side in a couple of minutes and looked back. She seemed to have shaken off her pursuers.

She peered cautiously out through the exit. She had almost reached the town centre. Another few hundred metres and she'd be in the main pedestrianised shopping area. She was tired, breathless. She knew she couldn't keep running for much longer. She looked both ways, saw nothing to alarm her, and jogged away up the street, a slight incline that sapped her remaining strength. She began to slow, gulping in air. There were shops on both sides of the road now, an estate agent's, a pub. There were people about. Annie felt safer.

At the top of the incline the road made a ninety-degree turn to the right. Off to the left was a pedestrian precinct. Annie turned into it and slowed to a walk. She was surprised — and relieved — to see how busy it was. It was gone 6.30, but many of the stores were still open — late-night opening, she guessed. She could mingle with the crowds, take cover in the shops if necessary. She started to relax a little. She was in the clear.

Then she saw the white Transit at the other end of the precinct. There must have been dozens of similar vans in the town, but Annie knew that this was the one from outside the Royal Oak. It was parked right across the street, the perfect location for checking everyone who went past. Annie stopped, pretending to study the display in a shop window. She turned away from the van, looking back the way she'd come. The man in the grey suit and purple tie had just appeared around the corner. He saw Annie at almost exactly the moment she saw him. He lifted his wrist as he ran, talking into his mike again. Annie glanced the other way. Two men were jumping out of the back of the white van, heading towards her. Both ends of the precinct were blocked. Annie was caught in the middle. She took the only escape route available to her — through the glass doors of the Regent Arcade.

The Arcade was like a tunnel, a long, narrow covered mall with two entrances, one at either end. Nothing in between except shops. Annie thought through her options, racing fast now along the marble-paved avenue outside the shops. There were men behind her at the north end of the Arcade. That left only the exit at the south end. If it wasn't covered already, they'd certainly have a vehicle on its way there now, men in place before she could get out. She could hide in one of the shops, but they'd check them one by one if they had to. There was nowhere else to go. She was trapped.

The shops, she thought suddenly.

She didn't need to hide. The shops must have back entrances, somewhere for delivery vehicles to pull in, for goods to be unloaded. Annie dived through the first available doorway — into a women's clothes shop. Raced across the shop floor, past the racks of clothes, the startled faces of the assistants and out through a door at the back marked 'Private — Staff Only'. There was a storeroom beyond the door, a further exit beyond that — double doors like a fire exit. Annie kicked them open and burst out into a cavernous service area, a vast enclosed space devoid of natural light, its roof so far above her that it was lost in shadow. A service road ran all the way along the backs of the shops until, in the distance, it emerged into daylight. Annie ran along the road. By the exit there was a waist-high lifting steel barrier and a security kiosk. A security guard stepped out of the kiosk as Annie drew near, blocking her path. She veered off to the side and vaulted over the barrier, then sprinted out into the street, blinking as the bright sunlight hit her in the face.

She kept going — across two lines of traffic, then down a side street, not pausing, not looking back. Only when there were several blocks of buildings between her and the Arcade did she slow down and change direction, circling around in a wide loop to the car park where she'd left her car. She crept into a yard overlooking the car park and slumped to the ground behind a low wall, too exhausted to move. For five minutes she lay there, struggling to regain her breath. Her lungs were burning, her legs in agony. When the pain had begun to ease off, she put an eye over the top of the wall and studied the car park. How much did the Faceless Ones know about her? Did they know she had a car? She thought back to her lunchtime meeting with Hanbury. She'd arrived at the café first, left after Hanbury. Were they watching him then? Had they seen her leave, followed her as she returned to her car? When she drove into the centre of Cheltenham, had they been on her tail? Had they been monitoring her all afternoon? Annie knew she'd been careful. She always was when she met Hanbury. She'd spotted nothing suspicious. Maybe they hadn't been watching her. Maybe Hanbury had made a mistake when he went back to his desk, done something really stupid, and it was that that had sparked off the surveillance. There were any number of possibilities. But it was rash to make any assumptions about which of them might be correct. Could she take a chance on the car? That was the only question that mattered.

There was no sign of the men in suits. If they knew about her car, knew where it was parked, surely someone would have shown up by now.

They'd have the place staked out, waiting for her. Wouldn't they? Or would they? That was the problem with this game of doublethink, of guess and gamble. She could be sure of nothing.

Annie could see no one in the car park. No one waiting in a car, no one hanging around on the periphery. But that didn't mean they weren't there. Was it worth the risk? The car was useful, but not essential. There were other ways of getting back to Sheffield. She had £500 in cash in her pocket. She could take a taxi all the way if she needed to. Abandoning the vehicle wasn't a problem. It couldn't be traced to either her or Moran. It was old, expendable. Hanbury was more troubling — if he talked, and he was the type who'd always go for a plea bargain. But what could he tell them? He knew her as Lucy, had no idea what her real name was, where she lived or whom she was working for. He'd never seen Moran, couldn't implicate him in any of this.

Annie weighed up her options. There were times to be reckless, times to play it safe. She took another cautious look around and slipped out of her hiding place, heading back to a taxi rank she'd passed on her way to the car park. There were two taxis waiting in line. Annie slid into the one at the front and slouched down low on the back seat so she was barely visible from outside. The driver twisted around to look at her. Annie passed him a £20 note.

'Just drive,' she said. 'I'll tell you where in a moment.'

18

On the Friday morning — three days after they'd arrived — the weather finally improved. Tom looked out of the front window of the cottage and was astonished to see blue sky and a whole range of mountains stretching west to the Irish Sea. Across the valley there was a v-shaped gap between two peaks, deciduous forest cloaking their bases, bare crags higher up. A thin vertical line of glistening silver marked a waterfall as it cascaded down a rock face. Through the gap, clear and stark against the distant skyline, was a sheer rock wall leading up to a sharp, triangular summit that Tom knew must be Snowdon.

He took in the panorama, not just the mountains, but the green fields in the valley, the waters of Llyn Gwynant gleaming in the sunlight.

'Quite something, isn't it?' Zac said, coming up to stand next to Tom. 'Worth all that rain.'

'I'm not sure about that,' Tom replied dryly. 'But it's pretty spectacular. That peak there is Snowdon, I assume?'

Zac nodded. 'As clear as I've ever seen her.'

'You been to the top?'

'A couple of times. Once up the Pyg track from Pen-y-pass, the other time up Crib Goch. You see that knife-edge ridge to the north-east? There's a path along the top. Well, not really a path, it's more like a climbing route. I did it in a howling gale. Didn't dare stand up. Went the whole way on my knees, praying I wouldn't get blown off. Not recommended.'

Zac sat down in a chair and started to put on his trainers.

'You going out?' Tom said.

'Shops.'

'Let me come this time.'

Tom knew what the answer would be, but he had to try. Zac didn't reply, so Tom went on, 'I won't draw attention to myself. What harm can it do?'

Zac laced up his trainers, not bothering to respond.

'No one will look twice at me. This is a tourist area, they must be used to strangers.'

'You want anything in particular?' Zac said.

'I could wear a hat. I'll put a paper bag over my head, if you like. Jesus, just put me in the bloody boot and drive me around for half an hour. Can't you see, I want *out* of here? I want to go home.'

'Another paper? A magazine?'

'Are you listening to me?'

'What about food? You fancy a curry tonight?'

'No, I don't want a fucking curry. I want a pizza, with my wife and kids. Don't you understand what I'm going through here?'

Zac stood up. 'Where would you rather be? Back in the Royal Hallamshire? You think *I* want to be here? Go on, pack your stuff. We'll leave this morning, if that's what you want.'

Tom looked at him, then turned away with a sigh.

'I'm sorry, Zac. I'm sorry I swore at you. A curry would be very nice.'

'You can sit out in the garden at the back,' Zac said, giving ground a little. 'Get some fresh air. That's not a problem. I'll be back soon.'

It wasn't much of a garden. Quarry would have been a more appropriate word. Hemmed in by stark sandstone cliffs, on which nothing grew except moss and the occasional clump of grass, it was a dark, uninviting little enclave. The soil was thin and infertile, only a few inches thick at best. In places the bedrock broke the surface in rough, angular slabs. There was a small paved patio immediately outside the kitchen door, but no other serious attempt to landscape the area had been made. There were no borders for plants, no tubs or containers, no lawn — not that even grass would have thrived in such impoverished conditions. Where vegetation grew at all, it was entirely wild species or weeds. It wasn't so much a low-maintenance garden as a no-maintenance garden.

Tom studied it from the kitchen window. Its aspect was south-easterly, but because of the surrounding high rock walls almost the whole area was in shade for most of the day. Tom pulled open the door. The sky might have been blue, the sun shining, but the air had a cold edge. It still smelt of the rain and mist that had only just dissipated. Make the most of the respite, he thought. Around here it won't be long. He stepped out on to the patio.

There was nowhere to sit, as Zac had suggested. No chairs, no bench. But Tom didn't want to sit down. He'd spent three days cooped up in the cottage, most of it slouched in the armchair by the fire. What he needed now was physical activity, the opportunity to stretch his legs, to uncoil the muscles that had begun to atrophy. The garden was small, but it still had more space than the living room of the cottage. Tom walked along the back of the house, past the open lean-to shed where logs were stacked in neat piles, then circled out around the garden, skirting the base of the rock walls. He repeated the circuit, feeling like a prisoner in the exercise yard. He wasn't normally one for purposeless exertion. He never went to the gym, though the university had one he could have used. The idea of rowing machines and treadmills was anathema to him. He could see no point in exercise simply for the sake of a heightened pulse, a healthier heart. There had to be more to it than that. If he walked, he wanted scenery to look at; if he cycled, he wanted a destination; if he rowed, he wanted a river sweeping by beneath his boat — not MTV on a wall of television screens in front of him.

But today he didn't care that there wasn't much of a view, he just wanted to work his muscles. Round and round he walked. Five brisk circuits, followed by a couple of slower laps, then another five at his original speed. He found it therapeutic, an antidote to the stresses of being confined in the cottage. Only when he became aware of an ache in his side did he stop. He'd forgotten all about his wounds. Conscious that perhaps he'd overdone it, he went back into the

306

kitchen and sat down, waiting for the throbbing to subside.

He wondered — as he had continually over the preceding couple of weeks — what Helen and the children were doing. Hannah and Ben would have been at school, of course. Ben had outdoor PE on a Friday morning. He'd be out on the school field playing football or something. Hannah would be doing maths or literacy. And Helen? She'd be at work. Tom thought about her, picturing her at her desk drawing up plans, writing out building specs. It was almost the weekend. Tom always looked forward to those precious family days. Saturday mornings, he and Helen generally had a lie-in. Well, as much of a lie-in as parents ever got. They didn't set the alarm, but allowed their bodies' natural clocks to wake them. That was the theory, anyway. In practice, the noise of Ben and Hannah getting up, coming in demanding breakfast, always roused them long before they would ideally have chosen to awake. Tom invariably went downstairs to feed the children, to settle them with their bowls of cereal before returning to bed with a couple of mugs of tea, Helen still drowsy. Helen warm and soft beneath the sheets . . .

Tom shut out the image. Not a good thought to linger on, much though he was enjoying it. He stood up and went to fill the kettle to make himself a cup of coffee. It was then that he noticed Zac's mobile phone on the worktop. Zac usually kept the phone with him in his jacket pocket, but he must have forgotten to put it back after making his daily check-in call to let Moran know all was well. Tom pushed the phone to one side, moving it out of harm's way while he spooned instant coffee into a cup and added milk. As he waited for the kettle to boil, his eyes were drawn back to the phone. Why not? Zac used it. What had he said earlier in the week? It was a pay-as-you-go phone. It couldn't be traced. You just had to be careful what you said, avoid anything that Echelon might lock on to.

Tom reached out and fingered the phone, toying with the idea. Was there any risk? If the phone couldn't be traced, couldn't be linked to him, then surely it was safe. There was unlikely to be a tap on Helen's office phone and, besides, it wasn't going to be a long call. He wanted to speak to her. He needed to speak to her. He picked up the phone and punched in Helen's direct number.

'Tom!' she exclaimed when she heard his voice. 'Oh, my God, are you OK? Where are you? No, don't answer that. Is everything all right?' Her voice cracked. She sounded as if she were going to cry. 'Oh, Tom.'

'I'm fine,' he said.

'You're safe?' He could hear her sniffing back the tears.

'Yes, I'm safe. How are you?'

'I'm OK. You shouldn't have called.'

'I had to. How are the children?'

'They're fine. Tom, we shouldn't be doing this. What if they're listening.'

'I'll be quick. I miss you.'

'Me too.'

'I'm going mad here. How much longer is

this going to go on?'

'I don't know.'

'Have you heard anything from — you know, our friend, the big man?'

'No.'

'He said he'd keep you informed.'

'I've heard nothing. We shouldn't linger, Tom.'

'Helen . . . ' This was difficult. He wished he hadn't called.

'I know,' Helen said intuitively. 'You don't have to say. Now go.'

'Yes, you're right.'

'Bye.'

The line went dead. Tom put the phone back down on the worktop and stared at it for a moment, as if hoping it might ring. That Helen might press 'dial back' and he'd be able to say all the things he'd intended to say. He hated phones. He hated communicating by words alone; distant, detached voices saying nothing to each other. He needed to see a face, to see eyes, expressions. To be able to touch and hold.

It had been a mistake. He'd thought it would make him feel better, but all it had done was depress him. He picked up the kettle and poured hot water into his cup, stirring the coffee with a spoon. He was angry with himself for being so stupid. The kitchen door was still open. He went out on to the patio with his coffee. A dark cloud was passing over the sun. He saw more black clouds behind it. As he looked up, it began to spit with rain.

★   ★   ★

'You know something,' Moran said. 'I'm beginning to wonder if we're on the right track at all.'

Russell helped himself to coffee from the cafetière on the table. They were in the box at Moran's office.

'Oh, yes?' Russell said.

'I've received more information about the Echelon listing of Danny Shields's name. The name was only placed on the system in February 2003.'

'As recently as that?' Russell was surprised.

'The question is,' Moran continued, 'why then? Shields was killed in June 1984. Why was his name only made a keyword almost two decades later?'

'Did Echelon exist in 1984?' Russell said.

'Not in its present form. But yes, the system existed. Echelon is just the name of the most recent software package. The NSA started building its global eavesdropping network back in the late 1960s, when the early INTELSAT satellites were put into orbit. First in America, at Sugar Grove, West Virginia, and Yakima, in Washington State. They built these huge dishes for intercepting satellite communications. Then they expanded the network to cover the rest of the world. They've now got listening stations in New Zealand, Australia, Japan, Puerto Rico and two in the UK — at Menwith Hill, in North Yorkshire, and Morwenstow, in Cornwall.

'Morwenstow is ostensibly GCHQ's monitoring station, but it was built largely with NSA money. Why Cornwall? Because, rather conveniently, only sixty miles away, also in Cornwall, is BT's commercial satellite ground station at Goonhilly Downs. BT transmits the messages, while just down the road GCHQ listens in to them.'

Moran's lip curled cynically. 'George Orwell would have loved it. But to get back to Danny Shields, what happened in February 2003 that made someone decide to make his name a keyword on Echelon? It must have been something pretty significant. The keyword list is big, but it's not that big. They keep it reasonably tight. They can monitor millions of communications, but at the end of the day some pen-pusher in Cheltenham or Fort Meade has to analyse the data, actually read the transcripts. So they only want the really important stuff.'

'Ibbotson?' Russell suggested. 'Was he a Cabinet minister then?'

'I did some checking,' Moran replied. 'He didn't join the Cabinet until the summer reshuffle in July 2003.'

'But he was a junior minister before that. A rising star. Someone the government would want to protect.'

'The Shields case was long dead and buried by then. Who was going to reopen it? What did either Ibbotson or Special Branch have to fear at that point?'

'Exposure?' Russell said. 'They were frightened that Ibbotson's role in the strike was going to be made public?'

'Made public by whom? Only Special Branch

311

— and almost certainly MI5 — would have known that Ibbotson was an informer. If they wanted to embarrass Ibbotson, they'd have leaked the information to the press long before 2003. Besides, I don't think it's something they would ever do.'

'No?' Russell said sceptically.

'Well, look at it from their point of view,' Moran said. 'MI5 has a file on Ibbotson containing compromising material. What would you do in their shoes? Leak it, force the bloke to resign and get someone else in his place — maybe someone worse, someone more principled? Or let him know you've got the file and exert a bit of subtle pressure on him?'

'Blackmail him, you mean?' Russell said.

'Nothing so crude or overt. You don't make demands, you just let him work out what course of action is in his own best interests — and that's something every politician knows how to do.'

Russell gave a humourless guffaw. 'You have a point.'

'I looked up Ibbotson's track record. Before he went to Trade and Industry as Secretary of State, he was Minister of State at the Home Office, with responsibility for — among other things — MI5. While he was there he gave Five more power than they'd ever had before — despite all the evidence showing that they couldn't organise a piss-up in a pub. He increased their budget, let them empire build, gave them carte blanche to snoop on us all, permitted them to snatch powers away from the police who, whatever you think of them, are at least publicly accountable. Anti-terrorism, organised crime, drugs, intelligence and surveillance, you name it, Five now have a finger in the pie. Ibbotson is the best friend they've ever had.'

'Doesn't that give them all the more reason to protect him then? To go after Tom because they think — erroneously — that he might be a threat to their creature.'

'But Tom wasn't a threat back in February 2003,' Moran said. 'What's this all about? We know that Ibbotson can't have killed Shields, so what exactly *was* he guilty of during the strike — betraying his workmates, his friends in the working-class movement? Please, that's not news. That's what they've all done. Giving up their class allegiances, their socialist principles, is an essential requirement for any New Labour minister. Think back to 1984. Arthur Scargill was the devil incarnate to middle England during the strike. Ibbotson doesn't represent a mining constituency, he has a safe seat in the Midlands. The revelation that he was stabbing Scargill in the back during the strike would probably increase his vote, boost his popularity. The *Daily Mail* would hail him as an English patriot, a folk hero. What could possibly be revealed that could really do Ibbotson irreparable harm?'

'You think we're barking up the wrong tree?' Russell said.

'I'm puzzled,' Moran said. 'Three questions worry me. One, why was the name of an obscure miner put on the Echelon keywords list? Echelon is used to identify serious threats to national security. I can't see anything so far to put Shields in that category.

'Two, why that particular date, February 2003? What happened then? What was the trigger for putting the name on the list?

'And three, something we haven't touched on yet. Why was the name put on the list by Menwith Hill?'

'Menwith Hill? You're saying the Americans listed Shields's name?'

Russell knew that the listening station at Menwith Hill was run entirely by America's National Security Agency. It was called RAF Menwith Hill but that was just a front. The RAF had nothing to do with it. The base wasn't marked on any Ordnance Survey map. Never had been. That was supposedly to stop the Soviets finding out about it during the Cold War, but of course the Soviets always knew where it was. The real reason it was kept off maps — and still was — was to stop the *British* finding out about it — a ludicrous, utterly pointless bit of official subterfuge considering you couldn't miss the place. It was on a public main road, just outside Harrogate, a vast sprawl of domes and antennae — a corner of an English field that was forever America.

Moran nodded. 'According to my source, and he's always been reliable in the past. But why? Why would the Americans be interested in a British miner who was killed during a strike twenty years ago? It doesn't make any sense to me.'

They were silent for a time. Russell sipped his coffee.

'Maybe there's more to the case than we realise?' he said.

'Maybe,' Moran said, but he didn't sound convinced. 'There's another possibility, though. We've got the wrong Danny Shields.'

19

Zac carried the bags of shopping into the kitchen and dumped them on the table. Tom drifted in after him and peered inquisitively into the bags like a child inspecting his Christmas stocking. Seeing what was there. Pulling items out and examining them. This is what I've become, Tom thought. This is what this place has done to me. The highlight of my day is the arrival of the groceries.

Zac was removing the cold items — the milk, some packets of ham and cheese — and stowing them away in the fridge.

'It's raining again,' he said.

'I noticed,' Tom replied grimly.

'Not much. Just a shower, I reckon.'

Tom took a packet of chocolate digestive biscuits from a carrier bag and opened it, helping himself to a couple before he even got the packet to the cupboard. He was eating more than he usually did. Nibbling constantly between meals. It was the boredom that did it.

'I brought you a paper,' Zac said.

'Thanks.'

Tom put a loaf of sliced wholemeal away in the bread bin next to the toaster.

'You want a coffee?'

'Why not?'

Tom went to the sink to fill the kettle. When he turned round he saw that Zac had picked up

316

his mobile phone from the worktop.

'You left it behind,' Tom said.

'It's on stand-by.' Zac was frowning. 'You haven't used it, have you?'

'Well . . . ' Tom found he couldn't meet Zac's gaze.

'Who did you call?' There was a sudden urgency in Zac's voice. '*Who did you call?*'

'My wife.'

'At home?'

'No, at her office.'

'Jesus! When? How long ago?'

'You said it was untraceable.'

'The phone can't be traced. But calls from it can be.'

'You think they're tapping Helen's work line? Why would they do that?'

'They don't need to tap her line. Echelon has a voice-recognition capacity. If the spooks have a recording of your voice — which they do from the tap on your home phone — they can get the computers to pick it out from all the millions of other communications they're monitoring, and pinpoint your exact location.'

Tom stared at him. 'Shit, I didn't — '

'When did you call?'

'I wasn't on for long. I was careful what I said.'

'*When?*' Zac was angry now. Tom had never seen him so roused.

'About an hour ago.'

'Christ! An hour?'

'Maybe less. Look — '

'Get your things.'

'What?'

'Your things. Get them packed.'

Zac spun round and ran through into the hall. From a low cupboard on the floor he took a pair of binoculars, then he went out to the front of the cottage and scrambled up on to the bluff at the side of the drive. He was high enough to see right down into the valley, to see the lower section of the road that led up to the cottage. He lifted the binoculars to his eyes and focused them on the valley floor.

There were vehicles moving along the main road towards Llyn Gwynant. A lorry, then a couple of cars. Which way would they come? Zac wondered. From the north-east? Or from the south-west? Probably both. They'd take no chances. They'd cast the net wide, then tighten it all round — attack from the front, with another unit waiting in the rear to cut off any path of retreat. The only question was when? How soon would they get there? An hour wasn't long. Snowdonia was remote, far away from any major centre of population. Zac saw a glimmer of hope, which quickly vanished beneath a cloud of realism. They'd have helicopters, cars waiting for them. Maybe an hour was all they needed.

Zac saw them.

Two dark-blue saloons moving fast along the road past the lake. Something about them — their speed, their convoy formation that seemed to indicate they were travelling together — told him he was right. He kept his binoculars trained on them. At the lower end of the lake he lost sight of them for a moment, a spur of the mountainside temporarily blocking his view.

318

He glanced up. The rain had stopped. The sky was clearing, the clouds breaking up. Just our bloody luck, he thought. The day it happens, we lose our cover. He knew they'd have a satellite in position. He almost smiled — for the camera in geostationary orbit a hundred miles above him.

The cars were racing back out into the open now. Zac studied them through the binoculars. There were two men in each car. Was this the whole team, or just the vanguard? Were there others already taking their places in the rear? Zac continued watching, resisting the overwhelming temptation to abandon his post. He had to know what they were doing.

The junction was coming up. The gap between the two cars widened. Zac guessed the rear saloon was slowing. He was right. The front car drove straight past the turn-off, heading on towards Beddgelert. The car behind slowed even more, then turned left, over the bridge and up the mountain road.

Zac slid down off the bluff. Where the hell was Tom? He ran into the cottage. Tom was still throwing his possessions into his holdall.

'In the car!' Zac ordered.

'I've just got to — ' Tom began.

'Now! They're coming.'

Zac grabbed hold of Tom's bag and ran out. Tom followed.

'The door — '

'Forget the door.'

Zac threw the holdall into the back of the car, then jumped into the front. Tom slid in beside him. The car shot forward, wheels spinning on the muddy drive, then slewed round on to the track. Zac accelerated. His eyes went to the rear-view mirror. Nothing behind them. Not yet, anyway.

'You're sure it's them?' Tom said.

'I'm sure.'

Tom twisted round in his seat.

'You saw them?'

'Two dark-blue saloons. One coming up the hill, one heading down the valley.'

'Can we get away from them?'

'I don't know.'

Zac was going as fast as he dared. He knew every road, every track on the mountainside. He had a detailed map of the area in his head. The car behind didn't worry him so much as the other one. The one circling round, coming up from the south-west. There was more than one road up the mountain on that side. Which way would they come? He had to take a gamble, guess which route they'd choose and take steps to avoid them. But there was the satellite to contend with too. The all-seeing eye in the sky. Was it locked on to them? He had to assume it was. Every move they made would be relayed to their pursuers. The cars he could evade. The satellite was a more implacable foe.

They were traversing the side of the mountain. The track was unmetalled, riddled with cracks and deep potholes. Zac concentrated hard, twisting from side to side to dodge the worst of the obstacles. Still nothing in the mirror, but that was slim consolation. The odds were stacked against them, Zac knew that. Simply running wasn't the answer, just driving recklessly down the hill in the hope that they could somehow get away.

'You got a pen?' he said to Tom.

'Yes. In my jacket.'

'Write down this number on your hand.' Zac called out the digits. 'It's a phone number. You'll need it.'

'Need it? What do you — '

'Just listen. I'm going to drop you off, lead them away from you. Give you a chance to escape.'

'Drop me off? Where?'

'There are some woods up ahead. Dense woods. Plenty of cover to stop them seeing us from above.'

'A helicopter, you mean?'

'Satellite.'

'A satellite can see us?'

'Look up and open your mouth, it can count the fillings in your teeth. It's almost certainly following our movements right now. But it can't track us in a forest.'

Zac touched the brake pedal. They were starting to descend now. The track became steeper, its surface slippery with grit and water. Zac turned the wheel for a corner and felt the car begin to slide sideways towards the drop next to the track. He eased on the brakes, corrected the skid. The car wasn't built for this kind of terrain. He really needed a four-wheel-drive up here.

'When I drop you,' Zac went on, 'get clear of the area. Stay under cover as much as you can.

With any luck, the satellite will focus on me, on the car, and you'll be able to disappear. When you get somewhere safe, call that number and leave a message for Moran. But don't do it yourself. Don't speak on the phone. Get someone else to leave the message. You OK for cash?'

'I've plenty in my wallet.'

'Don't use credit cards or a cashpoint. They can locate you through those too. OK?'

Tom nodded. He was feeling queasy. He was going to be on his own for the first time. He didn't know whether he could cope.

'And you?' he said.

'Don't worry about me.'

Zac wrenched the wheel over for another tight bend, accelerating through the corner. The wheels started to spin again, the rear end of the car slewing across the track. Tom grabbed hold of the door, clinging on as he waited for the car to tumble over the edge. Somehow the wheels held. The car shuddered, straightened up. Ahead of them were the woods.

'Get ready,' Zac said.

He braked and careered off on to another track, this one steeper, muddier than the one they'd left. It was barely a track at all, more a wide footpath through the trees. The ground was littered with leaves and twigs and channels where rain had washed away the soil. The car skidded down the slope, the wheels finding no purchase on the treacherous surface. Zac had the brakes on, but it seemed to make little difference. Slowly, inexorably, the car began to slip sideways off the track. The trunk of a tree loomed up in front of them. Zac pulled down desperately on the wheel. The side of the car grazed the bark of the tree. Zac struggled to control the vehicle. He rammed the brake pedal down. The wheels locked. The car went into a glide, sliding smoothly over the greasy ground. There was nothing they could do. Tom hung on, one hand on the door, the other gripping the edge of his seat. Zac released the brakes, letting the wheels unlock, then gently applied them again. The gradient began to level out. The car started to slow. Zac was back in control. The brakes were biting. The track was almost horizontal now, cutting across the side of the mountain, the branches of the trees overhead blotting out the sky.

Zac squeezed the brakes harder and brought the car to a halt.

'Go!'

Tom threw open his door and hauled himself out, feeling a twinge of pain in his injured side. He started to say something — a thank you, a farewell — but Zac was already reaching across to close the door. The car pulled off, speeding away down the track. Tom looked back. Still no sign of any pursuers, but how much time did he have? He dropped down off the edge of the track and plunged into the undergrowth beneath the trees.

20

Tom slithered down the steep incline, forcing a path through the dense swath of vegetation — huge clumps of rhododendron, thickets of dark holly which clawed at his clothes as he pushed his way past. Brambles straggled low over the ground, catching his ankles, ensnaring his feet in their thorny tendrils. It was dank and gloomy, the canopy of trees, of oak and beech and sycamore, obscuring the sun. It had been raining for days, but the forest floor was surprisingly dry. Drifts of dead leaves, of fallen twigs and shrivelled beechmast crunched and crackled beneath his shoes.

He moved fast, anxious to get clear of the track, to find cover in the depths of the wood. In the heavy silence, he was aware of the noise of his own breathing, a harsh, strained panting sound that seemed to reverberate inside his head as he struggled down the slope. A low branch sprang back and whipped him across the face, stinging his cheek. He held up his left arm to protect himself and felt a sharp pain as another branch snapped back against his injured forearm. His side was hurting too. The exertion, the laboured movement of chest and lungs, the constant twisting motion as he manoeuvred himself through the undergrowth were all aggravating the knife wound. He pressed a hand to the spot. He could feel the surgical dressing beneath his clothes.

Momentarily distracted by the pain, he lost concentration, took his eyes off the ground. His foot caught in a bramble and he toppled forwards. He tried to regain his balance, leaning back into the hillside. But on the loose, unstable surface he lost his footing. His legs shot from under him and he tumbled heavily to the ground. He landed on his left side — his uninjured side — but the impact still jarred, sending a bolt of agony across his lower body. He lay still, gritting his teeth, trying not to move, trying not to even breathe while the pain subsided.

Then he heard the car.

A distant noise of an engine drawing nearer. He rolled over, looking back up the hill. Through the trees, perhaps a quarter of a mile away, he caught a glimpse of a vehicle. A dark-blue saloon moving at speed through the forest. The car disappeared for a moment behind a wall of high shrubs, but Tom could still hear the low-gear whine of its engine. He saw the glint of sunlight on glass, a reflection in the side windows of the car as it raced fleetingly back into view and then was gone again, the engine noise fading away to nothing.

Tom remained where he was for a while. He thought about Zac. How much time had elapsed between Zac's departure and the arrival of the blue saloon chasing him? Five minutes? Certainly no more. Was that long enough for him to get away? Maybe. But Tom couldn't rely on it. If they caught Zac and found he was alone, it wouldn't take them long to work out where Tom had been dropped off. It was tempting to stay in the woods, to lie low for a while, but that was the worst thing he could do. He had to move on.

He sat up slowly. His side hurt still, but the pain was bearable. Very carefully, he pulled himself to his knees, then stood up. His legs felt unsteady. His head was swimming. He waited a moment for the dizziness to pass before he pressed on through the forest.

The steepest part of the descent was over, but Tom still found the exertion draining. He'd been a long time recovering from his wounds, had not done anything so physically demanding for even longer, but he was nevertheless surprised how weak he felt. He tried to keep the pace high, to ignore the aches in his arm, his side and his legs. After ten minutes' hard walking, the gradient began to level out and he found himself in a shadowy glade beside a small stream. He paused to rest for a moment. He had no clear idea where he was. Obviously somewhere on the hillside to the south-west of Moran's cottage. There was a valley below him, he could see traces of it through the trees, and it seemed logical to assume that there was a river in the valley, probably a road too. Staying where he was wasn't an option. But nor was simply walking on and hoping he managed to end up somewhere safe by chance. He needed a plan, or if not a plan, at least a viable objective. Find other people, he thought. Find a village, a town, somewhere he could blend in. Somewhere he could find transport — hitch a lift, take a bus — to get away from the area. He had to get down into the valley. That was where he'd find people.

He stood on the rise overlooking the stream, watching the water cascading away down a narrow, stony channel. He had encountered no footpaths in the wood, no well-worn trails showing him the way to go, but all streams eventually found their way into rivers. This was his guide. Climbing down the slope to the banks of the stream, he began to follow its course as it flowed away down the mountainside and into the valley.

Towards the base of the hill the forest began to thin out. No longer was there an impenetrable shield of branches over his head. Tom kept close to the trunks, moving from tree to tree in an attempt to stay under cover, but soon even that precaution became impossible and he was forced to venture out into the open. He climbed over a dry-stone wall and struck out across a field of grazing sheep. He was acutely conscious of being exposed. If the satellite Zac had mentioned was locked on to this one tiny square of land, then there was nothing he could do to escape its all-encompassing gaze.

He tried not to hurry, to draw attention to himself. Just walked steadily across the field and out through the gate at the far side. He saw buildings ahead of him. A farmhouse, a barn, outbuildings. A woman in wellington boots and a green waterproof jacket was putting a sheepdog into the back of a Landrover. She saw Tom walking into the yard from the fields and stared at him coolly.

'This isn't a public right of way, you know,' she said sharply as he reached her. She had a narrow face, pinched lips that gave her a peevish look.

'I know, I'm sorry,' Tom replied. He smiled apologetically. 'I was up on the hill. I fell. I think I must have twisted my ankle. I took the shortest way down, to get to the road.'

It sounded plausible enough. He knew he was walking awkwardly. The woman wasn't to know that his limping gait was caused by a stab wound to the abdomen rather than a twisted ankle.

'I don't suppose you could give me a lift?' he asked. 'I don't think I can walk much further.'

The woman studied him. Tom realised he must have looked a curious sight. Town shoes, a thin jacket, no rucksack — he wasn't exactly equipped for a hike in the Welsh hills.

'Do you need a doctor?' the woman asked, her expression softening.

'No, I'll be OK. It's not that bad.'

She considered his request for a lift.

'I'm only going to Beddgelert.'

'That'll be fine,' Tom said.

'Get in.'

Tom slid into the front of the Landrover, working out what he would say if the woman asked him any questions. If she wanted to know where he'd started from, where he was heading, if he had a car and where he'd left it. But she didn't seem to be the inquisitive type. She drove in silence down the track, clearly feeling no overwhelming need to talk. Tom was relieved. He was already thinking ahead, to what to do when they got to Beddgelert. He didn't even know where Beddgelert was. Snowdonia was unfamiliar country to him. He knew none of the towns in the area, had only the vaguest idea of the road network. Were there any railway stations nearby? Was there a bus service? He contemplated asking the woman, but decided against it. The less she knew about his intentions the better.

At the end of the rutted track from the farm, they turned out on to a narrow, metalled road. They'd gone only a short way when Tom saw a car in the distance heading towards them. A dark-blue car. His heart gave a jolt. There was no time to wait and see. He had to assume it was one of them. He bent forward and reached down to the floor, pretending to massage his ankle. His chest was pressed to his knees. He was below the windscreen and with any luck he would be hidden from sight when the blue car went past.

'Are you all right?' the woman asked.

'It's a bit sore, that's all,' Tom replied.

'You should strap it up, give it some support.'

'I'll do that.'

He listened. Heard the other car approaching, then pass by. He twisted his head, watching the car recede in the wing mirror. Only when it had disappeared around a bend in the road did he straighten up.

Beddgelert was closer than he'd thought. They turned left at another junction, out on to a wider road, and almost immediately he saw a sign on the verge reading, 'Croeso — Welcome to Beddgelert.'

'Where shall I drop you?' the woman asked.

'Oh, anywhere. Wherever you're going.'

'The village centre, is that all right?'

'That's fine. Thank you.'

They turned off the main road, going across a pretty stone bridge which had thick ivy growing up its arches and over the parapets. The Landrover pulled in fifty yards beyond the bridge and Tom got out, thanking the woman again before she drove off. He could tell at a glance that Beddgelert was a tourist centre. Hotel, guest-house and B&B signs were everywhere. There were cafés, tearooms and shops selling ice cream and picture postcards.

Tom felt instinctively that he should get off the street. He was too visible, too obvious to any passing car or pedestrian. But where to go? There were plenty of pubs and cafés. He could go into one and wait. But what was he waiting for? The last thing he wanted to do was prolong his time in the village. He considered going back across the bridge to the main road and trying to hitch a lift, but rejected it as too risky. Standing in the open at the side of the road he was too vulnerable. What if one of the blue saloons happened to drive past? What if he . . . ?

Jesus Christ! There was one of them. Coming over the bridge. Tom ducked swiftly into a shop, concealing himself behind a rack of paperback books. The car came crawling slowly past. Did they know — or guess — he was there, or were they simply driving around on the lookout? There were two men inside the car. Tom recognised them from the Royal Hallamshire — from the night Zac had come to get him. He wondered where Zac was, whether he had

330

managed to shake off his pursuers.

Tom peeped out through the shop door. The blue saloon had disappeared from sight up the street. Across the river, on the main road, he saw a small single-decker bus come round the corner and pull in at a stop. Straining his eyes, he could just read the destination board on the front of the bus — Betws-y-Coed. That would do him. They'd passed through Betws-y-Coed on their way from Sheffield.

Tom stepped out of the shop and stumbled awkwardly over the bridge, the ache in his side slowing him up. He was only halfway across when the bus pulled away and headed off up the main road. Tom slowed, but kept going, walking up to the bus stop and examining the timetable fastened to the post. He checked his watch. It was just after one. How had it got so late? The next bus to Betws-y-Coed wasn't until 14.30. An hour and a half, that was a long time to wait. Then he noticed that there was a bus in the opposite direction, to Caernarfon, at 13.24. That made more sense. But what to do for the next twenty minutes? Waiting at the bus stop didn't seem wise. He needed somewhere to hole up. He looked around. On the other side of the river was a row of buildings: a café with a terrace, an art gallery, a wood-craft gallery and — right at the end — public toilets. The perfect place to hide.

Tom went back over the bridge and walked down the lane beside the river. On the wall of the woodcraft gallery was a fancy plaque inscribed, 'Many scenes for *The Inn of the Sixth Happiness* were filmed in this area in 1958. The film, starring Ingrid Bergman, told the story of Gladys Aylward who worked as a missionary in China.' Tom remembered the film from television, remembered also some story he'd once heard about how all the Chinese restaurants on Merseyside had closed down for a few weeks while their staff went to North Wales to play extras in the movie. He looked up at the hills surrounding the village, the clumps of rhododendrons on the slopes, the rocky outcrops and damp, misty air. It took a little imagination, but he could see how the area — with some judicious angling of cameras — might have passed for rural China.

The plaque, according to a further inscription, had been unveiled in May 2004 by Burt Kwouk, who had co-starred in the film. Burt Kwouk? Tom thought as he walked past the gallery. Didn't he play Kato, Inspector Clouseau's insane oriental manservant in the Pink Panther films? For an instant he had a ludicrous vision of Burt Kwouk chasing Peter Sellers around Beddgelert, leaping out on him unexpectedly from doorways, Sellers shouting, 'Not now, Kato,' in his absurd cod-French accent.

He went inside the public conveniences, the door marked 'Dynion — Gents', screwing up his nose as the familiar pungent scent of urine and disinfectant assaulted his nostrils. There was a urinal against one wall and three cubicles, all unoccupied. Tom went into one of the cubicles and locked the door. The stench of urine was stronger in here than outside. There was piss on the floor all around the bowl, more liquid on the seat. Tom pulled down the seat lid. It wasn't much cleaner. He couldn't bring himself to sit down on it, even fully clothed. Instead he leant back on the wall and glanced at the graffiti scrawled on the back of the door. At least he had something to read.

The time passed slowly. The overpowering smell turned his stomach, almost making him gag. There was a window above the bowl but — as he discovered when he attempted to open it — it had been nailed shut, presumably to deter vandals, though why anyone would want to break into such a stinking cesspit of a place was beyond him. Only when the main door was opened did any fresh air blow in to dilute the noxious atmosphere. And that had its drawbacks, for it meant that someone wanted to use the toilets. Each time he heard the door bang open, the footsteps on the tiled floor, Tom held his breath, waiting for whoever it was to try the handle of the cubicle. Once someone did and Tom growled testily, succeeding in driving him away.

At 1.20 he emerged from the toilets and walked swiftly across to the bus stop, inhaling deeply to flush out his contaminated lungs. A couple of other people were waiting at the stop. Tom stood in line behind them, the tension in his belly only easing when he saw the yellow and white bus swing round the corner and pull in to the kerb.

He bought a single to Caernarfon and found a vacant seat near the back of the bus. He slouched down low against the window, his collar pulled up, his chin tucked into his chest, half expecting someone to come on to the bus and haul him off. For a couple of minutes the bus waited at the stop, the engine still turning over. Tom kept his gaze fixed on the floor, listening to the passengers around him conversing, some in English, some in Welsh. Finally, the door hissed shut and the bus pulled out on to the road, heading north-west towards the coast.

★ ★ ★

The journey took a little over forty minutes, the bus winding its way along the valleys, mountains rising steeply on both sides, until quite suddenly the road emerged above the coastal plain and began a gentle descent into Caernarfon. Below, in the distance, were the greyish waters of the Menai Straits and, beyond them, Anglesey, green and flat, not a mountain to be seen.

From the bus station, Tom walked into the centre of the town. Outside the massive stone walls of the castle was a square full of market stalls and shoppers. Tom found a bench at one end of the square, by the entrance to the pedestrianised main shopping area, and sat down to think. The castle was an impressive sight, but the rest of the view was singularly unprepossessing. The same drab chain stores as you got in England — Woolworths, Boots, W. H. Smith — and the same ubiquitous banks and building societies. Even the smell, of baked potatoes and burgers, was the same. Only the bilingual signs — Parth Cerddwyr, Pedestrian Zone; Stad

Fasnachwyr, Estate Agent; Swyddfa'r, Post Office — told him he was in Wales. The signs, and the voices around him speaking Welsh, their incomprehensible conversations broken up by the occasional jarring phrase in English.

Tom held out his palm, studying the telephone number he'd written down. Call it and leave a message for Moran, Zac had said. But don't speak on the phone. Get someone else to do it. How was he supposed to do that? Tom wondered. Just go up to some stranger in the street and ask them to make the call? Tom couldn't think of any other way. He looked around, searching for someone with a mobile phone. There were usually dozens of them around. Almost every place you went these days there were people with mobiles glued to their ears — walking down the street, loitering on corners, sitting in cafés. But not in Caernarfon. He couldn't see a single person using one.

Getting up from the bench, he walked into the shopping precinct, past KFC, Poundstretcher and a shop selling Welsh souvenirs — Welsh flags, garish inflatable green dragons and boxes of 'Welsh' shortbread which looked as if they'd been shipped in from Scotland complete with their tartan packaging. A young man — early twenties, might have been a student — was leaning on the wall next to the Cheltenham and Gloucester Building Society, talking into a mobile. Tom watched him from a distance. When the young man had finished his call and slipped the phone into his pocket, Tom walked over to him.

'Excuse me. I'm sorry to bother you, but I notice you've got a mobile phone.'

'Yeah. What of it?' the young man said guardedly.

'I need to make an urgent call.'

'There's a payphone just up the street.'

'I need someone to help me. I can't make the call myself.'

The young man gazed at him uncomprehendingly. 'Sorry, mate.' He started to move away.

'Please,' Tom said hurriedly. 'I'll pay you for it.' He took out his wallet and removed a £5 note.

The young man looked at the fiver. Tempted, but suspicious.

'What's the catch?'

'No catch,' Tom said. 'Take it. I promise it won't be a long call.' He thrust the note into the young man's hand. Then he held out his palm. 'This is the number I want to ring.'

The young man hesitated. Was this bloke off his rocker? He didn't look like a nutter, but you could never tell. Still, a fiver was a fiver. The young man shrugged, took out his phone and punched in the number.

'Whoever answers, I want you to give them a message,' Tom said. 'From Tom.'

'Tom?'

The young man had the phone to his ear. Tom heard the call connect, a woman's voice saying faintly, 'Yes?'

'I've a message for you,' the young man said. 'From Tom.'

'Tell her I'm in Caernarfon,' Tom said. 'The cottage is blown.'

The young man relayed the message, then listened for a moment before switching off his phone.

'She said call back in an hour.'

'That's all?'

'That's all.'

'Oh.' Tom was disappointed.

'That it?' the young man said.

'Yes, I suppose it is. Thanks for your help.'

'Thanks for the fiver.'

The young man made a quick escape, as if fearing that Tom might demand a refund of part of the money. Tom felt deflated. He'd expected something more, some kind of instant solution to his problems. This was all too much for him. What the hell was he supposed to do? All these precautions seemed ridiculous, the stuff of escapist films and paranoid thrillers, yet he knew they were essential. That was one thing he'd come to realise in the few weeks since this nightmare had begun.

He glanced around, suddenly on edge again. Was someone watching him even now? Had they somehow managed to locate him with all their sophisticated technology? Were they biding their time, awaiting the right moment to move in? There were plenty of witnesses around — shoppers, pedestrians, a busker playing Bob Dylan on a guitar — but was that really a deterrent? Tom felt an urgent need to seek cover again, to find a safe refuge. He was tired. He hadn't had anything to eat or drink for hours. A café, that would meet all his requirements. He went back into the square, to a coffee shop he'd noticed earlier. He ordered a sandwich and a pot of tea and sat at a table, eating slowly, drawing the meal out to last as long as possible.

Towards four o'clock, his hour elapsed, Tom went back out on to the street to find another willing helper with a mobile phone. The sky had clouded over and it had started to drizzle, a cold, insistent downpour that Tom — from his recent experience of Welsh weather — knew would probably go on for days. Returning to the main shopping zone, he targeted another young man — a teenager this time — who was sheltering in the doorway of Woolworths. The teenager was texting on his mobile, his thumb jabbing at the keys. Once again a £5 note proved irresistible. The teenager punched in Tom's number and waited, listening to the voice on the line.

'Yeah,' he said and passed the phone to Tom.

'He wants to talk to you.'

'Don't say anything.' It was Moran's voice. 'I'll ask questions. Just murmur or grunt to say yes. You still where you were?'

Tom made an affirmative noise.

'You OK?'

Another grunt.

'Your companion at the cottage. Is he OK?'

Tom couldn't answer that, so he remained silent.

'He's not OK?' Moran said.

Tom said nothing.

'You don't know how he is, one way or the other?'

Tom murmured his assent.

'I've been looking at a map of the place. Be outside the main entrance to the castle at eight this evening. Someone will pick you up. Stay out of sight until then. OK?'

Tom grunted. The phone went dead. He had four hours to kill. Four hours in Caernarfon on a wet Saturday afternoon. The prospect did not fill him with overwhelming joy.

★　★　★

Moran was troubled. This wasn't supposed to happen. He'd been so sure about the cottage, so confident it was secure. What had gone wrong? How in God's name had it been blown? Not that the cottage was his main concern. Losing it was inconvenient, annoying, but he'd soon find another remote hideaway. The people were the problem. Whitehead was safe. That was something. But what about Zac? Moran was worried about Zac. He'd tried his mobile a couple of times but got no reply. Nor had Zac reported in. That was disturbing. Moran knew he'd get a better picture when he brought Whitehead in. That was the next problem. Who did he send? It was the kind of job he'd normally delegate to Zac. Annie would have been his second choice. But she was compromised. The debacle in Cheltenham had seen to that. She was a known face now. The spooks had her description, even though they didn't know her identity. It was far too risky to send Annie.

He could go himself, of course, but that, if

anything, was even more fraught with danger than using Annie. Moran knew he was probably under surveillance. At any rate, it was sensible to assume that he was being watched. Going to Wales would have been a rash move. So who did that leave? What he needed was someone anonymous, reliable and absolutely trustworthy.

★   ★   ★

Staying out of sight in an alien city wasn't easy. Tom wondered about finding another public convenience and locking himself in again, but his experience in Beddgelert put him off the idea. Twenty minutes in a toilet was one thing, but four hours?

He killed some time in a couple of shops, just wandering around pretending to look at price labels, then went down towards the harbour. He found a pub close to the waterfront and went inside, ordering a half of bitter which he nursed carefully for more than an hour before moving on to another pub. This one was more crowded, a lot of young people drinking in groups. Tom hid himself away in a corner, eking out a second half of bitter until it was nearly eight o'clock.

It was dark as he made his way over to the castle. Street lamps shimmered on the surface of the Afon Seiont as it flowed out into the Menai Straits. Across the water the shoreline of Anglesey was punctured by tiny pinpricks of light from isolated houses. There was a damp chill in the air. On the wall of one of the buildings was a CCTV camera. Normally Tom

340

would have walked by it without noticing it was there, but he had become more observant in recent weeks. Zac was right. There was almost nowhere in any town centre where you could evade the gaze of these prying cameras.

Outside the main entrance to the castle, he stopped and waited. Almost on the dot of eight, a car pulled up in front of him. The driver wound down her window.

'Hello, love,' said Mrs Moran. 'Hop in the back and lie down on the floor.'

21

The moment they walked into the house, Tom knew it didn't belong to Mrs Moran. The bare floorboards in the hall told him that. Mrs Moran, he guessed, would have had a carpet, probably something patterned and deep-piled. The sitting room supported his theory. More bare floorboards around the edges, a worn but still colourful rug in the centre. Turkish, or maybe Indian, Tom reckoned. There was a bright Impressionist print over the fireplace, shelves of books in the chimney alcoves and a futon against the wall draped with an ethnic-looking blanket. It was a woman's house, Tom was sure, but a much younger woman than Mrs Moran.

As if to confirm his conclusion, there were footsteps out in the hall and a girl walked in. She was slim and lithe, with spiky black hair and a silver stud in her nose. She was wearing a loose black top and jeans, a pair of flat black pumps — like a child's plimsolls — on her feet. Tom recognised her as the driver of the car the night he'd fled the hospital.

'Hi,' she said.

'This is Annie,' Mrs Moran said. 'Hello, love.'

'You staying?' Annie said.

Mrs Moran shook her head. 'It's late for me, I ought to get off home. Dave'll be over soon.' She turned to Tom. 'Annie will take care of you now.'

Tom   clasped   Mrs   Moran's   hand   tight.

'Thanks for everything.'

Mrs Moran gave him a pat on the arm.

'You look after yourself.'

'You want a drink?' Annie asked when Mrs Moran had left.

Tom nodded. 'You got something strong?'

'Come into the kitchen.'

The kitchen overlooked the small yard at the rear of the house. It was dark outside, but Tom could see the brick walls, a few terracotta pots of plants in the light from the kitchen window. There was no blind or curtains. Annie opened a cupboard and took out a bottle of brandy. She poured Tom a large shot.

'You hungry?'

'A bit.'

'Toast OK?'

'Yes, thank you.'

Annie cut a couple of slices of wholemeal bread and popped them into the toaster. The kitchen smelt of coffee and spices — a subtle blend of aromas that reminded Tom of the wholefood grocery near the university where he often bought provisions in his lunchtime or after work. Work? Lunchbreak? he thought. Distant memories of a different world.

He took a sip of his brandy, letting it trickle down slowly, burning his throat.

'You OK?' Annie asked. She was studying him closely.

'Tired, that's all.'

'You can get to bed soon.'

'I'm staying here?'

Annie nodded.

'Is this your house?'

'No, I just rent a room from a friend. It's her house, but she's away for a few days. You can have her bed.'

'She won't mind?'

Annie smiled dryly. 'You're not the first bloke to sleep there.'

She spread butter on his toast. Tom accepted the food gratefully. He'd eaten nothing since four that afternoon and it was now — he glanced at his watch — gone midnight. The drive from Wales had taken four hours. The first half-hour had been the worst. Lying down in the back of the car until they were clear of Caernarfon, but the remainder of the journey — Tom in the front passenger seat now — had still been draining.

Tom was on his second slice of toast when Moran arrived. The private investigator came the back way, across the yard, slipping in quickly through the kitchen door. He pulled out a chair and sat down, unbuttoning his jacket and stretching out his legs.

'You want anything? A beer?' Annie asked him.

'No, thanks.'

Moran was gazing at Tom. Tom knew this was going to be an unpleasant few minutes. However you looked at it, the blame for the entire sorry mess rested on his shoulders alone. He wanted to get that off his chest right at the beginning.

'I was stupid,' he said. 'I'd seen Zac using the phone. I thought it would be safe for me to use it as well.'

'Who did you call?' Moran asked.

'My wife.'

Moran's body remained still, but his eyes rolled upwards in disbelief.

'Zac told me the phone was untraceable. I called Helen at her office. I didn't think there was any risk. I've never heard of voice-recognition software.'

'Why did you call her?' Moran said.

'To find out what was going on. I was cut off, in the back of beyond. No one was telling me anything. I was going insane. Can't you see, I just wanted to know what was happening?'

'And Zac?' Annie said. 'Where did he go?'

Tom sensed from the tone of the question, the anxious look in her eyes, that she had more than a professional interest in the answer.

'I don't know,' he said. 'He dropped me off in the woods, tried to lead them away from me.'

'They were on your tail?' Moran said.

Tom nodded. 'A dark-blue saloon. Two men, I think.'

'Just the one car?'

'There was a second, down in the valley.'

'When did Zac drop you off?'

'This morning. Around noon.' Tom realised how long ago that was. 'You haven't heard from him then?'

'No,' Moran said.

'He hasn't called in?' Tom rephrased his previous question, hoping — absurdly — that it might produce a different answer.

'No.'

'Where was he headed?' Annie asked.

'I don't know. He carried on down the hill. I suppose he must have gone through Beddgelert,

345

but after that I have no idea where he might have gone. His only concern was to take the heat off me, allow me to escape.'

'Did you see the cars again?' Moran said.

'I saw a dark-blue saloon on the road below the woods, then another in Beddgelert. I don't know if it was the same car. You think they caught Zac?'

Moran and Annie exchanged glances, some fleeting message in their faces that Tom saw but couldn't understand, as if they knew — or feared — something he did not.

'It's late,' Moran said. 'There's nothing we can do now. Let's see what the morning brings.'

★　★　★

Tom lay awake for a time, wondering about Zac, the guilt and the anxiety stopping him from getting off to sleep. Whatever had happened — and Tom didn't want to dwell too much on the possibilities — it was all undoubtedly his fault. He'd been incredibly stupid, unpardonably naive. And Zac was paying the price. Yet, despite his troubled mind, Tom very soon drifted off into a deep sleep. He was too physically exhausted to remain awake for long.

It was 10 a.m. when he came round. He could hear noises downstairs in the kitchen. He still felt tired, heavy-limbed, but he made himself get up. He knew that remaining in bed, far from alleviating his lethargy, would only make it worse.

Annie was at the kitchen table, drinking black coffee. She had dark shadows under her eyes as

346

if she'd had a disturbed night. She started to get up when she saw Tom, but he waved her back down.

'I can do it.'

He added more water to the kettle, reboiled it and made himself a pot of tea. Annie watched him in silence. Tom could gauge nothing from her expression, but he sensed undercurrents. He guessed their root cause had to be Zac.

'He's a friend of yours, isn't he?' Tom said.

Annie nodded. She didn't need to ask who he meant.

'He'll be OK,' Tom continued. 'He's clever, resourceful. I'd put my money on Zac any day.'

Annie looked at him. 'I want the details,' she said. 'Everything that happened yesterday.'

Tom sat down at the table and went through the events of the previous day from the moment Zac had returned from the shops. No justification or apologies, just the plain facts.

'You know the area around there?' he asked when he'd described their descent into the woods.

'Yes.'

'You've been to the cottage?'

'Yes.'

Tom didn't ask — it was none of his business — but he was pretty sure she'd been there with Zac.

'Zac was worried about satellite surveillance,' Tom said. 'That was why he wanted to drop me off under cover of the trees.'

'How far behind you was the car, the dark-blue saloon?'

'A few minutes. I was down the hill, still in the woods, when I saw it come past. I don't think they can have caught up with him, you know.'

'No? Why not?'

'Because I saw one of the cars later, prowling around Beddgelert. They were watching out for him.'

'For him?' Annie said. 'Or for you?'

The click of the back door opening prevented him answering. It was Moran. The private investigator paused on the threshold, looking out into the yard. Watching for something. He waited a few moments, then relaxed a little and stepped inside the kitchen. He turned to face them. His expression was grim. He put a newspaper down on the table and pointed to a short News In Brief item headlined, 'Car Crash Mystery'.

Annie looked at the article first. She turned pale, her hand going to her mouth to stifle an exclamation. She stood up quickly and hurried out of the room. Tom heard her running upstairs. He pulled the newspaper towards him.

'Welsh police are trying to identify the driver of a car which crashed into a ravine in Snowdonia yesterday afternoon. The driver, described as a young white man in his early twenties, was killed when his car plunged off the road in an isolated valley near Beddgelert. There were no witnesses to the accident. The driver was carrying no form of identification and his car was fitted with false number plates.'

Tom closed his eyes. He said nothing. There was nothing to say.

22

Moran walked across to the kitchen sink and stared out through the window into the yard. His hands were curled around the edge of the sink, gripping it tight.

'They took him out,' he said, his voice low and intense. 'The bastards killed him. Either forced him off the road, or stopped him, knocked him out and then pushed him into the ravine. Faceless Ones, Zac called them. Well, I'm going to put a face to them. This is personal. I'm not stopping until I've nailed the fuckers.'

He paced restlessly across the kitchen, then returned to the sink and stared out of the window again, his shoulders hunched, every muscle of his body tensed.

Tom said, 'I want to know everything that's been going on while I was in Wales.'

Moran didn't reply.

'What's happened that I don't know about?'

'Zac worked for me,' Moran said without turning round. 'I was responsible for him. I'll deal with it.'

'No. This is *my* fight,' Tom said.

Moran shook his head. His gaze was still fixed on the yard. 'Not any more it's not.'

'Don't be stupid,' Tom said impatiently. 'This is all about me. It has been right from the beginning. Not you, or Zac, or anyone else. *Me*. And it's still about me.'

Moran said nothing. Tom's irritation turned to anger. He thrust back his chair, stood up and strode across to the sink. He grasped Moran by the shoulders and turned him around forcibly.

'Don't shut me out,' he said fiercely. 'I have a right to know. I *need* to know. Just give me the facts. You're not sidelining me any longer. I'm the cause of all this. It's my life that's been destroyed by these bastards. I'm tired of hiding, tired of running. I want to hit back. But I need your help.'

Tom looked him directly in the eye. 'We have to work together on this. It's the only way.'

Moran held his gaze. Then he gave a nod.

'You'd better sit down again.'

★ ★ ★

Tom stared in silence at Moran, trying to absorb, to make sense of, everything he'd just heard.

'You should have told me sooner,' he said.

'You were in Wales,' Moran replied.

'*Another* Danny Shields? A different one? Is that possible?'

'The email you sent your boss, I've been looking at it again.' Moran reached into his inside jacket pocket and pulled out a sheet of paper. 'The wording is very ambiguous.

' "*Douglas, Re my research — as we discussed last week — I intend to take a closer look at the Danny Shields case. I want to see if I can discover exactly what happened the night he died. The circumstances were highly suspicious and my gut feeling is that there was much more*

350

to the whole affair than was revealed at the time. I suspect, in fact, that there may have been an organised cover-up by the authorities.

''This might be a controversial line of research. Some people won't want me reopening such a sensitive case. I'll need to talk to Danny's relatives, and the police — see if I can get them to disclose their file on the case, though I'm not optimistic about succeeding.'

'Nowhere in the email do you specifically say *which* Danny Shields you're referring to — presumably because your boss already knew that. You talk about the Danny Shields 'case', but you don't say what the case was about. At no point do you mention a miner, or the miners' strike. You give no dates, no details at all. You just mention a death, suspicious circumstances, an 'organised cover-up by the authorities'.'

'So the security services could have thought I was looking into some other case, some other death involving a Danny Shields?' Tom said.

'I think it's worth checking out.'

'How?'

'By hard graft,' Moran said. 'Going through records, databases, newspaper archives. Tracking down all the Danny Shields who get a mention and then seeing if there's anything about them to warrant an Echelon listing.'

'That could take a long time.'

'I can't think of any other way.'

'Where do we start?'

'We? I'm not sure that's — '

'I'm not asking, Dave, I'm telling. From now on, I'm at the heart of this investigation.'

'You should be resting. Those knife wounds — '

'Are just fine,' Tom interrupted. 'I'm not an invalid.'

'They'll still be looking for you.'

'Then we'd better get a move on.'

★ ★ ★

Moran pulled the blind down over the window of his office before signalling to Tom that it was safe to enter. They'd come in via the basement garage, Tom lying down in the back of the Jag, then up the internal stairs to the first floor. Moran walked across to his desk and sat down, switching on his computer. Tom pulled up a chair next to him.

The Google search page appeared on the screen. Moran typed 'Danny Shields' into the search box and they waited a few seconds for the first page to come up. Moran winced as he took in the figure at the top of the page.

'Three hundred and sixty-eight thousand results. Shit, that's not what I wanted to see.'

He clicked on the first entry. It was the personal website of some American student named Danny Shields. The site was only a page long and consisted simply of information on the college courses he was taking that semester. There seemed to be absolutely nothing in it of any significance.

Moran moved on to the next entry. This was even less interesting, being the website of the Minnesota Junior Golf Association, which

352

happened to have a member named Danny Shields who'd scored a seventy-eight in the previous weekend's tournament.

The third listing concerned a contributing editor to *Sportscar* magazine named Danny Shields, the one after that was holiday snaps of the Shields family from San Diego enjoying themselves in Mexico. Then the search engine seemed to give up on Danny Shields altogether and started highlighting the latest film projects of Hollywood actors Brooke Shields and Danny Glover.

Moran sighed. That was the trouble with the net. A plethora of information, almost all of it rubbish.

He clicked on to the second page of results. This was, if anything, even duller and more obscure than the previous page. None of the entries, from a Danny Shields who ran a pool cleaning firm in Palm Springs to a Barry Shields who was marketing manager for an IT company in Sacramento, seemed to be remotely relevant to their needs.

'They're all American,' Tom said. 'Narrow it down to just the UK.'

Moran returned to the Google home page and typed in their new search parameters. This time there were only ninety-eight thousand results.

'Well, that's an improvement,' Moran said dryly.

The top entry was for an adult swingers' club in South Shields, and the three entries below it for a mail-order supplier of S&M bondage gear, a massage parlour and a lap-dancing club, all in

South Shields as well.

'South Shields seems to be something of a hotbed of deviant sexual activity,' Tom said.

'I know,' Moran replied. 'I must go there some day.'

They tried a few more pages, but there was nothing that struck either of them as worthy of closer scrutiny. They had nothing more to go on than a name — Danny Shields. They had no additional information with which to qualify the name, to try to narrow down the scale of their search. It seemed pointless continuing. The results were just a vast, uncollated jumble of data. Without knowing more about what they were looking for, they were unable to reduce that sheer overwhelming quantity of information. Going through the results — even a few hundred — would take forever and would not necessarily get them any further. The Danny Shields they were searching for — and how would they recognise the right Danny Shields when they saw him? — might be number 100 in the results, or he might be number 98,000. They were wasting their time.

'Let's try one of the online news services,' Tom said.

In the search box Moran typed 'Times Online', then, when the site appeared, clicked on 'Archive'. The archive page asked for keywords. Moran typed in 'Danny Shields'. There were boxes, also, for specifying the date range of the search.

'What do you think?' Moran said. 'February 2003, that's the key date — when the name

354

Danny Shields was put on the Echelon list. Let's expand the timeframe a little.'

He set the limits at January 1ˢᵗ 2003 and March 31ˢᵗ 2003. The archive came up with twenty-one articles for the period.

Moran called up the articles one by one. The first was a business page story about a Danny Shields who was the finance director of an obscure manufacturing company in Halifax; the next two were from the sports pages, reports on football matches in which a Danny Shields, a forward for Grimsby Town, had scored goals.

'No deaths there,' Moran said. 'Though watching Grimsby Town must sometimes feel like it. You mentioned a police file in your email. We're looking for something the police were involved with, some kind of criminal investigation.'

He clicked on the next article. It was dated Wednesday February 19ᵗʰ. The headline read, *'Moors Search for Missing Boys'*. The article began: *'Police yesterday launched a major search operation for two 14-year-old schoolboys who mysteriously disappeared while on a cycling holiday in North Yorkshire.'*

The two boys, both from Doncaster, had left home on the previous Saturday, February 15ᵗʰ. Their names: Danny Shields and Rory Hill. They'd put their bikes on the train and gone to York, spending Saturday and Sunday nights in the youth hostel in York. On the Monday they'd cycled to Helmsley, staying the night at the hostel there, then on the Tuesday they'd cycled over the North York Moors to the youth hostel at

Boggle Hole, on the Yorkshire coast just south of Whitby. They'd checked into the hostel, eaten the evening meal provided by the hostel staff, and that was the last anyone saw of them. The following morning the hostel warden discovered the boys' luggage in their dormitory, next to their beds, which clearly had not been slept in. Their bicycles were found to be missing from the hostel bike shed. The warden had immediately called in the police.

'I remember that case,' Tom said. 'It was on the national television news, in all the papers. I don't think they ever found the boys, did they?'

'No, they didn't.'

Moran clicked on each of the remaining seventeen articles in turn. Four could immediately be dismissed as irrelevant. The other thirteen were follow-up stories concerning the disappearance of the two boys. In the initial stages the police inquiry had centred on Boggle Hole Youth Hostel and the immediate area. The hostel was in an isolated cove, almost literally on the beach. There was speculation that the boys might have gone down on to the beach after dark and been accidentally swept away by the tide. But that theory was soon discarded, undermined by the absence of their bicycles.

It seemed more likely that on the evening of the 19th, after dinner, the boys had taken their bikes from the hostel shed and gone for a ride somewhere. But where? The police inquiry was widened. They began to search the coast on either side of Boggle Hole, then moved further inland to the vast, bleak expanse of the moors.

Hundreds of police officers and volunteers were drafted in to help. Helicopters and specially trained dogs were used in the search, which continued for three weeks without success. There was no trace of either the boys or their bicycles.

This was all documented in the newspaper articles. In extensive detail to begin with, accompanied by photographs of the two boys, interviews with their families, with the youth hostel warden, the police and others. But as time went by the articles became shorter. There was less to report. The police were making no progress. When it became clear that Danny and Rory were not going to be quickly found, there was a flurry of speculation that they'd been abducted and almost certainly murdered. *The Times* focused on that particular angle for a few days, then that too ran out of steam. By the date of the last article, on March 28th, almost everyone involved in the case — except the boys' families — seemed to have accepted that it was futile to continue searching.

Moran went back to the Archive home page and changed the date parameters, extending the timespan to the present day. Four more articles on the boys were the result. The earliest was from April 2003, when the police finally abandoned their search, saying there was nothing more to be gained by continuing to scour the moors. The file, however, would remain open. Another report — from September 2003 — dealt with the discovery of a bicycle in a remote gully a few miles from Boggle Hole. It was thought at first that it might have belonged to one of the boys, but a second article closed the door firmly on that conjecture — it was the wrong make of bicycle.

On the first anniversary of the boys' disappearance, *The Times* had run an interview with their parents in which they said they still hadn't given up hope of seeing their children again. It was a heart-rending piece, but no amount of optimism could conceal the underlying reality that Danny and Rory were dead. That was the final article. There had been nothing since.

Moran pushed his chair away from the desk and stood up, walking around the office to stretch his legs and give his eyes a rest from the glare of the computer screen.

'What do you think?' he asked Tom. 'There's a death, two deaths — probable deaths, anyway. There's a police file. Is this our Danny Shields?'

'I don't know.'

Was it what they were looking for? Tom wondered. Was this the Danny Shields on the Echelon computer system? Was this the Danny Shields whose name had torn his life apart? A boy missing on a cycling holiday in North Yorkshire? How could that possibly be of concern to the security services? What could it have to do with national security?

'Let's try a few other places,' Tom said.

He logged on to three more online news databases and typed in the name Danny Shields with the same search parameters. Each time only one story of interest to them was found — the two missing boys.

'That seems to be it,' Tom said. 'The only new avenue for us to explore.'

'It seems a hell of a long shot,' Moran said.

'We don't have anything else.'

Tom went back to Times Online and took another look at the anniversary interview with the boys' parents. Their home addresses were mentioned.

'Can we get a phone number for the Shields family?' Tom said.

Moran nodded. He walked through into the box, rang Directory Enquiries from the phone on the table and obtained the number.

'That line's secure?' Tom said.

'It's got a distortion unit on it,' Moran replied. 'Neutralises any voice-recognition software. And it has a trap to stop it being tapped.'

'A trap?'

'Wire taps are activated when the voltage of your phone line drops as you pick up the receiver. The trap stabilises the voltage on the line electronically so that the tap isn't activated. And if, by some chance, the tap does kick in, then the trap produces 'pink noise' — sine-wave interference — that makes it impossible for the call to be recorded.'

'Give me the number, I'll do it,' Tom said.

A woman answered, Danny's mother. Tom explained why he was ringing.

'About Danny?' Mrs Shields said. Her voice was flat and listless.

'I'm calling from a private investigation firm,' Tom said.

'Private investigation?' Mrs Shields's tone

changed. She suddenly sounded more animated. 'You've found something? Something new?'

A parent never truly gave up hope, Tom reflected. I'd be the same. No body to lay to rest, no conclusive proof, I'd have the same irrational belief that my son might still be alive.

'No, I'm sorry,' Tom said regretfully. 'We don't have any new information. I was hoping that you could help me. I've read newspaper articles about Danny's disappearance, but I was wondering if you could tell me more.'

'What, now? On the phone?'

'If it's convenient.'

'Well, not really. We're just going out for the day.'

'Later then.'

'Tomorrow would be better. I don't like the phone. Where are you?'

'Sheffield.'

'That's not far. You could come here, if you like.'

Tom put his hand over the receiver and turned to Moran.

'I'm going to see her. Can you fix me up with a car again?'

'No problem.'

Tom went back to Mrs Shields.

'How do I find you?' he said.

★ ★ ★

The woman who answered the door looked to be in her late forties. Yet Tom knew from *The Times* articles that she was actually ten years younger

360

than that. She had straight greying hair and a thin, pale face. Her eyes had the dark, hollow look of an insomniac. There was something damaged, almost ravaged, about her appearance.

They went through into the sitting room at the back of the house. Beyond a pair of French doors was a small enclosed garden laid to lawn, the borders around the perimeter sparsely planted with shrubs. Over the fences, on all sides, were more identical red-brick houses with integral garages, only a few yards of open space separating them from one another.

Tom looked around the room — at the thick cream carpet, the pink three-piece suite with patterned braid along the edges of the cushions. Everything was spotlessly clean and tidy. The walls were bare, save for a gilt-framed mirror over the fireplace. Even the television was hidden away inside a mahogany-effect cabinet. It might have been the showroom of a new 'executive' development if it hadn't been for the photographs on the table under the window. One showed a couple outside a church on their wedding day. The bride was unmistakably Mrs Shields. Younger, prettier, her hair a glossy dark brown, her eyes radiant. Others pictured the couple with a little boy, then with the same boy a few years older and a younger girl — undoubtedly his sister. There was another framed photograph of the boy. He looked about twelve or thirteen, his facial features changing, thickening out as he approached puberty. He was smiling awkwardly, as if embarrassed at having his picture taken.

361

'Is this Danny?' Tom asked.

'Yes, that's him.'

'He's a nice-looking lad.' Tom realised at once his slip with the tense and tried to cover his mistake. 'And this must be his sister.'

'Yes, that's Rachel.'

'How old is she?'

'Twelve. Do you have children?'

'Two. A girl and a boy. Ten and eight.'

'Why are you interested in Danny?'

Tom lowered himself into one of the armchairs and waited for Mrs Shields to sit down before he replied.

'It's complicated,' he said. 'We're looking into another case, I won't bore you with the details. Knowing more about Danny might help us with it. I'm sorry to be so vague.'

Mrs Shields gave a distracted nod. She seemed satisfied with the answer, for she moved on without pause to her own preoccupation.

'We looked into using a private detective . . . after it happened. You know, Danny going missing. When the police weren't getting anywhere. We wondered if someone else might be able to find him. But the police had hundreds of people on the case. What could a private detective have done?'

'I'm sure the police did everything they could.'

'Oh, yes.'

Mrs Shields lifted her hand to brush her hair away from her forehead. Tom noticed that her fingers were unsteady. Mrs Shields seemed to be aware of it too, for she put her hands between her knees and squeezed them tight to stop them trembling. She rocked back and forth on the edge of her chair like an autistic child.

'It hasn't been easy,' she said. 'I used to have a part-time job. Secretarial, PA, you know. But since all this happened I haven't been able to work. My nerves, depression.'

She glanced anxiously at Tom, as if she were worried she'd said too much, revealed something too personal to a stranger.

'I got everything out for you,' she went on quickly, a brighter note in her voice that sounded forced.

She stood up and went out into the hall, returning with a cardboard box.

'I kept it all. Cuttings, letters. I thought you might want to look at them.'

She took some folders out of the box and flipped one of them open, pulling out a wad of old newspaper cuttings relating to her son's disappearance. She spread the cuttings out on the coffee table. To Tom, there seemed something peculiar, almost macabre, about this collection of mementoes. But Mrs Shields obviously found it a comfort.

'It was in all the papers,' she said. 'Front-page headlines, on the television news. Look.' She pointed to some of the articles, as if she were saying, 'See how important it was, how momentous, the loss of my son.'

'They all covered it, all the papers, the BBC, ITV.' Mrs Shields sank back in her armchair, her face clouding, a twist of bitterness touching the corners of her mouth. 'They've all forgotten about it now, of course. No one wants to know.

363

It's yesterday's news.'

'Are the police still looking into it?' Tom asked.

'They haven't closed the case, if that's what you mean. The police officer in charge, Chief Superintendent Maxfield, rings us every once in a while. To see how we are. To let us know what's happening. A nice man.'

'And *is* anything happening?'

Mrs Shields looked away, staring out of the window into the garden.

'It's been a long time,' she said eventually. 'You don't give up hope. You don't *want* to give up hope. But it gets harder to believe as the months go by. Everyone else thinks he's dead.' She paused, her brow furrowing. 'Maybe he is.'

'The police have no new leads?'

Mrs Shields shook her head and looked back at Tom. There was a bleak lifelessness in her eyes, like the cinders of a long-extinguished fire.

'There's been nothing. Not since they abandoned the search on the moors. At the beginning I was sure they'd find him. Rory too. I mean, they were sensible lads. Careful. We wouldn't have let them go off on their own if they hadn't been. They wouldn't have done anything stupid. I thought they'd probably got lost. At worst I thought they might have had an accident. You know, a puncture or a crash or something. But Danny would have phoned someone. He had a mobile phone with him.'

'When did you last hear from him?'

'When they got to Boggle Hole. He called from the hostel just after they arrived. Said they'd had a great day cycling over the moors.'

'He didn't say they were planning to go out again that evening?'

'No.'

'And no one saw them?'

'There were people earlier on in the day who remembered them, but no one who saw them in the evening. The police put out an appeal for witnesses, put posters up all over the area, but no one came forward.'

'No one at all?'

'No. It's pretty remote up there. Don — my husband — and I went up during the search. There's lots of fields and woods by the coast, and then just inland there's the moors. There aren't many villages or houses. And it would've been dark.'

'Had they been away by themselves before?'

'They'd been youth hostelling and camping with the Scouts. And they'd had a couple of nights away together in the Peak District the year before, camping out.'

'You must have trusted them a lot.'

'Like I said, they were sensible lads.' Her tone had an edge of defensiveness about it now. 'You've got to let kids off the leash, haven't you? Give them a bit of independence. We molly-coddle them too much these days. You worry. Of course you worry. But I thought they'd be all right. I never thought anything like that would happen to them. I blame myself now. If I hadn't let them go . . . '

For the first time her voice wavered. She blinked a few times, then wiped the corner of her eye with her finger.

'It's the not knowing that's the worst thing,' she said. 'Not knowing what happened to them. I know, I suppose, that Danny's probably gone. The police think that. But they've never found the bodies. I've got nothing to grieve over, no way of saying goodbye.'

She broke off, turning her head away, fighting back the tears.

'I'm sorry,' Tom said. 'This must be hard for you. I don't want to reopen old wounds.'

'You're not reopening them. They never healed. I don't think they ever will.'

'No, perhaps they won't,' Tom said sympathetically, trying to imagine how he'd feel if Ben or Hannah went missing. It was beyond imagining.

Mrs Shields sniffed, rubbing her eyes. Then she leaned forward, removing more papers from the cardboard box.

'People understood what we were going through. You wouldn't believe how kind they were. The house was full of flowers people sent. We had dozens of letters, a lot from complete strangers. Look at them all. It felt as if the whole country was hoping and praying with us. The local MP wrote to us. We had letters from government ministers. Someone from the Home Office came to see us, to see what they could do to help.'

'Someone from the Home Office?' Tom said.

'Yes. Ever such a nice man.'

'Do you remember his name?'

'I remember all their names. It was Templeman. John Templeman.'

366

23

'Read them,' Mrs Shields said. 'I can't tell you how beautiful some of them are.'

She took an elastic band off a bundle of cards and handed one to Tom.

'Mrs Shields, what I really — ' Tom began, but she didn't let him finish the sentence.

'That's from a vicar in Whitby. He wrote very early on to offer his condolences. Isn't it lovely?'

'With deepest sympathy' it said in gold lettering on the front of the card. Beneath the words was a drawing of a posy, and there were more flowers in a border around the edges. Tom couldn't concentrate on the images. He felt short of breath, his heart was palpitating. All he could think of was that name — Templeman.

'Mrs Shields — '

'Have a look inside,' Mrs Shields insisted. 'Go on.'

Reluctantly, Tom opened the card and read the short, handwritten message: *'We are praying for the safe return of your child. Trust in the Lord and He will deliver.'*

'We had a lot of letters from clergymen,' Mrs Shields said. 'They were very sympathetic. Look at this one. This was from a Catholic priest in York. He didn't need to write, but it was so nice that he did.'

She extracted a card from the pile without looking inside it. She seemed to know every item, could probably recite their contents from memory.

'*Our thoughts and prayers are with you,*' the priest had written. '*In this difficult time you must have faith in the Lord. He will hear your prayers and come to your side when you are most in need of Him.*'

Tom put the card back down, making no comment. The wishes expressed in the card were sincere and well-meaning enough, but he couldn't help reflecting that the Lord had not been exactly successful in answering the prayers of the Shields family.

'There are many more like that,' Mrs Shields said, producing another bundle of cards and thrusting them into Tom's hands. 'It seemed to touch people's hearts.'

But Tom wasn't going to be diverted any longer from his central concern.

'This man from the Home Office,' he said. 'John Templeman. What did he want when he came to see you?'

'Mr Templeman?' Mrs Shields had to pause for a moment, adjusting to the sudden change of direction. 'Well, to offer his sympathies, of course. He said the Home Secretary was taking a personal interest in the case.'

'That's all. It must have been a short visit.'

'Oh, no, he stayed some time, I seem to recall. Asking about what had happened. You know, about where Danny and Rory had been, whether they'd said anything on the phone to us. This was early on, when they'd just gone missing. I suppose they were the same questions the police

368

asked really. But that's what the Home Office is, isn't it? They're in charge of the police. He said they'd pull out every stop to try and find the boys.'

'He came just the once?'

'Yes. Well, it's a long way from London.'

'No one else visited you? From the Home Office or any other part of government?'

'No, Mr Templeman was the only one. Here, take a look at this card. It's from a woman, a mother of three, in Orkney. Imagine, writing to us from all that distance.'

Tom took the card, and the others Mrs Shields proffered, and read the messages in them. Some were genuinely moving, full of heartfelt emotion, simply expressed. Others were mawkish or banal, compilations of every cliché associated with bereavement or loss. '*The little darlings will be singing with the angels,*' was one more nauseating contribution, a sentiment echoed in various permutations as the writers assured the Shields family that Danny was undoubtedly in Heaven, where a divine reunion awaited them all.

Tom put the cards discreetly to one side. His brain was seething, his thoughts focused on only one thing: Templeman had been here. The security services had been asking questions about the two boys. Why? Missing children was well outside their remit.

Tom picked up some of Mrs Shield's newspaper cuttings. Maybe there was something in them he'd missed, something the online news archives hadn't mentioned.

'There's a lot to go through,' Mrs Shields said. 'Why don't you stay for lunch?'

'That really isn't necessary.'

'It's no trouble. I'll make us a sandwich.'

She seemed to have recovered from her earlier agitation. Far from upsetting her, talking about Danny now seemed to be a welcome distraction, a catharsis. Over lunch the memories flooded out, of Danny as a baby, as a schoolboy, of the events leading up to his disappearance and everything that had happened since. Tom tried to concentrate on the cuttings, but it wasn't easy.

They ate in the sitting room, their sandwiches on their knees, Mrs Shields delving continually into her cardboard box of mementoes to show Tom another newspaper article, another letter of condolence from a stranger. Tom saw the mementoes now through Mrs Shields's eyes. They were less an unhealthy manifestation of a parent's reluctance to face up to the truth of losing a child than a desperate means of hanging on to him. Mrs Shields knew all too well that Danny was gone, but she needed a life raft to cling to. She needed a reminder that he had once been there, once been her son.

'Here's a couple that really touched us. This one was from Miriam Bishop. She was the peace camp woman. You know about her?'

Tom nodded. On their way across the North York Moors, Danny and Rory had stopped briefly at the informal 'peace camp' that anti-Star Wars protesters had set up near Fylingdales early warning station. Tom had read quotes from Miriam Bishop in the newspaper cuttings. Apart from the Boggle Hole Youth Hostel staff, she was probably one of the last people to talk to the boys.

Tom read the letter she'd sent. Miriam talked in warm terms about her encounter with Danny and Rory and expressed her hopes that they would be quickly found.

Tom handed the letter back. 'Are there any more cuttings you haven't shown me?'

'Not cuttings. But you must read this letter. Another complete stranger who felt moved to write to us.'

Mrs Shields thrust the letter into his hand. It came from a Karen Harding, from an address in Pickering, North Yorkshire. Tom glanced unwillingly at the words. He'd read too many of these emotional missives. He was impatient to get away.

'*Sometimes tragedies happen for no good reason,*' the correspondent had written. '*Sometimes the innocent get hurt. But when there is no evil intent, we must show compassion and find it in our hearts to forgive. I hope you will think of this as you grieve, and try to put aside the pain and anger I know you must be feeling.*'

What was the woman talking about? Tom wondered as he passed the letter back to Mrs Shields. It was astonishing how incidents like these could elicit such a widespread, often irrational, effusion of feelings from people who had absolutely no connection with the case.

'I really have to be going,' Tom said.

Mrs Shields came with him to the door, looking at him with her moist, torpid eyes.

'I hope it's been of some help to you. Give me a call if you need anything else.'

'I will,' Tom said.

★ ★ ★

Moran was slouched behind his desk with a cup of tea and a large slice of what looked like home-made chocolate cake — his mother's, Tom presumed. No wonder he was so big.

'Afternoon snack,' Moran said, taking a bite of the cake.

Tom watched him from the doorway of the office, keeping well back so he couldn't be seen through the window. He'd come in via the basement garage again. He was on edge, a little nervous.

'Let's go into the box,' he said.

Moran looked at him. Then he picked up his slice of cake and finished it as they went into the secure chamber.

Tom told him what he'd found in Doncaster, what Mrs Shields had said.

'There's something there,' he said. 'Templeman tells us that. Only I don't know what it is.'

'Two missing kids,' Moran said. 'If it was something straightforward — you know like an accident or misadventure — they'd have found the bodies by now.'

'We don't know for certain they *are* dead,' Tom said.

'I think we can assume it.'

'What if they were abducted?'

'Doesn't wash. The only cases where kids

372

disappear and don't end up dead is when some estranged parent kidnaps them, takes them abroad. But there's nothing like that here. It was a couple of years ago. If someone took them, they won't still be alive.'

'We need to follow this up,' Tom said. 'Find the national security angle, try to get access to the police file on the case. Do you have contacts with the North Yorkshire police?'

'Outside my area.'

'The officer in charge was a Chief Superintendent Maxfield. I've read the newspaper reports, but there'll be a hell of a lot the press weren't told, or didn't print. I know we're on the right track here. A bit more information and we might be able to see where we're headed.'

Moran gazed at him thoughtfully. 'I'll make some calls.'

★   ★   ★

Detective Chief Superintendent Jim Maxfield was in his early fifties, Tom guessed. A tall man with a big frame that somehow needed more flesh on it. His shoulders were broad, but the body below it seemed out of proportion, as if he'd once been much heavier but had lost a lot of weight. His charcoal-grey suit hung loosely on him, the trousers flapping around his legs, the jacket sleeves dangling down over his hands, giving the impression that he'd borrowed the clothes from some heftier friend. He had a thin, sallow face, unremarkable except for his eyes, which radiated a mixture of

373

shrewdness and integrity. A reliable man, an honest man, Tom thought, as they shook hands.

'Take a seat, please,' Maxfield said. 'Can I offer you a cup of coffee?' He spoke with a gentle North Yorkshire accent, not the hard cadences of the conurbations, but a pleasant rural burr.

'No, thank you,' Tom replied. 'Thank you for seeing me. I know you must be very busy.'

'Your Mr Moran is a persuasive man. We also share a mutual acquaintance on the West Yorkshire force, an old colleague I owe a few favours. That helped. What is he, Moran? Your boss? He was rather vague on that point.'

'Not my boss,' Tom said. 'I suppose, in a way, he works for *me*, but I don't see it like that. He's the private investigator, but I'm doing some of the legwork myself.'

'Keeps the bills down,' Maxfield said.

Tom smiled. 'Something like that.'

He looked away for a second, wondering how he was going to broach the subject that had brought him to North Yorkshire. They were in Maxfield's office at Newby Wiske, the headquarters of the North Yorkshire Police Force. Through the window, Tom could see a car park, a scattering of houses and a distant vista of cornfields.

'You want to know about Danny Shields and Rory Hill,' Maxfield said, starting the ball rolling himself.

'Yes,' Tom said.

'May I ask why?'

Tom hesitated. Maxfield seemed like a man he

374

could trust, but he was wary of trusting anyone too much.

'Would you mind if I don't answer that directly? There's no mystery. It's just that some of the reasons are personal to me, some of them are tricky to explain. Will you believe me if I assure you that my motives are entirely honourable?'

Maxfield studied him intently for a time. Tom felt his eyes appraising him, assessing his character.

'I'm intrigued,' he said. 'Yes, I'll talk to you on those terms. But I'm not sure I can help.'

'Thank you.'

'It was a difficult case. Very traumatic for the parents. And for us. Missing children, no one likes that.'

'You're still working on it?'

'You want the truth? Not actively. In the beginning we poured everything we could into it. That's when you need the resources, the manpower. You have to move quickly, not waste those vital first few hours. They could have been out on the moors somewhere, dying of hypothermia. It was February. The moors are treacherous in winter. If the weather closes in — and it was foggy the night they disappeared — you can easily get lost. The temperature drops — it was below freezing that night — a couple of inexperienced youngsters could easily have died of the cold.

'But as we searched and found nothing, that's when you start to consider the other possibilities, the things you don't want to think about at the beginning. They were kids, but they were competent, old enough to know what they were doing. Danny had a mobile phone. It wasn't with his things at the youth hostel, so we assume he had it with him. Why didn't he call someone?'

'Did you try ringing him?' Tom said.

Maxfield nodded. 'Of course. No answer. Even if one of them had had an accident, say fallen somewhere, broken something, even knocked themselves unconscious, the other one could still have called for help. And what happened to their bikes?'

'Do you have any theories?'

'There are plenty of theories,' Maxfield said. 'Just not many facts to support them. But they're dead, that's one thing we can be sure of.'

'You know that?'

'It's the only rational conclusion you can come to. It's not nice to think about it, but someone killed them, and disposed of the bodies. What else could have happened? That's why we've wound down the investigation. Even if we could spare the personnel and resources — and we can't — there's nothing further for anyone to investigate. We've been over everything countless times. Re-examined the evidence, the statements, all the facts. There are no leads for us to pursue. Basically, we're just waiting for the bodies to turn up.'

Tom shuddered a little at the thought. 'Who would have wanted to kill them?'

Maxfield shrugged. 'Who knows? Some nutter. A psychopath. A paedophile. Maybe more than one man.'

'I've read a lot of newspaper cuttings. Spoken to Mrs Shields. Was there anything you didn't tell either her or the press? About the investigation, I mean.'

'Surprisingly little,' Maxfield said. 'It was an unusual case. There are normally all sorts of things we don't disclose — and I'll say now that if there had been anything like that, I wouldn't be telling *you* it either — but in this particular instance there wasn't much to withhold. We had no witness statements, at least no helpful statements, because after the boys left the hostel no one at all saw them. We had no forensic evidence from the scene of the crime, because we had no scene of crime. They vanished into thin air, leaving absolutely no clues behind for us to work on.'

'Was someone called John Templeman involved in the case?' Tom asked. 'From the Home Office.'

'Templeman? No, I don't know the name.'

'The Home Office never interfered?'

Maxfield eyed him narrowly. He wasn't stupid. He knew this was the crux of the matter, the essential point of Tom's visit.

'They took an interest in the case,' he said carefully. 'I'd expect that. It was very high-profile. There was a lot of public interest in it. But they never interfered, as far as I'm aware. No pressure — no *improper* pressure — was ever put on me by anyone. There was pressure, of course. Everyone wanted a result.'

'No one ever suggested you followed a

particular line of inquiry, or *didn't* follow a particular line?'

'No. Why do you ask?'

'Templeman visited Mrs Shields early on in the case.'

'Yes?'

'A friendly visit, to offer his support, see what she knew.'

'That doesn't surprise me. I know the Home Secretary received regular briefings on our progress — or lack of it. There were questions in Parliament he needed to be able to answer. Sending a civil servant to talk to the family would have made sense — if only for PR reasons.'

'Yes, I suppose so,' Tom conceded. 'Still, it's a little strange, isn't it?' He paused. He'd never met Templeman, but he disliked him intensely. No, hated him. His was the only name he had, the only Faceless One with an identity. The only target on which he could vent his anger. It was time to put his name on the record.

'Strange?' Maxfield prompted.

'To send an assistant director of MI5.'

★   ★   ★

Tom was inside the North York Moors National Park, approaching Helmsley, when he became aware of the car behind him. A dark-blue saloon — he wasn't sure of the make — that was following him about sixty yards away. His pulse quickened. Was it them? How the hell had they latched on to him? They couldn't know the car

378

he was driving — a nondescript VW Polo Moran had borrowed from a friend. They couldn't know he was in North Yorkshire. Could they?

Maxfield? Had Maxfield tipped them off? Tom didn't think so. Maxfield had seemed straight, principled — an old-fashioned honest copper. Besides, even if Maxfield *had* betrayed him, there hadn't been time for the Faceless Ones to get there.

Tom felt his heart rate settle down. He was overreacting, being needlessly paranoid. It didn't have to be them. There must have been thousands of dark-blue saloons on the road. It wasn't particularly strange that one of them should be behind him. He looked in his rear-view mirror. He couldn't see who was inside the car. It kept its distance. When he slowed, the dark-blue saloon slowed too. When he accelerated, it stayed with him. That, in itself, wasn't suspicious. They were on a narrow, winding road. It was almost impossible to overtake. The traffic was stretched out in a long line, every vehicle, by necessity, going at roughly the same speed. The dark-blue saloon was almost bound to remain behind him. And yet . . .

The cars in front began to slow. They were entering Helmsley. Tom saw a crossroads ahead, traffic lights on green. The lights changed — amber now. Tom put his foot down. Went through on red, just squeezing across the junction before an articulated lorry came the other way. He glanced in his mirror. The lorry was covering his movements. Tom braked hard and took the first turn to his left, accelerating away up the road. After half a mile he swung off into a small complex of industrial units, circling round into a yard behind a warehouse where he was hidden from the road. He came to a stop and turned off the engine.

Closing his eyes, he breathed in and out slowly, trying to relax. Was he being stupid, letting his imagination override his reason? Recent experience had taught him to be cautious, but was he taking it too far?

He waited in the yard for twenty minutes, then drove back out, skirting round the edges of Helmsley to rejoin the main road on the far side of the town. He headed east to Pickering, then turned north on to the A169, the road climbing up on to the moors. Five miles on, descending the steep escarpment at Hole of Horcum, he suddenly saw the Fylingdales early warning station on the horizon.

It was years since Tom had last been this way. When he was a child they'd gone to Whitby a couple of times for their summer holidays. He had vivid memories of seeing the radar station's three huge geodesic domes glistening a brilliant white in the sunshine, a sea of purple heather all around them. There had been something beautiful about them, something magical that excused their incongruity, these fantastic gleaming spheres perched on the bleak moorland as if deposited there by extra-terrestrial visitors. But the 'Golf Balls' were no longer there. They'd been replaced by a large, truncated concrete structure which resembled a pyramid with the top chopped off. It was still an incongruous feature in the landscape, but it had no redeeming aesthetic qualities. It was functional, ugly, a hideous scar on the otherwise unblemished surface of the moors.

Tom drove past. The 'pyramid' was less than half a mile away, surrounded by a complex of other buildings, all much lower. He saw the turn-off into the station, the high wire fence with a checkpoint at the gates. A sign read, 'RAF Fylingdales'. Tom had brought an Ordnance Survey map with him. He knew the base wasn't marked on the map, another curious example of the baffling pathological secrecy that pervaded official circles. Was this another instance — like Menwith Hill — Tom wondered, of an RAF base being something entirely foreign?

Running parallel to the road, just off the carriageway, was another fence — this one only a metre or so high — enclosing a vast area of moorland outside the base itself. At intervals along the fence, there were signs reading, 'Ministry of Defence Property — Keep Out'.

A car overtook him — a battered Landrover with mud spattered up its sides. Tom checked his mirror. The road behind was clear. He'd seen no sign of the dark-blue saloon since Helmsley, no evidence of any other vehicle tailing him.

The 'pyramid' was behind him now. The road started to dip down into a broad depression. In the bottom of the depression, nestling among undergrowth and a few stunted silver birches, were a couple of tents. Strung between two of the trees was a large white banner emblazoned with the words 'NO STAR WARS HERE'. This had to be what the newspapers had referred to as a 'peace camp'.

Tom braked. The road was turning to the left, crossing a small beck. On the other side of the carriageway was a dirt lay-by. Tom pulled off the road and climbed out of his car.

The peace camp was only a few yards from the road, on a tiny patch of open land beside the beck. Two ancient canvas ridge tents, their sides faded and mottled by the sun, were pitched a few metres apart. In between, a makeshift canopy had been constructed from tarpaulins slung over wooden poles to form a sheltered area for sitting out. There were two women in it now, squeezed into metal-framed camping chairs. There was a small wood fire burning just in front of them, but it seemed to give off more smoke than heat, for both women were swaddled in several layers of jumpers, anoraks and scarves and wore hats. They had blankets around their shoulders and across their knees. One was reading a book, the other was knitting, her hands half wrapped in a pair of fingerless gloves. They looked up as Tom approached.

'Hello,' Tom said.

'Hi.'

The woman reading the book regarded him warily. She was in her forties. She had a small head and delicate features. The rest of her body was probably built in proportion, but it was impossible to tell because she was so thickly enveloped in clothes and blankets.

'I'm looking for Miriam Bishop,' Tom said.

'I'm Miriam.'

The other woman put down her knitting. She was older than her companion, in her sixties, Tom guessed, with a ruddy, weather-beaten complexion undisguised by make-up. Strands of coarse, greying hair poked out from beneath her woolly hat.

Tom told her who he was, why he was there.

'The boys?' Miriam said. 'What do you want to know?'

'Just what happened that day. If you can remember.'

'I can remember all right. It's not something you forget. I think it was the banner that made them stop — the 'No Star Wars' sign. They thought it referred to the film and came to take a closer look. They were going to fill their water bottles from the beck, but I advised them not to — there are sheep up on the moors, there's always the danger of liver fluke in the streams. I gave them some water from our canister instead, a couple of biscuits too. They stayed and had a chat.'

'About what?'

'They told me about their trip. You could see they were having a great time. Away from home on their own, with their bikes. It was one big exciting adventure for them. They were nice boys. Intelligent, curious, interested in everything. I told them why the peace camp was there, what Star Wars was. Explained to them what's going on at that place on the hill.'

She inclined her head towards Fylingdales. The early warning station was a dark, sinister silhouette on the skyline.

'They didn't know anything about the US National Missile Defence system. Well, they wouldn't, would they? Our government doesn't want anyone to know exactly what they're doing at Fylingdales. The British people haven't been asked whether they want to have a US radar station on British soil. The government tells us Fylingdales is British, of course, but that's just a smokescreen. The Americans dictate what happens there, the radar information goes directly to the North American Defence Command in Cheyenne Mountain, Colorado. The Americans allow us to share a few crumbs from the table, but the NMD system isn't going to protect the UK from missile attack. Its only purpose is to protect the USA.

'And yet it's made us a target. We've rolled over, given the Americans whatever they want — like the good little poodles we are. Does anyone seriously think these rogue states the Americans talk about as such a threat — and they do seem to have appeared at rather a convenient moment, with the Cold War over and the US looking for new enemies to justify their enormous defence spending — does anyone think these states are going to overlook Fylingdales? If they really want to hit North America, they're going to make damn sure they take out the defences first.'

'You told Danny and Rory this?' Tom said.

Miriam smiled wryly. 'They wanted to know. They wanted to know what we were doing out here, freezing our backsides off. I told them it was important to speak out against what you

384

believe is wrong. Most people think we're mad. NMD is going ahead whatever we think. Whatever the British people think. But it's important the government knows that someone objects to what they're doing here. It's important they know that we're watching what they do. Just because no one's listening, that doesn't mean you have to stop shouting.'

Tom looked around at the ramshackle camp — the tatty tents, the sagging tarpaulin canopy, the fraying banner hung between the trees. It seemed a pathetic, ultimately futile gesture of opposition to something that was going to happen no matter what, but Tom admired these women for making it. For suffering in support of their principles.

'How long were they with you?' he asked.

'Fifteen, twenty minutes probably. They filled their water bottles, ate their biscuits, then cycled off to Boggle Hole. That was the last I saw of them.'

Miriam frowned, her face clouding. 'Then *that* happened. I couldn't believe it. It was so awful, so tragic — we overuse that word, but in this case it's right. It really was tragic. They were just boys. Young boys exploring the countryside, having fun, learning to be independent. Why is it always the innocent that get hurt?'

'The boys didn't say anything to you about their plans? What they intended to do in the evening, for example?'

Miriam shook her head.

'I'm sorry I can't tell you more. I only met them briefly. I know the police did everything they could to find them. The search parties were all over the moors. I was in one of them. There must have been hundreds of volunteers searching alongside the police. There wasn't a trace of the boys.'

The younger woman eased herself out of her camping chair and walked across to a Calor-gas stove mounted on a couple of wooden crates. She filled a kettle with water from a plastic container and put it on the burner to boil.

'You want a cup of tea?' she asked Tom.

'No, thanks, I ought to be going.'

'Where are you parked? In the lay-by on the bend?'

'Yes.'

'You're right, you'd better not linger. It's a restricted zone. The Modplods will tow you away.'

'Modplods?'

'Ministry of Defence police. The whole area is crawling with them.'

'They bother you?'

'They tolerate us. They come by every so often — to let us know they're monitoring us. It's amazing how a home-made banner and a few bolshie women can make them piss their pants.'

'The government will close us down eventually,' Miriam said. 'Find some obscure by-law, or create a new one, that says we're not allowed to camp here. They'll send the police in, get them to break the place up, threaten us with jail if we come back. That's how politicians think. They can't stand opposition, can't stand being questioned. They either ignore public opinion which disagrees with them, or try to suppress it. That's what democracy means to them.'

Tom thanked the two women and walked back along the beck to the main road. He couldn't be absolutely certain, but he was pretty sure he knew where Danny Shields and Rory Hill had gone the night they disappeared.

★　★　★

A couple of miles beyond the peace camp, Tom left the A169 and cut across country on minor roads to the coast. The road down to Boggle Hole was narrow and steep, fringed by hedges and fields. In front of him, Tom could see the greyish sweep of the sea, the horizon blending seamlessly into the overcast sky.

A quarter of a mile from the coast he came to a small car park. The road continued beyond this, signposted to the youth hostel, but it became much narrower, a lane barely wide enough for a single vehicle. Tom left his car in the car park to complete this last part of his journey on foot.

The lane was a gentle downhill to start with, then it turned a corner and began to descend steeply into a cove hemmed in by two rocky headlands. Below Tom, to his left, was a deep, wooded valley leading down to a stream. Through the trees, he caught a glimpse of a tall, honey-coloured stone building that he knew must be the youth hostel. The lane had straightened out now, still dropping steeply into the cove. At the bottom end it ran straight out on to a pebbly beach, like a slipway for launching boats.

The hostel was almost on the beach, on the far side of the stream. It was an old converted corn mill that had once been powered by water. There was no sign of the wheel that had turned the millstones, nor the mill race, but in the valley just above the building were the remains of the wall that had enclosed the mill dam. To reach the hostel you had to cross a narrow pedestrian bridge suspended six feet above the stream. Tom went across the bridge, glancing out into the cove. The sea was a hundred yards or more away, but he could see from the waterlines on the headland that the tide came right in, very nearly high enough to wash the foundations of the hostel. It was very quiet, remote. The hostel was the only building in the cove. Tom could hear birdsong in the trees, the roar of the waves breaking along the shore.

There was a concrete ramp leading up around the side of the hostel to the main entrance. On the hillside above it was a complex of dilapidated prefabricated buildings, presumably some kind of annexe to the hostel. Tom walked up the ramp to the main entrance. The door was locked, a sign on it reading, 'Reception open from 5 p.m.'

Damn! Tom gazed at the sign. He'd forgotten that youth hostels were closed during the day. He should have telephoned, made an appointment. But the sign didn't mean there was no one there. He rang the bell beside the door and waited. Rang it again. Nobody answered. Tom looked at his watch. It was approaching three o'clock. Two hours to wait.

He walked back down the ramp towards the beach, wondering if he could kill time exploring the cove. As he approached the bridge across the stream, he stopped dead.

There was a man on the far side of the bridge.

Tom thought at first it must be the hostel warden returning. Then he took in the man's face, features he'd seen before — that night at the hospital. He felt a tight spasm of nausea in his stomach. The man gazed at him implacably, with all the quiet confidence of a hunter closing in on his cornered prey.

Tom retreated, his eyes still fixed on the man. Then he heard footsteps on the ramp behind him and spun round. A second man was coming down the hill from the rear of the hostel. He must have crossed over the stream higher up. The man paused. The corner of his mouth twitched. A sneer, a smile, Tom couldn't be sure which. Then the man came towards him. Not hurrying. There was no need.

Tom glanced back at the bridge. The first man was coming across. No way out there. Nor behind him. Tom did the only thing he could. He dashed across the bottom of the ramp, splashed through the stream where it flowed into the cove, and ran out on to the beach.

24

The two men came after him. Looking back, Tom saw them heading on to the beach. They were an ungainly pair, overweight and unathletic. They ran awkwardly, stumbling on the loose bed of shingle and pebbles that covered the shoreline. Tom felt a surge of hope. He knew he was faster than them, could probably keep running for longer, even in his present injured state. It was only as he raced further out into the cove that he realised his mistake.

There was nowhere *to* run.

The tide was coming in. Coming in fast. Already the headland on the south side of the cove was being washed by the waves. And on the north side the sea was breaking over the rocks at the base of the cliffs, surging into the crevasses, hissing and foaming over submerged boulders. The whole length of the shoreline beyond the headlands was now under water.

Tom came to a halt, staring around desperately. The sea was in front of him. The headlands on either side must have been seventy feet high, their faces sheer and unclimbable. Behind him were the two men. Tom watched them. They'd slowed to a walk. They were close enough for him to see their gaping mouths, their flabby bellies and chests rising and falling as they gasped for breath. They'd realised too. They'd realised he had nowhere to go.

Tom searched for a way past them. They'd split up, spread out to cover more territory. The cove was narrow. There was little room for manoeuvre. Tom knew he'd never outflank them and make it back up the lane to his car. They were slow, but there were still two of them. They'd catch him for certain.

He looked back at the sea, trying to think. The fear, the adrenalin, were urging him to run. His brain felt sluggish, all the blood concentrated elsewhere in his body, in his heaving lungs, his throbbing heart, in the taut muscles of his legs. The water was lapping his feet, curling around the soles of his shoes. Could he swim for it? Too risky. There were rocks everywhere. He could see the lines of them further out in the bay, see where the waves broke over them. Big, rolling breakers leading in a swirling, treacherous sea, the hidden currents beneath the surface as deadly as the frothing maelstrom on top.

He spun round again. The men were moving closer, taking their time. All they had to do was wait. Wait for him to come to them. Or wait for the sea to do their job for them.

Tom felt the bile rising in his throat, an anger starting to seethe, to boil over.

'What do you want, you bastards?' he shouted. 'Who the fuck are you?'

The two men watched him impassively, no emotion, no anything in their faces. Tom looked around for a weapon to fight them off, a rock or a piece of driftwood, but he was standing on a patch of smooth sand. He had his fists, his feet, but he was wounded, in no condition to launch an attack.

Frustrated, shaking with fury, he bent down and picked up a handful of wet sand. He hurled the sand at the men, aware how feeble a gesture of defiance it was, how hopeless, how ludicrous.

The men didn't move. They waited beyond the waterline. The sea was over Tom's ankles now, soaking the bottoms of his trousers. His gaze went to the tops of the cliffs, to the back of the cove, seeking a way out, seeking someone to come to his aid. The landscape was deserted. It was just the three of them on the beach.

Then, away to his right, he saw a slight chance of escape. At the base of the north headland there were still rocks uncovered by the sea — a ledge like a step that was being battered by the waves but had yet to be submerged. If he could only get up on to it. Scramble round the headland into the next bay.

He didn't give himself a moment to consider the risks, just acted on impulse. He sprinted away through the shallows. The move seemed to take the men by surprise. They stood rooted to the spot for a moment, unsure how to react. Then, finally, they roused themselves and lumbered clumsily after him.

The ground near the headland was pitted with hollows and pools, all filled with water. Tom plunged into one, soaking his trousers to the knee. A wave hit him at thigh level, making him stumble. He was wet from waist to toe now, his clothes sticking to his skin in a cold, clammy embrace.

The men were thirty yards behind him, giving chase but only half-heartedly, as if they couldn't quite believe he was going to try to get round the headland. Tom couldn't really believe it either. It was madness. The sea was crashing in with a thunderous roar, the spume frothing, the air saturated with spray. Another wave hit him, washing right over his head and knocking him off his feet. He fell sideways, salt water stinging his eyes, surging into his mouth. His hands touched sand, then his knees. He struggled to stand up. The undertow was tugging at his body, dragging it out deeper. He was just regaining his balance, trying to get his head above the surface when another breaker slammed into him, propelling him in towards the headland. He caught a glimpse of a rock ledge through the cloud of bubbles and swirling sand and thrust out his arms to protect himself. His palms hit the edge of the ledge. He felt a stab of pain as the skin scraped off. He couldn't breathe. His mouth, his lungs, were filling with water. He fought desperately to find the ground with his feet, but the force of the sea was turning him over, thrusting his head even deeper. He went dizzy. He didn't know which way was up and which down. He was choking, blacking out.

Then for one brief instant the water around him seemed to ebb, one wave retreating before the next cascaded in. He felt a breeze on his face, just had time to cough up water and gulp in a mouthful of air before he was tossed against the rocks again. His shoulder hit the ledge, jarring him to the bone, the pain shooting through his injured side. Water smashed into his face. It was like being hit with a spade. He reached out, grabbed hold of a rock outcrop and clung on. The water rolled him over, flipping his whole body on to the ledge as if it were no heavier than a cork. A jet of icy water shot up his nostrils. He gagged, managed to get his head clear of the surface and snatch in another breath. The water was boiling around him, pummelling his body.

He felt rock beneath him, hard and uneven. He scrambled to his knees, steadying himself. Saw a wave rolling over his head and braced himself for the impact. Felt the wall of water collapse on top of him, burying him in a dark, whirling vortex. What little air he had inside his lungs was forced out. He was as limp as a piece of seaweed, twisting helplessly in the current.

He thrust his head above the surface, took a deep breath and staggered to his feet. Another barrage of waves came crashing in towards him. He couldn't see the two men. Didn't care where they were. He had more pressing threats on his mind. He turned round, bowing his head, taking the force of the breakers on his back. A deafening roar filled his ears. The wave picked him up and threw him forwards like a piece of flotsam. He held his breath, his eyes tightly shut, letting himself roll with the wave.

The rock came up to meet him. His shoulder took the force of the impact again. The vibrations shuddered through him. He felt a sizzling pain that seemed to burn his flesh. He reached out instinctively, clawing at the rock, looking for a handhold before the undertow swept him away. His fingers found a crack, hooked into it. The water was rushing back off the ledge, sucking him with it. He held on. The force was like a hawser pulling on his limbs, threatening to tug the joints from their sockets. He clung to the rock, his teeth clenched, his fingertips losing all sensation. One hand started to slip. He held on tighter with the other. His body felt as if it were being torn apart.

Then the sea receded abruptly. Tom was spreadeagled on the ledge, water streaming from his clothes. He twisted his head round, saw another massive wave looming up behind him. He got to his knees. He was weak, exhausted. He couldn't take much more, knew the next breaker would sweep him away. The wave was curling over him. He pushed himself to his feet and scrambled across the ledge, hauling himself up on to the boulders around the base of the headland just as the wave broke below him, engulfing the ledge in a seething torrent. Water poured over the boulders, but Tom was above the worst of it. His legs and thighs took another battering, but his torso and head were clear of the wave. He could breathe, could feel air on his face. He climbed up higher, out of reach of the waves, and clung to a rock until he recovered his breath. The two men had been forced to retreat further back into the cove. They were fifty or more yards away, an impassable barrier of raging water separating them from him.

But Tom couldn't afford to linger. The tide was sweeping relentlessly into the adjoining bay too. There was a strip of beach still exposed, but it was fast being submerged by the pounding waves. Tom could see the houses of Robin Hood's Bay in the distance, less than half a mile away. The sight gave him a renewed surge of energy. He clambered quickly over the boulders and around the headland into the bay. Without pausing, he started to run along the beach towards the houses.

★   ★   ★

Looking back from Robin Hood's Bay, Tom saw that the entire beach was now underwater. He'd run the last twenty or thirty yards with the waves coiling around his ankles, scrambled up the ramp on to the small quay only minutes before the ramp too had been submerged. He gazed around breathlessly. A couple of fishermen stacking lobster pots stopped what they were doing and stared at him curiously. He knew he must have looked a bizarre sight. Dripping wet from head to toe, his clothes drenched, his hair sodden and matted. Ignoring the interest he was arousing, Tom walked across to the road, to a block of public toilets, and went into the Gents. He locked the cubicle door behind him, stripped off all his clothes in turn and wrung them out into the toilet bowl. When he put the clothes back on, they were still damp, but at least they no longer left a trail of puddles behind them. Tom shivered. The immersion had made his body temperature plummet. The knife wound on his side was throbbing painfully. He needed to warm up, get dry clothes. And he needed to recover his car from the car park near Boggle Hole.

What would the two men do? Remain at Boggle Hole, waiting for him to come back for his car? Or come after him in Robin Hood's Bay? Tom didn't know, but his instincts told him to keep moving, to get out of the village.

He went back out into the street. There was a general store just beyond the toilets, one of those typical seaside stores that sold just about everything — buckets and spades, windbreaks, suntan lotion, sweets, groceries, even clothes. On a metal rack outside the door was a collection of sweat-tops. Tom selected one and paid for it, slipping it on over his wet jumper. Immediately he felt warmer.

He walked up the steep hill through the village, thinking hard about his next move. He was on foot, he had no transport. How exactly was he going to get away?

At the top of the hill, near the visitors' car park, he came across a small kiosk with a man sitting inside reading the paper. Parked in front of the kiosk was a minicab with a yellow taxi sign on the roof.

Tom checked his wallet. He had £25 in cash. That wasn't going to get him very far. He really needed his car.

'Is that taxi for hire?' he asked the man in the kiosk.

The man gave him an odd look. 'No, it's just for show. One of them modern sculptures.' He put down his paper. 'Where do you want to go?'

The taxi driver took him back to Boggle Hole, having first draped the passenger seat with a plastic bag to protect it from Tom's damp trousers.

'I made a mistake, got caught by the tide,' Tom said.

'You want to watch yourself,' the taxi driver replied. 'That beach can be lethal.'

Tom didn't contradict him. He was watching the road, keeping an eye out for the two men, calculating what he would do if they were waiting for him at Boggle Hole.

But the car park above the cove was empty except for his own car. Tom looked around cautiously as the taxi driver pulled in beside the Polo. The surrounding area was quite open, mostly fields divided by hedges. There was nowhere another car might be hidden, where the men might be watching for him.

'Would you mind waiting a moment?' Tom asked the taxi driver. 'Then following me back up to the main road.' He handed him a soggy £10 note from his wallet. 'Keep the change.'

'Whatever you like.'

Tom slid out of the taxi and into his own car. As he inserted the key into the ignition, he noticed his hand was trembling. The engine turned over and fired. Tom gripped the steering wheel hard, trying to calm his racing pulse.

The taxi driver stayed behind him all the way back up the lane and out on to the coast road. At the turn-off for Robin Hood's Bay, he gave Tom a parting toot of his horn, then Tom was on his own. He kept to the coast road into Whitby — no short cuts cross country this time; he wanted the reassuring presence of other traffic around him.

From Whitby he headed inland, back towards the moors. He put the car heater on full, letting the warm air dry his clothes.

The drive over the moors was a nerve-shredding ordeal. Tom drove fast, his eyes continually flicking to the mirror, searching the road behind for suspicious vehicles. The sun was dipping low in the sky as he approached the peace camp on Fylingdales Moor. The high concrete walls of the distant 'pyramid' were catching the light, glowing a pale orange. The surrounding moorland, in contrast, seemed unnaturally dark — a dense, black sheet devoid of recognisable features.

Tom was tense. He couldn't take his eyes off the 'pyramid'. It was fascinating, frightening. He could almost feel its emissions creeping out across the heather, enveloping his car, contaminating his body. Only when the early warning station was far behind him, its menacing bulk hidden by the rolling hills, did he relax a little. The road was clear. He'd seen no sign of the two men, no sign of any vehicles on his tail.

He tried to think about something other than the men, to blot out the traumatic incident at Boggle Hole. Focus on the boys — on Danny and Rory. He could guess, he could speculate about what had happened to them, but his theories were valueless without evidence, without proof. And he had no proof. Two innocent young boys had died. Their bodies had never been found. A gut feeling about what exactly had occurred wasn't enough. He needed more . . .

Innocent . . .

It hit him suddenly.

Innocent boys . . .

What had Miriam Bishop said? *Why is it always the innocent that get hurt?* Where had Tom heard that phrase — or something similar — before? *Sometimes the innocent get hurt.* It had been in a letter — one of the letters Danny Shields's mother had shown him. Tom remembered it now. It had been an odd letter. Something about it had been different from all the others. Tom tried to recall the contents. What else had it said? Something about when there is no evil intent, we must show compassion and find it in our hearts to forgive. Tom hadn't given it much thought at the time. It had seemed just another self-indulgent letter from someone with no connection to the case. But now he wondered. *When there is no evil intent.* What did that mean? What did the letter writer know about anyone's intentions? What *could* they have known? The writer had been a woman, Tom remembered. From an address in Pickering. He was descending the hill towards Pickering now. *When there is no evil intent.* The phrase troubled him. He was on the spot. What did he have to lose by checking it out?

He turned off the main road into the centre of the town. Dusk was falling. The shops were closed. There were few people about. Near the top of the main street Tom found a payphone. He rang Mrs Shields in Doncaster, asked her to dig out the letter and give him the name and address of the sender. He waited impatiently for her to find the information. He knew he was taking a risk by phoning. Echelon would pick up his voice and pinpoint his location, but did that really matter now? The Faceless Ones knew where he was anyway. The satellite had probably been tracking him every inch of the way from Boggle Hole. Tom glanced up at the sky. It was almost dark. Could the satellite follow him in the dark?

Mrs Shields came back on the line. The letter had come from a Karen Harding of 3 Willoughby Close, Pickering. Tom thanked her and hung up, then went into the pub across the road to ask for directions.

★　★　★

Willoughby Close was a cul-de-sac of small maisonettes and flats tucked away behind a row of shops. Tom rang the bell of number three and moments later the door swung open to reveal a middleaged woman in a blouse and pleated skirt, her feet encased in a pair of fur-trimmed moccasins.

'Karen Harding?' Tom said.

'Karen?' The woman shook her head. 'She doesn't live here any more. Moved, oh, about fifteen months ago.'

'Do you have her new address?'

'Somewhere, yes. We still get mail for her. Let me have a look.'

The woman disappeared into a room and emerged with a scrap of paper in her hand.

'She's changed her name. Got married. She's Karen MacIver now. Lives at 8 Richmond Gardens.'

'Is that in Pickering?' Tom asked.

'Follow the road out. It's on your left.'

Karen MacIver's house was one of about ten or fifteen starter homes on a small estate on the outskirts of the town. The young woman who answered the door seemed flustered, under pressure. Her face was pale and pasty, her hair lank and in need of a wash. She was wearing jeans and a T-shirt which had a fresh stain on the front that looked like mashed carrot. Down the hall, from the kitchen at the back of the house, came the sound of a baby bawling.

'Karen MacIver?' Tom said.

'Yes.'

'I wonder if I could — ' Tom's words were drowned out by a sudden crash from the kitchen and an explosive howl from the baby.

'Oh, hell!' Karen exclaimed. 'Look . . . wait on a minute . . . ' She went to the foot of the stairs. 'Wes!' she yelled. 'Wes!'

There was music playing somewhere upstairs. Loud country and western.

'Wes!'

The music stopped in mid-track. A man came into view at the top of the stairs.

'You calling, honey?' He had an American accent.

402

'Can you see to the door? The baby needs me.'

Karen hurried away down the hall. When she opened the door to the kitchen, Tom caught a glimpse of a chubby baby boy in a high chair, his face smeared with puréed carrot.

The man was coming downstairs now. He was in his early twenties, broad-shouldered and heavily built. His size, the muscles bulging beneath his sweatshirt, gave him an intimidating presence, but his expression was warm and open.

'Hi, what can we do for you?' he said amiably.

'My name's Tom Whitehead. I wanted to speak to your wife about something that happened a few years ago. The two boys who disappeared on a cycling trip near here.'

Tom had never seen the colour drain from someone's face so fast. Wes's cheeks and forehead turned white, as if the blood had been sucked out of them. Even his lips went pale, giving him the pallor of a corpse.

'Oh,' was all he managed to say. His eyes were wide open with shock.

'She wrote a letter,' Tom went on. 'To one of the boys' mothers.'

Wes stared at him. Tom saw something else in his eyes now. Not just shock. But fear. The young man was frightened.

'You know the letter I mean?' Tom said.

Wes found his voice. It was soft, hoarse, barely audible.

'Letter?'

'Maybe I could ask her?'

'She didn't write any letter.'

'Yes, she did. I've — '

Tom broke off abruptly. He twisted round, hearing the noise of a car. A dark saloon was coming slowly up the road. Tom saw the two men in the front. Then he saw a second car coming up behind it, another two men inside. He stepped over the threshold into the house and closed the door behind him. The Yale lock clicked shut.

'Hey, now look — ' Wes began, but Tom cut him off.

'Just listen to me. Please. Those men out there, they're trying to kill me.'

'Now wait a — '

'Hear me out. I'm serious. They've tried it before. I don't know why. But I know it's something to do with the two boys.'

Outside in the street, a car door slammed.

'You have to believe me,' Tom continued quickly. 'This is important. You know something, don't you? Your wife does too. What is it? You know what happened to the boys, don't you?'

Tom edged away down the hall.

'Is there a back way out?'

Wes was rooted to the spot, staring fixedly at him.

'They're coming, Wes,' Tom said urgently. 'There isn't much time. Wes? Jesus, are you listening to me?'

Tom took hold of Wes and shook him violently.

'You're in danger. So is Karen. We have to get out. Wes! Your lives are at risk. Do you hear me?'

Tom moved swiftly down the hall and into the kitchen. Karen was sitting by the high chair, spooning food into the baby's mouth.

'You have to get out, Karen. Trust me.'

Karen glanced up, frowning uncomprehendingly.

'What . . . ?'

Her eyes flickered to Tom's shoulder. Wes pushed past hurriedly and bent down, lifting the baby out of his seat.

'It's happened,' he said.

'What do you — ?'

'What we always thought might happen. We have to go, Karen. Now!'

Wes threw open the back door. He took a jacket down from a peg and wrapped it around the baby.

Tom pulled Karen to her feet.

'Quickly.'

He pushed her towards the door. Wes took hold of Karen's shoulder and practically dragged her out into the garden. From the front of the house Tom heard a heavy thud as if someone were trying to break down the door. He ran out into the garden. Wes and Karen were halfway across the lawn. Tom caught up with them as they pushed through the low hedge at the bottom of the garden. There were open fields beyond, trees in the distance. It was pitch-dark, the moon hidden by clouds.

The wooden gate at the side of the house rattled as someone tried the handle.

'It's locked,' Wes said. 'It'll hold them for a few minutes.'

He clutched the baby to his chest and ran across the field. Karen went with him, Tom just behind her. His side was hurting again, his legs still aching from his ordeal at Boggle Hole. He looked back momentarily. He could see the kitchen window of the house illuminated. It seemed a long way off. The silhouette of a man moved briefly across the square of light.

The field they were crossing was pastureland, ankle-deep grass, rough and uneven. Tom turned his gaze back to the ground, watching for hollows, for obstacles. His eyes were adjusting to the darkness. Wes and Karen were a few yards in front of him. Karen was slowing, panting noisily. Wes grabbed her arm with his free hand and pulled her along beside him.

They reached the dry-stone wall that marked the boundary of the field and paused. Wes clambered over a stile, the baby still nestled against his chest, then turned to help Karen over. Tom climbed over behind them. He glanced back. Shadowy figures were flitting across the field towards them.

'You know somewhere safe we can go?' Tom asked breathlessly.

Wes nodded. 'This way.'

The ground fell away on the other side of the wall, the hillside cloaked in woodland. There was a public footpath through the trees. Wes took the path, moving easily down the slope, familiar with the route. It was darker here, branches overhanging them as they descended.

At the base of the hill, the woods and open country gave way to the fringes of the town. The footpath took them along a passageway between houses and then they were out on a street, parked cars by the kerb, lights glowing in curtained windows. Tom could see no one behind them.

'Hurry,' Wes said, urging them on.

The baby started to mewl. Wes jogged him up and down, murmuring softly to him as they ran down the road. Two junctions on, just before a pub, they turned off into a street of terraced houses. Wes hammered on the front door of one of them.

'Wes? Karen?'

The woman who opened the door gazed at them in surprise.

'Sorry, Val.'

Wes pushed past her into the hall. Karen went in after him. Tom took a last look around outside. The street was deserted, no people, no cars on the move. He stepped into the house and closed the door behind him, checking the lock was engaged before ramming home the bolts at top and bottom.

* * *

Wes was hunched forward over the kitchen table, his hands clenched tightly together. Karen came in from the hall and sat down beside him.

'He's fallen asleep,' she said, talking about the baby. 'Val's keeping an eye on him.'

She prised her husband's hands apart and kept hold of one of them. Her lower lip was quivering. She looked as if she were close to tears. Wes was pale. His face was taut, anxious. Tom waited.

'You know I'm American,' Wes said, more a statement than a question.

Tom nodded.

'I'm a mechanic now. Work in a garage in the town. In Pickering. But a few years ago I worked at the base.'

'At Fylingdales?'

'Yes. The early warning station. I was in the Marines. One of the people responsible for guarding the base.'

'The base is guarded by US Marines?'

'The high-security sections, yes. There are Ministry of Defence police there as well. The cars that patrol the perimeter of the base and the surrounding public roads, they're all MoD. But the inner core, the radar installations and the SATCOM compound, they're protected by Marines. It's a sensitive issue. The British government doesn't want anyone to know the Marines are there. I shouldn't be telling you this, it's all classified information.'

Wes glanced at his wife. Karen squeezed his hand and gave him a brief smile of encouragement.

'That night the two boys disappeared,' Wes continued, 'I was on duty at the base. I was with a buddy, another Marine, named Chris Kaplinsky. We were patrolling the inner perimeter fence.'

Wes paused. 'You have to understand a few things about what it was like back then. It was just before the second Gulf War, the invasion of Iraq. All US bases around the world had been on a high state of alert since 9/11, but security was

408

tightened even more in the lead-up to the war in Iraq. Fylingdales was a potential terrorist target, we all knew that. We were reminded of it constantly, warned to be extra vigilant.

'That night, about half past eight, Chris and I got a radio call from the base control room telling us that the outer perimeter fence had been penetrated. It's just a metal chain-link fence a couple of yards high, not difficult to climb. It's not alarmed. But just inside that fence is another one — the middle fence, which *is* alarmed. That too had been penetrated. The infrared CCTV cameras had picked up a couple of intruders heading for the inner fence. It was dark and very foggy. Visibility was terrible, even with night sights. The fog up there on the moors, it's sometimes so thick you can't see more than a few feet. We caught sight of the two intruders. They were wearing ski masks. You call them something different here.'

'Balaclavas,' Tom said.

'Yeah. They were wearing balaclavas. We didn't know who they were. We certainly didn't know they were kids. They were tall, they looked like men. We challenged them, shouted a warning. They ignored us, started to run.'

Wes licked his lips. He gripped his wife's hand tight.

'Shit, I know now it was an overreaction, but you have to appreciate our state of mind back then. Everyone was on edge. We thought we might be hit by terrorists at any time. The base is surrounded by fences and warning signs saying keep out. The kids shouldn't have been there.

They shouldn't have been within two hundred yards of the inner perimeter fence. In the dark, in bad weather, how do you distinguish between two kids messing around and two terrorists trying to break into the base?'

Wes looked at Tom. Tom could see the anguish, a plea for understanding, in the young man's eyes. Tom nodded, urging him to go on.

'Chris . . . my buddy . . . he opened fire. The kids were hit . . . '

Wes put a hand to his face, covering his eyes. He was shaking. Karen put her arm around his shoulders and held him.

'I'm OK,' he said. He uncovered his eyes and blinked a few times. 'You try to forget it, but you can't. You'll never forget it. Seeing those kids . . . ' He couldn't finish the sentence.

'What happened afterwards?' Tom asked.

'The bodies were recovered, the British authorities notified. Chris and I were taken down to Lakenheath the next day and flown back to the States.'

'Was there an inquiry?'

Wes nodded. 'I don't know what happened here, but there was a military inquiry back home. We admitted what had occurred. Chris was shattered by it all, in a bad way. He needed counselling, some help, but the Marines did nothing. We were nineteen years old. We were just kids too. We wanted to come clean about the whole incident, but the US authorities — and the British — wanted it covered up. We were discharged from the Marines, told we'd be prosecuted if we said a word about what had happened. We didn't know anything about what had gone on here — the search for the boys, all that. Karen only told me when I came back last year.'

'And your friend Chris?'

Wes swallowed. 'He committed suicide a few months after the inquiry was over. Went out to a lake and shot himself. He couldn't live with it, with the knowledge of what he'd done. He told me that every day and every night he saw the faces of those two boys in the morgue. The guilt was too much. I guess that's why I'm telling you this. To ease my own guilt. I didn't kill anyone, but I was there. Chris was my friend. Maybe I could have done more to help him.'

'You knew, didn't you?' Tom said to Karen.

'Yes,' Karen replied. 'We were going out, planning to get married. Wes called me from the base, told me what had happened before they flew him out.'

'And that's when you wrote the letter to Mrs Shields.'

'I wanted to defend Wes, and Chris. They weren't evil. It was an accident. I knew Chris. He wasn't a killer. He was a gentle, considerate guy. He had a younger sister the same age as those two boys. What happened . . . they thought their lives were at risk. They thought the base was under attack. It was a tragic accident. The government should have come clean, that's what Wes and Chris wanted. It wasn't their fault.'

'We went along with it,' Wes said. 'We shouldn't have done that. I guess it was a cowardly thing to do.'

411

'And the bodies?' Tom said. 'Do you know what happened to them?'

'No, I don't know.'

'Will you go on record with this? Write out a full statement for the police and sign it?'

Wes looked at Karen. The tears were trickling down her face. He put his arms around her.

'Yes, I'll go on record. It's time I did what's right.'

25

Detective Chief Superintendent Maxfield put down the thin sheaf of paper he was holding and sat back heavily in his chair. He took a deep breath.

'That's quite a read,' he said softly.

'Every word of it is true,' Wes MacIver replied.

'Are you prepared to stand by it, on oath?'

'Yes.'

Maxfield looked at his watch: it was approaching 11 p.m. It was almost two hours since Karen — acting on Tom's instructions — had called North Yorkshire police headquarters, a little less since the duty officer at force control had paged Maxfield at a choral concert in Ripon Cathedral. It had been an anxious wait for Tom and the MacIvers before the superintendent arrived at the house in an unmarked car, alone. More plainclothes officers had come since, also in unmarked cars. No one wanted to draw attention to the house. There was a detective constable sitting just inside the front door now, another in the porch at the rear.

Maxfield took a pen from his jacket pocket and handed it to Wes.

'Would you initial all the pages and sign at the bottom, please?'

Wes nodded. 'Sure.' He glanced at his wife. They were both looking drawn and tired.

The kitchen door swung open and the

detective watching the front of the house walked in.

'There's a Mr Moran outside, sir,' he said to Maxfield. 'Says he's expected.'

'Show him in,' Maxfield said.

A moment later Moran came into the kitchen, dark suit jacket swinging open, a sapphire tiepin sparkling in the middle of his chest.

'You made good time,' Maxfield said.

Moran shrugged. 'No traffic at this time of night.'

Maxfield gave him Wes's statement. Moran read through the pages in silence, still standing up by the door.

'Finally it all makes sense,' he said.

'Only if you live in a particularly sick, perverted world,' Tom said.

'But they do,' Moran replied. 'That's exactly where they live. No wonder they were scared, no wonder they wanted this kept hidden. Look at the timing. Those two poor boys couldn't have been killed at a worse moment, for either our own government or the Americans. The build-up to the invasion of Iraq. There was massive public opposition to a war. Blair was struggling to win the argument, to get support from the people, even his own party. The Americans needed us on board, they needed a partner to take some of the flak from the rest of the world. Can you imagine what a public outcry there would have been if it had come out that a US Marine — guarding a so-called British military installation — had shot two British teenagers? It might well have made it impossible for Blair to go along with the Americans.'

Moran handed the statement back to Maxfield.

'That's powerful explosive. A lot of people won't want to see it detonated.'

'But it will be,' Maxfield said with quiet determination. 'I'll see to that. After what those families went through, I'm not going to allow anyone to block me.'

'I admire your guts,' Moran said. 'But you move too soon and you won't see the big boys for whitewash.'

Maxfield peered at him quizzically. 'Meaning?'

'Don't start at the top. You'll never get near them. They'll have covered themselves too well. They have too many friends to protect them. Go for the foot soldiers, the ones on the ground, out in the open. They're the weak point. They know they're vulnerable. They know their masters will hang them out to dry. You can do a deal with them. Prise them open. Once you've got a crack in their defences you can work away at it, open it wider and maybe, just maybe, you'll find a route to the top.'

'The foot soldiers?' Maxfield said.

'You trust me?'

'What did you have in mind?'

★ ★ ★

Tom walked twenty yards into the field and stopped. The grass was long enough to cover his shoes. He could feel the dew seeping into his socks. He looked around. The cloud cover split open for a moment. Moonlight washed over the earth, daubing the undulating grass, the darker lines of the stone walls, with a silvery frosting. He was in a meadow between two roads. In front of him, down the hill, he could see the lights of Pickering. Behind him, fifty or sixty yards away, was a broad stand of deciduous woodland.

He checked the luminous dial of his watch. It was 2.30. Time to make the call. Time to wake the man up. He'd be disorientated, not thinking too clearly. That was what they wanted — a reflex action.

Tom pulled the mobile phone from his pocket and punched in the number Moran had given him. He waited, listening to the ringing tone, which seemed weak and faint in comparison with his own heartbeat. It rang ten or eleven times before a voice answered. A man's voice, sleepy but with an edge of irritation.

'Yes?'

'John Templeman?' Tom said.

'Yes. Who is this?'

'Tom Whitehead.'

There was a pause. Then Templeman said sharply: 'Where did you get this number?' The drowsiness had gone. He sounded wide awake now.

'I want to talk,' Tom said.

'Do you know what time it is?'

'Does it matter?'

'Just a minute. Let me get to my study.'

The line went silent. Templeman had pressed the 'mute' button. Tom wondered what he looked like, tried to put a face to the voice, picturing someone tall, someone aloof, arrogant.

It was a minute or more before Templeman came back on the line.

'What is it you want?'

Tom glanced at his watch. A couple of minutes, Moran had said. That was all they needed to make the trace.

'I want you to call off your dogs,' Tom said.

'Dogs? I don't know what you're talking about.'

'I've had enough. I've been through too much. So has my family. I want my life back. Do you understand? I know what happened that night. I know what happened to the boys.'

'What boys?'

'Danny and Rory.'

'I don't know what you mean.' He was cool all right, gauging every word, giving nothing away.

'The two teenagers,' Tom said. 'You remember them, don't you? I know they went to Fylingdales. I know a US Marine shot them. What I don't know is who ordered the cover-up. Was it your idea? Or was it someone higher up?'

'I'm afraid you're losing me,' Templeman said.

'Someone in the government? Was it a minister? Did the orders come from Downing Street? Or maybe the White House?'

Tom had his eye on his watch dial, the second hand ticking inexorably round. He'd given them long enough, surely.

'As I said before, Dr Whitehead, I really have no idea what you're talking about.'

'Doesn't your conscience trouble you? Don't

you ever wonder about those two boys? Don't you ever imagine what it must be like for their families?'

'This is all very interesting, but I can't see what it has to do with me.'

Tom lifted his gaze from his watch. He could see headlights coming up the hill. Two sets. One on the road to the left, one away to the right. Just over three minutes. They were good, he had to give them that. He could hear the engines now. The cars sped over the brow of the hill and skidded to a halt.

'Have to go,' Tom said, thumbing the 'off' button and slipping the phone back into his pocket.

There were four of them. Two from each car. Tom gave them time to get through the gates into the field, then he turned and ran towards the woods. Pacing himself, giving them a chance to catch up. As he reached the first of the trees, he glanced back. The men were bunched together only five or six yards behind him. Tom swerved around a tree trunk and ducked down suddenly into a patch of dense undergrowth. At that moment two powerful beams of light shot out from the depths of the wood, hitting the pursuing men full in the face. They stopped dead, arms raised to shield their eyes from the dazzling glare. Temporarily blinded, they failed to see the encircling police officers until it was too late. They broke apart and bolted, but were brought down heavily to the ground before they'd gone a couple of paces.

Tom straightened up, watching expression-lessly as the four men were handcuffed and led past him to the waiting police van.

Moran emerged from the intense darkness behind the spotlights and walked over to Tom.

'You OK?'

Tom nodded, his eyes still following the four men. He felt exhausted, light-headed. The relief was almost more than he could bear.

'Maxfield will nail them,' Moran said.

'You think so?'

'I know a good copper when I see one.' He touched Tom on the shoulder. 'Come on, it's time you went home.'

* * *

An area of ground the size of a badminton court had been cordoned off with red and white plastic tape strung between the trees. Maxfield stood on the edge of the area, just outside the tapes, watching the men in white overalls going about their work. They were removing earth from the centre of the clearing, digging slowly, carefully, pausing occasionally to examine the soil. They'd been at it for twenty minutes. It was important to be methodical, to make sure no evidence was overlooked, but Maxfield was getting impatient.

He'd thought this moment would never come. The four men had proved difficult to break, as tough and intractable a quartet as he'd ever encountered. But he'd gone to work on one of them — Finch, the only one with the semblance of a conscience. Even when Finch had begun to

419

crack under the pressure, Maxfield hadn't dared hope it would end like this. He still wasn't sure. Finch had shown them the spot, but until Maxfield saw the evidence with his own eyes he wasn't going to believe it.

One of the scene-of-crime officers shovelled out another spadeful of earth and stopped. There was something different about his movements this time. He removed a bit more earth, then looked up, staring across the clearing at Maxfield.

Maxfield ducked under the tape, sensing from experience that this was the moment. He skirted round the edge of the hole and stopped next to the Soco. The officer swapped his spade for a trowel and knelt down, scraping the earth away gently to one side to expose a slender stick of pale bone — the finger of a hand, the flesh long since eaten away. Then an armbone came into view — a boy's arm. Maxfield looked away through the trees, feeling no sense of elation, only a cold, empty sadness.

26

Tom heard the alarm go off from a distance, as if he were buried deep beneath the earth. The noise seemed faint, a tiny, repetitive beep echoing around the confines of his head. He couldn't, at first, identify what it was. Then the noise got louder. It was no longer so far away. It was there right next to him, hammering away at his eardrums.

'Tom?'

It was Helen's voice.

'Tom, you awake?'

He realised where he was and stretched out his arm, his finger jabbing at the 'off' button of the alarm clock. The silence was blissful. Tom rolled over, his arm curling around his wife's warm body. He started to slip back into his subterranean tomb.

'Tom, it's gone seven.'

He felt Helen throw back the covers and slide out of bed. He opened his eyes, watched her putting on a loose top and padding out to the bathroom. He sighed. He'd got out of the habit of rising early.

It took him a few moments to summon the energy to swing his legs out from under the duvet. The wound to his side was almost fully healed now, but he was still aware of a slight soreness and was careful how he moved. The gash on his forearm didn't trouble him at all.

Only the livid three-inch scar on his skin reminded him that he'd ever been wounded there.

He put on his dressing gown and went downstairs, boiling the kettle to make tea and filling bowls with cereal for the children. It seemed strange to be back into his old routine.

The newspaper arrived shortly afterwards. Tom picked it up from the mat and spread it out on the table. The joint funeral of Danny Shields and Rory Hill was the front-page lead. There was a photograph of the two coffins being carried into the church in Doncaster, the boys' families leading the procession of mourners behind.

Tom read the story as he ate his toast. He had been invited to attend the funeral by the Shields family but had declined. He hadn't known the boys, would have felt like an intruder on a very private occasion. It was a time for the families and friends alone, the intensive media interest notwithstanding. Reading the article now, seeing the families' tear-streaked faces in the photograph, he was glad that he hadn't gone. It wouldn't have been right.

On an inside page there were other articles on the background to the case. The four men — all confirmed as employees of MI5 — had been charged and remanded in custody, but there were no signs that anyone higher up in authority was likely to join them in the dock. A statement from Downing Street reiterated earlier denials that the government had known anything about the boys' deaths and the subsequent cover-up, and implied that it was all the work of 'rogue elements' within the Ministry of Defence and security services. Washington had taken the same line, pointing the finger of blame in the US at unnamed Pentagon officials. A full public inquiry in the UK was promised at some unspecified time in the future. Tom's lip curled. Governments only ordered public inquiries when they could ensure — by rigging the terms of reference, appointing only the 'right' people to the inquiry panel — that nothing damaging to them would ever emerge.

Tom closed the paper and pushed it to one side as Ben and Hannah came in, Hannah as smart as ever, Ben still looking as if his school uniform had been trampled underfoot by a herd of wildebeest.

They chatted comfortably as they ate their breakfast, then Tom went upstairs to wash and get ready for work — putting on a suit and tie for the first time in weeks.

For once they were early dropping the children off at school. Tom gave Ben and Hannah a big hug, then watched them with tears pricking his eyes as they ran through the gates into the playground. There'd been a time when he'd thought that he would never again hold his children, never again be a true father to them. Just before they disappeared into the school building, both Hannah and Ben turned and waved to him. Tom smiled and waved back.

On the bus into town, Helen's hand found his.

'God, it's good to get back to normal,' she said.

Tom leaned over and kissed her.

'Tell me about it.'

There was no one around when he arrived at the History Department. Tom was relieved. He didn't want a welcoming party, didn't want to speak to anyone. He went upstairs to his office. He put his briefcase down on the desk and switched on his computer. There was a printed label stuck to the side of the monitor, a South Yorkshire police identification tag. Tom pulled the label off and threw it in the bin. Then he checked his timetable, pinned to the cork board on the wall. He had no lectures or tutorials until eleven. That gave him a couple of hours.

He wandered around his office for a while, looking at the books and files on the shelves, touching a few of them, familiarising himself again with his environment, with a part of his life that he'd feared he'd lost for ever. Then he took down a couple of files and placed them on the desk. It all seemed a very long time ago, but wasn't he supposed to be writing a book?

We do hope that you have enjoyed reading this large print book.

Did you know that all of our titles are available for purchase?

We publish a wide range of high quality large print books including:
Romances, Mysteries, Classics
General Fiction
Non Fiction and Westerns

Special interest titles available in large print are:
The Little Oxford Dictionary
Music Book
Song Book
Hymn Book
Service Book

Also available from us courtesy of Oxford University Press:
Young Readers' Dictionary
(large print edition)
Young Readers' Thesaurus
(large print edition)

For further information or a free brochure, please contact us at:
Ulverscroft Large Print Books Ltd.,
The Green, Bradgate Road, Anstey,
Leicester, LE7 7FU, England.
Tel: (00 44) 0116 236 4325
Fax: (00 44) 0116 234 0205

Other titles published by
The House of Ulverscroft:

FLASH POINT

Paul Adam

In McLeod Ganj, home of the Tibetan government in exile, the Dalai Lama is secretly dying. When fearless camerawoman Maggie Walsh receives the tip-off, she smuggles herself into the compound and films the pictures that will make her fortune. But her escape is thwarted by Tsering, an idealistic young monk. When Maggie is released, the Dalai Lama's death has been announced, so she heads for Tibet. Tsering, too, is heading there. The reincarnation of the Dalai Lama has already been born, and visions in the oracle lake will reveal the chosen child. As their paths overlap, Tsering and Maggie are drawn together. For, once the Chinese Army discover who they are looking for, there is no way they'll be allowed to leave Tibet alive . . .